I0591012

Stay With Me

Becca Blue

Stay With Me

The Guardians Of Your Heart Series

Copyright 2025
Lincoln, New Brunswick
CANADA

Stay With Me
(The Guardians of Your Heart Series)
Written by Rebecca Carrigan (author pen name: Becca Blue)

Copyright © 2025 by Rebecca Carrigan
Published by Rebecca Carrigan
Lincoln, New Brunswick, Canada

All rights reserved. This book is protected under the copyright laws of the United States of America and applicable international copyright treaties. No part of this book may be reproduced, stored in a retrieval system, or transmitted in any form or by any other means without prior written permission of the publisher. Reviewers and other writers are hereby granted permission to use brief quotations in articles and reviews, provided proper credit is given to the author and the publisher.

The characters and events portrayed in this book are fictitious. Any similarity to real persons, living or dead, is coincidental and not intended by the author.

To contact the author please email:
sakurabluestudios@gmail.com

Cover Design & Typesetting by:
Rebecca Carrigan under her company Sakura Blue Studios

Facebook.com/beccablueauthor
Facebook.com/sakurabluestudio
www.sakurabluestudios.ca

Printed in the United States of America For Worldwide Distribution

ISBN 978-0-9878132-9-9

"Most of us never allow ourselves to want what we truly want, because we can't see how it's going to manifest."
Jack Canfield - The Power of Focus

1
Perfection

Perfection. It was the only word I could think of to describe him as he lay there sleeping quietly beside me. Although he had just learned to sleep in the past few months, I still caught him most nights watching over me as he used to once before. The room was quiet as the sun pushed its way through our windows and began to warm his perfect face. I reached over and carefully touched his cheek with my hand. His eyelashes fluttered and a soft smile grew on his lips.

"Morning, crazy girl."

I smiled and moved in closer to lay my head on his chest. He breathed in deeply, holding me tight. His heartbeat, the warmth of his body against mine, even his scent stimulated every hair on me. A light wind blew in from the window and sent a chill down my spine. He shivered slightly reaching down to pull up the covers tight around us.

"I still can't get used to this," he whispered, finally opening his eyes to me.

"I'm doing my best to keep you warm," I said, wrapping my arms around him.

"I appreciate it," he replied.

Slowly, I began to kiss his chest, making my way up his neck to his perfect lips. Sliding myself over top of him, my hair hung low. He laced his fingers through the strands, pulling it over to one side as we continued to consume each other.

1

His hands slid down my sides and gripped onto my hips securely for a moment before he pushed me over and down against the bed. Then he paused, looking down at me and smiled. The same smile since day one. The one that made me melt inside. The one that could make me do anything now that we had the freedom we did. Something we were still getting used to. He leaned in and kissed me gently, lingering his lips on mine.

"We should stop here," he whispered, but my body wanted to keep going. It always did.

Nathan lowered himself next to me. His fingers traced my jawline over to my lips. He then pulled me in for another captivating kiss. My cold fingers pressed up against his chest before they slid around his back to pull him in tighter. As much as Nathan and I desperately wanted each other, sadly, we had never gone all the way. But he never pressed me on the matter. After the first time I stopped us, he just got the hint. I wasn't ready yet. Although we were official now and technically a new relationship, Nathan and I had known each other for quite some time. He understood me and sometimes predicted every thought in my mind. He had a way of easing all my worries and concerns. He showed compassion and love like I've never experienced before, and more importantly, he kept the nightmares away. He kissed my nose playfully before pulling away and getting up from the bed.

"Want some breakfast?" He asked, with a sudden burst of energy. I sighed, pulling the covers around me from the cold air.

"Come on crazy girl, get up. Let's eat. Then we'll take Bruce for a walk. It looks nice out today."

I watched as he tossed on a T-shirt, then exited the room. A few steps down the hall, I heard him call out to our little dog Bruce. Taking a deep breath in, I stretched out in the bed.

"Sophie! Get up!" Nathan called again, louder this time. "I'm making pancakes!"

Walking through Stanley Park, Bruce tugged at the leash as he normally did. Nathan snapped his fingers, then gave a slight pull back. Bruce eventually slowed down. Nathan worked with our little dog every day. Training him to heal, fetch and do ridiculous tricks no dog needed to know. Like getting a blanket from the small ottoman in our living room. I didn't understand why it was so important for Nathan to teach him this, but I certainly found it entertaining.

"So, I've been thinking," he said, politely.

I raised an eyebrow as he took my hand in his.

"I'm thinking it's time for me to go back to school and finish my degree." He paused, waiting for my reaction.

"School," I finally said. "I mean, sure. If that's what you want."

"It is Soph, and I'll get a job as well so I can contribute to our life."

"Nathan, I'm not worried about the bills." I replied. "We're fine. Like I said, if that's what you want, I completely support you."

He stared at me for a moment, studying my thoughts.

"Stop it," I slapped him playfully, "I'm not worried about anything. You just caught me off guard with the whole school thing. I just want to make sure you're ready." I paused. "Do you feel like you're ready, Nathan?" I asked, in a slightly more serious tone.

"I'm ready," he replied confidently.

"Okay then," I smiled.

"I mean it Soph. I'm healthy, and I'm getting used to life again. You don't have to worry about me. I can do this—I need to do this."

I took a deep breath, a little unsure about his decision but before I could speak again he continued.

"This is my second chance Sophie. I want to do it right. I won't let you down. I promise."

I sighed, feeling a little guilty for doubting him.

"I know you won't." I agreed, pulling him down to me.

Our lips didn't stay connected long before Bruce pulled him from my grip.

We made our way towards the seawall and found a bench to rest on for a moment. Nathan took my hand in his and lifted it up to meet his lips.

"I'm going to make you so happy. I promise."

"You already make me happy." I smiled.

"I know, it's just, I want to do as much as I can for me and for you—for us, understand?"

3

"I get it. I do." I replied. "Let's just go slow though, okay? It's already hard enough for me to believe that you're actually here, that we're a real couple, and now you want to do stuff like go to school and be well—normal." I said, feeling a little overwhelmed by the conversation now.

"You don't want me to be normal, Soph?" He laughed.

"No, I do. It's just, now I have to share you with the world, when I'm used to being the only one who can see you."

His eyes softened.

I suddenly felt awkward for being so needy. I got up from the bench thinking I'd change the conversation when he quickly stood up, grabbed my wrist and pulled me back towards him. My hands gripped onto his toned arms.

"You don't have to share me with anyone. I'm still yours." He whispered, then gently kissed me on the lips. "You just have to let me live. I'll be okay, Soph. Don't be scared for me."

As usual, Nathan's words and gentle touch calmed my inner fears.

"Sorry," I whispered.

"It's okay." He smiled, "I forgive you for being so needy."

I gave him an unimpressed look for reading my thoughts.

"I thought you said you weren't doing that anymore. Whatever happened to acting like a human being?"

"I'm not. It was just this once," he said. "For old times' sake."

I continued to stare at him.

"Come on, let's get some slushies." He said, pulling me down the path with Bruce running full speed ahead.

Later that night, I watched Nathan fill out a couple of College and University applications Online while I folded laundry on the bed. Seeing him so excited made me happy, even if I was little nervous about the whole idea. Nathan had told me many times how much he loved writing and that he wanted to finish his English degree he had started long ago.

When he first returned to me, I had bought him a beautiful thick leather journal one day when we were out browsing through the local bookstores. Ever since, I can't seem to peel him from it. He writes poems and short stories, then reads them to me late at

4

night. He's a wonderful writer. His ability to capture the emotions of each of the characters he creates always amazes me. It's probably because he spends most of his quiet time reading any and every book he can get his hands on. It doesn't matter the genre either. Fiction, a love story, fantasy, or a mystery—he reads them all. I feel like Nathan truly has a gift for understanding people, which is probably why he made such a fantastic guardian angel. At least in my experience he was.

When Nathan was finished with his applications, he got up from the chair, stretched out and turned to me. I smiled. He joined me on the bed and began to fold some towels.

"I love you, Sophie Reid." He said, not making eye contact.

"I love you more, Nathan Hayes." I teased, pulling the horribly folded towel from his hands. He quickly yanked it back from me. My eyes tightened, feeling challenged by him. I reached again for the towel, but he quickly tossed it on the floor, then tackled me back against the bed.

"Love me more? Not possible…" he laughed, pinning my arms back over my head. His face then softened as he released one hand so he could touch the side of my face.

"Sophie, no one will ever love you like I do. That, I promise."

My heart melted whenever he said things like this. I too, had never loved someone so much in my entire life.

Pulling him back in, I kicked the folded laundry onto the floor as we scrambled up on the bed. I pushed back the covers as Nathan tugged the shirt from over his head. His lips connected immediately with mine as I reached to pull the covers over us.

My hands slid over his lean, athletic body as he hovered over me. His scent was intoxicating, and every inch of his body was perfectly sculpted. I pushed him over and straddled his torso. I then pulled the cotton tank from over my head. His hands slid around my waist as I leaned down to kiss him again. I could feel his fingers move to the back of my bra. I knew he wouldn't undo it, so I reached back and released the connection.

Tossing my bra to the ground, the warmth of our skin began to make me nervous. I started to tremble, feeling the softness of his lips on my neck. For some reason, every time I thought I could go a little further with Nathan, my mind wouldn't cooperate with what my body wanted.

"Are you alright?" He whispered, surely feeling the tension in my body.

I stopped for only a moment to look him in the eyes—trying my best to assure him that I was okay with this. Then I proceeded to kiss him. My hands slid down to his waist where they connected with the drawstring on his gray track pants. I tugged at them until he removed them. With nothing left between our bodies but Nathan's black boxers and my tiny blue pajama shorts, I felt myself start to choke up. My hands were shaking. I quickly gripped onto his arms to steady them.

"Soph," he said, trying to speak between our kisses. "Stop,"

But I didn't. I wanted to keep going. I needed to push past this. I could feel Nathan trying to separate us, but I resisted as best I could. I hated doing this to him. At first, I thought that maybe our love was a little too powerful for real life. Only because of how rare it was to exist between a previous angel and a human being. That the excitement and freedom of being together now had made things so electric between us that it might take some time to get used to. However, when things didn't change, I had to admit to myself that it wasn't something between us. It was something to do with me alone. The truth was that the idea of us fully being together scared me.

Suddenly, I found it hard to breathe. I tried my best to concentrate on my boyfriend, but my eyes began to widen in fear. Then I began to gasp for air. I sat up and grabbed my chest from the pain. Nathan's hands cradled my face.

"Sweetie, breathe," he spoke calmly. "You're fine, take a breath." My eyes connected with his for only a moment before he pulled me in tight against him.

"Soph, listen to my voice," he said. "I'm right here,"

I gripped onto him desperately, trying to catch my breath.

"Breathe," he repeated.

I could feel the warmth of this hand rubbing my back.

"Breathe,"

Eventually, I did. My breathing finally slowed to a reasonable speed, but I hadn't let go of him yet. I hated this. It was ruining everything, and it was completely embarrassing. He began to loosen his grip—I tightened mine.

"I can't. Not yet…" I said, quietly. I couldn't look at him.

"Soph,"

He knew I was embarrassed, and I worried even more that Nathan might read my mind at some point, hearing all the insane thoughts inside my head. But he kept his promise tonight. For the most part, Nathan respected my thoughts and stayed out of my head since becoming my official boyfriend—with the exception of playful times like in the park.

"I love you," he said, squeezing me tight.

He let me hang on for a moment longer, then gripped onto my arms and forced me back to face him. I stared awkwardly away from him.

"Do you know how beautiful you are?" He whispered, turning my chin back to face him.

He couldn't possibly know how horrible this felt inside. No matter how much he said he understood. I really wanted him, and I didn't want him to think there was something wrong with him—or us. I knew it was killing him not to read my mind in that very moment.

"Sophie," he whispered again, lacing his fingers through my hair.

I knew at some point I'd have to talk to him about this. I just couldn't do it now—not yet. We were too new, and I was certain at some point I could straighten myself out.

His lips pressed against mine, staying connected this time as he pulled me back down to the bed. Keeping me close against his chest, his arms wrapped around me tight as they always did, creating a protective barrier. One that calmed everything inside of me— instantly.

2
A Past Life

Five years have passed since Nathan first appeared in my life—or should I say in my dreams. He arrived just when I needed someone the most. It was my last year of high school and sadly, it didn't end the way I'd imagined. My best friend since kindergarten had slept with my boyfriend of four years just before graduation. Also at that same time, my parents had announced they were getting a divorce. Everyone went their own way after high school and my family quickly fell apart. I was lost and heartbroken.

When the nightmares first began, they were just scattered meaningless dreams blended together with random images of people I used to know and conversations I once had. Then they started to change. They grew longer and more detailed, almost like a scene from a movie. The dream would always start out beautiful and relaxing, but quickly changed. They became dark and scary— even for a horror movie fan like myself. That's when she showed herself for the first time—the girl in my dreams.

I've never seen her face up close. She always keeps her distance from me—just a silhouette in the sunlight. But sometimes, I think I hear her voice calling out to me. A few times, I tried to communicate back, but for some reason I can't speak. She also doesn't linger, always managing to disappear right before the darkness takes over. I kind of feel like she's trying to warn me about something because although she seemed to have a very calm demeanor about her, there was something haunting—something frightening about this delicate girl I saw at night.

To be honest, the idea of her being my conscience had crossed my mind many times. Maybe I was trying to tell myself something. But that girl wasn't the only thing that was visiting me in my dreams at night. There was someone else—or should I say something else. A horrible feeling deep inside would fill my gut as the sky around me turned dark. That's when I couldn't see her anymore, but I could hear them. Their frightening screeches and inhuman-like screams sent chills up my spine, enough to make me run for my life. That feeling… that horrible, daunting feeling of what pursued me as I ran made me want to throw up in fear. I could barely breathe when I heard them and feared mostly of tripping over my own feet. From the sounds they made, I didn't want to imagine what they looked like or what it might feel like if they actually caught me. I constantly worried that every time I closed my eyes, it might be the last for me.

But then he would come. Right when I thought it was surely over, before my heart would stop from fear alone. The touch of his warm hand on my shoulder would bring the world around me to silence, and slowly the sky above would lighten to its original shade of blue. I immediately felt safe and protected by his presence. His dark, beautiful brown eyes and long eyelashes softened his sharp facial features. They were hypnotizing and he always made sure to never lose eye contact with me until my heart returned to a steady rhythm. His medium length hair hung slightly to the left side, partially covering his eye with a few wispy pieces. He had this energy about him that paralyzed me from the moment he appeared. Then, in the next second, he'd be gone, and I'd feel a part of me leave with him. That's when I'd wake up.

Every night it was the same thing for two years and although I worried about the stress the dreams were adding to my life, I also looked forward to seeing him. He was a positive thing for me at that time, someone to rely on. For I had never felt loneliness like I did back then. He was perfect. The perfect image and being of what I could only imagine a guardian angel would be—if I believed in them—and he was mine.

Shortly after that, Nathan appeared for the first time in real life.

A day I will never forget. I was on my way to Vancouver, British Columbia to attend acting school. My grandmother had secretly helped me apply because my parents were completely against it. They didn't think it was a real career path for me, but I had dreamed of it since I was little.

I remember how amazing I felt the day I opened the envelope and read the acceptance letter. I was so happy but scared as hell to tell my parents. My gram stood by me the entire way—encouraging my dreams. I thought this new path would help me feel better about life, but I soon found out, it wasn't that easy.

Since that horrible last day of high school, darkness had begun to grow inside of me and it wasn't long before depression had taken over my mind. I was embarrassed for the way I felt inside, so I did my very best to hide it from the world. I didn't think anyone would understand. I was convinced there was something seriously wrong with me. The thoughts I was experiencing were indescribable. They were heavy to carry and left room for nothing else in my life. Some days, it even made me physically sick to my stomach. That annoying feeling in my gut, twisting with the thoughts in my head was overwhelming. Every once and a while, I thought about ending it—escaping the pain and nightmares that haunted me day after day. At one point, I couldn't see any other way out, but then Gram called. She must have had some superpower, because she always knew when I needed someone to talk to. I could tell she was worried about me—I was worried about me. I was letting the darkness take over my life. I was a completely different person. Vancouver was supposed to be a step in the right direction for me, a path that could possibly change my outlook on life—as Nathan once said.

On the day he arrived in my real life, I was just dozing off on the plane to the West Coast when I heard his voice, something I had only heard a few times in my dreams but would recognize anywhere.

● ● ●

"You see? So far so good, eh?"
I opened my eyes. To my left, was the guy from my dreams.

10

"You!" I stuttered, freaking out by his ghostly presence.

"Shh… No need to shout. People will think you're crazy. No one else can see or hear me—just you." He spoke. "So I wouldn't make a scene."

I quickly rubbed my eyes thinking this had to be a dream, but when I opened them again, he was still there smiling at me.

"You're not dreaming, Sophie." He assured me.

I glanced around to see if anyone else had noticed his arrival, but he was right. It didn't seem like anyone could see him. I looked back at him oddly. There was something different about him. His words were simpler in my dreams, but now he was much more casual as if we were old friends.

"What are you doing here?" I asked, unsure of what else to say.

"Just checking in on you. That's all." He responded.

That's when the flight attendant interrupted.

"Would you like a drink or some crackers?" She asked, politely.

I froze awkwardly. I couldn't believe it. She couldn't see him, and he was right there in front of her. I looked over at him and then back at the flight attendant.

"Are you all right, dear?" She asked with concern.

"Yeah, oh yeah. I'm fine." I stuttered. "Water and crackers please," The flight attendant handed me everything, then slowly stepped away.

"Wow," he teased, shaking his head.

I'll admit, I didn't handle that as smoothly as I would've liked, but what did he expect?

"Can I have a cracker?" He then asked, holding his hand out.

"Can you even eat? I mean, if you're not really here… I mean—I don't know what I mean. I'm so confused." I said, covering my face. I felt like a lunatic. It had to be from my lack of sleep.

"What are you confused about?" He asked, as I peeked between my fingers.

"You!" I said loudly, dropping my hands to my lap. Frustrated now, I struggled like a child to open the package of crackers. When I finally got the bag open, I pulled one out and slowly handed it to him.

"Thank you," he said, taking the cracker from me.

His touch was very cool against my skin. Not like in my dreams where it was usually warm. I waited impatiently as he ate the cracker. I needed to know why he was here. Not that I minded—he was still fascinating to look at and to be honest, very easy on the eyes. But how was he here—in the daytime? It wasn't like I was in any danger or having a nightmare—at least I didn't think I was. I paused, waiting to see if everything was about to go dark like it normally did in my dreams. When it didn't, my mind flooded with questions I wanted to ask him.

He stopped chewing when he noticed me staring at him.

"What? You've never seen someone eat a cracker before?" He teased, taking the bottle of water from my hands, opening it, and taking a sip.

"How can you? If you're not real—how can you be touching me and eating things?"

"Because I am real. I'm real to you. To everyone else, I'm not real. So they can't see me. It's a guardian angel thing." He smiled again. "Sophie, relax. Sometimes, you won't understand everything in life, so just go with it—all right? Trust me."

"Trust you? I know nothing about you," I paused. "Wait a minute, how did you know my name?"

It was the first time he had actually said my name. In my dreams, I had never had the chance to talk about such casual things as names. I didn't even know his. The only thing he told me was that he was my guardian angel and he was here to guide me on the right path in life.

He smiled, clearly entertained.

"Well, what do you want to know?"

I thought for a moment, a little thrown off with his offer to explain.

"Okay, for one, what's your name?"

"Nathan. Nate. Either works."

"All right... How old are you, Nathan?"

"When I died, I was 24. But that was years ago." His smile faded.

"When you died?"

"It's a long story, not important right now," he said, changing the subject. "Are you ready for acting school? Seems like a pretty cool place."

"I think so," I replied taking the hint.

"I know so. You're a fun person, and Vancouver is a beautiful city, especially when the cherry blossoms fall—it looks like pink snow." He paused for a moment.

"Really? Have you been there before?"

"Briefly," he replied. "A good friend told me about the cherry trees, so I had to see them for myself—to see what she was so obsessed about,"

I stared at him—confused as to whom he was talking about. I suddenly wanted to know more about him and his past life.

"This school is going to be amazing for you and just what you need to change your outlook."

"Why? What's wrong with my outlook?"

"You're becoming too isolated." He spoke. "It's not good for you. You need to get out there and become more independent. This will be a good experience—if anything."

"What do you mean if anything?" I asked worried. "What the heck, Nathan. Did I not choose the correct path, or..." I felt myself begin to choke up a bit.

"Sophie, you're going to give yourself a heart attack. Relax, crazy girl," he joked. "It's fine. You're supposed to do this, and I'm going be here the entire time in case you need me."

"You're going to be here, with me?" I repeated.

"Well, I won't exactly be in sight all the time. People will definitely think you're crazy if you're always talking to me."

I looked around again remembering where I was. No one seemed to notice, but I did catch one person staring at me. I needed to keep my voice down. This whole thing was overwhelming for sure.

I took a deep breath, trying to relax. As much as those burning questions still flooded the back of my mind, a sudden warmth began to fill my body after our short but kind of helpful interaction.

"You know, this is going to sound a little crazy..." I began, "but ever since you first appeared in my dreams, I've strangely felt comfortable around you. I feel like maybe I've met you before. Maybe in another life or something?" I couldn't believe I was telling him this. I didn't even know if I believed in reincarnation.

"Maybe," he responded. "You do remind me of someone I used to know. That's why I chose you."

I smiled at the thought of Nathan choosing me.

I desperately wanted to ask him even more questions now, but this was a big step for us. It was the most conversation we had ever had. I didn't want to push it. I took a moment to think of my next few words before turning to him again.

"If you truly are what you say you are," I paused, thinking about how this might sound. "Then please, don't let me down. Okay?" This meant more to me than he would ever know. Given the last few years, if Nathan was suddenly a part of my life now, I really needed him to come through. I wanted desperately to trust someone again—to know that someone had my back. It seemed like a lot of pressure. Especially to put on a guy that wasn't even real, but it was truly what I needed to help me move forward and to possibly get on that right path my guardian spoke about.

"I won't." He promised.

● ● ●

Nathan had been there just like he said he would the entire way through my schooling to become a professional actress. He watched silently over me every day, and at night we would have conversations about life. Sometimes, I would even wake up to find him watching over me while I slept. Knowing he did this helped me sleep a little better.

He was right, school was a good step for me. It helped me change. I became a little stronger as a person, even with the darkness still lingering inside of me. I sometimes felt as if it was waiting for me to fall. Waiting for the moment that life beat me down again, for the moment Nathan wasn't there so it could creep up on me and consume me once again. But Nathan always did well with keeping my spirits up any time I began to look down on myself.

Throughout the school year, I faced many growing pains. Ones I wasn't prepared for. I made many new friends in my acting class. One amazing friend in particular—my roommate, Julie. She was fun and a positive person to be around. Every second I spent with her I felt more like my old self. We enjoyed many of the same things which included a passion for movies, music, shopping and more importantly going out for a night of dancing. There was only one thing that frustrated me about Julie… She unfortunately had a very poor relationship with my other roommate, Natalie. They completely hated each other and every time they got in a room together, it was a full out war—an exhausting competition between two beautiful and talented girls. Especially when it came to boys at the clubs.

On the evenings Natalie would join us at the bar, Julie's attitude would completely change. Natalie made a scene anywhere we went, even when our entire class was there. Most of the time the guys from class were able to separate my roommates, enabling us to have a solid night of fun. But they weren't always there to save us. The closer Julie and I became, the more jealous Natalie grew. She was degrading to Julie at times and frankly, if it were me, I probably would have crumbled by now. But Julie was tough. At least I thought she was. I guess eventually, even the strongest people can crack. It took one weekend away visiting my family in Ontario after graduation for my roommates to almost kill each other.

It happened late one evening. I received a phone call from Julie saying she couldn't take it anymore. She told me she had to move out immediately, that she would be gone by the time I got back. I begged her to wait until I got home. I wanted to move out with her, but she didn't wait for me. She packed up all her stuff and didn't just move out—her parents drove up from Alberta and took her home. She moved right out of the province.

I'll never forget the moment I walked into our apartment. Her bedroom was bare. It was like she never existed. I had lost my best friend—again. What I didn't know then was that Julie too was fighting her own demons inside. She apologized profoundly in a letter she left on my bed. It broke my heart to lose her and not only that, I wish I would have known about her secret depression, so I could have been there for her. It made me stop and think about myself. Wondering, if I opened up about my depression, would someone want to be there for me? Was this all that I needed to do to make things different in my life? Then I remembered how hard it was to even admit it to myself, let alone anyone else. I was way too scared. Scared that people would judge me, not want to be friends with me—or worse. It was just too awkward to speak about. Even Nathan couldn't break me. That was the last thing I wanted to discuss with my guardian angel, a guy I had grown very fond of in many ways.

When Julie left, it was towards the end of the month and our lease was almost up. It was time for me to get my own apartment now that school was over. I was confident I could afford it with my job at the music store and a few acting gigs on the side. I had originally hoped that Julie and I would embark on this new journey together, but I was on my own now and I wasn't mad at her for leaving either. I understood her pain completely. Nathan then reminded me of how some people are meant to come and go from our lives. How some of them leave footprints in our hearts forever, and how all of them enter for a specific reason, even Natalie. What he said was true. Julie's friendship had carried me through school and allowed me to have many new adventures. I only hope that someday we might meet again—when we are much stronger inside.

Nathan and I had grown very close over that year. We connected in ways I had never done before with anyone in my entire life. But he was soon called on by the Archangels for our so-called close connection. They warned him that he was spending too much time in my real life. That his actions might seriously affect me and my choices. They reminded him that he was only there to be my guardian angel—and not my best friend. Nathan assured them that he was only doing what he felt was needed. I trusted him and listened closely to everything he said—even if I didn't understand it completely.

He had mentioned to me at one point something about a pure heart. I wasn't sure if he was talking about my actual heart or my soul. He said that was the reason I needed more attention from him, the reason the Archangels were constantly on his back. He kept saying how important it was for me to feel like my old self again. But I just couldn't figure out how I was going to get back to that—not with what I was carrying inside. To do so would mean really opening up and facing everything I feared within myself.

It wasn't possible. Not right now at least. I just felt that every time I tried to help myself, I took one step forward and four steps back, and it wasn't just Julie's absence that affected me deeply that year. My relationships were even worse.

Throughout the school year, I met two guys. Both crushed me. The second more than the first. It began with Jake. I met him at the beginning of school. He was a grad from the class before mine. He instantly swept me off my feet with his charming ways and gentleness. He had an edgier exterior but a gentle heart—or at least I thought he did. We shared a love of music and felt very much like old friends. He was the first guy I had been interested in since my high school boyfriend. It was a big deal for me to date him, and I felt proud of myself for taking a huge step forward in life. I wanted to trust him. I wanted him to help me believe in people again. But unfortunately, that idea backfired. Jake had lied to me the entire time we were together. As it turned out, he had a girlfriend that he hadn't really broken it off with quite yet. Because his hometown was so far from school, his girlfriend didn't have much of a chance to visit. Convenient now that I think about it. He said they were in between right now—not really together and when he met me, things changed for him. I really didn't understand it, but I knew I was being played. I was just a backup for when she wasn't there. It crushed me. All of the lies instantly brought back many of those horrible feelings and memories from high school. I remember hiding away for a day in my bathroom after learning about Jake's girlfriend—crying my eyes out. Then my graduation from acting school happened.

My class was celebrating with a huge house party. That's where I met the second disaster—Devon. He was much different than Jake. He was bold, said everything on his mind, and knew exactly what he wanted. He approached me as I lingered alone in a corner feeling out of place because unfortunately, Jake was at the party too. Devon had this ability to pull things out of me. He made me explain why I was so upset, then insisted on showing me a good time. I couldn't believe how much I told him, but his pushy ways were almost attractive. He said there were plenty of other fish in the sea and perhaps even one here tonight—clearly hinting

17

to himself. I thought that was pretty smooth of him. We didn't get to chat long before a huge fight broke out again between my roommates. I tried to break it up but only ended up being elbowed in the mouth. Luckily, Devon was more than happy to care for my bleeding lip. He was sweet and immediately protective of me. It kind of reminded me of Nathan.

Devon and I really hit it off and his roommate Carter was really into Julie. The four of us had a blast together and for a little bit, life felt normal again. But what wasn't normal was the distance it was creating between Nathan and I. My guardian angel was becoming short with me, appearing at random times, and not long enough for us to talk about anything too deeply. I almost felt like he was jealous of my relationships, and perhaps holding something back which really confused and upset me. But what Nathan didn't tell me back then was that he could see into my future, and he knew what was coming next for me with each choice I made. Which means, he knew that Jake had a girlfriend, and he knew what would happen next with Devon too.

About three months into seeing each other, the four of us went out to a club one night. That night was much different than our normal nights out. Carter and Devon met up with some "friends" and basically left Julie and I alone for most of the night. It was completely rude, and I couldn't figure out why Devon wouldn't want to introduce his girlfriend to his friends. It was the first time I was angry with him and at one point, Julie and Carter got into a huge fight and left screaming. I suddenly found myself alone at the bar. I remember wandering around the club, searching for Devon. I was drunk and really upset. After an hour, I gave up and caught a cab outside the bar to his apartment—hoping at least Carter and Julie were heading home.

When I arrived, I walked in on Devon and his new "friend" more than close on the couch. Julie and Carter were also there, fighting in the bedroom. Completely humiliated, I knew exactly what was happening. He was done with me. The rage inside of me grew quickly. I was fed up with being treated this way. I stormed out into the rain that night and quickly began my long walk home. Not really a safe choice to do in Vancouver, especially when you aren't too stable on your feet. But I couldn't bear the thought of being there for a second longer. I only assumed Carter and Julie were fighting over the same issue.

I remember feeling that heavy weight building up in my chest again as I made my way home. I couldn't figure out why people treated others like this, and why it was constantly happening to me? I wondered if I deserved this? Maybe I had done something wrong in life to have this happen to me over and over again? Or maybe I was just not as good as I thought I was at picking out good people. There was no explanation that made sense in my head.

As I continued to stumble my way home, I came across a man wandering through the park towards me. I remember thinking that this was a shortcut. I thought I could get home faster if I cut through the pathway in the park, but it ended up being the worst decision. As the man got closer, I noticed him wobbling a little on the path. He was drunk, but looking straight at me. A sickening feeling grew inside of me the closer he got until I passed him. I released a sigh of relief. Then I heard him call out to me.

His words slurred and that horrible feeling ran through me again. As I turned to look at him, he was already there—right behind me. He quickly attacked me, knocking me to the ground. His dirty hands ripping at my clothes. I screamed, fighting him off as best I could, but he was too strong. His weight alone held me down against the ground. I screamed again, but he quickly hit me across the mouth, silencing me immediately. I thought I was done for. I couldn't escape no matter how hard I tried. My mind continued to race with horrible thoughts. I deserved this. I wasn't good enough in life. This was going to be the brutal end to my existence. Then something worse clicked inside of me, and the thoughts stopped. I remember being scared as hell, but also mentally and physically exhausted. I stopped fighting. I gave up.

Then suddenly, Nathan appeared. This time in rage. He threw the man off me and immediately appeared beside him again—beating senseless. I had never seen him this way. It scared me. Hearing Nathan's voice growl as he beat this man—I'll never forget it. He was a completely different person.

When he was done, he turned back to me. All I could do was stare at him with tears in my eyes. He approached slowly. He seemed to have a soft red glow surrounding him in that moment. As he drew closer, I shuffled back on the ground from him, nervously. He froze for a moment, his entire demeanor changed instantly. Even the red glow began to fade. He must have known how scared I was and not from the attack alone, but from him. He stepped towards me again and spoke very softly. "Sophie, come here."

My hands trembled. I quickly covered my ears, curling my knees up tight to my chest. I didn't want to hear his voice.

"Sophie," he begged, kneeling down to me, being ever so careful as to how he was going to touch me. Eventually, I felt his hand touch the side of my face.

"No!" I screamed, scrambling back from him again.

But Nathan was right there, just as quick. He snagged me up from the ground and pulled me into arms. I screamed in fear, desperately trying to fight him off.

"It's okay, calm down. I'm right here." He said, holding me tight.

"But you weren't, Nate!" I cried.

"I know, I'm sorry."

"You weren't there. You let him…" I broke down crying in his arms to the point I couldn't breathe.

"I'm so sorry," He whispered. "Forgive me."

His hold on me was too strong. I couldn't fight him anymore. My hands shook against his chest until I gripped onto him for dear life.

"I won't leave you alone again—not ever." He whispered.

That was the last thing I heard him say before my body gave way and I collapsed in his arms.

After that horrible night, I became cold towards Nathan. Especially after he told me he could see into my future—but also couldn't tell me about it. He said all things needed to play out, like the attack in the park. Knowing that only made things worse because I didn't understand why he even bothered interfering then? If he was only here to guide me, then why did he step in at all? And if he was going to go against the rules, why not step in earlier and change the situation completely? None of it made sense.

He said he was doing his best to be there for me, but he was also saying one thing and doing another. I couldn't listen anymore. I trusted him. He was my very best friend, but he had let me down. I quickly began to double think how much Nathan actually cared for me. Maybe I really was just another one of his hopeless humans he had to guide in life. Maybe he really was just doing his job.

I remember Nathan spending days trying to convince me otherwise. He swore that he would never let anything else bad happen to me, no matter what the Archangels said, but I didn't believe him anymore. I had completely shut down and if that wasn't bad enough, I received a phone call from back home that my grandmother was in the hospital with pneumonia and wasn't doing very well. I scrambled to organize things at work and get a flight back home. I'll never forget that phone call. I remember crawling into bed that night and closing my eyes. Instantly, the nightmares that had been less casual throughout the year thanks to Nathan suddenly flooded back, all in one night—and they were worse than ever. Even that girl was back, but this time, she was different. I remember finally hearing her voice loud and clear that night. The girl from my dreams warned me that I was going to fall, and that I would take Nathan down with me. She suddenly didn't seem so delicate anymore and I no longer saw her as a possible self-warning, but a threat.

Nathan was always there when I woke from my nightmares. But oddly enough since the attack in the park, he didn't appear in my dreams anymore and he's never seen the ghostly girl. Something was changing between us.

He had many questions about my dreams—like what was happening in them and what I saw. He seemed more worried than ever for me and that scared me the most. Then, while visiting my grandmother in the hospital, things got worse. The doctors explained that the pneumonia had taken over her lungs and they didn't expect her to live much longer. I remember being a complete wreck. I spent the entire day at the hospital by her side, then went to my dad's house that night only to sleep.

On the last night of my grandmother's life, the girl from my dreams visited me once again. I was in the bathroom. It was close to one in the morning. My Dad was still at the hospital taking shifts. I splashed my face with cool water, trying to calm my anxiety that was building up inside. I had just woken from another nightmare drenched in sweat and Nathan wasn't there. I had forced him to leave earlier in the evening so I could have some time alone. I dried my face with a towel and when I looked up in the mirror, the lights went out.

I reached for the wall, searching for the switch. When I found it, I flicked it on. The lights seemed to work fine. Then I turned back to the mirror and staring back at me was the girl from my dreams. But she wasn't just in the mirror, she was there in real life—right behind me.

"I warned you," she said, sharply.

I whipped around just as she lunged at me. We fell back hard against the sink. I struggled as the girl's fingers grasped around my neck. I immediately attempted to call out to Nathan, but her grip on my throat was too strong. The girl ripped me from the sink and tossed me to the floor like a rag doll. I slammed against the tub hitting my head hard. I felt a dizziness take over me as I touched my forehead. Blood.

There was blood on my fingers now. I looked up just in time to see the girl reach down for me again. She crouched over me with a smirk on her face. Her long blonde hair touching my arms as she leaned in close. Her thin fingers tightened around my neck. She was strong. I could feel her nails digging into my skin. I remember crying—wishing Nathan was here—wishing I hadn't forced him away. I was horrible to him earlier, blaming him like a child for most of what happened to me. I didn't mean it though, but it didn't matter now. It was too late. Suddenly, the lights went out again and I heard a crash. It shook the walls of the bathroom and sounded as if someone was fighting—right in front of me. Then I heard a horrific scream that sent chills down my spine as I sat blinded in the darkness. I covered my ears in fear, wondering if it came from the girl. It sounded like she was in pain. But the bigger question was, who was inflicting the pain upon her? I remember quietly praying for the first time ever—desperately—for Nathan. But he still didn't come.

More thunderous bangs rippled around me as I curled up against the tub in fear. My eyes squeezed shut. Then everything went silent. I began to breathe very quietly, scared to make any sound or movement. Then a voice spoke.

"I warned him," he said. "Why must the two of you insist on defying me?"

Sporadically, the lights flickered until they eventually remained on in my now destroyed bathroom. My eyes widened to the beautiful man kneeling before me. He reached out and touched my shoulder gently.

"Are you alright?" He asked.

His features were sharp like Nathan's and his body was toned. His flawless skin, calming voice and white attire could only mean the presence of one thing—an Archangel. He was exactly how Nathan described.

"Do not be afraid young one, my name is Gabriel. I'm an—"

"Archangel," I interrupted, staring into his piercing blue eyes.

His eyebrow raised, "I thought you didn't believe."

His response embarrassed me a bit. Although it was true, I was seriously reconsidering my beliefs lately, especially after these past few years.

In our late-night talks, Nathan told me a little about the Archangels and Heaven. All of it seemed pretty impossible to believe, but on the other hand, an Archangel was right here— staring back at me now. Nathan always spoke highly of Gabriel and his wisdom. So, although I was intimidated by my moment alone with him, I also felt very safe.

"I'm going to take him from you." He said, making my heart stop for a moment. His hands then reached for mine and he slowly pulled me up from the ground. I remember looking around for the girl from my dreams.

"Do not worry. She's gone. She will not be bothering you again."

I took a breath, then quickly connected eyes with the Archangel again. I wasn't sure what to say to him, or if I was even allowed to speak to him freely. But I had to. Especially if there was a chance he was going to take Nathan from me. I slowly pulled my hands from his and spoke very politely.

"Please don't take him. I need him." I said. "Nathan is the only one who can help me. I won't survive without him." I begged. I didn't realize how badly I needed Nathan in my life until I was faced with losing him. All my anger towards him immediately washed away. I didn't care what else I had to go through in life or whatever other challenges were still to come for me. I just needed to know that Nathan would be there by my side.

The Archangel took a step back from me, staring deep into my eyes. He then snapped his fingers and suddenly my bathroom was back to its normal state. His silence scared me. So much that the correction of the room around me didn't even make me blink.

"I'm sorry. I'm so sorry." I said, hoping the stories my grandmother had told me were true. That the great Angel of Mercy Gabriel would give me another chance.

"There is something very dark following you," he said, glaring at me. "Tell me, why is it that Nathan cannot see it?"

I paused, confused as to what he was getting at. Did the Archangels know of my nightmares as well?

"I don't know," I eventually answered.

I kind of hoped that the Archangel might be able to shed some light on what's been happening to me over the past few years, but he just continued to glare at me.

"This is very interesting," He finally said, then Nathan burst through the bathroom door.

"Gabriel?!"

The Archangel glanced over his shoulder. "There you are,"

I remember how badly I wanted to run to Nathan at that moment, but Gabriel's presence froze us both in fear.

"Nathan, why is it that you're just getting here now?" He asked, politely. "Could it be, that you cannot see into her future anymore? Have things become too dark for you?"

My eyes shot to Nathan's in fear. "Is that true?" I asked.

His eyes returned to Gabriel's, he nodded.

My heart stopped again.

"I'm so sorry, Soph. I couldn't see you anywhere, or hear your call," he paused.

"It is as I said," Gabriel spoke again. "You have stepped too much into her real life, and have now become a reality to her. She sees you as an everyday human and treats you as one too. You cannot protect her anymore if you cannot see into her dreams or hear her thoughts."

My eyes remained frozen on Nathan who was tensing up from the Archangel's harsh words. But everything Gabriel was saying was true. Nathan and I had become best friends—maybe more than that. We had experienced friendship, jealousy, arguments and more in our time together. Everything a normal human would experience. He wasn't just appearing in my dreams with a few kind words of wisdom. We were a permanent part of each other's life now. Our once and a while talks at night, had turned into daytime hangouts. Walking through the parks of Vancouver, talking and sharing secrets—being normal. After my breakup with Jake, Nathan had tried to cheer me up with a stroll through the cherry blossom trees at one of the botanical gardens within the city. That's where I had tried to learn more about his personal life, but Nathan would never budge on the subject. While sharing some traditional Asian treats under the pink sky, I had also asked Nathan if he ever missed being alive. If there was any possible way for him to come back after he passed on. I remember his reply perfectly, "I wish."

Sometimes, I secretly felt guilty for Nathan watching over me. I wondered if it was ever painful for a guardian to watch over humans for so long. To watch them live their life while he stayed in limbo. He said that was one of the reasons they needed to pass on after a certain amount of time. I then asked him if watching over me ever made him feel sad. He responded in a way that made me feel deeper for him than ever before.

"I'm not jealous of your life Soph," he began, "but I am jealous that I can't be in it."

Those words changed everything between us that day—at least for me it did.

"I can still watch over her, I can still—"

"No you can't, Nathan. You didn't even see what was happening to her until it was too late. It's fortunate for you both that I stepped in. You almost lost her this time."

I remember feeling helpless as the angels argued before me. I had to do something. Nathan was the entire reason I was still living this shitty little life I had.

"Gabriel. I am so grateful for your help—"

"I'm not helping Nathan, and I will not stand for those who continue to defy His orders and show themselves in this way. It is a disgrace to us and to Him. Do you wish to become one of the Fallen?" Gabriel's tone was much stronger now. "You can't even see what is truly happening to her. You mustn't lose sight of what you've been assigned to do." He warned again.

"It me," I interrupted. "I'm making it harder for him. It's me you should be mad at. I'm so sorry. I'll do better. I promise. I'll try—"

"Sophie stop," Nathan said, cutting me off.

Gabriel stepped towards me. I felt my body tense up. His hand reached for my face and I froze in fear. I could see out of the corner of my eye Nathan step forward, surely worried for what might happen next. As Gabriel's soft hand touched my cheek, he looked deep into my eyes.

"You should be very grateful for what you have," His hand then slid up slowly to my forehead where the blood was still dripping from my wound. I felt a sudden warmth, then a bright glow that made my eyes squint from the light.

"You need an angel," he said as the light faded.

I reached up to my head—nothing. The blood and pain was gone.

"Thank you." I said, staring back at him.

"You've changed young one. You must be very careful of your thoughts and what they might bring to your life. Be aware, especially with that connection you two share." He then turned to Nathan, "That includes you,"

I looked at him, worried for what the Archangel meant. Was Nathan hiding something else from me? Or was he talking about me in general? Or maybe it was the secret ghostly girl I saw at night. I hadn't even told Nathan about her yet.

"Humans and their actions can have an effect on many lives for a very long time." Gabriel then said. "We must be aware of what surrounds us and the choices we make—especially when it deals with matters to the heart. The mind is a very powerful thing, but the heart can be blinding." Gabriel looked at me once again.

Studying me carefully. Unfortunately, I still couldn't decode what the Archangel was trying to say.

"This is very interesting," he repeated, then he was gone.

That night, Nathan stayed with me. We didn't talk. He just sat next to me on the bed while I attempted to sleep. Tossing and turning, the words from Gabriel continued to spin in my mind. I remember not wanting to close my eyes in case Nathan was taken from me. I kept looking up at him, making sure he was still there. He eventually slid down next to me and placed his hand on my cheek.

"Stay with me," I said quietly.

"I'm not going anywhere, Soph. Go to sleep." He assured me.

I moved in close to his chest, wrapping my arm around him. I didn't care about the rules anymore. I wanted to be as close to him as I could get.

The next morning, my grandmother died. She passed quietly in her sleep. Just when I felt like there was nothing else for me to lose, nothing left for me to cry about—this happened. I had lost the most important person in my life. She would never be able to see me grow up or get married, or achieve the dreams we spoke about. We would never have one of our long phone conversations again or play cards, or even watch one of those ridiculous soap operas she loved so much anymore. She was never coming back. The funeral was beautiful. I remember not being able to cry right away. I was numb and quiet—very quiet. I didn't know what to do with myself. I truly felt like I had nothing left. But Nathan said differently. He spoke very honestly to me that day at the grave. He told me that I needed to continue on with life. That it was okay to be sad. That I needed to let it sink in for a bit, but then I had to move on. He wanted me to continue to work at my dreams like my grandmother hoped I would. At first, I wasn't sure if I could. I was still terrified of losing him. I couldn't imagine what I would do after all this if he wasn't here to guide me. So, I asked him again, "Nathan, did you mean what you said earlier?" I spoke nervously.

"I mean everything I say," he replied with a smile.

"Did you mean it when you said that you weren't going anywhere? That you would be here for me—always?"

I still remember the expression on his face as I secretly panicked about my future.

"I'm right here. Always." He replied.

"But what if Gabriel—"

"We'll cross that path when it happens. He hasn't called on me yet. So maybe he sees something in us—in you. Let's not worry about that right now."

"But what about us?" I asked, taking another shot at a hard question. Clearly, we couldn't deny it anymore that our connection had changed into more of what I felt might be love. But his response said differently.

"It's probably best if we just move on from this idea that has been building up inside of us. It's just not realistic, Soph. You and I both know that deep inside. Right?"

His words broke my heart that day. As much as I understood what he was talking about, I still wished it could have ended differently.

After that, Nathan forced me to return to Vancouver and continue my life. It was hard at first—very hard. Especially with Julie gone. But Nathan remained close and continued to encourage me through the rough nights and slowly, as he said, it got easier.

I eventually learned how to survive on my own and move on with life after everything that'd happened—as painful as it was. He kept reminding me that it was a clean slate. That when these hard things happened in life, it was kind of a blessing to be able to start over and learn from our experiences.

He was right—as always, and I finally understood how lucky I was to have a guardian angel by my side. I only wished that I could give him something back for all the things he had given to me. But there was nothing I could give him and as usual, Nathan knew exactly the right words to calm my worries.

"Crazy girl, you've given me the only thing I've ever lacked—passion." He smiled. "I never had that until now. Not when I was alive, and not even as a guardian. I've always just gone through the motions with no real passion for what I was doing. But somehow, you've made me feel something different. It began the moment I met you. There was this fire inside of you that sparked me. You made me care more about one thing than I ever have before—and I mean you. I desperately didn't want to fail you. There's something about you that makes me feel so much deeper than I ever have before and only you could have done that, Soph. So for that, I'll always be grateful."

His kind words couldn't have been more perfect. But then he spoke again.

"We both know we can never be together, but don't you think our time together has been incredible and kind of a miracle?" He smiled again. "It made me feel like I had a second chance in life, and it was good. Really good. So seriously, thank you."

I knew Nathan meant every word he said to me that day. It was then that I decided to change my life. I began to try—at everything. I made an effort to make new friends. I auditioned more, and I lived my life to the fullest. I faced anything and everything life had to throw at me, and I eventually felt like the old me again. I was happy and it was all thanks to him—my guardian angel. But even happiness comes with a price. I learned that lesson with what came next.

It happened late one night while I was up playing around on my digital piano in my new apartment. I had just left my best friend Charlotte after a girls' night out. The apartment echoed with the soft sound of my melody, until I heard his voice.

"Hey you,"

I turned on my stool.

"Hey," I smiled, happy to see Nathan.

"Have a good time with Charlotte?" He asked, making casual conversation. I nodded, then got up to walk over to him but he raised his hand to me. "Can we talk?"

I looked at him curiously, confused by his question. We talked all the time. What would he need to talk to me about now that would require him to ask for permission? I suddenly felt nervous as I stepped closer. He reached for my hand.

"I have to go," he said, quietly.

"Okay. Well, do you want to talk later then?" I asked, still confused. His hands began to rub mine and eventually he looked up at me again.

"No. I mean, I have to go." He repeated. "It's time, Soph."

I stared at him, swallowing the lump in my throat that was starting to rise. I had feared this moment secretly for a very long time. I wanted to jump into his arms and tell him not to go, but I couldn't move.

"Oh, that kind of go." I said, trying to think of something better to say. "But what if I still need you? I mean, I could... anything could happen, Nate. What if—"

"No, Soph," he interrupted. "You're good. You're so good. You don't need me anymore."

I could feel the tears swelling up in my eyes. There had to be a way I could stop this, or at least prolong it a bit longer. I wasn't ready yet.

"But you're my best friend." I said, sadly. "I'll always need you."

He closed his eyes. I could tell my words hit him hard. I wanted them to. I wanted him to think about what this really meant for us.

"And you'll always be my best friend, Soph." He replied.

It wasn't the response I wanted.

"I'm going to miss you so much." I began to cry.

His eyes locked on mine, "Me too, crazy girl," he said. "Come here."

I stepped into his arms immediately and held him tight.

"I'm sorry Soph, it's over. It's really over."

His arms tightened around me as we stood embracing each other for the last time. My fingers dug into his shirt—holding on desperately.

"Be strong," he whispered.

I cried harder into his chest from his perfect words. He then leaned back and lifted my chin up so that he could stare into my eyes once again. I couldn't believe that this was the last time I was ever going to see him. The last time I was going to touch him or hear his voice.

"Nate," I said, quietly. "If this is really it..." I paused, there was something I still wanted from him. Something I desired deeply. "Then kiss me,"

He looked into my eyes sadly.

"Please…" I whispered as another tear slid down my cheek. Slowly, he leaned in closer. I could feel his warm breath on my lips. My eyes closed, preparing myself for this long awaited and overdue moment. A moment I knew we both secretly wanted. I wasn't sure if I could see him go if this didn't happen. I needed closure for us. His hands slid down my arms to lace his fingers between mine. I could feel the electricity between us racing through my veins. For some reason in that moment, I could smell lavendar in the air. It began to relax me as Nathan's lips hovered close to mine. It felt like a dream. Like this couldn't really be happening—but it was. I was standing before my guardian angel, my best friend, the one I had fallen in love with, saying goodbye—forever. Then I felt his lips touch down gently against my forehead for what seemed like only a second, then he was gone.

3
A New Life

The next morning began as it usually did. Nathan woke up bright and early. He walked Bruce and then went into the kitchen to make the two of us breakfast. Most mornings, I had to snap myself out of the past and back into the present because my history with Nathan constantly raced in my mind whenever I was alone. I was grateful for my current life with him, but also just as scared of losing it.

Slowly, I got out of bed, showered and eventually made my way to the kitchen. Nathan was already sitting at the table with pancakes, fresh fruit, and juice. He always made the most impressive breakfast. I enjoyed our morning routine. Mainly because I hated cooking and Nathan definitely had "mad skills" as he likes to say. I sat down beside him and smiled.

"I'm going to grab Bruce some food today. He's almost out."

"Sounds good," I said, taking a bite of my pancakes.

I never let Nathan in on my worries. I always did my best to clear my mind before entering a room with him.

"What do you have on the go today?" He asked, shoving a pile of food into his mouth.

I always found it cute watching him eat. He told me once that he had forgotten how tasty food was and how much he enjoyed it now that he was alive again.

"Well, I have to drop off my new headshots to my agent, then I was going to meet Charlotte for an afternoon movie. Want to join us?"

"Sure, I'll shoot you a text after I bring Bruce's food home and I'll take him out again before I go."

"Good. We definitely need to work on Charlotte a little more." I spoke again.

"I know." He said, reaching out and taking my hand. "I'm sorry this has been so hard for you. We'll keep trying. She'll come around eventually."

Since Nathan had reappeared in my life, everything was perfect—except for one thing. I had to explain to my new friends where he came from and why suddenly this strange guy they had never met before had moved into my place and was living with me as if we were a married couple. My story was that Nathan was a very good friend from back home and we had stayed in touch ever since I moved out here for acting school. Then recently, after many emails and phone conversations, we decided that we meant more to each other than we thought. So now we were trying out our new relationship here in Vancouver. Most of my friends had bought the story—except Charlotte. This bothered me a lot because Charlotte's friendship meant the most to me. We had met through one of the girls in my acting class a while back and connected immediately. It reminded me a little of my friendship with Julie. We told each other everything and she knew all about my past, except for the supernatural aspect. But I knew from the beginning that Charlotte wouldn't buy my story. She knew me too well and even if she did, she wasn't going to make it easy on Nathan.

She was constantly questioning him because she didn't want me to be used or mistreated like I was in my past relationships I told her about. I loved that she cared so much, so I could never be mad at her no matter how exhausting it was at times. I know she thinks that Nathan is just freeloading off me and I can see why. I wanted Nathan to ease into his new life and not get carried away too fast. Which is why I had told him in the beginning not to look for a job. I told him that he should just get used to living again. So I pay for everything. In my opinion, I owed him—for saving my life. I could never repay him for what he's done for me, and it never bothered me to take care of him. I liked it. It also gave me time to adjust to him being here. When Nathan returned to me a year after he left, it was a beautiful summer's day. I still remember it like it was yesterday...

I was walking home from the corner store with a slushie in my hand. Something Nathan and I shared many times during our long walks through the park. I had gotten myself a little dog, a Cairn Terrier and named him Bruce. I was doing well in my acting career, and I was healthier than ever. I even moved into a new apartment. At night, I slept soundly. Ever since Gabriel's last appearance, I hadn't had another nightmare—just like he promised. But I still thought of Nathan. Hoping by some chance he might appear by my bedside—but he never did.

As I crossed the street towards my apartment, Bruce bolted from my grip and ran towards the front steps. I quickly chased after him, trying desperately not to spill my slushie. When I reached the tall steps that led up to the entrance, I stopped halfway up, noticing someone crouching down and petting my little dog. His dark hair hung low, covering his face as he scrubbed Bruce playfully.

"He got big fast, eh?"

That voice...

My slushie dropped from my hand and exploded everywhere against the ground.

"Hey Soph," Nathan said with a smile.

He was dressed much differently than I was used to. He now wore a dark pair of blue jeans, black docs and a charcoal gray T-shirt. He was so handsome, better-looking than ever before—if that was at all possible. I stood frozen, unable to speak.

"Sophie? You in there, crazy girl?"

"Nate?" I managed to get out. "Is that really..."

I rubbed my eyes, then took a step back from him nervously unable to comprehend what was happening.

He chuckled a bit. "Yes, it's really me."

"No way," I whispered.

"Just relax, let me explain." He replied, taking a step towards me. This was going to be huge, I could feel it.

"It turns out that when a guardian angel follows his heart for all the right reasons and never falls astray, then he's truly done all he can for the person he's watching over."

I stared at him, confused. He took another step down towards me.

"But the ultimate goal, is for the person they are guarding to truly understand his or her life for what is, was, and what it could become in the future. Facing all reality and truly accepting it in their heart. You see, most people are content with whatever they can get in life because most great things are hard to achieve. So, they can't see how it could possibly manifest, but they're just accepting things instead of understanding what they can change,"

He waited for my reaction. When I still didn't speak, he went on. "Very few people in this world end up truly happy with life, Soph. But you have. You accepted your life for all that it was and still pressed on to see what you could do with it wholeheartedly. You listened to every single word I said and because of you, I got my second chance."

For the first time in a long time, my eyes teared up.

"You mean, you're really here?" I whispered, "Alive,"

He smiled, then nodded. "I guess you were a better friend to me than you thought, eh?"

I covered my mouth, trying hard to hold in the cry that was pushing its way out.

"An angel getting a second chance in life is really rare Soph, but apparently we beat the odds. So, when my time came to an end as a guardian, I was offered a choice. A choice that only a couple of angels long ago were ever given." He paused. "I chose to live. I'm really here, Sophie. For good this time."

A tear slid down my cheek as I stepped down again and almost slipped on the remains of the slushie beneath me.

He smiled, entertained by my clumsiness.

"So… I was kind of thinking." He said, stepping towards me again. "That maybe we could take that chance we used to think about. I mean, if you still think about it…"

I had dreamed of hearing those words for so long.

"Maybe, if you would let me, maybe I could be the one to make you happy. I mean, maybe I'm the one you were meant to be with. What do you think?" He asked nervously, then finally stepped down beside me and slowly laced his fingers between mine that were trembling before him. His touch was warm and made me feel very weak. If this was a dream, it would have been the worse one yet.

"Sophie, I know you're doing great right now, but I'd still like that chance to be with you. I know I can make you happy. Please let me prove it to you."

My heart was racing, beating frantically inside. Slowly, I shook my head no. He looked at me confused and a little worried.

"Nathan, you have nothing to prove to me." I said, my voice shaking now. "I already know that you make me happy. Of course I want to be with you. It's all I've ever wanted," I said, releasing his hands to run mine up his chest and around his neck.

"I can't believe you're really here,"

He let out a sigh of relief. Then leaned his forehead against mine.

"I'm so happy you said that," he whispered, pulling me in close against him.

I held him tight. He was really here, and he was alive.

"I can feel your heartbeat," I whispered. A smile grew on my face. I closed my eyes for a moment. I wanted to listen to his heart forever, but he stopped me.

"There's one more thing," he said. "Something I should have done long ago, and it's been killing me."

"What?" I asked, looking up at him.

"This," he replied, leaning in and kissing me on the lips. He took his time kissing me over and over again. I loved how he tasted. It was exactly how I had pictured it—and more—if possible. When we finally paused for air, I opened my eyes. He was still there.

"Nathan, I—"

"I love you Sophie," he said, cutting me off.

"I love you too." I smiled.

His face lit up in a way I had never seen before. He was full of life. He leaned in and kissed me again. How was I ever going to get used to this? Finally, with one last kiss, he pulled back from me.

"Looks like you need a new slushie." He paused and then licked his lips. "Berry, cola mix?"

I smiled again stepping down from him, but he unexpectedly pulled at my arm.

"Wait, one more," His lips locked with mine again.

My hands gripped his shirt, taking in everything that was him.

He then slowly pulled back, "You might get sick of me wanting to do this all the time,"

"I don't think that's possible," I replied.

"Good, because there's so much time we need to make up for." He then bent down and grabbed Bruce's leash.

When we reached the corner store, Nathan waited outside with Bruce as I went back in to get us slushies. I looked over the selection of flavors before deciding on my usual mix of cola and berry from the order board above the counter.

"Can I help you?" The cafe girl asked.

"Two... Berry cola mix please," we said in synchrony.

I glanced to the right.

A beautiful girl with long blonde hair tied up in a tight ponytail and big sunglasses on smiled down at me. The glasses were almost too big for her face.

"So sorry, go ahead," she said politely, stepping back.

"No, you go. It's fine," I insisted.

The girl smiled and ordered her drink.

It took the cafe girl only a second to dispense the drink and hand it over. The girl then grabbed it from her hand and placed some change down on the counter.

"Thanks again," she said, turning quickly to leave.

The cafe girl then turned again to get started on my order. That's when I noticed that it wasn't change that the blonde girl with the long hair left on the counter that day, but a green bracelet with beautiful little cherry blossoms on it. I picked it up and turned to see if she was still in the store, but she was long gone. I quickly placed the bracelet in my pocket, noticing the cafe girl bringing over my drinks. I then tossed down some extra money with my own to cover the girl who had taken off without paying. The cafe girl didn't seem to notice at all and to be honest, it wasn't a big deal to me either because Nathan was waiting just outside and I couldn't wait to start our new life together. I thought my life couldn't possibly get any better than the day Nathan returned to me, but I was wrong. Every day we've spent together since has made me even happier.

Snapping myself out of my daydream, I got up from the table and put my dishes in the sink. I was running a little late today.

"Text me later?" I said, then stopped in my tracks. "Man, that's still so weird to say to you—text me. Who would've thought I'd be telling an angel to text me," I continued to giggle as I collected my things.

"Previous angel, Soph." Nathan corrected me.

"I know," I smiled, looking over at him. "Seems funny, all these simple things that I do every day, you're going to be doing now too. I think, I only think it's weird because I never knew you before when you were alive in your first life. It's hard for me to see you as anything other than an angel."

"I know what you mean." He responded. "I feel like I've lived too many lives already."

"We have a lot to get used to—you and me." I said, making my way back over to him. I then leaned down and kissed him, tasting a slight hint of syrup on his lips. Then I headed out for the day.

It was another nice day in Vancouver, British Columbia as I walked to the SkyTrain. The ride to my agent's office was about twenty-five minutes. It was in Gastown, a beautiful historic area in downtown. There were many entertainment offices, coffee houses, head-shot printers and more here for the local artist to indulge in.

After getting off the SkyTrain, I walked down the street past the historic smoking clock to the gray stone building just another block away. I pulled at the heavy doors and headed up the stairs to Vancouver Coast Talent. As I reached the reception desk to check in, my agent Audrey was just coming out of her office.

"Sophie, good timing. How are you today?" She asked, motioning for me to follow her.

"Good thanks. How are you?"

"I'm great. It's busy, so that's exciting. My favorite time of the year."

"Yeah, for sure." I replied, sitting down on a chair in front of her desk. "Speaking of which, I brought you my new headshots."

Audrey took the envelope from my hands and glanced through the pictures.

"They're great Sophie. Seriously. Who did these again?"

"Actually, my friend Charlotte. She's a local photographer in town." I smiled.

Even though Charlotte was still a new photographer, she was making a pretty good name for herself with a few actors and some indie production studios.

"I think we will use… these two." Audrey said, putting the rest back into my envelope. "They show off a nice soft look for you and an edgier one too. Send me the digital files of these when you get home so I can upload them into our system. We need to start getting you some stronger roles."

"I would love that." I agreed.

"So, did you take that workshop I recommended? The voice-over one?"

"Yes, I did. Last month. It was fantastic. I'm working on a few scripts they gave me now, then I'll do my voice-over reel soon."

"Great. Send me a copy as soon as you get it back, alright? We need to get that up on our site as well."

"Definitely." I assured her.

"Alright, well that's all I need from you right now. Lots coming up this summer, hope you're ready." She said, getting up from her desk.

"Oh, and Sophie…"

"Yeah?" I responded, stopping in the doorway.

"I feel like this is your year. You've improved so much, and I really think people are starting to see that."

I smiled back at her.

"Get me that reel ASAP." She repeated.

"I will, thank-you Audrey."

As I strolled down the street, I took in a deep relaxing breath. I had never felt so calm in my entire life and every time I heard exciting news like this from my agent, it only motivated me more to keep working hard at my dreams. Then I thought about my grandmother. I wished she was here. I wanted to tell her about everything—but mostly about Nathan. My thoughts were quickly interrupted by the sound of my cell phone, it was a text from Nathan. I quickly responded with an address to meet me at. It always made me smile being able to talk with Nathan every day, even by text. I reached into my purse again and pulled out a small bracelet. It was the very one I had found the day Nathan returned to me. I had kept it after the girl left it in the store. The pink blossoms on the little green beads reminded me of when Nathan and I had walked through the cherry blossoms years ago. I loved it, even if it wasn't mine. I quickly slipped it on and headed for the train again.

When the SkyTrain pulled to a stop minutes later, I got off and walked a few blocks down to a small bubble tea shop. Waiting out front was Charlotte. She was on time as usual.

"Hey Soph!" She yelled as I got closer, then hurried over to give me a big hug.

"Hi, how are you?" I laughed.

"I'm great. It's so nice out today, huh? Good day for bubble tea and a scary movie."

"Of course, what else would I do with a perfectly nice day," I joked, as she led us inside.

"So, where's Nate today?"

"Actually, he should be here soon. I hope you don't mind, I invited him to join us."

"Sure…" She spoke.

I could tell by her tone that it wasn't, but I ignored her and went on with our conversation,

"Nathan applied for school last night," I mentioned as we stood there quietly.

"Really? School?" Charlotte repeated. "What's he going to school for?"

"English." I replied. "He wants to finish his major he started a while back."

She stared at me. "Why didn't he finish the first time?"

I paused, a little lost in my lie for that part of the story. I hadn't thought of something to say if people asked why Nathan was going to finish what he didn't long ago. I should have just said he wanted to go to school and left it at that.

"Well, he was a little tight on money. So, he had to drop out." It was the only thing I could think of.

"But now he's living with you and he doesn't pay for anything, so he has lots of money to go to school, right? Is he going to get a job while he's in school?"

"No, I told him not to." I paused, I knew where this was going.

I tried to stay positive.

"He should just concentrate on getting his degree and if things get tight, then he can get a job. But for now, we're okay with my income."

Charlotte stared at me as if I wasn't listening to the words coming out of my mouth.

"Char, it's fine. I promise. It was my idea."

"I know you do well Soph, and I'm so happy for you because you deserve everything you have right now. But you need to make sure he isn't just freeloading off you. You're too nice, too trusting, and sometimes you let people use you." She paused. "I mean, I can't help but think that he conveniently moved in with you and, it's just—"

"I know Charlotte. I do. I swear." I said cutting her off. "I know how this looks, but he isn't using me. He offered to get a job, but I told him no." I needed to get out of this conversation fast.

"Look, I know you don't trust him, and I love you for looking out for me, but like I said before, Nathan isn't someone you have to worry about. He's kind and never expects anything from anyone. He really wants to do well and he's trying very hard to make me happy and to get you to trust him. So please, can you cut him a little slack?"

"Sophie," Charlotte replied, worried still.

"Please." I begged. "I love him."

Just then Nathan entered through the doors. I could feel his presence before I saw him. He seemed to just glide in, weaving his way through the people to join Charlotte and I in line.

"Hey girls, hope you weren't waiting long," he said, giving me a kiss on the cheek. My hand immediately reached for his.

Charlotte smiled, then stepped up to order.

"What are you going to have?" I asked, while Charlotte paid for her drink.

"I'm feeling... the same as you—thanks," he said, rubbing my shoulders. I turned back to the counter and ordered our drinks. I then pulled a twenty from my wallet and paid the cashier. I noticed Charlotte in the corner of my eye giving Nathan a secret glare— surely for not paying. Charlotte was all about chivalry. Something she said was pretty much dead nowadays.

"So how are things with you, Charlotte?" He asked, sliding down the counter beside her.

Even though Nathan had promised not to read my mind, I knew he was constantly reading hers. Which is why he always had a quick response for her. This ability was the only thing left of his guardian powers, something that actually came in handy for situations like this.

"Those headshots you took of Sophie were fantastic." He spoke again.

"Thank you," she said politely, taking her drink from the shop girl.

"Hopefully your agent loved them?" She asked, looking back at me.

"She did." I replied.

"Good," she smiled. "Business is going great actually, it's steady. I actually have a big photo shoot with a new television series coming up this weekend."

"Really? That's so cool, what's the series?" I asked, grabbing the drinks from the cashier and taking my change. I handed Nathan his as we walked outside.

"It's confidential. I can't say yet, but it's a new series. I think it's about a group of high school friends. Apparently, it's going to be huge. Lots of big names on it. You should ask your agent about it. It might be something you can go out for."

"Yeah, definitely." I replied, intrigued.

"It's great having friends in the industry, isn't it? You can get the inside scoop!" Charlotte winked at me. "I'll mention your name if I get a chance."

Charlotte was really good for that. She always lets me in on gossip from the entertainment world. She had not only done many photo shoots on her own but also assisted in a few larger Hollywood ones when they were in town. She always volunteered for anything and everything she could. She was great at networking and sometimes took me along as her assistant.

I felt Nathan's arm rest gently around my shoulders. He then leaned down and kissed me on the top of the head. He knew how excited I got about these things and completely supported me. He had stayed up with me many late nights, running lines and making sure I was ready for every audition.

"So what movie are we going to see today, girls?" He asked.

"Well, there's a horror film fest going on at the theatre, so our plan was to head there and randomly pick one to watch. Half of the excitement is not planning." I joked.

"I see. Well, whatever you pick is fine with me."

"Good, because we weren't going to give you a choice anyways," I teased again. Charlotte laughed, agreeing with me.

"Oh? I see how it is," Nathan said, taking my drink and holding it high into the air where I couldn't reach it. I jumped at it a few times before giving up and grabbing him by the shirt. I pulled him down close to my face, then leaned in to kiss him. But right before our lips touched, I quickly grabbed the drink from his hand. On the way down, my bracelet accidentally scraped the side of his face.

"Ouch," he said, touching his cheek.

"Oh my god, I'm sorry Nate. I didn't mean to… my bracelet…" There was a small scrape on his skin.

"I'm fine," he laughed, "But what are you wearing today? Some kind of armor on your wrist?" He grabbed my hand and lifted it up to see. He then froze, staring oddly at my bracelet.

"What?" I asked. "What's wrong?"

Nathan didn't answer.

"He's fine," Charlotte said. "Come on you guys, we need to get to the theatre." She then grabbed my hand and pulled me down the street.

When we arrived at the theatre, we stood in line patiently for tickets. I listened as Charlotte gabbed on about how we should pick today's movie, but I was slightly distracted by how quiet Nathan had become. Charlotte jumped as her ringtone suddenly blasted from inside her purse.

"Soph," Nathan whispered, as Charlotte took her phone call. I turned to him.

"Where did you get that bracelet?" He asked.

"What, this?" I said, looking down at my wrist again.

Suddenly, the teller called out to us. I stepped forward, ignoring Nathan's question. Charlotte was still on the phone, so I quickly chose a movie.

"I'll take three for whatever horror movie is coming on next." I spoke.

I felt like that was a pretty random choice. Charlotte would definitely approve. The teller printed out the tickets and handed them to me. I then headed into the theatre with Nathan and Charlotte close behind.

"Okay, so what did we get?" Charlotte asked, hanging up her phone call.

I looked down at the ticket.

"Looks like... Blood Runs Cold."

"Ooh, sounds gruesome." She laughed. "Shall we get snacks? They're on me since you grabbed my ticket."

I turned to Nathan,

"I'm okay." He replied.

"Me too." I agreed.

"Well, I need something." Charlotte said, racing towards the lineup. Nathan quickly grabbed my arm.

"Sophie, where did you get that bracelet?" He asked again.

"I found it a while back." I answered. "How's your face? Let me see." I then reached for him, but he stepped back from me.

"Nathan, what's with you?" I said, a little annoyed. "I said I was sorry."

"No Soph, I don't care about the scratch. I'm fine." His face softened. "I just don't remember you getting that bracelet. Where did you find it?"

I continued to look at him oddly.

"Nathan, what does it matter?" I asked, confused about his sudden interest in my jewelry. I didn't want to tell him that it was a stolen keepsake.

"Nathan?" I said, still waiting for him to respond.

I reached up and touched his chest. "Nate, talk to me."

"It's fine. I was just wondering, that's all." He paused, "I'm sorry, I didn't mean to be rude."

Just then Charlotte returned with a large popcorn, a pop and some chocolate candies, they were my favorite.

"How did you know?" I joked, taking the box of candies from her hand. We then headed into the theatre.

Later that night, Nathan slid into bed next to me, still pretty quiet from earlier. He rested his head down on the pillow then reached out for me. I moved in closer, lying my head down on his chest.

"Nate," I said, quietly. "Are you feeling alright today?"

"Of course," He replied.

I felt his hand begin to rub my back.

"You seemed quiet at the theatre. Are you angry with me?" I asked again.

"Sophie, I could never be mad at you." He smiled and then leaned in to kiss me on the forehead.

I didn't buy it though. Something was off.

"Are you nervous? I mean, about getting into school?"

"A little." He replied.

"Don't be. I'm sure you'll get in." I said, honestly.

He then sighed and closed his eyes. In the evenings, Nathan and I usually had long talks in bed before we went to sleep, but tonight was different. He was unusually quiet.

"Nate…" I spoke again, trying to make a conversation happen.

"Yeah," He replied, with his eyes still closed.

"Can you tell me a little more about your past?"

His eyes opened slightly.

"Tell me about the people in your first life. Do you ever wonder what happened to them? I mean, did you ever—"

"Sophie, it's late." He said, cutting me off.

"Sorry." I replied, a little taken back.

I took his hint and turned over in bed—pulling the covers up tight.

"Soph…" He spoke again, moving in close behind me. "Don't be mad."

I didn't reply. Nathan was open to me about everything. His feelings, ideas, thoughts and more. Everything except his past life and the people that were in it. Which was frustrating at times. Knowing little things like him loving English class, reading and breakfast wasn't much to go on. I wanted more. I felt him tug on my shoulder a bit, but I didn't move.

"Crazy girl, come on."

I could never fight him for long. I wanted to stare into those beautiful brown eyes. I turned over, and the second I did he met my lips with his. "I love you." He whispered.

"I love you, too." I replied.

"Look, I'm sorry. I know you want answers. But to be honest, when you become a guardian angel, part of the deal is that you can never look back into your past life—ever again."

"Never?" I replied.

He shook his head no.

"To be a guardian, I must always move forward and be grateful for the work I was doing. My life was to serve Him alone and watch over those who are in need."

What a horrible thing, I thought to myself. To die and then be reborn in a beautiful new way, but to never be able to look back on the ones you loved. To never know what became of them. It must be so hard.

"It's as if my past life didn't exist. The Archangels made sure of that too. They said I couldn't look back even if I tried. They even warned me again before I returned to you. The rules still stand in my new life."

"Nathan, that's horrible." I reached up to touch his cheek.

"I'm not trying to avoid the conversation when you ask me about my life, Soph. It's just, since I never knew what became of anyone, it kind of hurts to even try and think about it. Understand?"

I suddenly felt horrible for pushing Nathan constantly about the subject. I wish I knew this earlier.

"I'm so sorry, Nate."

"It's fine. Maybe someday I'll be able to talk about it. But for now, you're my family and this is my new life. That's all that matters, right?" He then leaned in and kissed me again. Pressing his lips hard against mine.

Nathan was right. He was alive now and that's all that mattered. He deserved a fresh start.

"I will tell you this though," He spoke again, "I have never loved someone so much like I love you."

A smile grew on my face.

"Same," I replied. "You're my world, Nathan."

"Your world?" He smirked.

"What?" I giggled, "I just mean—"

"No, no, I like that." He smiled, kissing me once more. "I'm happy

to be your world, because you are definitely mine."
He then embraced me again.

4
Unforgotten

The next morning Nathan didn't wake as early as he normally did. I quietly slipped out of bed to take Bruce for a walk. I could hear him whining faintly from his kennel in the living room and I felt like Nathan deserved to sleep in for once.

After walking my dog, I quietly showered up and got ready for the day. I then made my best attempt at preparing breakfast.

Quietly, I snuck back into the bedroom, doing my best not to spill anything on the tray as I walked. I placed it down on the nightstand, then crawled over Nathan into bed. I gently kissed him on the lips. His eyes opened slowly. "How graceful of you to topple over me…" He joked, pulling me close.

"Morning, sleepy head." I giggled.

He breathed in deep before smiling back.

"You feeling alright?" I asked, noticing how warm Nathan's body was.

"Yeah, I think so." He said, feeling his forehead.

"You must be sick, because there is no way I could be up before you."

"That's true." He laughed, then pulled me in for another kiss. "I think I'm just tired. I didn't sleep too well last night."

"Well, humans do need rest to function, Nate." I then touched his forehead, making sure he didn't have a temperature. He was a little warm, but nothing too serious. "Maybe you should just stay in bed today and get your energy back," I suggested.

Nathan then glanced over at my tray. "Is that breakfast?"

"Indeed." I replied.

I crawled over him again, making him moan in pain to grab the tray from the nightstand. I carefully placed it on his lap. On the tray was a glass of orange juice, an English muffin with butter and peanut butter on it, and a bowl of cereal. Of course, it was my favorite cereal, the one with the rainbow marshmallows in it. But I was sure he would love it.

"I know it's not as fancy as you make, but I tried." I spoke.

"Soph, this is great. Thank you. You're sweet."

He then took a bite of the English muffin.

"Wow, there's a lot of peanut… butter... on this," he said, trying to get his words out.

I bit my lip nervously, then watched Nathan swallow the chunk of food. He then took a big gulp of juice.

"It's perfect."

"Really?" I replied, in disbelief.

He nodded, taking another sip of juice.

"Good! Maybe I do have the talent for breakfast then, huh?" I said, jumping off the bed to grab the last few things I needed from my closet.

"I have an audition today, but I'll be back before dinner. If you're still not feeling that well, I can make us something. Since my skills are improving." I joked.

"Okay, good luck." He said, as I slung my backpack over my shoulder. "And don't worry about dinner," he spoke again. "I'm sure I will be fine. I'd be happy to make us something. Just text me when you're on the way home, alright?"

"Kay! Feel better!" I shouted, then hurried down the hallway.

Around noon, Nathan finally got out of bed and got dressed for the day. He gathered up the tray of food and took it into the kitchen. He decided that maybe a good walk might make him feel better. He called out to Bruce and hooked him up with the leash.

It was cool outside as Nathan walked slowly behind the little dog. Taking a deep breath in, he tried hard to clear his head as he walked through the cherry trees in bloom. Just then, a thought crossed his mind. A faint memory from long ago. One he was not allowed to think about. He glanced up at the pink budded trees. Their scent filled the air as the wind whistled around him—bringing along another familiar scent. Hers. He choked a little in fear as his eyes searched the area but found no one. He then remembered her words, *"I love everything about them, maybe someday you can walk with me through them? Wouldn't that be nice?"*

His eyes closed. Her voice was so clear. As if she was right there beside him. Suddenly feeling weak in the knees, Nathan lowered himself to the ground. With his fingers resting on the cold pavement below, he took a moment to catch his breath. Bruce tugged at the leash a few times, but Nathan didn't move. The little dog returned to his side and whimpered, scratching his hand.

"I'm alright buddy, I just need a moment." He said, taking another deep breath in. Bruce clawed again at his hand, then nudged his nose against Nathan's face that hung low.

"Okay, I'm getting up." He said, taking another deep breath and patting the little dog on the head. "Sorry, let's go."

Slowly, he rose to his feet again. He had to keep his promise to the Archangels. He had done so well up until now, but what sparked this? Bruce howled and pulled at the leash again. They continued their walk through the park.

When Nathan arrived home, he jumped into the shower to freshen up. He let the hot water beat down against his shoulders, but the water wasn't helping. His mind began to race again with thoughts he wasn't allowed to have.

He remembered her body, beaten and bruised as she sat lifelessly in the bathtub. He remembered the water turning red as the blood washed away from her skin. He felt his chest clench up as it did at that very moment long ago. He remembered how fragile her body was when he lifted her from the tub, wrapping her in warmth and placing her down on her bed. Then he heard her voice again, *"Don't leave me…"*

Pain shot through him. "Stop," he whispered.

He didn't want to remember any of this. He didn't want to relive that horrible night. He quickly reached down and turned off the water.

Getting out of the shower, he snagged a blue towel hanging on the rack to dry himself off. He then wrapped it around his waist and stepped towards the mirror. He wiped the moisture from the glass.

"What are you doing?" A familiar voice said from behind.

Nathan turned in shock to see the Archangel, Gabriel.

"Your thoughts are changing, Nathan. Are you not happy with the new life we gave you?"

Caught off guard by the sudden appearance of the Archangel, Nathan found himself at a loss for words. He hadn't seen or heard anything from the angels since the day he returned to the real world.

"They just came out of nowhere, I can't—"

Gabriel raised his hand to him.

"Listen to me very carefully, Nathan. You are a miracle. Do you understand that?"

Nathan nodded.

"Not many guardians get a second chance at life. This young girl beat the odds for you. If you continue to indulge yourself in these memories, you could lose everything."

Nathan stared at him in fear.

"What did I tell you a while back?" Gabriel went on. "I told you to move on with your life and forget about the past." He took a step closer. "You fought so hard for Sophie. You love her, don't you? Or are you having second thoughts?"

"No. Never." Nathan answered. "I love Sophie—more than anything and I would never do anything to ruin us. I didn't mean for these thoughts to appear they just did, ever since…" He paused suddenly, deep in thought. "Gabriel, may I ask, just this once? What happened to… I mean, after I died…" He paused again nervously, looking at the Archangel. "What happened to her, Gabriel?"

The Archangel didn't respond.

"Please Gabriel, at least tell me if she was, okay?" He begged again.

The Archangel continued to stare at him.

"I can feel you right now. Your heart is racing." He replied.

"These feelings stirring up inside of you are not good. Don't you understand?"

"If you can feel me, then you know my intentions are true. Please, Gabriel." Nathan asked, again. "I just want to know what happened to her. Was she alright?"

After a long moment, the Archangel finally spoke.

"Serena is fine."

Nathan stared silently into Gabriel's eyes. The sound of her name aloud filled his body with various emotions.

"So, she's—"

"Nathan, stop. That's enough. I didn't give you a second chance for you to act like this. Do you want to stay here or not? Are you truly going to play with God's gift and make a fool of me?"

"Of course not. I'm sorry." He responded quietly.

Lowering his head, Nathan closed his eyes from exhaustion. He took a deep breath in and released his thoughts as the Archangel requested. When he finally opened his eyes, Gabriel was gone. Heading back into his bedroom, Nathan felt much more awake after his recent interaction and quickly got dressed. Standing quietly in the center of the room, he looked over to the dresser where a small jewelry box sat. After hesitating for a few minutes, he eventually made his way over and opened it up.

There it was, the green bracelet with cherry blossoms on it. He carefully picked it up to examine it closer. He was right. He hadn't seen it wrong. It was exactly the same. He remembered it being one of Serena's favorite pieces of jewelry—solely because of the cherry blossoms on it.

Serena had an obsession with Japan, their folklore tales and more importantly—the Sakura tree. She had shown the bracelet to Nathan the first time he came to her home to work on a project for school, and when she spoke about walking through the blossoms with Nathan by her side. It was the first time she had openly admitted feelings for him.

The memories rushed back quickly now, but what he couldn't figure out, was why Sophie had one exactly like it? He quickly slipped the bracelet into his pocket and headed for the living room.

Sitting down at the computer, he placed the bracelet down on the desk before him and began to type in her name. SERE-

The screen flickered.

He gave the mouse a little shake to wake it back up. The screen flickered again. He then leaned over, making sure the computer was fully plugged in. Everything looked good. When it finally calmed down, he hit the search button once completing her name. Suddenly, the screen went black. Bruce growled from behind couch, then peered out cautiously. Nathan continued to tamper with the computer. He even tried resetting it, but nothing worked. The power had completely cut out. He looked around the room nervously, wondering if Gabriel was still watching. Bruce growled again. Nathan quickly grabbed the bracelet and got up from the computer. He then hurried to the front closet to grab his jacket. The little dog scurried after him.

"I'll be back, Bruce. Stay here."

Nathan hurried to the local library, a place he had been to many times since returning to the real world. At the main desk, an old woman wearing thick red reading glasses glared at him.

"Excuse me, is there a computer free I could use right now?" He asked, politely.

The woman typed something into the computer, then looked up at him. "There's one at the back, to the left of fiction." She said, pointing the way.

Nathan quietly made his way through the library. It was very busy today. He suddenly felt a little guilty for the actions he was about to take. He knew Gabriel was right. He shouldn't be playing with the gift God gave him, but he just needed to know a little bit more—to calm his mind. His hands shook as he numbly sat down at the last computer available. Shaking the mouse to wake up the screen, Nathan carefully typed in Serena's name once again. So far so good. Just then, the boy sitting beside him moaned. Nathan glanced over to see the screen on his computer flicker off and on again. He took that as a warning and quickly slid the arrow over the search button. Just as he was about to click, Gabriel's voice thundered around him.

"Nathan!"

Nathan covered his ears, looking around. Luckily, no one heard the angel's warning but him. The boy beside him looked at him oddly. He smiled, then nervously glanced around the library again.

There was no sight of the Archangel. His eyes returned to the computer screen. He had to try, just one more time. He quickly hit the search button and just as a list of options came up on the screen, the entire library went black. Everyone began to complain and the boy beside him continued to stare at him. Slowly, Nathan got up— the boy watching his every move.

"Alright," Nathan said aloud. "I'm done,"

The boy quickly shuffled the chair back from him. Nathan stopped and looked down at him. "Sorry."

He then exited the library.

Walking down the street, Nathan tried desperately to fight back the thoughts of his past life. When he reached the corner, a small book café caught his attention. He stopped for a moment, staring through the window at the display of books, then decided to go inside.

The café was quiet and smelled of sweet tea and freshly baked pastries. The white walls were painted with dark trees that soared to the ceiling. Nathan stepped up to the counter and gazed across the order board.

"Would you like to try our new Angel's Dream tea latte today?" The girl asked from behind the counter.

Nathan smirked, "Why not."

After paying, he slid down to the end of the counter to wait for his drink. Behind him stood a tall bookshelf with an abundance of novels on it. His fingers traced the spines until he stopped on one. The Hero and the Crown. One of his favorites. He pulled it from the shelf and found a seat at one of the small wooden tables. He only read two pages before the café girl brought over his latte.

Nathan placed the book down and leaned in to smell the sweet scent of Angel's Dream tea. It smelt of lavender, vanilla and something else. He couldn't put his finger on it. Carefully, he picked up the cup and placed his lips on the rim. The thick foam coated his mouth as he took his very first sip. The first sensation to the tongue was quite bitter, but it only lasted a second before the sweetness settled in, filling his mouth with a beautiful taste. It was perfect. After a few more sips, he sat the cup back down and reached for his book again.

"How is it, Nathan?" A voice asked from behind.

He quickly turned to a girl with long auburn-colored hair. She smiled, then continued to wipe down the tables around him.

"I'm sorry, do I know you?" He said, staring back at her.

The girl looked at him confused. She stepped a little closer about to say something, but Nathan spoke again.

"Did you just ask me how my drink was?" He repeated, certain he heard her voice.

"No," She smiled. "But I will now. How is it?"

He stared a moment longer, then looked around the room.

It had to be her. There was no one else on his side of the café except one older gentleman in the far corner.

"Did you want something else?" The girl asked.

Nathan's glance slowly returned to hers. Her hazel eyes seemed to glow a little from the sunlight shining through the windows.

"No." He finally answered. "Sorry, this is perfect." He then returned to his book.

When I heard the front door open, I hurried down the hallway.

"Where were you?" I asked, meeting Nathan at the door. "I tried calling and texting, but you didn't answer."

"Sorry about that," He replied, giving me a kiss on the cheek. "I was at a café reading and I forgot my phone."

It was a reasonable answer, but I was still a little worried.

"Did you eat?" He asked, changing the subject.

I shook my head, no.

He then took my hand and led me towards the kitchen.

As Nathan began to make us dinner, I sat down at the kitchen table silently.

"You're awfully quiet over there," he said from the stove. "Aren't you going to come over here while I cook and chat with me?"

Normally when Nathan made dinner, I would join him. Not in the cooking aspect, but by sitting on the counter next to him. Here, I talked about anything and everything that was on my mind that day. It was our sweet, flirty time together. But today, his actions had spooked me a little and I was caught deep in my thoughts.

Nathan eventually stopped what he was doing and joined my side. When I didn't look up at him, he pulled out the chair in front of me and sat down.

"Talk to me,"

"It's nothing, you just scared me, Nate." I finally said.

"I scared you?" He repeated.

"Yes. I've never not been able to get a hold of you and it worried me. I mean, are you okay? Are you feeling better?"

"Soph, I'm fine." He smiled. "That's why I went out for a bit. To get some fresh air. I'm sorry, I didn't mean to worry you."

He then leaned in and kissed my forehead.

"Help me make something to eat. You must be hungry. I am."

I nodded, feeling a little embarrassed about overreacting.

"Come on, get up," he repeated, pulling at my arms.

He led me over to the stove.

I stood quietly as he continued to cook. He then turned to me and crossed his arms.

"Okay, I know I said I wouldn't do this, but you're worrying me now. So, I hope you'll forgive me." He began.

I looked at him oddly.

"I'm fine, and you're fine. This is something we are going to have to get used to in life. There will be times when one of us might be late, or will miss some messages, but we can't overreact. Okay? I know that we're not a normal couple, but you need to start thinking like we are. Otherwise, we will never have a normal life, Soph."

He had read my mind.

"I love you for how much you care about me, but I can take care of myself."

"You're right, I'm sorry." I replied. "It's just... scared."

He looked at me oddly.

I had never expressed this to him out loud before. I went on,

"I'm so happy having you here, but I'm also afraid of losing all of this at the same time. I'm afraid that I'll wake up one morning and you'll be gone, or something will happen to you one day when we're not together and—it drives me crazy." I blurted out.

Nathan pulled me in close.

"Soph, take a breath." He said, calmly. "Nothing is going to happen to me and we can't stop what is meant to happen to a person anyways, you should know that. We also can't spend every day being afraid of what might come. I need you to have faith in our

future—I do. Nothing is going to take me from you, alright?"
I nodded in his arms.

"Let's not spend our life together being afraid. I'm going to get sick and I'm going to have bad days, and everything else that happens to a normal person. We might even fight and that's okay. We will get through everything because we were meant to be. That, I'm certain of. That's why I didn't live very long in my first life. That's why I was your guardian, and that's why I'm here now. Don't you think so too?"

I smiled at him and nodded again.

"Oh Soph, what am I going to do with you—my crazy girl." He hugged me tightly. "I will always be here. You can't get rid of me."

I tightened my grip around him.

"Sorry," I repeated.

"We will get past this, but talk to me, alright? Don't keep stuff like this bottled inside. It doesn't help either of us. Even if you feel embarrassed about your thoughts, just say them, okay?"

I nodded again.

"Promise? Because if you don't, I'm going to start reading your thoughts again." He teased.

"I promise." I assured him, a little annoyed.

"Good, now how about some pancakes?" He asked, stepping away from me to pull out the mix from the cupboards.

I lifted myself up onto the counter.

"Can I help?" I asked, sliding myself over towards the stove.

"Whoa, um, no it's fine." He said, stopping my legs from moving any closer.

I glared at him.

He then winked at me. "I've got this."

"What do you mean by that? I made you breakfast. You said you loved it." I replied, grabbing the box from his hands.

"I have skills too."

"Yes, you do—definitely—but they just aren't as good as mine and this is my favorite meal. So I want it perfect."

"What? I think I'm offended by that," I laughed a little.

"No, no. Don't be." He said, taking the box back from my hands.

"I have just the job for you,"

He then handed me a bottle of syrup with a big smile on his face. "When they're ready, I like a lot on mine."

I sighed, shaking my head at him. "Fine, I get it."

5

An Understanding

The next day Nathan was back to his old self. He woke up early, walked Bruce and made breakfast for the two of us. He was doing his best to cheer me up from the night before and it was working. I felt pretty bad for overreacting, but Nathan handled it well. His perfect words and kindness helped me understand our relationship a little better. It seemed even the simplest of things was going to be a learning curve for Nathan and I, but he was right, we did have to start thinking like a normal couple—it was just easier to say than do. After finishing my breakfast, I kissed Nathan goodbye and headed out the door. I was off to help Charlotte with a photo shoot today.

As I hurried to the train, I tried my very best to really take in Nathan's words. I had to trust that he could take care of himself, that he would be fine, and he was definitely going to be there when I got home. I repeated this to myself as I hopped on the SkyTrain.

Moments later, I came to my stop. I headed down the street towards what looked like an abandoned industrial area of town—kind of creepy in my opinion. As I got closer, I noticed Charlotte sitting on a bench out front. Her sunglasses were big, hiding most of her face as she sat there staring up at the sky, bathing in the sunlight.

As I watched her, I worried for a moment that I wasn't dressed as nicely as I should be. Her skinny white jeans hugged her hips perfectly, and they were accompanied by a baby blue lace top. She looked like a model. She was always put together so well—so in style. Her finishing touch was a pair of flower printed heels that gave her at least two inches on her height. I never knew how she managed to work in those shoes, but she always did.

"Hey, you beach bum!" I hollered.

She quickly sat up and slipped her glasses up to the top of her head. Her long sandy-blonde hair blew elegantly in the wind as she got up from the bench.

"Hey," She laughed.

I saluted her playfully, "I'm ready boss! What do you need me to do?"

She smiled, "Grab a bag and follow me. Today is a very interesting shoot. It's for one of those artsy magazines."

"Oh yeah? Cool, what's the theme?" I asked, intrigued.

"You'll see," she teased. We then headed inside.

It was a long hike up the wooden staircase before we reached the doorway. Charlotte pushed open the doors with all her might. Inside, there was a room with a bright light shining in the middle of it. As we stepped inside, people were frantically running all over the place. Against the back wall were a few tall ladders and some odd vintage items. The warehouse was cold, and I immediately regretted not bringing a sweater. Charlotte led us to what I assumed was going to be the set and began to unpack.

"What's with the ladders?" I asked.

"I told you, Soph. It's artsy. I don't ask, I just deliver the goods and try my best to create their vision. But don't worry, there is a very good aspect to today's shoot."

"And what's that?" I asked again, passing her a tripod.

"That," Charlotte replied, motioning behind me.

I turned just as a very good-looking young man in white, walked up behind me. I froze for a moment. The last time I saw someone dressed like that was the night Gabriel appeared to save me. The young man stopped in front of me and smiled.

"Where would you like me?" He asked.

"Right over here," Charlotte said, guiding him onto the set.

I stood silently, still caught up in my thoughts of the Archangel. That quick moment flooded my mind with old memories—and fear. Just then, a lady pushed by me with a bag full of feathers and immediately began to scatter them all over the floor.

"Excuse me, are you ladies ready for me?" Another voice spoke from behind.

I turned again to see a second young man in white. He was tall and very handsome. His dark brown hair was freshly styled off to the side, and his piercing blue eyes and tanned skin glittered as if he walked right off the beach. I smiled, a little nervous by his presence.

"Soph, come on..." Charlotte laughed. "Send him over,"

"Oh, uh, right." I said, "Just, go over there," I pointed, trying to guide him in the right direction.

"Thanks," he replied politely, then stepped past me.

His eyes connected with mine again as he found his place on set.

"What is wrong with you?" Charlotte teased. "I mean, I know they're good looking and all, but we need to act professional,"

"Right, of course. Sorry Char." I said, giggling a bit. "I'm still confused though, what's the theme?" I asked again.

Charlotte stopped what she was doing and grabbed a feather from the ground.

"Duh," she smiled. "Angels from Heaven," She then blew a feather at me playfully. "So get a hold of yourself. We are about to be surrounded by a whole lot of good-looking!"

And just as Charlotte said that three more handsome guys walked past us. Every single one of them was in great shape, with perfect hair and perfect skin.

"This is definitely my favorite job." Charlotte winked at me.

I agreed. She then quickly grabbed my hand and led me towards the men.

Another lady joined us and began to scatter more feathers across the ground. Charlotte started positioning the five guys around the set.

"Hey Soph, get Alex to move a little closer to Matt, please." I looked around nervously, who the heck was Alex?

"Um, Soph is it?" A young man spoke up. "That's me, she's talking about."

I felt my cheeks grow warm; it was the beach boy again.

"Yeah, and I'm Matt." Another guy called out, clearly trying to help me out with my job.

I hurried towards Alex and guided him to where Charlotte wanted him.

"First time at a photo shoot I'm guessing," Alex laughed.

"Not really." I replied. "I help Charlotte out here and there when I can, but I've never been on one this big before."

"That's nice of you, are you a model too?"

"Definitely not," I laughed. "Actress, actually."

"Cool. I definitely would've thought model though. You're, um, pretty. I mean that nicely. Not in a creepy way," he joked. "I'm not a creep—I promise."

I laughed again. "Thank you, but no. I would never model. I'm really into acting, and I sing a little too. So, how long have you been doing this?" I asked as a makeup artist pushed her way past me. I felt awkward standing there as she unbuttoned his dress shirt and began to powder his bare chest, but Alex didn't seem to mind.

"Only for the past year or so. I'm actually thinking about getting into acting now. Maybe I can ask you a few questions after the shoot? Perhaps you could give me a few tips? Would that be okay?"

"Um, sure." I smiled. "I'll tell ya what I can."

"Sophie, off the set! We're starting now," Charlotte hollered from behind the camera.

I quickly stepped away as the lights went down and five soft white spotlights from above lit up the area. Each one of the guys had this heavenly glow around him from the white clothing and dark cold-looking set design.

I stood quietly to the side as Charlotte did her thing. She snapped what seemed like a million photos and before I knew it, they were done.

I couldn't help but think of Nathan the entire time. How funny was it that I was here on set with fake angels, when I had a real one waiting for me back at home.

I reached into my pocket to grab my cell. I wanted to text Nathan now that I was thinking of him. My fingers paused over the screen. I promised him I wouldn't worry. If I texted him now, would he think I was worrying too much? I sighed, then put the phone back in my back pocket. Just then, I felt it buzz. Reaching back for my phone my face lit up as I looked at the name on my screen. Nate.

"HEY CRAZY GIRL. HOW'S YOUR DAY? I JUST WANTED TO SAY I LOVE YOU AND I'LL SEE YOU TONIGHT— HOPEFULLY FOR DINNER. LET ME KNOW."

He must have read my mind, but I didn't care this time. It was exactly what I wanted. I quickly texted him back.

"I'll SEE YOU FOR DINNER, DEFINITELY. I LOVE YOU… MORE."

After tossing my phone away, I began to help the others clear the set area while the models changed back into their normal attire and washed themselves of any makeup still lingering on their body. Packing up the last bit of stuff into Charlotte's equipment bag, I was startled by a tap on the shoulder.

"Sophie?" Alex said, from behind.

"Oh hey,"

"Do you still have a second to chat with me? Maybe we can grab a coffee?"

Suddenly, I felt a little nervous about agreeing to sit down and chat with this very good-looking guy. I wondered if Nathan would be okay with it.

"Um, well, it's actually kind of late now," I said.

"Really? Oh, okay, that's cool. Maybe another time then?"

"Yeah, sure." I said, just as Charlotte snuck up behind him.

"Okay, well, hopefully I'll see you again soon." He spoke. "Maybe on another shoot? I've been in quite a few with Charlotte, she's really good."

"Yeah, she is." I said, looking over at her.

He smiled, then slid his hands into his pockets and slowly stepped away.

I felt a little bad for rejecting him.

"Oh my god Soph, why didn't you go for a coffee with him?" Charlotte finally spoke. "Alex is such a sweetie. He's not stuck up like other models. He's actually a really nice guy and... I think he kind of likes you."

"Char, come on, seriously?"

"What?"

"You know why. His name is Nathan—my boyfriend—who I love very much."

"I know that, but it's just coffee between friends and if you hang with him, then he might have some cute friends that I could meet." Her eyes widened with the thought.

"Maybe, he could hook me up with Matt. I hear they're good friends." Charlotte rambled on. "I've had a crush on him for a while now."

"Charlotte, you meet so many guys with this job. Why don't you just hang with them yourself?"

"Because it would be less nerve-racking if I had someone with me. I need a wing man, or wing woman—whatever they call it." She complained.

"I'm sorry, it's out of the question. I know you don't trust Nate, but he's everything to me."

Charlotte sighed, "I know. I believe you, but I'm just saying that maybe you shouldn't seal yourself with him just yet. There are so many people out there and after all the crazies you've had, perhaps you need to take your time and find a good person."

I crossed my arms, a little upset.

"I have, and Nathan and I are going to prove that to you—however long it takes us."

"Okay," Charlotte responded, throwing her hands in the air. "Don't get upset. I'm just looking out for you. Sorry," She frowned, giving me a sad puppy dog face. She then opened her arms, waiting for a hug.

I shook my head, then hugged my best friend. "Now let's get out of here. I can't wait to get home and eat."

Charlotte agreed, rubbing her stomach. We then grabbed the last of her things and headed on our way.

When I finally got home, I locked the door behind me. The scent coming from the kitchen was enchanting. Italian. My favorite. I hung my purse over the hook at the entrance, then followed the lovely scent into the kitchen. Nathan met me at the table with a kiss.

"Hi beautiful, how was the shoot?"

"Oh, it was interesting," I replied. "I missed you." I then kissed him again.

"I missed you too. So, what was so interesting about this photo shoot?" He questioned.

"Guess what the theme was?"

Nathan looked at me puzzled.

"Angels from Heaven." I said, with a giggle.

"Oh really?" He smiled. "So, I'm guessing it was a bunch of good-looking guys dressed in white and—there must have been feathers involved and—glittering bodies," he teased. "Definitely glittering bodies."

I laughed at how accurate he was.

"Pretty close, minus the glitter. We save that for the vampires."

He smirked, then turned to grab the dish full of pasta from the stove. He placed it down on the kitchen table.

"Have a seat, I just need to grab the garlic bread."

I did as he requested.

"Nate, can I ask you something?" I said, a little awkwardly.

He carefully pulled the garlic bread from the oven and slid them onto a large plate for us to share. He then joined me at the table.

"Does it bother you?" I spoke again.

"Does what bother me?" He repeated, placing a piece of bread on my plate.

"Does it bother you that I hung out with a bunch of guys today?"

He looked up at me with a smirk on his face.

"No, why? Should it?" He teased.

"No. I just mean, I don't know what our boundaries are. One of them asked me out for a coffee because he wanted to know more about acting. He was thinking of getting into the field. He had some questions for me, but I said no."

"Soph, you can hang out with whoever you want. I trust you." He smiled. "I love you and I know you love me, so I'm not worried about anything." He then paused, with a bunch of pasta wrapped around his fork and looked up at me again, "Unless there's something I should be worried about?"

His eyebrow rose slightly.

"Definitely not." I assured him. "No one compares to you. I just didn't know if that would upset you."

"It wouldn't have." He replied. "Like I said, I trust you and I would never tell you who you could or couldn't hang around with. As long as I know you're safe, I'm happy. I know in this industry you're going to have a lot of friends. I also understand with acting that you're eventually going to have an on-screen boyfriend, and you're probably going to have to kiss him, and I'll be okay with that too, as long as you tell me that I have nothing to worry about. Okay?"

I smiled back at him and took a bite of my food, feeling much better about the situation. A perfect response… again.

Later that night after dinner, Nathan and I crawled into bed and turned on a movie. These were my favorite nights. Just lying around in Nathan's arms made everything perfect.

"Nate?" I said, quietly.

"Yeah?"

"There's something else I want to tell you about today." I said, sitting up to look at him. "There's this guy, Matt. He's a model and Charlotte really likes him. She wants to ask him out on a date, but she wants it to be a group date so it's less awkward for her. She was going to invite his best friend, Alex. He's the guy I told you about earlier that wanted to go for coffee with me,"

"Go on," Nathan said, kindly.

"Well, if she asks Matt out, I want you to come with us."

"Soph, it's fine. You don't need to prove yourself to me. If Charlotte wants you to go, then go. Maybe she'll think I'm not trying to control you more if you tell her I was cool with you going out with them," he laughed.

"Well, it would impress her." I sighed. "I seriously think she's waiting for the day you snap on me so she can be right about her opinion."

"Snap on you? I don't think that's possible." He said, shaking his head. "You couldn't possibly make me mad."

"I might, someday…" I admitted, sadly—worried at the thought of disappointing him. "I mean, we're probably going to fight eventually."

"Nope, we'll never fight," he teased, pulling me in tight.

"Nathan, we might," I repeated, trying to be realistic about the situation.

"Are you trying to argue with me now?" He asked, in a more serious tone. "Because, do you know what I'm going to do if we ever start to fight?" He spoke again.

"I'm not trying to argue with you," I responded quickly.

"I'm just saying that—"

His lips met mine—cutting off my ability to speak. I yanked myself back from him.

"That's your plan to not fight? Every time we start, you're just going to—"

He kissed me again.

"Nathan, seriously?" I laughed. He did it again. "Okay, you win."

"See," He smiled. "It works. Problem solved, now be quiet. I love this movie."

"You've never seen—"

He kissed me one last time. I retreated quietly back down by his side.

6
Misguided Ghosts

The woods were silent and strangely beautiful as she made her way through the trees. As gloomy as this place was, she sometimes enjoyed it when everything was quiet—when the others were not around. The silence helped her think and sometimes see things a little more clearly. Especially without that voice in her head.

Deep in thought, she dragged her feet slowly through the dirt. She hadn't planned to be here this long. This place was starting to feel heavy and suffocating. She had promised the plan would work. She had promised that he would notice, but he didn't. Kicking her feet across the ground she let out a frustrated sigh. The trees rustled, listening in on her thoughts. She was stuck in this god-forsaken place.

"I agree, we need a better plan," a voice spoke from behind. Ready to defend herself, she whipped around quickly.

"Calm down, it's me." The young woman spoke again, "Your mind is really racing today, isn't it?" she asked.

"You promised it would work, but it hasn't—none of it." She complained.

The young woman stepped closer, her long auburn hair blowing in the wind.

"It will work. We just had a minor setback. I'll admit, I didn't think he'd actually get a second chance, but don't worry. We can get by that. These things take time,"

"But I've been doing everything precisely how you said. It's her, isn't it? She's blocking his mind."

"Don't worry too much about that, she already doubts herself. You will have another chance soon enough. She still dreams."

The two young women stared at each other.

"Promise?" She asked again.

"I promise." The other smiled, "Your time is coming. I can feel it. He's already begun to look for you."

"He has?"

The woman nodded, "I'm sure you will make contact soon."

She sighed in relief, "I miss him. It's been so painful."

The woman slowly glided by, a faint smile on her face. "Patience," her voice whistled in the wind.

Then she was gone

I could feel Nathan stirring in the bed beside me. With my back to him, I glanced up at the clock on the nightstand. 3:15am. I felt the bed move again as my eyes closed heavily, then I heard his voice.

"Soph? You awake?"

My eyes remained shut. I tried my best to respond, but nothing came out. I felt him move in close behind, his hands then slid around my waist.

"I love you." He whispered.

I wanted to turnover, but the weight of sleep was too much. I felt him kiss my bare shoulder. It sent a slight shiver down my arm. The exhaustion I felt was indescribable. My body felt like it was anchored to the bed and my mind was cloudy—very cloudy.

He carefully tucked a piece of hair behind my ear. A sudden jolt of energy trickled through me as I felt his breath on my skin again. I began to feel my body turning over towards him.

"Are you awake?" He repeated.

I felt my eyelashes flutter. He looked different to me tonight. I then felt his hand touch the side of my face.

"You're so beautiful."

I still couldn't speak. Slowly, I saw my hand reach out to touch his chest. Gripping onto his t-shirt, I pulled myself in closer. His hand slid down to my waist and around to my back. The touch of his warm fingers under my tank top tracing my spine gave me goosebumps. He pulled me in closer, connecting his lips with mine. I felt myself push him back down against the bed so I could climb over top of him. I stared into his deep brown eyes for a moment, before leaning in to kiss his soft lips. His hands ran down my hips to my thighs. I pulled at his shirt until he finally removed it. I then reached for my tank and slowly pulled it over my head. I didn't think twice about it. I was completely numb.

The air in the room felt very cool against my bare skin. I felt Nathan's fingers tracing my spine as our lips continued to connect. I gripped onto him, pulling him back over me on the bed. I felt my hands begin to slide my tiny shorts off. I tossed them from under the sheets onto the floor. His body hovered over mine as my fingers immediately reached for the waistband of his briefs. Pulling him down against me, my lips traced his neck with kisses down to his collarbone. I could feel the small hairs on his skin begin to stand up with every touch I made.

Suddenly, the room became heavy and the air thickened. I began to sweat and I soon found it difficult to breathe. My eyes shot open to the haziness around me as Nathan electrified my body. I couldn't stop. Something felt different—wrong, but my body continued to move with the motions.

I gripped onto his briefs as his eyes met mine.

"Are you sure?" He whispered.

Keeping my eyes connected with his, I could feel my heart begin to race. It felt as if it was going to burst out of me. Lacing my fingers around his neck, I pulled him down again to kiss me. His hands slid down to the small blue lace panties I had on. Seconds later, our skin was touching—everywhere. I could feel my body trembling now as the air in the room continued to thicken.

"Sophie, I love you more than anything." He spoke. "I know I said I can wait, but I just want you so badly," he breathed, deeply.

"I want you too, Nate. All of you." I heard myself say.

He leaned back down, closed his eyes, and connected his lips with mine. His touch was the gentlest it has ever been. His fingers laced into my hair and I felt my eyes roll back. With his warm breath on my neck, I heard a soft voice speak,

"This is how it should have been. With me. Not her."

He quickly pulled back to look at me. "What did you say?"

I stared back at him numb and unable to blink.

"Sophie," He said, carefully touching my face.

I didn't answer.

"Soph…" He spoke again.

Just then, the air around us turned cold. I blinked once.

"Don't you want me, Nathan?" I heard the voice speak again—this time, I felt my lips move with her words.

Nathan quickly pulled back in fear. It was definitely not my voice we were hearing. Something twisted inside of me. I moaned in pain but still couldn't move. Suddenly, I felt my body jolt up in the bed—launching Nathan off me. My head tilted back and I began to gasp for air. My fingers dug into my neck—panicking—I couldn't breathe!

"Sophie!" Nathan shouted, reaching for my shoulders. "Breathe, breathe!"

My eyes were wide in fear as I looked to him for help. He quickly pushed my body back down to the bed and cradled my head in his hands. I gripped onto him, trembling with fear. His eyes shut immediately, and he began to concentrate. It was silent for only a moment as he read my mind. Then his eyes shot back open.

"Serena," I heard him say. Suddenly, I caught my breath.

Coughing so hard I thought my lungs would crack, Nathan helped me sit up again.

"Deep breaths…" he said, stroking my cheek. I could feel his hands trembling against me. "You're fine. I'm right here."

Feeling the utter coldness in the room now, I gripped onto the sheets and suddenly noticed I was completely naked. I quickly pulled them up around me to cover myself. I had only ever been partially naked with Nathan. My eyes raced around the room.

"Soph?" I heard him say. "Look at me." He begged.

His hands grabbed onto my face to catch my full attention.

"What just happened?" I spoke, nervously.

"Are you alright?"

I didn't answer, I was still searching the room for that other voice. When I didn't find anyone, my eyes met his again.

"Sophie," He was worried, just like he was long ago.

"Did we…" I began to say.

His face softened. His eyes almost looked sad with what I was about to ask him. I began to tear up.

"No sweetie," He spoke quietly, then reached for me but I quickly slid back in the bed from him. His hand froze in mid-air.

"Soph," he said, a little upset.

"I'm sorry." I whispered, "I can't. I just—can't. I need to process this." I then quickly pulled at the sheet and slid myself from the bed, taking it with me.

I hurried into the bathroom and locked the door behind me. Slamming my back against the door, my body slid down to the ground. What happened back there? Whose voice was that and who was Serena? I felt the tears begin to pour down my cheeks. "That voice…"

I buried my face in my hands, letting my frustrations out. I heard Nathan rustling around in the other room before a quiet knock vibrated the door.

"Sophie," he said. "Open up,"

"Please go away," I asked, politely. "Please, Nate."

"I can't. You know I can't." He responded. "I need you to talk with me. Come on, open up."

I continued to sob from my side of the door.

"Sophie please, let me in."

With the sheets wrapped tightly around me, I began to wipe my eyes from the tears that felt like they wouldn't stop. Although I didn't want to see Nathan right now, I wanted to know about the name he mentioned.

"Who is she, Nate?" I managed to get out. "Who is… Serena?"

He didn't answer at first.

I then heard his body slide down the other side of the door. He sighed as I waited patiently.

"She was the girl I loved—in my previous life."

As much as I figured that was the answer coming, I was in no way prepared for it. I felt my heart crack inside of me. I had always known that Nathan lived a life before me—had other friends, family, and possibly loved someone as well, but I had secretly hoped that our love was much stronger than anything he'd experienced before.

That maybe our love was the first real thing for him and the only thing he could have ever wanted. But I wasn't the first. Someone else had stolen his heart long before me. We sat quietly for a moment in our own thoughts. I felt things instantly change between us.

"Did she love you, as well?" I asked, quietly.

"Very much." I heard him reply.

My eyes closed again as I turned to the door. I placed my right hand against it, picturing Nathan on the other side. I didn't want anyone else to love him. I loved him.

"And you loved her..." I repeated.

"Yes,"

My head dropped. It was hard to hold back the cries that wanted to burst out from inside me. Suddenly, I was filled with doubts again. Was our love good enough? Strong enough? Did he miss her more than he loved me? Did he wish he was with her, instead of me?

I began to cry harder. Holding my hand over my mouth, I tried my best to hide every sound from him. Then suddenly, I heard a rustle on the other side of the door. A loud bang startled me.

"Stop that, Sophie!" He shouted from the other side. "Stop those thoughts immediately! Open this door right now!"

I continued to cry, pulling myself away from the door.

"Sophie!" He shouted again, there was fear in his voice now. He banged again and again. "Open this damn door!"

But I continued to sit in the middle of the bathroom floor, curled over in pain.

"Sophie Reid. I'm serious, if you don't open this door right now, I'm going to break it down!" He warned.

My eyes widened from the floor. The rage in Nathan's voice scared me. It reminded me of the day in the park, where I was brutally attacked.

"I can't..." I cried. "I can't face you..."

He went silent—surely reading my thoughts again.

"Please...please, stop that Soph. Your thoughts are driving me crazy." He spoke quietly. "You know very well how I feel about you."

I didn't answer.

"Serena's in the past. I don't know why I said her name... Maybe I was half dreaming—"

"No," I said. "I heard it too."

He paused again for a moment.

"It doesn't matter what we think we heard, it means nothing— absolutely nothing, Soph." He suddenly spoke again. "I probably said her name because I've been flooded with old memories recently and I have no idea why. But it's only natural, right? I'm human now. I just wondered what happened to the people from my old life, like you asked me about—which includes Serena."

I listened to his voice more attentively now from the bathroom floor. "No one compares to you, Soph. Believe me. What we have, is… indescribable. I love you more than anything in this entire world."

I closed my eyes as another tear fell. Slowly, I reached up and unlocked the door. I heard Nathan turn the knob.

Sliding in and closing the door behind him, I felt his eyes lock on me. I couldn't look at him. Moving down in front of me, his hand reached for my face. I flinched for only a second, then let his fingers carefully brush the tears from my cheek.

"Sophie," He whispered. He then pulled me up towards him. I felt the tears begin to pour again from his embrace.

"I'm sorry. I'm so sorry," he continued to say.

My hands rested against his bare chest. I could feel his heart racing in time with mine.

"Nate, tell me the truth." I said, "Do you still love her? Do you wish that you were with her, instead of me?" I could barely get the embarrassing words out.

"Sophie, no! I don't at all." He shot back. "I love you and only you, crazy girl. This is the only place I want to be—here with you, forever, okay? I swear to god." He pulled me in tight again. "Please, stop those thoughts racing through your mind. Do you know how much it pains me to think that you don't understand how much I love you? How everything has happened because of you, because our love was true."

He looked down at me again, "How can I make you believe me?"

"I just," I began, "I'm scared, I wasn't ready and—"

"Sophie, this scares me too." He said. "I'm not sure what happened back there, whether I was dreaming or you had a panic attack, but I don't regret anything with you. Ever. Everything we do, no matter how fast or slow, I love. I love everything we have and experience together. Even if you decide last minute that you don't want to do anything. That's completely fine. Everything is alright—we're alright." He leaned in and kissed my forehead gently.

"Whatever is happening between us, we'll figure it out. But I never want you to be scared of anything—especially me."

I looked up at him, wiping my eyes.

"I read your thoughts, Soph. I'm sorry I scared you. But for the first time in a long time, I was scared too. Scared that you would build these thoughts up so much inside your head, like you used to long ago and you wouldn't be open to me anymore. I don't want you to ever feel like you did back then. I want to be the one who keeps your spirit bright. That truly scares me more than anything. I have no power to protect you like I used to, other than reading your mind and it makes me feel a little vulnerable. All I can do now is talk to you. But I have to be able to reach you. The thought of not being able to reach you—and Sophie," His line of thought instantly changed and caught me off guard. "It really pisses me off that you think that you're going to disappoint me,"

I wasn't expecting him to say that.

"Nate…"

"You just don't see what I see in you at all. I am so in love with you. There is no possible way that you could ever disappoint me, especially at night." He said, with a slight smile.

"Can't you tell how nervous I get whenever we touch? I'm just as nervous as you."

"I don't want to lose you, Nate."

"You're not going to and I'm just as scared that I'll lose you someday. I know I never say it, because I'm trying to stay positive, but the slightest feeling is there. So we're in this together, alright?"

"But what's so great about me, Nate? I mean, you—you're an angel that came back to life. You're perfect and that's a lot of pressure for a human. Do you get that?"

"I came back to life for you, because I want to be with you and I was human once too, Soph. You're forgetting that. You have to start seeing us as two normal people that are completely in love with each other."

"And Serena?" I asked, timidly. "I know nothing about her, Nate."

"Sophie, no." He said, pulling me back into him. "I've always been honest with you. If you really want, I will try to explain my past life to you, the parts I can. But then that's it. Gabriel warned me not to linger in the past and he'll probably keep checking in. We don't want to upset him.

I nodded. That was the last thing I wanted.

"But there's one condition if I do…" He paused, looking down at me. "If I talk to you about this, if I even can, you have to remember that I still love you the most. Our relationship is much stronger than the one I had with her. So please, stop the doubts in your head."

I nodded, agreeing to his terms.

"This actually started the other day," he then said.

"What started?"

"I was thinking of her, and when I say thinking of her, I just mean that I was wondering how her life turned out. I was hoping that she was alright and was just as happy as I am with you—that's all. And it was the first time I had thought of her in a very long time. She was an important part of my life and a good friend."

"I thought you couldn't think about your past life? Didn't you say that Gabriel hid it away or something?" I asked, still confused.

"He did, and for a very long time I couldn't think of anyone. But suddenly, the other day, a thought appeared in my mind. It took me completely off guard. The only reason I can think of, is that I'm human now and maybe the angels don't have as tight of a grasp on me and my memories as they used to."

Nathan pulled the sheet tightly around me, then helped me up from the ground.

"I'm sorry," I said. "For how I acted. I was just nervous about what was happening between us back there. I wanted it, but I didn't. Not that I don't want you Nathan," I assured him.

"I know what you mean," he smiled.

"When I heard her name. I guess, I just… immediately went to that dark place where every guy cheats on me and wants someone else." The words were humiliating to say aloud.

"Sophie, I would never cheat on you."

"I know, Nathan, but it scared me. I don't know what happened to my body. I just… I want it to be—perfect."

"It will be, no matter when it happens. Now listen, we'll sit down tomorrow, and I'll tell you everything I can. There will be no secrets between us anymore."

"Thank you." I whispered.

He then leaned down and kissed me. "But first, let's get some sleep." I could see the sun starting to rise from the window in the bathroom. Nathan slid his hand into mine and opened the door.

"Nate," I began, as I followed him back into our room dragging the sheets on the floor that were wrapped tightly around me. We climbed into bed. He handed me my tank top and bottoms to slide on under the covers.

"Yes?" He eventually replied.

"Guess what?" I smiled. "We survived our first fight,"

He smiled back, "I guess we did." He said, pulling me in to rest against his chest. "But let's not do that again—at least not with a door between us. I can't use my defense mechanism if I can't get to you."

I kissed his chest.

"Good night crazy girl," he said, looking out our window. "Err, good morning now?"

I wrapped my arm around him and closed my eyes.

"Good night."

7
The Unfold

The crystal-clear water poured down from the tall white marble fountain into a pool of water below. The water that glittered before him was not for the eyes nor the touch of human hands. It powered for angels alone.

"There you are brother,"

Gabriel turned to a tall, beautiful man in white.

"Michael," he said, calmly. "I knew it was only a matter of time."

"A matter of time?" The Archangel repeated. "You've been keeping a secret, haven't you?"

"This is my own matter, I'm handling it." Gabriel replied.

"It doesn't look like that to me." Michael spoke again, staring down at the fountain in front of them. "It looks to me like you might have a Fallen on your hands, one with growing emotions. Why are you taking so long to get rid of her? This is an easy process Gabriel, one that needs no thought."

"I understand that," Gabriel replied, turning to his brother. "But you must know how I work by now—don't you?"

"Oh, we understand how you work," another voice mocked from behind.

"Uriel, nice of you to join us." Gabriel smirked.

"You and your silly thoughts on humans and their souls." Uriel said, sarcastically. "You should understand by now that not all of them can be saved. Your job is simply to pass on the good ones and remove the bad."

Uriel then joined Michael's side. "If you like, I can take her out. It would be my pleasure." He smiled.

"No need," Gabriel spoke again, raising his hand. "I am studying something. Please brothers, leave her to me just a while longer."

"What could you possibly be studying, Gabriel? She isn't a pure heart, and she will not be joining us. Her actions have ruined her. You really must learn that these beings are not your toys to play with. Do you not wish to keep your precious Nathan safe?" Michael asked, guiding the conversation in a new direction.

Gabriel didn't answer.

"This girl, you had hoped to keep her as a guardian angel, correct? But her choices made her fall before you could even get started." Gabriel nodded.

"Such a shame when they don't see the light." Michael sighed. His eyes met Gabriel's again. "You must let her go. You cannot win every time, brother."

"I understand," Gabriel agreed, "but you must trust me. Nathan will remain safe and by Sophie's side."

He then turned to walk away.

"We know what you think he is meant to become, Gabriel." Uriel spoke again.

The Archangel stopped in his tracks and turned back to his brothers.

"If he is what you think he is, then there is a process we must follow." Uriel warned. "Sooner than later,"

"I understand," Gabriel replied. "I will let you know if things change."

Suddenly, Michael appeared before him, gazing down into his eyes.

"Brother," He said, in a deep tone, "if you are correct, and Nathan is the one, then you must make sure that his heart is not altered. This is important—for all of us." He spoke. "Letting that fallen soul have the freedom she does right now could alter his fate. Please tell me you understand this?"

"I understand completely." Gabriel repeated.

His assuring, ice blue eyes stared like stone back at his brother without a single blink. Then he was gone.

Michael stood silently, listening to the water pouring down from the fountain. It echoed in the great hall around them.

"He's going to get himself into trouble with that one." Uriel finally

said. "She's very persistent and reckless in my opinion."
"She is." Michael agreed. "It worries me a little. Keep an eye on him—and the girl."
Uriel nodded as his brother stepped past him.
"You are the protector of the gate, brother. The one we rely on to keep things where they should be." Michael spoke again, "If this gets out of hand, I want you to finish it."
He then vanished from sight.

It was around eleven thirty in the morning when my cell phone went off. My eyes barely opened as I reached over to grab my phone off the nightstand.
"Hello?" My voice cracked.
"Good morning my little flower!" The voice chimed.
Stretching out in bed I replied, "Morning Charlotte."
"Did I wake you?"
"Yes."
"Well good! It's too nice to be sleeping on this beautiful morning. Get up!" She shouted.
I sighed, then rolled over to look at Nathan. He was fast asleep.
"What's up?" I asked a little quieter.
"I did it Soph, I finally did it."
"Did what?" I asked, reaching over to carefully brush the wispy strands of hair from Nathan's face.
"I asked Matt to hang out with me, and he said yes!"
"Good." I smiled, staring at my angel.
"Well, actually, not just me. It's more like a group hangout that I asked him about." She stalled. "Meaning, you…and maybe Alex." My hand stopped. "What?"
"I mean, I told Matt that we were all hanging out today. You, me, him, and Alex…"
"Charlotte," I moaned.
"Of course, you can bring Nathan too. It's fine. But I really need a wing woman, please!" She begged.
I was exhausted and kind of hoped that Nathan and I would stay in bed for the day.

"It will be fun, I promise—please."

I rubbed my eyes, sitting up a little more in the bed.

"What exactly did you tell him we're doing today?"

"A hike!" She said, cheerfully.

"But you hate hiking. I hate hiking." I complained.

"But there will be a picnic too. A good one! And it will give me a chance to get to know him more. Please, Sophie. I'll owe you forever!"

Nathan's eyes began to flutter. Slowly, they opened, and his hand reached over to grab my leg. He pulled at me, trying to bring me in closer.

"Fine," I smiled, moving down towards him.

"Yay!" She shouted, "Okay, I'll meet you guys at Stanley Park this afternoon, two o'clock, near the Totem Poles. Don't be late!" Then she hung up.

I tossed my cell down on the bed and moved in closer to Nathan.

"Not enough sleep. Need more," He whispered, holding me tight.

I agreed.

"Was that Charlotte?" He asked.

"Uh huh…"

"Do we have to get up?"

"Unfortunately," I answered. "She wants us to join her for a picnic today. Turns out, she's asked that guy Matt out on a date, but she needs some back up."

"But I want to stay here, with you." He moaned, opening his eyes again.

"I do, too." I replied. "But the fresh air might do us some good and it would mean a lot to Charlotte."

I looked up at him, he stared back at me quietly. "Alright, you win."

I quickly leaned up for a kiss. Keeping his lips locked with mine, I began to feel him pull from my grip. I moaned, trying to hold on tight as long as I could. He smirked, then painfully got up from the bed.

"I need to wake up. I'm jumping in the shower." He said, grabbing a few clean clothes from the drawers.

"Hey," I pouted.

"Hey yourself. You're the one that wanted to go out for the day," He

81

teased. I crossed my arms as he headed for the bathroom. Stopping at the door he looked back at me and winked. I sighed flopping back in the bed.

"Stupid hike, stupid picnic, stupid…no bed day with Nathan." I mumbled, then rolled out from under the covers to get ready.

While Nathan cleaned up, I searched through the dresser for something bright to wear. Something that would feel positive and uplifting to combat my tiredness. I slipped on a pair of blue jeans, then found a pastel yellow t-shirt to slip on. It was getting a lot nicer out now, summer was right around the corner. I couldn't wait.

After throwing a brush through my hair, I looked at myself in the mirror. I thought I looked alright for getting up last minute. I just needed a touch of makeup and some perfume—then I'd be good to go. As I waited for Nathan to finish up, I lingered towards my dresser again. Straightening things up a little, I opened up my jewelry box to play around with my collection inside. Tracing my index finger through the small items, I noticed something missing—my bracelet with the cherry blossoms on it. I quickly looked around the room. I looked under and around the dresser—nothing. I headed to the closet and searched through my sweaters, jackets and more to see if I had left it in something. I began to panic a bit.

How I could lose this? It was an important reminder of the day Nathan returned to me. Where was it? I heard the bathroom door open.

"Hey Nate?" I said as he entered the room. "Have you seen my bracelet? You know the one I wore that day at the movies? The green one with the cherry blossoms on it? It's missing."

"Um no," he said, staring at me. "Where did you have it last?"

"The movies, I think."

"I'm sure it will turn up, I wouldn't worry." He said, tossing on a shirt.

"But I need it," I said, beginning to pull the clothes out from our dresser. I then felt Nathan's hand on my lower back.

"Sweetie, go have a bowl of cereal. We'll look for it when we get back."

"But—"

"We're going to be late if you don't."
I sighed, looking down at my watch.
"We'll find it." He assured me again, then kissed the top of my head.
"Go."
I dragged my feet slowly out of the bedroom.

"Sophie!" Charlotte called, running towards us.
I felt my heart begin to race. I was a little nervous for Nathan and
Alex to meet. Charlotte greeted me with a giant hug, then smiled at
Nathan.
"Hey Nate." She said, leaning up to hug him awkwardly. She then
pulled back just as Matt and Alex approached.
"This is Matt and Alex," she said, pointing to each guy.
Nathan reached out and shook both their hands.
"Alex, yes, Sophie told me about you. I'm Nate."
"Oh really?" His eyebrows raised at me playfully.
They stood silent for only a second before Matt chimed in.
"Well Charlotte, where are we heading?" He asked, grabbing her by
the shoulders. She blushed from the touch of his hands.
"Well, to be honest… I'm—um," She paused, looking over at me
for help. I stared back at her with a smirk on my face. Like me,
Charlotte wouldn't know where to begin on a hike. We didn't even
know if there was actually a trail here in Stanley Park other than the
seawall. We were the last people that should be guiding a tour in the
woods today or any other day for that matter. I continued to stare
at her, waiting for what possible answer she was going to come up
with.
"I know a good trail," Nathan spoke, pleasantly. "It's just up this
way." He pointed.
"Perfect!" Charlotte responded, "I brought my camera!" She said,
flashing Nathan a quick smile as she passed by. Matt followed, then
Alex.
I quickly grabbed Nathan's hand and let the rest get a few good steps
ahead of us.
"Don't be nervous," he whispered, squeezing my hand.

"I'm fine with this."

"I'm not." I sighed looking up at him. He really did seem fine, so I tried my best to change the mood.

"I'm guess I'm just excited to get going..."

He stopped and looked at me, a surprised expression on his face. "You hate hiking,"

I was about to argue back when Matt yelled to us. "Come on you two," Pulling his heavy backpack up higher on his shoulders he motioned for everyone to hurry up. Fortunately, he and Alex had offered to carry the meal Charlotte had prepared for us. One that apparently needed two backpacks.

The five of us hiked the trail for about an hour before we finally stopped for our picnic. I dropped to the ground, gasping for air while the others began to set up. I hated this. My head hung low as I leaned against a nearby tree. Glancing over at the group again, Charlotte had out done herself with a major spread of delicious food today. She was definitely pulling out all the stops to impress Matt.

"Here, drink this." Alex said, appearing before me. "Looks like you need it."

I reached out and grabbed the bottle. Desperately, I chugged down the water.

"Thanks." I said, wiping my mouth.

"So, hiking... not your thing, huh?"

"No, it's just..." I sighed. I couldn't lie. It was written all over my face. "I hate it."

"Me too," he laughed, sitting down beside me. "Matt makes me run with him in the mornings. He's a major fitness guy. Which I guess models need to be. But me, I'm just, well—lazy."

"Really?" I quickly looked him over. "I wouldn't have guessed that about you. You look like you work out every day,"

I felt my cheeks grow warm.

"I do?" He smiled, "Well thank you. That means a lot. My secret diet must be working."

"Secret diet?" I laughed, "What does that involve?"

"It's a secret. Can't tell," he smiled back.

I rolled my eyes.

"No, it's actually nothing." He then said. "I don't do anything. I just eat healthy and go about my day. Once and a while I run with Matt when he bugs me to death. But other than that, I'm just an active person. Always on the go. That's good enough to keep me fit, I guess. How about you? How come you look so good?"

My face burned again. Tucking my hair behind my ears, I shook my head in denial.

"Come on," he smiled, giving me a little elbow to the side.

"I really don't do anything either." I replied. "I'm always acting or helping Charlotte with photo shoot stuff. It's probably the reason I'm out of shape. But I do eat well. Nathan cooks for me all the time."

"Yes, Nate." He repeated. "He seems like a good guy."

"He is."

"Well good, I'm happy for you Soph. You deserve someone great. You seem like a genuine person."

"Thanks," I said. "He's my world." My eyes suddenly widened. I didn't mean to say that out loud.

"Your world, eh? That's pretty serious." He replied. "I haven't found that person yet—someone to be my world as you say," he teased.

I smiled back at him.

"You will. You're a nice guy. I'm sure there's someone great out there just for you and it may surprise you who she is, and where she'll show up. It did for me at least."

He stared over at Nathan, then glanced back at me.

"That's definitely a sweet thought to keep in mind. Thank you."

We sat for a moment as I took another sip from the water bottle. I then handed it back to him.

"Thank you again for the drink, you saved my life." I joked, then began to get up. "Shall we eat?"

"Please." He agreed, following me over to the big mats that were spread out on the ground.

Charlotte had recently done the photography at the Vancouver Cherry Blossom festival this spring and bought a few large petal mats that you could zip together with others of its kind, creating beautiful pink and white diamond shapes on the ground.

She mentioned that in Japan, when the cherry blossom petals begin to fall, it symbolized the beginning of spring. For hundreds of years, it has been the custom to set up a picnic beneath a blossoming cherry tree and participate in Hanami (cherry blossom viewing), a custom that to this day brings all types of people out into the world to toast the changing seasons and the rebirth of nature in the warming months. A tradition Vancouver was happy to emulate.

We each found a spot on the mat as Charlotte passed around some small cups.

"A little champagne to toast?" She smiled.

Nathan raised his cup looking over at me. "What shall we toast to?"

"How about to new friendships, success and clarity in each of our lives." Alex said, politely.

"I like that." Charlotte smiled, looking over at Matt.

"And to love and new beginnings." Nathan added.

I smiled back at him. I felt the soft touch of his hand on my lower back as we tapped our cups with everyone. In the corner of my eye, I saw Alex's eyes look up from his cup, directly at me.

"Oh shoot, I need some water to boil for our special treat…" Charlotte said, digging through the bag for a bottle, but found nothing.

My eyes shot to Alex again, we both giggled.

"You…" Charlotte's eyes tightened.

"There's actually a stream not too far from here," Nathan said, getting up from the ground. "I don't mind grabbing it," He then snagged a large bottle from one of Charlotte's bags to take with him.

"Thanks so much," she said, a little surprised.

He winked at me, then headed off.

It wasn't long before Nathan reached the stream. The woods seemed to part slightly as he entered an open area filled with tall grass. His body slid through it towards the stream. He had been here before with Bruce on a walk and came across this stream. Leaning down to the water, Nathan began to fill the container.

"Nathan…" a voice whistled through the air.

He turned quickly. Nervously, he looked around—listening carefully.

"Nathan…" the voice whispered again.

Startled, he dropped the container to the ground.

"Serena…" It was almost impossible to say her name aloud.

A rustle in the grass behind him made his heart begin to race. His eyes continued to search the area but found no one.

"Serena?" He repeated, a little louder this time.

Rubbing his eyes from exhaustion, Nathan laced his fingers through his hair, wondering if he was still that tired from his lack of sleep that he was hearing things now—maybe like he did last night. Suddenly, his hands dropped as another thought crossed his mind. He reached down into his right pocket and carefully pulled out the cherry blossom bracelet that he had hidden away.

"You found it," the voice said from behind.

Nathan swung around to see Serena standing behind him. Her long blonde hair seemed to glisten in the sunlight. A slight smile grew on her pale pink lips. Her eyes, a dark brown—just like his, softened as she stared back at him.

He trembled, gripping tight to the bracelet in his hand.

"It can't be…" He whispered.

Slowly, she stepped towards him. His body froze in fear. Standing directly in front of him now, she didn't blink.

"I've missed you," she said.

Her hand rose slightly and reached out for his. The touch of her skin electrified every hair on his body. His eyes closed quickly.

"No. This can't be. I must be dreaming,"

Although he was human now, he still remembered what it felt like to touch the soul of another right before he sent them onto their rightful place. It was exactly what she felt like in this moment. Her cold hand laced around his as his eyes began to water.

"No…" A tear slid down his cheek. He felt another cool touch as her hand gently caressed his skin and wiped the tear away.

"How am I seeing you?" He asked, opening his eyes to her. "How did you… I mean," He paused, a little overwhelmed.

She smiled. "One question at a time, Nathan." She spoke very softly. She then opened his hand to where the bracelet lay.

"I'm so glad you have it. I've missed this—my favorite thing in the world." She was about to take it from him but stopped. Looking back up into his eyes, she smiled again, "No. My favorite thing is you."

Her hands returned to the sides of his face.

"How is this possible?" He asked, again.

"I've been trying to contact you for quite some time, but you've been hard to get through to." She said, her smile fading slightly.

He stared at her. She was as beautiful as she was the day he left her. If not more. Her delicate fingers traced his skin as she moved in closer.

"Nathan, have you missed me?" She asked, leaning her forehead against his. Her cool breath floated over his lips.

He nodded, sadly. "I'm so sorry…"

"Don't be," she whispered. "We're together now, and I still love—"

"Let him go," a voice spoke from behind.

Nathan's eyes shot to Gabriel's standing not too far from them.

"I mean it Serena, let him go and be gone!" He warned again.

Serena's eyes widened in fear. She held onto Nathan tightly.

"No, this is the way things should have been," she said, standing her ground.

"She can't be here Nathan, you know that." The Archangel spoke again. "She's messing with the order of things."

Serena continued to hold onto Nathan. Lacing her arms around his waist. He looked down into her frightened eyes.

"Please, I need him," she said, staring up at him.

"What happened to you?" Nathan asked.

Gabriel took a step towards them, ready to attack.

"Gabriel, please!" Nathan's hand rose to the Archangel. "Please, just let me talk with her for a moment."

The Archangel's eyes widened, "Are you forgetting our conversation from earlier?" He asked. "You're going mess everything up if you—"

"Mess what up?" Nathan snapped. "What's going on here, Gabriel? Tell me now!" He demanded.

"She's dead, Nathan." Gabriel finally replied, taking a moment to let it sentence sink in.

Nathan's eyes returned to Serena's. His hands slid down her shoulders and moved to her very thin waistline. She felt cold and weak—too weak.

"She's stuck between the real world and the next realm. She's stuck in purgatory—holding onto you. Don't you see that?" Gabriel spoke again.

Nathan's heart stopped for a moment.

"Stuck." He repeated, quietly. "For how long?"

He could barely get his words out. His hands rose to her face.

"Why," he asked. "Why would you linger? It's no life—not for you.
I can't bear…" He paused again as his eyes filled with tears.

"She killed herself shortly after you died," a new voice spoke.

Nathan's eyes shot up to the Archangel Uriel.

"Do not speak, brother. It is not your place." Gabriel warned. His
eyes met Nathan's again worried.

"Why?" Nathan asked, looking down at Serena.

Her eyes softened.

"Why would you kill yourself?" Another tear fell from his eye. He
quickly pulled her tight to his chest. "Why would you do that?"

"I'm sorry. I couldn't do it. I couldn't live without you." She cried,
nuzzling her face into his neck.

Suddenly, Uriel appeared beside them, "Enough of this,"

Nathan pulled back with Serena in his arms just as the Archangel
reached for the ghostly girl. Gabriel vanished then reappeared in
front of Nathan and Serena.

"You will not touch them. Now go!" He demanded his brother, but
Uriel stood his ground.

"You have no power over me."

"This is my business—not yours!" Gabriel growled, his body
lighting up before them all.

Uriel's eyes gleamed with delight. "Fine," He replied, turning to step
away.

But just as he did, he suddenly changed his direction and
unexpectedly came back for Serena. He ripped her from Nathan's
grasp and tossed her hard to the ground. He then quickly snagged
her by the arm again and yanked her up to her feet. Gabriel slammed
into the Archangel—knocking him back a few feet and pushing
Serena to the side.

Nathan ran to her immediately.

"Do not touch her, boy," Uriel's voice thundered through the tall
grass. Lifting his hand towards Nathan's direction, a bright light
suddenly blinded them. Nathan felt the blow, then soon found

89

himself a few yards away on the ground, in severe pain.

"Nathan!" Serena called, dashing towards him.

She was soon by his side, helping him back up to his feet. She gently reached for his face. A small cut had begun to bleed and drip down from his eyebrow.

Uriel's hand rose again, but Gabriel quickly appeared before the blast could be released and snatched Serena up. They then disappeared from sight.

"No!" Nathan shouted, searching the area desperately.

Uriel grunted from his brother's actions, clearly annoyed. His eyes then shot to Nathan's—but only for a moment—before he too vanished into thin air. Nathan fell to his knees, feeling a little lightheaded. His eyes rolled back into his head as it went dark, but only for a moment.

"Nathan?" I said from behind. "What are you—" I stopped, then hurried to his side noticing his current state. Lifting his head gently, he eventually opened his eyes and looked up at me. There was blood running down his cheek. I had never seen Nathan bleed— ever. I froze in fear as he stared at me silently. He began to get up. I snapped myself out of it as he laced his arm around my shoulders to stabilize himself, I lifted him up as best I could. His body was trembling.

"Nathan," I said, gripping onto his chest with my free hand. "What happened?" My other hand held tight around his waist, but his weight soon became too much for me. We fell to the ground. I rested his head against my chest and held on to him for a moment. I had never seen him like this. I brushed his hair back from the bloody eyebrow. His skin was flushed.

"Nate, what happened? What's wrong with you?" I repeated, again. I didn't know how to help him. "You're scaring me."

His eyes finally met mine. "I… I slipped." He spoke.

"What?" I didn't believe him.

"I felt exhausted, like I was going to pass out. Then I guess, I did," He reached up to touch the cut on his eyebrow. "I must have hit my head,"

"Don't," I said, grabbing his hand.

"I think, I'm okay…" He said, attempting to get up again.

"Hold on," I replied, pulling him back down. "You don't look good. Maybe we should take you to the hospital."

"No, I'm okay. I promise. It's just a little cut."

"Well, it sure shook you up for just a little cut, Nathan." I said, still worried.

"I fine, I swear." He assured me. "I'm sorry I over reacted. I guess it scared me a little—the thought of getting hurt, I mean."

I still didn't believe him. "You sure that's it?"

"Yeah," He replied, with a half-smile.

Reaching into my pocket, I grabbed a napkin and pulled it out.

"Wait here a second." I said, sliding out from under him and walking over to the nearby stream. I dipped the napkin into the water, then folded it up.

Coming back to Nathan, I knelt down and began to clean up his face. He flinched as I dabbed the cut on his eyebrow.

"Sorry," I said, gently blowing on it.

Finally, it stopped bleeding. But Nathan was looking pale now.

"Soph," he said, quietly. "I want to go home—if you don't mind."

"Of course," I agreed. "I'll tell everyone you're not feeling good. Let's get you home to rest." I braced myself again to lift him. Thankfully, he had gotten a little strength back. I rested his arm around my shoulders, and we carefully began our walk back to the picnic sight.

After spilling our little lie to the group, Alex surprisingly took over and helped Nathan back to our car that was parked just below the Totem Poles. I was thankful that Nathan and I decided to drive ourselves today.

"Feel better, Nate." Alex said, closing Nathan's door and looking over the car at me. "Soph, he doesn't look that good,"

"He'll be fine, he just needs some rest." I replied, opening my door. I then stopped and glanced back at Alex.

"Thank you… for helping me."

He smiled, "Of course,"

With a slight wave to the others, I got into my car and left.

Later that evening, I waited for the water to boil before pouring it into a cup. I let the teabag steep a bit while I pondered over what really happened to Nathan in the park. There was something he wasn't telling me—I could feel it. When the herbal tea was ready, I carefully carried the mug into our bedroom.

Nathan was still fast asleep when I placed it down on the nightstand next to him. I then touched his forehead. It was still very warm. "What happened to you?" I whispered.

I went to my dresser to change into something a little more comfortable. Looking into the mirror above my dresser, I realized how exhausted I looked myself. The dark circles under my eyes told me I too could use some sleep, but I suddenly heard a knock at the door. Quietly, I exited the room.

When I reached the front door, I peeked through the hole to see Charlotte waiting patiently. I opened it quickly.

"Hi," she said, quietly.

Rubbing my eyes, I smiled back at her. "Hey, what's up?"

"Nothing, I just wanted to see how you and Nate were doing. Is everything alright?"

"Yeah, every thing's fine. Nathan's sleeping now. He hit his head pretty hard when he passed out. He wouldn't let me take him to the hospital either. He's just been trying to sleep it off."

Charlotte looked at me confused.

"If he hit his head, he probably shouldn't sleep, Soph."

"Yeah, I know," I replied, knowing it was more than that. "Do you want to come in for a bit?"

"Sure, if it's not too late for you."

"Come in, please." I pulled her inside and closed the door.

The two of us made our way into the kitchen to make some more tea. Charlotte sat down at the table as I grabbed two mugs from the cupboard.

"I wonder what made him fall? I mean, he didn't seem sick when we first got there and…" Charlotte paused, tapping her finger to her bottom lip.

"It was probably a mixture of lack of sleep and the hot sun today," I lied, filling the kettle with water. I then tossed two tea bags into the cups. "If he's still like this tomorrow, I'm taking him to the hospital."

"Good idea," Charlotte replied. "Maybe the doctors can tell us what happened."

I had to admit, it was kind of nice to see Charlotte worry about Nathan like this. Maybe he had finally gotten on her good side?

"So, on another note, do you want to hear something very cool?" She asked, a little more energetically.

"Always," I replied.

"Well, after you left, Alex didn't stay much longer, which left Matt and I on our own. He insisted on hanging out some more. So of course, I agreed."

"Of course," I giggled as the kettle whistled from the counter.

I poured the water into the two mugs and brought them over to the table.

"Well, I was taking some pictures as usual, and he suggested that we take one together. So, I placed the camera on a stump. That way I could set the timer and get in front of it, right? Then, just as we sat down, he put his arm around me and...." Her face lit up.

"And what?" I asked, sitting down beside her.

"He leaned in and surprised me with a kiss just as the camera flashed. How cute is that?" She shrieked.

"Really? Aw, Charlotte, I'm so happy for you!"

"Yeah, apparently, he's had a crush on me for a while now and was too afraid to ask me out because it wouldn't be professional. But he decided to just take a chance after I invited him to hang out. How awesome is that?"

"Very awesome. So, what's next then?"

"He asked me to go out later this week—on a real date." Her cheeks were blushing with delight. "Sophie, seriously, this just made my life. He's so cute and nice and—yay!"

"Yay!" I repeated, happily.

I was so thankful that we didn't end up ruining my best friend's date after all.

"So maybe we can double date now, huh? What do you say? You and Nate—me and Matt?"

"Sure, but not until Nathan's better."

"Yeah, no prob." Charlotte agreed with another huge smile on her face.

"So, how was it—with Alex? Not too awkward with Nathan there was it?" She then asked.

"What do you mean?"

"I just mean, it's kind of obvious, I think Alex likes you, Soph."

"No way." I said, "Alex is nice, but we're just friends and I'll definitely help him out with some acting info if I can, but that's all."

"And what does Nathan think of all this? Or have you told him?"

"He's fine with it." I replied.

"Well, that was nice of him." She spoke again. "I'm glad he's so cool with it all. Like I said, Alex is a great guy. You should at least be friends with him."

"I am, Charlotte." I said, getting up from the table to get a snack. As I reached for the cupboard, the lights went out.

"What the—" I stubbed my toe. "Dam it!"

"Are you alright?" Charlotte asked. "What happened?"

Suddenly, we heard the sound of footsteps coming down the hallway. "Nate?" I called out, searching the darkness for his figure. "Nate, is that you?" I asked again. I heard Charlotte get up from her chair.

"There you are," she said.

"There who is?" I asked confused. "I'm over here," I replied, just as Charlotte's phone lit up the room.

"Wait... I just..." She stuttered, then smirked at me. "Very funny, you got me."

"What are you talking about? Will you quit fooling around and help me find a flashlight or some candles," I said, covering my eyes from the bright light. I began to dig through the cupboards.

"Bring that light over here so I can see better."

Charlotte carefully walked towards me.

"Here," she then handed the phone to me.

Another creak from behind made Charlotte and I both jump.

"Did you hear that?" She said, grabbing me. "It sounded like it was coming from the hallway again." Her voice trembled.

I continued to search, ignoring her words.

"This is getting a little scary. It reminds me of that horror movie we watched a few weeks ago. Remember?"

"Char, don't even say it. It's just going to freak us out more,"

Suddenly, a loud crash made us both jump into each other's arms. With our backs to the cupboards now, Charlotte slid us down to the floor. Silently we sat like fools, listening to the dead air in the room.

"What was that?" Charlotte whispered.

"I don't know," I replied, just as nervous now.

The footsteps continued. They got closer and closer. The kitchen floor creaked as the footsteps entered the room. Charlotte's nails dug into my arm as we tried our best to be silent.

Just then, the lights flicked on, and Nathan stood before us.

"What are you two doing?" He asked, staring down at us. "And why are you in the dark?"

I let out a huge sigh of relief. "Nathan, thank God."

Reaching up to the counter, Charlotte and I rose to our feet.

"It was really odd Nate, the lights just went out and we heard footsteps coming towards us… " I said, a little embarrassed.

"You must have just bumped the switch, the rest of the lights work fine." He said, a little amused. "I think you two have been watching too many horror flicks lately. Seriously."

"I guess so," Charlotte replied, taking a breath. "So Nate, how are you feeling anyways? Better now?"

"A bit. My head still hurts," he replied, stepping past her. "But nothing some pain medication and a good night's sleep won't heal." Reaching into the cupboards, he grabbed a small bottle.

"Thanks for the tea, Soph." He smiled, giving me a kiss on the head as he walked past us again.

"No problem, do you need anything else?" I asked as Nathan popped two pills in his mouth.

"No, I'm good. Are you coming to bed soon? Or are you two going to stay up and watch movies?" He teased again.

"Actually, I'm going to head out. I have a shoot tomorrow, so I really should get some sleep." Charlotte replied, heading to the front door. "Feel better, Nate."

When Charlotte was gone, I followed Nathan back to our bedroom. I still had many questions, just like Charlotte, but I decided that it might be best if we just went to sleep for the night. Tomorrow we would talk. Tomorrow I would figure out what really happened to Nathan.

8
Pieces of the Past

The next morning, before I jumped in the shower, I checked on Nathan's wound. I was careful not to wake him. It looked a lot better today. It was healing fast.

After cleaning myself up, I went to the computer to check my email. There were a few messages from my agent about a bunch of auditions coming up. I noted them down on a piece of paper and then printed off the scripts she sent along with them. I needed to land a few gigs. I hadn't worked too much at the music store this week. It was a good thing Charlotte had paid me for assisting her in the photo shoot earlier. Usually, I was always pretty good at keeping up on the bills and I kept a secret stash for backup in case anything happened. But I was falling a little behind this week. Stretching out in the chair I looked over at Bruce, he seemed bored.

"Let's go for a walk, buddy." I said, getting up.

The little dog leaped from the couch and ran after me.

It was another nice day out. I needed this fresh air, and Nathan needed more time to sleep. The blossoms were falling quickly now. They never lasted long enough in my opinion, but that was what made them so fleetingly beautiful. I took my time walking through the pink snow with my little dog.

Later that afternoon, I snuck the laundry out from our room while Nathan continued to sleep and started a load. As I checked the dryer getting it ready for when the wash was done, I felt a cool breeze across my shoulders. Which was odd because our washer/dryer set was in a closet in the hallway. There were no windows in sight.

It was so quiet in our place today, like it used to be when I lived alone. A soft mumbling of voices made me stop what I was doing for a moment. I thought for a second that they came from the hallway outside our apartment, but then I heard it again.

It was him. One of the voices was Nathan's. It sounded like he was talking to someone, but I couldn't make out what he was saying. I tossed the lint from the dryer into a small garbage can and headed back towards our room. Leaning my ear against the bedroom door, I listened again for the voices. I could hear Nathan rustling around. It sounded like he was dreaming or something. Then I heard his voice again,

"Why would you do that? How could you?"

I carefully pushed the door open to peek inside. He was fast asleep and definitely dreaming. I stepped into the room and made my way over to the bed. Sitting down on the edge, I watched Nathan's facial expressions changed as he continued to dream. It must have been an intense dream—he seemed very bothered.

"Nathan," I whispered, then touched him gently on the shoulder. When he didn't respond, I carefully climbed in next to him.

"Nate." I whispered again. "Wake up."

His eyes flickered a bit, then opened slightly.

"What are you doing?" he asked, softly.

"You were having a bad dream, so I woke you up." I smiled, then reached for his face, but he grabbed my wrist before I could make contact.

"Where's your bracelet?"

"I told you, I couldn't find it the other day—remember?"

I continued to stare at him, confused. Was he still dreaming? His eyes then softened and looked as if they might cry.

"Why did you do it?" He asked again.

"What are you talking about?" I replied. "Do what? Nathan, are you awake?"

My thumb gently stroked his cheek.

"That must have been some dream,"

His sweet complexion in that moment reminded me of what he looked like when he was an angel. When he would appear by my bed late at night. It was much fairer—flawless even.

"It's all my fault. I did this to you." His eyes then closed on me.

"Nathan, what are you talking about. Open your eyes. Look at me," I insisted, giving him a slight shake. His eyes shot back open.

"Hey," I smiled, again. "Are you in there?"

"Sophie?" He finally said, his eyelashes fluttered a few times before he pulled from my grip and rolled to his back. He was silent for a moment, breathing deep as he orientated himself with the room again.

I arched up on my elbow, "What were you dreaming about?"

"Nothing. It was just a stupid dream," He sighed.

I stared at him, then moved in to rest my head on his chest. But he didn't embrace me like he normally did.

"You sure you're alright?" I asked, again. "You seem—"

"I'm fine." He replied, sharply. "Soph, please... let's not play the hundred questions game right now. I'm tired."

I removed myself from his chest. Nathan had never brushed me off before.

"Okay, sorry. I was just worried."

"It's fine. I'm fine. Can you just give me a sec, alone?"

I sat up clearly upset, but he didn't care. I didn't know what to say. I slid myself from the bed and headed towards the door. I could feel a welt building up inside me. Why was he being like this? I looked back at him, but he continued to lay there staring up at the ceiling.

"I'll just be... out then." I finally spoke. "I'm going to make a run to the grocery store. Feel better." I said, then left.

● ● ●

When Nathan reached the library, he quickly hurried over to an open computer and began to search for obituaries published shortly after his death. He couldn't sleep, he needed to face what was on his mind. He continued to click through many pages, until he saw his face.

The article read:

"24-YEAR-OLD DIES FROM GUN SHOT WOUNDS"

On Friday October 15th, 1993, Nathan Hayes, a 24-year-old student was killed following a brutal shooting outside his girlfriend Serena Reilly's house.

Police recently found out that Reilly was attacked by the same killer the night before Nathan died and claimed Mr. Hayes had protected her from the brutal attack. Although his girlfriend describes Hayes as a quiet, kind young man, sources say that he was wrapped up in unknown dealings with the murderer for quite some time which could have instigated the first attack.

Being a foster child from a young age, there was very little info found on Hayes other than what Reilly told reporters. The two of them were newly dating and completely caught off guard by the sudden attack the night before Hayes' death.

Dempsey—the murderer, was arrested a few days after the killing and sentenced to life in jail on numerous accounts of dealings and first-degree murder.

Mr. Hayes' funeral will be held this Tuesday, October 19th, 1993, at eleven in the morning. Reilly was clearly torn apart by the tragic death of her boyfriend and has taken over all funeral arrangements. Sources say she is now in counseling to help her deal with the grief and depression that has taken over her life.

Nathan stopped for a moment and sat back in the chair. It was a lot to take in. The memories of their very short relationship flooded his mind. The attack, the gunshot, all of it was so hard to think about. His stupid choices—getting mixed up with the wrong people had inevitably ended his own life and caused even more pain to the one person in the world who loved him. He couldn't believe after everything Serena had been through, she still loved him. She had even planned his funeral. He bravely swallowed the lump growing in his throat, sat back up and continued to click further onto the next few pages. Feelings from his past began to rise inside of him. He had once loved Serena so much. She was his first true love, and no one compared to her at that time. That is, until Sophie came along. The emotions stirred inside of him, making him feel a sick to his stomach. He knew Sophie was his life now, but Serena was unfinished business. He clicked again, and this time saw her face. She was right there, beautiful as ever. Beautiful and now dead. He closed his eyes, taking a deep breath before reading the sure to be upsetting article. The title alone, made his heart stop.

"TRAGIC SUICIDE"

We are saddened to report that Serena Reilly, age 24, ended her life two days ago. After the death of her boyfriend Nathan Hayes last month, Reilly sought aid for her depression. Doctors speculate that the attack and loss of Mr. Hayes caused her to inevitably fall into a dark place—something she was unable to recover from.

Reilly's parents told reporters that Serena was known as a happy individual. Her parents also claim not to have known anything of her boyfriend Hayes, or the attack that happened. Having spent most of their time working out of town, they were completely shocked by the horrible ending to their daughter's life.

Reilly was found on November 21st, 1993, dead in her bathroom after slitting her wrist in the bathtub. Her parents found her lifeless body after returning home from work one evening. Heartbroken, Reilly's parents have moved away from the area and ask for privacy during this difficult time.

Nathan sat with tears in his eyes, slit her wrist? How could she? He blinked the tears away and remembered to breathe again. He then quickly printed the article, folded it up into his pocket and slid back from the computer.

"I have to find her," he said, getting up from the chair.

As Nathan walked down the street, anger began to build inside him. He cut through the park onto a small path. A figure suddenly appeared before him.

"Nathan,"

He felt a surge of adrenaline spark from within at the sight of the Archangel.

"How could you not tell me, Gabriel?" He shouted. "She killed herself, over me! She slit her wrist and bled to death in the bathtub!

How could you not tell me that? You said she was fine!"

"Nathan, calm yourself," Gabriel replied, blocking his path.

"Calm myself? Are you kidding me? I can't even process what's happening! Or... what happened," he fumbled over his words. "You lied to me, Gabriel! I knew there was a reason I kept thinking of her, I'm so stupid. I should have looked for her as soon as I became an angel. I should have made sure she was okay. How could I have just believed that she would be fine? I have to find her. Tell me where she is—now!"

"You couldn't have looked for her even if you wanted to. Remember what I said to you long ago. Once you become a guardian angel, you cannot look back into your old life. It's kept hidden from you—forever."

"Then why now? Why can I see it all now? Because Uriel spoiled your secret? I mean, did you expect me to just hear that and not look into it? It's kind of a big thing. I trusted you, Gabriel." He paused, hurt from the betrayal. "I was a loyal Guardian. How could you do this to me?"

Gabriel's expression softened. "Because it was her fate. Just as yours was to die. There was nothing you could have done to change it. Nathan trust me, looking back and lingering in your past will only cause more damage and heartache." He spoke calmly.

"Serena is holding onto the past, which is why she continues to linger in purgatory. A place that can only darken her soul," He warned again. "She has somehow created a doorway into the real world and it's effecting you—something she was clearly trying to achieve for quite some time. I didn't expect her to do that. It was a slip up on my part, I apologize." He sighed. "Somehow she got past me, and once you admitted to yourself the possibility that she was still around, it opened your mind to hers—creating an instant connection between you now." He paused for a moment, "It probably doesn't help that your human now either. The human mind is much more vulnerable than an angel's."

"A doorway?" Nathan repeated, completely confused with the conversation. "What are you talking about?"

"I've been tracking her since she first attacked Sophie in her dreams, years ago. She is stuck now. She's stuck in between. I need to release

101

her so she can pass on, but I believe there's something else holding on to her—and it's not just you."

Nathan stared at him, "Something else?"

Gabriel nodded, "You must let go of any thoughts of her. It will only make things worse for you and for Sophie."

"I want to help her." Nathan said, sternly, "Tell me everything, Gabriel," he demanded.

"No, it's much too dangerous. There's no telling what a Fallen..." He paused to correct himself, "What a spirit like hers can do the longer she resides in purgatory."

"Fallen?" Nathan repeated, disgustedly. "There's no way she's a Fallen, Gabriel. It's not possible."

"She ended her life, Nathan. That is a sin in God's eyes. You should know that. Her spirit was so angry when I approached to help her pass on that she fought against me and hid herself from the angels. I had hoped to save her gracefully and possibly make her a guardian, but she's been on the run from us ever since. Her soul is clearly upset and darkened now. There's nothing left we can do for her. She must pass on."

Nathan couldn't believe what he was hearing. Is this what had become of his beloved Serena? A darkened spirit, full of rage and hate? It couldn't be true.

"I just don't believe it, Gabriel."

"Nathan, this conversation is becoming tiresome. You know how Fallen ones are created. Remember, one of the reasons Lucifer fell was because he wanted what didn't belong to him. Just as Serena wants what doesn't belong to her anymore."

"Then what, Gabriel? What does she want?" Nathan hollered once again.

"You," Gabriel said softly. "She wants you. It has now become an obsession, and whatever is in there with her, guiding or holding onto her, is very strong. Do you understand the severity of this Nathan and what could happen? Do you understand whose life is in danger here?"

"I'm not in any danger, Gabriel. She would never hurt me."

"I'm not talking about you. I'm talking about Sophie." he was frustrated now. "Have you forgotten about her?"

"What? Why? She wouldn't," Nathan replied, in disbelief.

"You are not hearing what I'm saying here, Nathan," Gabriel repeated, in a stern voice.

"Yes, I am. I just don't believe it," Nathan argued back.

"No, you're not. I told you that I had been watching over Serena ever since she first attacked Sophie in her dreams. You didn't even flinch at what I said. You are so caught up in her evil that you are not seeing the larger picture here. She is coming for Sophie, to get to you, and she will kill her if you are not on your guard. You will lose her, Nathan. I promise you that if you continue on this way," Nathan stared back at the Archangel.

"Do you think I'm that stupid? Sophie won't die! How could you even say that?" His chest pained at the horrific thought, "Serena would never do that to me,"

"Nathan, her jealousy has consumed her. She sees Sophie as a way for her to enter this world. She found you through her, when Sophie's soul was at its weakest point. She's waited a long time for this connection. Spirits can easily attach themselves to those who have doubts in their heart and mind as Sophie did long ago. And even though she is stronger now, it's too late. Serena has made her connection to you—through her. She now has you both to hang onto. It's her doorway in and out of this world—permanently, and she will definitely kill Sophie without a second thought."

"But how did she find me?"

"I'm not sure. We did our very best to hide you from her once you became a guardian. But perhaps whatever is in there with her… has more power than we anticipated." Gabriel stopped to think. "There's something else to this that we are still missing..."

Nathan's mind raced with possible ideas. He then thought of the bracelet. The one that looked identical to Serena's from long ago. That had to be it.

If it truly was Serena's, then that could be the connection. He had to get rid of it as soon as he could. It might not solve their problem completely, but it would definitely help. He just couldn't piece together how Sophie had gotten her hands on it. She said she had found it—but where?

Gabriel stepped closer, then placed his hand down on Nathan's shoulder.

"You must not give her anything else to go on, understand?" His voice was stern.

"The more you link yourself with her, the more power she has to enter this world. You will lose everything you've worked for—your second life, your chance at happiness, and more importantly, Sophie. You need to keep her safe and happy. Do not let her mind stray or she too will be at the mercy of purgatory."

"Gabriel, it's just so hard to believe that Serena is doing this. Maybe if I could just talk to her, I could—"

"Absolutely not." Gabriel said, cutting him off. "We gave you this second chance to make something of yourself. Do not make a fool of us by throwing it all away. I will handle this, but to do so, I need you to back off. I want to help her as much as you do. So let me do my job, for if I do not get to her fast the other Archangels will and I cannot say what they will do to her."

"But I can help you, please!" Nathan begged again.

"No." Gabriel then stepped back from Nathan, "Sophie needs you. You owe it to her to keep her safe. She gave you back your life, Nathan. She loves you. Serena is your past. Let her be."

Nathan looked at him sadly.

"Please, I need you to trust me. I know how you feel." The Archangel touched his hand to his chest and closed his eyes for a moment.

"I feel everything you are feeling, and I feel her emotions as well. It is very sad what happened between you, but sometimes, people are not meant to be." His eyes then opened, staring blankly at the ground below him. "Some people, are meant to be alone..."

Nathan stood quietly for a moment, deep in thought. He didn't want Serena to be alone in the world. Gabriel then glanced up with a slight smile on his face.

"Lucky for you—you are meant to have love. You should be grateful. You are meant to be with Sophie, and she loves you dearly." Nathan's eyes softened at the thought.

"You must look at what is right in front of you. Look at what you have. I beg you, Nathan. You are like family to me." He paused, "I have hopes for you, I will not stand by and watch you ruin everything. Forgive me for being so hard on you, it is truly in your best interest."

Their eyes connected once more before Gabriel disappeared from sight. Without a second to waste, Nathan took off towards home. He needed to get back to Sophie—now.

When Nathan reached the apartment, he frantically searched for Sophie, but she was no where in sight. Bruce leapt from the couch to greet him, but he ignored the little dog. Grabbing his cell from his pocket, he rang her number.

No answer. "Damn it!"

Thoughts began to race through his mind as to where she could be. It was far too long for her to still be at the grocery store. What if something happened? What if he was too late? What if…

He stopped, dropping his head into his hands.

"I swear to god, Sophie," He breathed deeply. "Where are you?"

He slammed his fist against the wall, then dialed her number again. He repeated this twice more before tossing the phone to the floor. He then searched the apartment one more time to be sure he hadn't missed anything, then grabbed his jacket and headed out towards the grocery store, hoping to retrace her steps.

It was close to eleven o'clock at night when Nathan returned back home. He had looked everywhere but found nothing. As he locked the door behind him, everything inside of him hurt. He didn't know what else to do. He had called all of her friends with no luck. He even called Charlotte, but she immediately blamed him and went straight to Matt's to look for her missing friend. He was at a loss as he made his way down the hallway—Bruce trailing sadly behind. The little dog scratched his leg a few times, but Nathan continued to ignore him. He entered the bedroom and sat down on the mattress.

"Gabriel?" He said, very loudly. "I know you can hear me. Please, I need your help. Please, help me find her." His voice cracked.

"Gabriel," he called again, "Please, I'll do anything..."

No one answered.

He got up from the bed and began to pace around the room.

"Damn it, Gabriel!" He yelled, "I seriously need you. I promise

I'll listen! Please, just help me! I'm sorry," He began to cry, "I'm so sorry, Soph,"

"Why are you calling to Gabriel?" Nathan turned quickly to see me standing behind him in my bathrobe—my wet hair dripping down to the floor below.

"Where did you come from?"

I looked at him oddly.

"Where have you been?" He growled again. "I've been looking everywhere for you! Why didn't you answer your phone?"

"I—"

"I thought you said you were going to the grocery store?" He shouted, cutting me off again.

I stood quietly, a little taken off guard by his sudden anger towards me.

"Well?"

"I went for a walk instead," I replied, quietly.

"You just went for a walk for like six hours, Soph? That's so stupid of you! You could've been killed or kidnapped—anything could've happened. I thought we agreed to keep in contact at all times," he continued to yell as I stood there taking in his hateful words.

"Yes. I did walk around for six hours," I shot back at him finally. "I needed air, and you said you needed time to yourself. So I walked." I was upset with him now.

"Soph, you can't do that. Do you hear me? When did you get back?"

"About an hour ago. I had a bath to relax. You weren't here. I thought you were out taking time to yourself."

"Jesus Sophie, do you know what you did to me? I had no idea where you were, and I couldn't get a hold of you. That's straight out stupid of you!"

I couldn't take it anymore. He wasn't supposed to talk to me like this. This wasn't how our relationship was supposed to go. I turned to head back into the bathroom, trying hard to keep my tears from falling. But just as I was about to shut the door Nathan was there—blocking it.

"No you don't!" He said, pushing it open.

I stepped back from him, a little frightened.

"Don't you dare close this door on me. You scared the shit out of me

106

tonight, Soph. I'm so mad at you!"

The anger in him was out of control. Suddenly, his eyes began to tear up.

I wasn't sure what had come over him, but I didn't like it.

"Say something!" He shouted again. "Don't you even care?"

My lips trembled as he waited impatiently for my response.

"You're scaring me, Nate,"

"What?" He replied, trying to catch his breath.

"You're changing and it scares me," I repeated.

Nathan stood there for a moment, then slammed the door shut behind him in frustration. He fell back against it and slid to the ground. I felt like things were breaking between us—for real this time. I watched as Nathan rested his head in his hands.

"I don't know what's happening," he whispered.

I stood quietly, unsure of how to respond. I didn't know what was happening between us either. I hated this, every second of it.

Slowly, I knelt in front of him.

"Soph," he lifted his head. "You scared me so bad tonight. It's not like you to disappear on me. I thought something had happened or… you had—"

"Had what?" I asked, feeling a little guilty now. "I thought that maybe, you had left me,"

The fact that Nathan even thought of the idea, broke my heart.

"I wouldn't leave you—not ever. But I do feel like you're hiding something from me and it's pulling us apart. I'm scared that what we have won't last."

"So am I," he admitted, quietly.

I didn't like that either of us were thinking this way. I had a horrible feeling building up inside of me.

"Why were you calling to Gabriel?" I asked again. "Tell me the truth,"

He looked up at me. There was fear in his eyes.

"He paid me a visit one morning, checking up on me I guess." He took my hand in his. "It's messing with my head, Soph. I want to be strong for us and not worry, or make you worry, but I just can't handle it anymore."

"Nate, why didn't you just tell me?"

It frustrated me—all the secrets he felt he had to keep for me to feel safe. He wasn't an angel anymore. We were a team. We were supposed to rely on each other for strength. I moved a little closer to him, then pulled his hand up to my lips. Kissing his fingers gently, I spoke again.

"You know, you're allowed to be scared, right? You're the one always telling me that I need to treat us like a normal couple. Well, that means you have to be normal and normal people worry. Normal people are scared at times,"

He nodded.

I wanted desperately to dive into his arms. I hated seeing him like this. I didn't understand why Gabriel's presence rattled him so much. I leaned up and kissed him on the forehead gently.

"I want to protect you Soph and give you everything...." He said. "But I have some unfinished business to deal with first and I need to figure out some stuff with Gabriel—to ease my worries. Okay?"

"You will, and I'll help you." I replied trying to be supportive, even if I didn't fully understand what he was talking about.

9
Saviour

Even the light shining through the window failed to stir us. We were mentally and physically exhausted. My arm rested over Nathan's bare back as the heat of the sun continued to warm our faces. Suddenly, a shadow moved in front of me, creating a cool breeze.

"Wake up," he said.

Nathan quickly turned over.

"Gabriel?" I said, my eyes adjusting to the sight before me.

"What are you doing here?" Nathan asked, nervously. I moved in closer to him.

"We need to talk—now." He demanded, turning his back to us. "Get dressed."

Nathan got up from the bed and tossed on a hoodie as I ran to the bathroom after grabbing some clothes from my dresser.

It only took me a second to change. I then stepped back into the room nervously. Slowly, I passed Gabriel. My eyes were glued to his until I reached Nathan's side. He took my hand in his.

"When I gave Nathan his second chance at life, I did not do it for something so silly to mess it up. These little quarrels between you two will stop."

I frowned, a little disappointed that Gabriel was upset with us. It was our life, what did he care if we argued a bit?

"Was it not you that said you would do anything to be with her?" His eyes met Nathan's.

"Of course, but—"

"And you," His eyes shot to mine. "You wanted him so badly you were willing to defy our warnings? Well, now you have him, and you don't trust him?"

"I do trust him, it's not like that," I argued, unsure of where this conversation was going.

"Then why do you doubt him? The two of you constantly worry about everything you have being taken away from you, when you should be just living your life," he said, starting to pace.

"Gabriel," Nathan began, "we're very thankful for what we have. I assure you and—"

"Do not interrupt me," he said, sharply. "I want to tell you a story that I have never told anyone before now and I want you to listen to it very carefully." He said. "Sit down,"

Nathan and I did as the Archangel requested.

"A long time ago, while I was leading the Archangels, I met a young woman. She wasn't one I had chosen to watch over, but one I came across by accident. She was alone in the world, her family was killed, and she had wandered until she had become very weak and collapsed. Her skin was beaten and cut from walking in bare feet, and it looked as though she had been through a few encounters with some men who had not treated her so well. I took it upon myself to help her. She was kind and gentle-hearted, even after all she had been through. When I found her, she was lying unconscious in the grass in the middle of the woods. I healed her and brought her some water and food to give her energy. She was very grateful and begged to return the kindness. But there was nothing she could give me. Nothing that I needed or required. For some reason, her presence intrigued me very much and I wanted to see more of her. I wanted her to have more in life. So I spent many days after that following her around and having conversations as if I was alive—ultimately protecting her from anyone that threatened her life. She made me feel—different inside."

Gabriel's voice continued to change as the story went on. The way he spoke about this woman seemed too weak for an angel. It was too human—too real.

"The Archangel Chamuel noticed my absence first and followed me one day. Being the angel of love, of course he would understand what was happening to me. But as quiet as he remained about my situation, it was only a matter of time before the rest of the Archangels found out about her. When they did, they warned me about spending too much time with her. That I needed to remember my duties to the higher power first and foremost. Of course, I never forgot about Him. He is what I live for, but she had, for a moment, distracted me. She was beautiful and I had never had feelings like this before. I wanted to see her every day, but in the end, the Archangels forbade me. They feared that I would lose myself to her. The rules were clearly given to me. I was the messenger for God, the leader of Archangels, and I lived to serve only Him for eternity." He stopped again.

I couldn't believe the story Gabriel was telling us.

"I knew I could never be with her because of what I was, but somewhere in the back of my mind, I hoped that maybe, just maybe, I could be a small part of her life—just as you had once hoped Nathan when watching over Sophie."

I felt Nathan's hand tighten around mine.

"But Michael soon stepped in and put an end to everything I had hoped for. He threatened to end my services to God and banish me if I continued to see her. If I were to abandon Him, I would then become one of the Fallen, which was something I never wanted to be. So, I went to her. I went to say my goodbyes. She begged me to stay. She said she didn't know if she could live without me. She said she needed me, and it broke my heart to leave her. But I had no choice. I returned to the angel realm with Michael and the rest, and I never saw her again. That was the day that I stepped down as leader and Michael took over." He sighed.

"The reason I tell you this is because they do not see things as Chamuel and I do, so they will not have mercy on your choices or actions."

I looked to Nathan and suddenly felt embarrassed about how we'd been acting. It seemed like Gabriel understood us much better than we could have ever known.

"I'm sorry, Gabriel," Nathan repeated, sadly.

The Archangel stepped closer to us, crossing his arms deep in

111

thought for a moment.

"Months later, I felt a sickness inside of me. It was a sudden rush of emotion for her, so I secretly searched for her whereabouts. This was before that rule came to be, the one about angels not being able to look into their past," he said, looking at Nathan. "When I finally found her, she was dead."

My heart stopped for a moment, and I covered my mouth. How horrible for him to come across the one he loved—dead. I immediately thought of Nathan and how it would ruin me indefinitely.

"Beaten by a man and left helplessly by the water. I can't describe the feeling, holding her lifeless body in my arms."

I felt a tear fall from my eye. I quickly wiped it from my face as he continued.

"If I had denied them, could I have saved her? Or was this her fate all along? These thoughts haunted me for a very long time. But I couldn't live like that. I had to move on."

"That's horrible," I said, sadly, "it seems so unfair,"

"I agree." He said, looking over at me. "But Fate has a path for everyone—even you two—which is why I tell you my story. I do not fight for you two for no reason. You are meant to be together. I believe that Nathan was meant to watch over you and you were meant to give him his second chance which is why your first life didn't work out for you." He said, glancing back at Nathan.

I suddenly felt much different about the Archangel. The fear I once felt was replaced by sadness and—respect for all that he knew. He had been rooting for us the entire time, not trying to pull us apart like I thought.

"There are things in this world that will test you both, including your relationship. You must stay strong. You must work as a team and fight for what you deserve."

The Archangel was right. We needed to be smarter. We need to make better choices—starting right now.

"I'm called the Angel of Mercy for a reason. I give mercy to those who continue to lose their way in hopes that they will eventually find the right path again."

His eyes adjusted to Nathan's.

"Do not waste your time with silly things that could disrupt the order of Fate. She is not to be reckoned with. Believe me."

"Gabriel, this Fate, why have I not seen her? I mean, you and the Archangels talk of her, but I just don't understand how She controls all?" Nathan asked.

I was confused again, was Nathan saying that Fate was a real being?

"Be thankful you have not met her yet, Nathan. She is more powerful than He. God may have created humans, but Fate has designed their path. It was agreed by the two of them long ago, before the first man and woman were created. The two of them ruled this earth, constantly bickering over how things should be. This agreement draws the lines between them—at least for now. We hope to change this in the future."

"But why can't you just talk to her?" I heard myself butt in.

"Because we have no power over her. She ultimately rules everyone and everything, and her ways of dealing with things are not as true as His. If she feels you are swaying from your fated path she has designed for you, she will step in and change it for the worse."

My eyes widened in fear. Who gave this Fate such power I wondered? I thought God controlled everything. Why couldn't the Archangels just stop her? There was no way she could defeat them all on her own—could she?

Gabriel strolled over to the window and looked outside to the beginning of another beautiful day.

"It is a good life you two have here," He said, glancing back at us. "Do not ruin it. I beg you." Then he was gone.

After having breakfast and taking Bruce out for a long walk, the two of us lounged around the apartment for the rest of the day. Neither of us in need of going anywhere. We just wanted to be close, and we didn't speak about Gabriel's visit or his tragic story.

Nathan sat on the couch, a book in his hands as I lay with my head in his lap, flicking through the channels on the television. Every once and a while I felt him stroke my hair, a feeling that calmed me.

"How's the book," I asked, turning off the television.

I then turned on my back, so I could stare up at him.

"It's good, you should read it."

113

I scrunched my nose up, "Why don't you read it to me." I teased.

"How about I tell you a new story?" He replied.

I sat up, intrigued a little.

"Remember when I told you long ago, that you were a pure heart?" I nodded.

"Well, it's true. You see, a pure heart can only omit love and light and are most powerful when they are in the right state of mind."

He then reached up and placed his hand in the middle of my chest. My heart began to race from his touch.

"Your heart, your beautiful pure heart gave me my second chance." Although I still didn't fully understand how, the idea made me very happy inside.

"There are very few of you left on this earth, and I was lucky enough to fall in love with one."

"What are the chances?" I smiled.

"Very, very slim." He replied. "I'm so grateful to have found you Sophie. To have you in my life, to be able to love you like my heart wants to."

The thought of Nathan being thankful to me was unbelievable, because in my mind, I was so thankful that he found me. He had picked me out and decided to help me. He had no idea how much he meant to me. I leaned up and kissed him. He truly was my world.

Later that night, while Nathan and I ate in front of the television my cell phone went off. I hurried over to the kitchen to grab it from the counter. It was Charlotte. I felt Nathan's eyes on me the entire time. He was reading my mind as I spoke to my best friend. She was upset and ripping my ear off about going missing.

With everything that had happened in the past few hours, I had completely forgot about calling her to tell her I was okay. I completely understood her worrying, but I also wasn't in the mood an argument right now. There were bigger things on my mind. Eventually, I was able to get off the phone with her. I sighed, placing the cell on the kitchen table.

"Everything okay?" Nathan asked, from the living room.

I made my way over to him and flopped down on the couch.

"Yeah, just the same old stuff. This is exhausting. I'm running out

114

of lies for our life, Nathan." I joked, sadly.

He took my hand in his.

"I wish she would ease off you. I thought for sure we had made a breakthrough with the hike, but I guess I ruined it by calling her frantically last night, didn't I?"

"No, it's fine. You were worried and I'm just as much to blame."

"Can we agree we're both to blame then?" He spoke again, "Let's promise right here, to move past all this. We know what we've done wrong, and we know what we should be doing moving forward, right?"

"Agreed."

We didn't need to say anything else. We just needed to start doing things right. I leaned in and wrapped my arms around him.

"I love you," He said, kissing the top of my head.

"Good," I sighed, pulling back from him.

He looked at me oddly.

"Because Charlotte's on her way over. She said she has to see me in person to make sure I'm alright."

Nathan's head dropped back against the couch.

"Remember, you love me," I reminded him.

He sighed, "I have to give her props, she never gives up."

I climbed onto his lap and pulled his head back up.

He smiled, then kissed my nose. "You're lucky to have such a good friend though,"

I nodded, then linked my lips with his once again.

"Well, I guess I could use a new book." He then said, lifting me off him. I watched as he got up from the couch and took our dishes into the kitchen.

"I'm going to head over to the library and pick out something new. It'll help me relax. I'll leave you two to your girl talk,"

"Nate, you don't have to leave just because she's coming over." I said, entering into the kitchen behind him.

"You can stay with us. I'm sure things can be smoothed out."

"No Soph, it's not that. I think I should just let you two talk. I won't be late."

"Okay, sorry." I said, feeling a little guilty.

"Don't be, this is the part where we do our own thing, right?" He smiled, "I'll see you soon."

Before Charlotte arrived, I put on a pot of tea. This conversation was sure to be a tiresome one. I prepared myself as best I could for what she might say. I needed a good story, something that she would buy. Something that wouldn't make her disapprove of Nathan any more than she already did. Just then, I heard a knock at the door.

"Come in!" I yelled.

I heard the door open and then shut quickly after. Listening to Charlotte's footsteps coming down the hallway suddenly made me nervous to defend my relationship again. She plopped herself down at the table beside me, dropping her big purse to the floor. Here it comes.

"Alright Sophie, spill the tea. What is so great about Nathan that you insist on staying with him? I mean, come on. He doesn't work. He lives here free and now you're fighting so bad that you ran out on him last night? Nobody could find you. It scared me half to death! What if something happened to you? That's not how people in love treat each other, ya know?"

She sounded like Nathan a little.

"I know that Charlotte," I responded, reaching out for the mug I had ready for her on the table. I carefully poured some tea into it, then into my own. She took my hand quickly.

"Sophie, sometimes in life people are blinded by infatuation and when that happens, they don't see the things that are bad in their relationship—things that seem small and meaningless soon grow to be a very horrible thing. I'm not saying Nathan's abusive or anything because I know he's not, but I do know he's someone you've had to take care of. Soph, it should be the other way around right now. You've had too much happen to you over the years." She sighed. "You need someone who can take care of you. He's just at a different level than you in life. I really don't think that he's the person for you. He's nice, but you need—"

"Please stop," I said, looking down into my mug.

I then pulled my hand from hers.

"He is the only one for me, Charlotte. So get over it. I know

Nathan and I are at two different places in life. I know more than you think. There's so much about him that you wouldn't believe it even if I told you the whole truth. But it's not mine to tell."

"What do you mean?" Charlotte asked, confused. "What can't you tell me? I mean, I know I've been hard on you lately about him, but you can always talk to me. No matter what. You know that, right?" She insisted, grabbing my hand again.

"No, I can't." I sighed, pulling from her grip again. "Nathan's life was tragic, and I'll respect him by not spilling his history all over the table to everyone. He's been working through a lot and he's been close friend of mine for many years now. He helped me through so much and now it's my turn. I want to give back to him, and he can take as long as he needs to straighten himself out. He was just upset the other night and kept it to himself which is what he always does, and I took it as him not trusting me enough to talk to me."

It was partially true. I took a long sip of my tea.

"I felt like he didn't love me enough to want to work through his issues with me. But I overreacted, Char. It was my fault entirely. I didn't give him his space. Maybe if I did, he might have come to me. Nobody's perfect and everyone has issues. But like you and me, we need to be there for each other, even when we don't understand everything." I stared at her, hoping to get through to her.

"I just need you to trust me that things will work out. It makes everything so hard on Nathan and I every time we get together. He feels like he's never going to win with you and it upsets him very much. Then it upsets me, because I want my best friend and my boyfriend to get along. Why can't you just cut him a break?"

"Sophie,"

Charlotte was a little lost for words. I had never been this brutally honest with her, but she needed to hear it. Nathan and I were changing, and I needed my best friend to get on board.

"I'm sorry. I just—" Suddenly the lights went out.

"What the hell? Again? What's wrong with your building, Soph?" Charlotte said, grabbing her phone from her purse on the floor. She tapped on the flashlight App.

117

"I'm not sure." I said, a little annoyed. "Guess we'll just have to wait it out."

Carefully, I got up and found my way over to the counter drawers. I was prepared this time with a lighter and some candles.

The smell of cinnamon filled the air as I made my way back over to the table. Our faces glowed from the warm light.

"Sophie, listen, I don't want to fight. I—"

Just then, a loud bang came from the end of the hallway, startling us both.

"Is Nate home?" Charlotte asked.

"He can't be," I replied. "He went to the library. Maybe the wind from the window blew a door shut."

Another two bangs came from the closet doors in the hallway, making us both jump again. Bruce whined, racing over to hide between my legs.

At first, the sounds were sporadic, then they happened every second. They became louder and louder. As the doors continued to bang, I grabbed Charlotte by the wrist to pulled her up and back towards the counter. Bruce ran close behind us.

"What the hell is going on? I'm really freaking out. Should we call the cops?" Charlotte trembled—fumbling her cellphone in her hands.

I was just as scared. With my record of supernatural encounters, and the recent return of Gabriel, it could be anything.

Suddenly, everything went quiet. I began to feel something I hadn't felt in a very long time. That eerie, horrible, dark feeling inside. The one that used to keep me up at night after my last year of high school.

The sound of footsteps in the hallway kept us quiet. Charlotte's fingers froze over the phone. We could hear every creek on the floor as the sound moved closer. I quickly grabbed the cellphone from Charlotte, trying to stop her from calling the cops. We continued to listen, our bodies shook uncontrollably. I took Charlotte's hand in mine, and we slowly made our way over towards the living room to give us a better view of the apartment.

"Soph, I want to call Matt or someone—please," She whispered.

We couldn't see him, but we could hear Bruce growling from the other room. I stood my ground, carefully searching the apartment with my eyes. There weren't many places for someone to hide if someone had really broken in.

The banging started again, making Charlotte quickly yank the cell phone back from my hands.

"That's it, I'm calling the cops!" She said, trying her best to handle the phone with stability.

The living room floor creaked in front of us and made our bodies freeze up again as a small figure appeared before us. The window behind illuminated her shape.

"Nice try," The girl said. Then suddenly, she was gone from sight.

"Where did she go?" I whispered. My heart was racing.

"She?" Charlotte repeated.

Deep inside I knew who it was. I hadn't seen her since Gabriel removed her from my life long ago. But there was no mistaking that haunting, fragile girl from my dreams.

Just then, a very thin arm reached between us from behind and grabbed the cell phone from Charlotte's hand. I whipped around quickly, backing away from the dark figure in front of us again. Her pale skin glowed in the moonlight as she took a step towards us. I fearfully pulled my friend back.

"Who the hell are you?" Charlotte shouted.

The girl smirked, and just as her mouth opened to respond the sound of the front door unlocking, startled us all.

"Soph? I'm back." It was Nathan. "I forgot my—"

"Nate! Help!" I shouted.

"Nathan," I heard the girl repeat quietly.

He immediately raced down the hallway at the sound of my desperate voice.

"Soph? Sophie, where are you?!"

Just then, she appeared in front of him.

"Nathan," she whispered.

He froze from the sight. Then suddenly, the lights flickered back on and the girl was gone. Bruce ran around the room frantically, searching for the intruder. Nathan's eyes shot to mine. I quickly ran to him, throwing myself into his arms.

"Are you alright? What the hell happened here?"

119

"Someone broke in!" Charlotte shouted, "What does it look like? But where the hell did she go? She has to still be here! Nathan, we need to call the cops!"

Charlotte then began to search frantically for her cell phone.

"Did you get a good look at who it was?" he asked, nervously.

"No. But it was definitely a girl—if you can believe it and it looks like she took my cell phone. Damn it!" Charlotte complained.

"I'll take a look around to make sure every thing's clear," Nathan replied, trying to pull away from me, but I wouldn't let him go.

"It's okay, Soph. You can come with me."

He slid his hand into mine and cautiously guided us around the apartment, opening every door and every closet. Charlotte crept close behind. We found nothing. There was no sign of her.

"I think it's clear," he said.

"That doesn't make sense at all. How could she have just disappeared?" Charlotte yelled, throwing her hands up into the air.

"What should we do?" I asked, still holding his hand tight.

"There's no point in calling the cops. There's no proof." Nathan said, trying to lead Charlotte from the idea.

"What? Nathan, someone broke in. That's crazy, we should definitely call the cops!" She replied, still freaking out.

"No Char, it's fine. Nathan's right. It's pointless." My voice shook. I tried desperately to calm myself. "We're fine,"

"You are not fine," She argued. "What if he's not here next time? I'm not letting you guys stay here alone tonight. I'm sleeping over. I don't understand why you won't call the cops," Charlotte continued to complain flopping down on a chair.

"Because Char, it's fine. If it happens again, I'll call the cops. I promise."

"Let's hope there's not a second time. I mean, what did she want? Just to steal my cell phone? So stupid."

We headed back towards the kitchen.

"Charlotte, you're welcome to stay here tonight if you want, but I assure you Sophie's safe. I won't let anything happen to her."

Charlotte took a deep breath, putting her head into her hands.

"Soph, can I please call Matt? It would make me feel so much better."

"Of course," Nathan said, reaching into his pocket and handing her his phone.

"Please don't tell him about this Char," I started to say, but Nathan squeezed my side.

"It's fine." He assured me.

Charlotte then hurried off into the spare room to make her call.

Nathan turned to me, gently holding my face in his hands.

"Are you alright?" He asked, again.

"Nate, it was her. I know it. It was the same girl from my dreams! How is she here? Why now? I thought Gabriel had gotten rid of her? I'm freaking out, it's about to happen all over again, isn't it? I know it," Tears filled my eyes.

Suddenly, I realized I had never told Nathan about the girl from my dreams. He was probably confused as to who I was talking about. My mouth opened, I tried to think of where I should begin and how to explain her, but nothing came out.

"Sophie, stop sweetie. You're fine, I'm right here. Nothing is going to hurt you."

I shook my head, "No, you don't understand." I began, "She used to haunt my dreams long ago. She was the one—the one I always saw before everything went dark, before you came to save me. She attacked me. She was the one in the bathroom that day—the day Gabriel saved me." I rambled on.

His arms wrapped around me, cradling me tight against his chest.

"She's coming for me again…" I said, trying to catch my breath.

"Please, don't let her get me,"

"Never," He whispered. "No one will touch you."

His embrace scared me a little. Now that Nathan wasn't an angel, I was worried for how exactly he was going to protect me from her.

"Come, let's go to bed. We'll talk more there. We can't do this with Charlotte around."

Just then Charlotte returned. She stopped at the sight of me, then hurried over and pulled me from Nathan's grip. She hugged me tight.

"I knew you were freaked out." She said, sadly. "Are you sure you don't want to call the cops? It might make you feel better—make you feel safe—ya know?"

I tried my best to clear my throat.

"No, I'm fine. I just want to go to bed." I replied, quietly.

Charlotte loosened her grip to look at me.

I stepped back from her nervously, I needed a moment alone.

"Soph?" I heard Nathan say. The room began to sway.

"Maybe you should sit down for a sec," Charlotte suggested, stepping towards me, but before she could touch my hand, I dropped to the ground.

Everything was dark, the distant sound of voices rang in my ears, but I could see nothing. My breathing became very slow. The air was thick and hard to breathe. Then I heard his voice.

"Sophie!" It startled me, "Open your eyes!" I felt my body shaking.

Then suddenly, a blast of cold water hit my face. My eyes shot open and I gasped for air.

"Good girl, sit up." Nathan spoke again.

His hand forced me up so I could rest in his arms.

"Are you alright?" Charlotte asked, worried.

I felt Nathan's arms slide under me as he lifted me from the ground.

"She needs some rest." He said, carrying me from the kitchen.

I dazed in and out until Nathan gently placed me down on the bed. I could feel the heat coming from him. He pulled the covers up close around me.

"Sophie," he said, making my eyes open again to his voice. "I need you to stay awake, alright? Are you listening to me?"

I was listening, but I couldn't respond.

Eventually, I nodded, taking a deep breath in. I then attempted to adjust myself up on the pillow more. Nathan's hand guiding me slowly. He then brushed a few strands of hair from my face.

"Don't go to sleep, alright?" He repeated.

"I'll be right back."

I felt the bed move as he got up and left the room.

Back in the kitchen, Charlotte waited patiently with Bruce on her lap. "Is she okay? Maybe we should take her to the hospital, Nate?"

"No, she's fine." He replied. "She hasn't had much sleep lately. She just needs some rest. If she's still not well by tomorrow evening, I'll take her then—I promise. Okay?"

Charlotte paused, thinking over his offer.

"Alright. Keep an eye on her. I'll stay tonight, but I have a photo shoot tomorrow morning. Matt's picking me up here at nine sharp. Will you please text me later in the day to let me know how she is? Please, Nate." She begged.

"Sure." He agreed, turning to walk away.

He stopped before entering the hallway to look back at Charlotte. "I know you don't trust me because you don't understand me, but know this, I love Sophie more than anything in the world. We're going to have our good days and bad, but she will always be in good hands. That, I promise you."

Charlotte stared back at him.

"I hope you'll give me a chance to prove that to you, because I think you're a great friend Charlotte and I want you to see what a great friend and boyfriend I am too." He smiled, "The bed is all set up in the spare room. Help yourself to anything. Good night."

"Night," she replied softly.

10
In Her Eyes

"Nate, you stayed awake." I said, opening my eyes to him.
"Barely," he yawned.
"You need some sleep. It's daytime now, rest for a bit," I said.
"I can't. I can't watch over you if I'm asleep, Soph."
"Nathan, I'm fine. I'm going to shower and freshen up.
Nothing will happen. Please, just sleep a bit," I begged. My
hand reached up and brushed his hair from his eyes.
"Go to sleep, Nathan," I said again, watching his eyes slowly
close. His body slid down in the bed to get more comfortable.
I leaned over and gently kissed his forehead.
"Thank you." I whispered, then quietly got up from the bed.
Tip-toeing down the hallway, I peeked into the spare bedroom.
The bed was made perfectly, and Charlotte was gone. I
only hoped she wasn't too upset about last night. So much
happened that I couldn't explain to her. I wondered what she
was thinking today.
    Walking towards the bathroom, I still felt anxious about
everything. That eerie feeling from last night was still with me
and I couldn't help but look over my shoulder every few steps.
    Closing the bathroom door behind me, I began to fill the
tub with hot water. I needed to relax. I felt tense, stressed,
and I still had a chill running throughout my body. I began to
undress. My legs wobbling a little beneath me. Even though
I told Nathan to rest, I really didn't want to be too far from
him. I was scared. Scared that everything was going to begin

again. All of the nightmares, the stress—the depression. I had worked so hard to deal with it and change my frame of mind like Nathan told me to long ago. As good as I felt these past few years, I secretly always worried about it coming back. But thanks to Nathan, I never worried for too long. He always managed to keep me distracted.

Stepping into the water, I felt myself instantly melt from the heat. I rested my head back against the tub. My mind began to race with thoughts of that girl. How had she managed to come back into my life? Why was she set on attacking me, and now Charlotte? None of it made any sense and why had Gabriel not saved me like he did before? Couldn't he see or sense her? How was I supposed to protect myself now that Nathan was human? The more I thought about everything while soaking in the warm water, the more overwhelmed I became. My eyes became heavier and eventually closed.

Her body trembled with fear as she sat in the water that had run cold now—crying. Her hands shook as she splashed some water up against her face. She had tried for so long to let go of everything and move on, but it was just too much. These feelings were consuming her every second of every day. They didn't have enough time together. It wasn't fair. How could life ever be normal again? How could she ever feel happiness like she did before? Her hands traced the water, remembering the last time she was in this very tub. She was bloody and numb after a brutal attack from an intruder, but he had taken care of her and not left her side for a single moment—until the next morning. When everything changed.

Her body sank lower into the tub as she stared up at the ceiling—tears staining her cheeks. She glanced to the side of the tub where a razor sat on the edge. Her breathing slowed. She took the razor in her hand. Staring at it, she considered her options carefully.

Nathan turned over in bed, deep in sleep until a soft voice spoke.

"Nathan. Nate, wait up!" Her voice called out. "Hey, you forgot your pen!"

Nathan turned to a beautiful young woman running up behind him.

"You're coming over tonight, right? Maybe you can make us some dinner with your mad skills?" She joked.

He closed his eyes in disbelief. When he opened them again, he was back in his bedroom. Nathan rubbed his eyes and turned over again, his emotions began to stir. He tried desperately to hold himself together as he closed his eyes another time and fell quickly back to sleep.

"Nathan, I love you," the voice whispered.

His eyes shot open again, and there in front of him was Serena. Lying quietly beside him, she reached for his face, but Nathan quickly pulled back in fear.

"Shh, don't wake her. I just want to talk." She said, reaching for him again, but he pulled away further.

"What are you doing? What's happening?" He couldn't get his words out. There were so many questions. He had no idea where to begin.

She moved in closer.

"Don't be afraid, Nathan. It's just me." She took hold of his hands and wrapped them around her waist so she could pull herself in closer to his chest. "I've missed you so much," she said, looking up at him.

"Serena, what's happened to you? I mean, I read an article. Is it true? Did you kill yourself? Why would you do that? Why would you end your life—over me? You had so much going for you. You could've made something of yourself. It was me that messed up. I just don't understand any of this," he said, sadly.

"None of it was worth having if I didn't have you, Nate." She replied. "It wasn't fair. I tried so hard to go on without you. I was so alone. I had no one. I needed you, but it's okay now because I found a way back to you. Haven't you missed me?"

"Of course. But you're not really here, are you? And my life—I'm so sorry—it's with Sophie now." He said sadly.

Her eyes blinked once before she leaned up and kissed him on the lips. At first, he fought against it, but she was persistent and kept moving towards him. Her lips felt cold. His hand slid up her back as she pulled him in close.

"How am I able to hold you? How are you here?" He whispered between their kisses.

"Because you still love me." She smiled, "I have a special link to you. We were meant to be together."

She continued to kiss him over and over again, until he pulled back.

"I want to help you, Serena. What can I do to help you?" He asked.

"This..." she answered, connecting her lips to his again. She then pulled his shirt from over his head and tossed to the ground. Gripping onto his pants, she continued to kiss his warm skin.

He couldn't control the urge he felt for her. He remembered their connection from long ago and it was intoxicating. Serena made her way on top Nathan—a beautiful vision that tempted him with every touch.

"Forget about everything. It's just you and me here now. I love you and you love me. There's nothing else," she whispered into his ear. The sound of her voice numbed his body. "I want you, Nate." She kissed his chest, then slowly made her way up his neck to his chin, then back to his lips.

"I want you too," he heard himself say.

● ● ●

I felt the razor gently touch the skin on my wrist. I felt sad and confused, and unable to wake myself from these horrible thoughts.

"I can't live without you, I won't." I heard myself say before feeling the sharp burn of a blade slicing through my skin.

My body jolted in pain just as I felt another quick slice in the same area. I tried to scream but nothing came out. It was like my body wasn't listening to me. I couldn't stop it. I strained to make a sound again as another cut ripped across my wrist, this time deeper than before.

"Sophie, open your eyes!"

The voice startled me and finally woke me from my horrible dream state. My body shook violently in the cold water as I watched it turn red around me. I immediately felt lightheaded. The pain in my chest was unbearable and my wrist burned as it continued to pour blood into the water below. I attempted to reach for the side of the tub, thinking I could pull myself out, but I was too weak. Crashing back down into the water, I hit my head on the way down.

"Nate..." I whispered, "I need..." But it was too late.

I felt myself slide down under the water. My lungs began to fill as I choked for air. The pressure was unbearable.

Then suddenly, I felt a harsh grip on my arm before my body was yanked from the water. It was followed by the warmth of a towel wrapping around me tight as he held me in his arms.

"Fight young one, you can do this." His soft voice said. "Open your eyes."

I felt myself choke, then cough dramatically gasping for air. I glanced up, "Gabriel?"

"Are you alright?"

"What happened? Where's Nathan?" I said, lifting my hand to my head. I was still dizzy. I was about to speak again but the fuzziness made the vision of the Archangel disappear fast.

"Sophie!" Nathan shouted, bursting through the bathroom door. He froze at the sight of Gabriel holding the lifeless body in his arms and the blood dripping onto the floor below him.

"Finally, you woke to my warning!" Gabriel said, in a stern voice.

"I don't know what happened. I couldn't wake up Gabriel, not until your voice broke through and I saw what you were seeing in that moment. I thought she was dead," he replied, running his fingers through his hair.

"Is she alright? What happened?" He asked, kneeling next to the Archangel. "Please, let me take her,"

Gabriel carefully handed over the body to Nathan. He then pulled the damaged arm out of the towel. His fingers lit up with a soft glow as he slid them gently across the cuts and sealed them instantly, making every sign of the slits disappear. "Put her in bed to rest." He ordered.

Nathan carefully did as the Archangel said and headed quickly into the bedroom.

He covered her shivering body with every blanket he could.

"This is getting out of control." Gabriel spoke from the other side of the bed. "You need to keep your eyes on her." Nathan didn't answer.

"This needs to end now or I fear that something more horrible will happen to Sophie."

Nathan's eyes grew wide.

"Stay here. I'll be back soon with a plan." He then turned from Nathan and paused. "If you cannot learn to control yourself around Serena until we can fix this, then I will have to teach you. I'm prepared to work with you—for Sophie's sake. Until then, please do as I say."

Then he was gone.

Nathan stood silently in the room, looking down at the girl he loved. Anger grew inside of him. He quickly made his way over to the closet. Digging through a few pairs of pants, he finally found the bracelet he had hidden away in the pocket of his blue jeans.

"Nathan..." Serena's voice startled him, making him drop the bracelet.

His eyes searched the room but found no one. Sophie stirred in the bed before him. Waiting for Gabriel would be too nerve-racking. He had to try and figure this out now—on his own. Glancing back over at the bed, he quietly slipped out from the room to make a phone call.

"Hello?" Charlotte answered. "Hey, it's Nate."

"Is everything alright? Did you take Sophie to the hospital?"

"No, she's still resting. Listen, I know you're working, but do you think you can come over a little later and stay with her for a bit? I want to go to the police station and report that intruder like you said, but I don't want to leave her alone. She's still a little spooked and I don't want her waking up alone in the apartment."

"I think that's a good choice, Nathan. I'll be over by four, is that okay?"

"Sure, thanks Charlotte."

Around four, as Charlotte promised, Nathan heard a knock at the front door. He hurried to answer it, anxious to get out and find some answers.

"Hey Nate,"

"Alex...." Nathan replied, surprised to see him. "What are you doing here?"

"Charlotte's going to be stuck at work a little longer, so she asked me to stop by and help until she gets off. She told me about the intruder. Scary stuff."

"Oh, okay, well thanks for coming." He said, opening the door to let Alex in. He followed Nathan into the kitchen.

"I won't be too long. I promise."

"No problem, where is Sophie now?"

"Sleeping, and most likely will continue to sleep for a while longer. But can you check on her every fifteen minutes or so? She hasn't been sleeping well and sometimes wakes in a panic."

"I will, for sure." Alex responded, confidently.

"Thanks again," He replied. "And Alex, remember to check on her. It's very important."

● ● ●

When Nathan reached the library, he went straight to the computers and began his search. He pulled the bracelet from his pocket and studied it closely.

"Serena, where are you?"

He placed it down on the table and read the next article that popped up on the screen. Nothing was giving him what he needed. As he glanced back at the bracelet one last time, he thought of the cherry blossoms and Japan, so he quickly typed in "Japanese Folklore" for the hell of it.

There were a few articles that spoke about people who had tragically died by suicide due to a loss. It spoke about the heartache and rage the soul feels just before someone commits to this. He then came upon a link entitled, "Reikons" so he clicked on it. The article read:

"According to traditional Japanese beliefs, all humans have a spirit or soul called a Reikon. When a person dies, the Reikon leaves the body and enters a form of purgatory where it waits for the proper funeral rites to be performed, it will then join its ancestors. But if the person dies in a violent manner, such as suicide or if they are influenced by powerful emotions such as revenge, love, jealousy or sorrow at the time of death, the Reikon is thought to transform into a Yūrei. A strong spirit that has the power to bridge a gap back into the physical world. There is only one way to lay a Yūrei to rest, one must resolve the spirit's conflict and ease their emotions back to a reasonable state. Only then can they pass on. If unsuccessful, the spirit could continue their haunting—indefinitely. There are two ways a Yūrei can connect themselves to the real world. One being a loved one that won't let go. The other being a cherished, sentimental item once owned by that spirit."

Nathan paused, looking down at the bracelet. It was the most precious thing to Serena when she was alive and alongside his feelings that were building up again quickly—no wonder Serena had such power now. But it didn't answer how she had linked onto Sophie so long ago in her dreams. There had to be something else. Nathan glanced over at the clock on the wall. He had to get back. He quickly printed off the articles, grabbed the bracelet and left.

●●●

I heard the floor creak, "Nate?" I felt hazy as I attempted to open my eyes to the movement in my room.

"No, Soph. It's me, Alex. Nate stepped out for a moment. Do you need anything?" He asked, stepping towards the bed.

I turned over in bed to face him.

"Alex?" I said, rubbing my eyes. "What are you doing here?"

"Nate asked me to watch over you. He didn't want to leave you alone while he stepped out. How are you feeling?" He asked, sitting down on the mattress.

I stared at him nervously. Something felt wrong. Why would he leave me? Especially after what just happened. I suddenly felt too far from him. I wanted him here—now.

The hair on my arms began to stand up as a cold draft filled the room. Everything inside of me was tingling now. I quickly sat up and looked at my wrist. I remembered being in the tub now and slicing my skin with a razor, but there was no evidence left on my body. Carefully, I touched my skin, wondering if maybe it was just a horrible dream.

"Sophie? What's wrong?" Alex asked again.

I stared around the room. I could feel it again—her presence. My breathing became short, and that awful gut feeling returned. Anticipating what was surely about to happen next, I found myself slowly shuffling to the edge of my bed.

"Soph? Sophie, look at me." Alex said, very calmly. "What do you see?" He asked. "Is she here?"

My eyes darted to him—confused. "What did you say?"

"Do you see her now?" He asked again, reaching for my hand.

There was no way Alex was talking about the same thing I was thinking about. He couldn't possibly know what I was fearing. I quickly jumped from the bed and threw myself into a corner on the other side of the room. I didn't want him to touch me. I needed to see everything.

"Sophie, you're fine. I know all about her..." He said, getting up from the bed.

"What? You couldn't possibly...." I responded in fear. I glared at him for a moment. "What are you?"

It was only a matter of time. I had experienced this before in my dreams.

"I'm just Alex, I promise." He replied, with his hands raised high in the air. "Come here, please. You need to listen to me." He took a step closer. I didn't move.

Glancing over at the door, I pondered if I could make it there before him. His hands eventually lowered, and he straightened himself out before me. Sliding his hands into his pockets he said very calmly, "You won't make it,"

Suddenly, the door slammed shut. I swallowed in fear and took off towards the exit. Alex jolted from the other side of the bed and quickly grabbed me by the arm. I screamed, trying my best to fight him off. He quickly released me, letting me fall hard to the ground.

"Get away from me!" I screamed as he reached for me again.

His hands were strong as he tried to pull me back and pin me to the ground. I continued to fight until I finally maneuvered myself free from his grip by giving him one hard kick to the chest.

His body slammed back against the wall and I scrambled to my feet, making a run for the door again. Just as I reached it, I heard her voice behind me.

"Hello Sophie,"

I whipped around just as the girl from my dreams appeared before me. Her eyes locked on mine. I screamed as the girl reached for me. Just then, Nathan's voice bellowed down the hallway and the bedroom door burst open behind me.

"Sophie?!" He yelled, I turned and threw myself into his arms. Hanging on for dear life, I couldn't breathe—I couldn't speak. I wanted out, now! I began to push back at Nathan, trying to get us through the door but he didn't budge. I glanced back in fear.

The girl had vanished from sight and Alex was slowly pulling himself up from the ground.

"She was asleep when I checked on her. I brought her some tea. Then she felt something in the room. She looked spooked, Nathan. I tried to help her, but she bolted from me. I didn't mean to startle her. I was only trying to help," Alex said, out of breath.

I stood there trembling in Nathan's arms. I wanted to say so much but I couldn't get anything out. I wanted to tell Nathan about Alex, but Nathan had no powers now as a human. We couldn't defend

133

ourselves from Alex, or from whatever else might show up.

"It's fine Alex, don't worry about it. Thank you for your help. You can go now," Nathan stepped to the side to allow Alex to leave. I squeezed tighter against Nathan as he stepped past us, then paused.

"I'm sorry Soph, I didn't mean to scare you."

When he left the room, I quickly slammed the door shut behind him.

"Nate! Something is happening! It's really bad and it's not just the girl from my dreams. It's so many things." I yelled, throwing myself against the door to hold it shut. "I can't sleep. I can't sleep ever again. But that won't even help me because she comes when I'm awake now too. Nathan, I'm not going to make it. She's going to get me and Alex, he said something. I couldn't tell what he was getting at, but it crept me right out. There was this presence in the room, and I could feel..." I paused, looking round the room nervously again. "I can't do this. I can't," I felt my knees become weak beneath me.

"Sweetie, calm down." Nathan's hands reached for me again, "Come here for a second, let me see you."

He wasn't listening. I quickly yanked the door open and took off towards the kitchen.

Leaning against the counter, I reached up, grabbed a glass from the cupboards and quickly filled it with water from the tap. It felt good against my dry throat. I then felt Nathan's hands touch my arms. I lowered the glass and turned to him, still trying to catch my breath.

"What happened back there?" He asked.

I took another deep breath, trying to collect my thoughts before speaking.

"Alex asked me if she was here,"

Nathan looked at me oddly. "Why would he say that?"

"I don't know! How does he know about her, or my dreams? It was like, he just knew what I was seeing and feeling. Then I tried to run because I had this horrible feeling like I get in my dreams and he said I wouldn't make it. He knocked me down. So I kicked him, but as I reached the door, the girl from my dreams suddenly appeared behind me. That's when you came in. Then she just vanished—like she always does!"

Nathan slowly rubbed my arms. "You're sure it's the same girl, the one from your dreams, and the other night with Charlotte?"

I nodded.

"And did you feel like Alex might hurt you or..." he paused, trying to piece this all together.

"I couldn't tell, but he was after me. Maybe he's on her side!" My mind began to race. "Or maybe he's an Archangel? I have no idea. I'm scared, Nathan."

"Sophie, I know the Archangels, but I don't know him. Unless one of them took over a new body." He paused again. "It's a possibility."

"Where did you go?" I then asked, trying to calm myself.

"I just went to research something at the library."

"Research what?" I asked.

He stared at me for a moment.

"Just some facts about spirits and stuff. To see if it would help us at all. I didn't want to leave you alone, so I called Charlotte. She was supposed to come, but Alex showed up. He said Charlotte sent him until she could get here herself."

None of it felt right—nothing he was saying. He then stepped back from me and reached into his pocket for his cell phone.

"What are you doing?" I asked.

"Texting Charlotte, I wonder what happened to her?"

She replied almost immediately, and Nathan's face went white.

"What?" He was making me paranoid.

"Charlotte says I never spoke with her at all today. She said she didn't send Alex over either."

I felt sick to my stomach. "What is going on here?" I said, leaning back against the counter.

"I'm not sure," He replied.

I reached out for him. I wanted him to be closer. He stepped into me and wrapped his arms around me tight.

"Don't worry, I won't let anything happen to you. We're going to get through this, alright?" He said, very clearly. "Promise me, promise me you won't give up."

"Promise..." I replied, quietly.

I was sick of this. Sick of feeling scared and vulnerable. I had worked so hard to get over my past, but now I was more terrified than ever.

"There's something else I think we should talk about," He then said, interrupting my thoughts. "And I don't want you to be mad at me. We promised we'd be honest with each other. Right?"

I leaned back from him a bit, "Of course," I agreed, intrigued by his words.

"We need to have this talk with Gabriel—all of us—together. We're going to need him. We can't do this alone. I don't have the power anymore, Soph."

"Nathan, what's going on? Just tell me now. I can handle it." I begged.

I didn't want to wait for Gabriel.

He let me go, "Let me get cleaned up first. It's going to be a long night. I'm also going to take Bruce over to the neighbors for a few days. That nice couple down the hall loves him. I'm sure they won't mind watching him for a bit."

"Why do we have to get rid of Bruce?" I asked, confused.

"Just trust me, our plates are about to get very full. We won't have time. He'll be fine, Soph. Why don't you boil some water so I can make us some spaghetti? We'll need our energy. I know that neither of us have eaten yet and we can't afford to be weak—not now. Then we'll talk about everything, I swear." He stepped away from me, then stopped again. "Oh, and change into something comfortable," he said, grabbing a few of Bruce's toys off the floor. I watched silently as he snagged a big bag of food from the closet next. He then attached Bruce to the leash and led him towards the front door. My little dog whined as the door slid shut behind them.

11
Hidden Truth

As Nathan showered, I found myself wandering around the kitchen mumbling to myself. I didn't understand any of this. Why was this happening to me? Why was she back? What did she want, and how could Nathan think of food at a time like this? Why wasn't he asking more questions about this ghost that was haunting me? Why did it not worry him as much as me? I couldn't cook anything—not right now. But I did as Nathan suggested and decided to change into some comfy clothes.

In the bedroom, I found myself digging through my drawers aimlessly. There was nothing I could wear that would make me feel comfortable right now—nothing. I turned to Nathan's hoodie lying on the bed before me.

I walked over and snagged it up. As I attempted to pull it over my head, I saw a few pieces of paper fall to the ground before me. Adjusting the sweater down on me, I bent over and picked them up. I could still hear the shower running as I slipped on a pair of fresh jeans. I then sat down on the bed to see what Nathan had hidden away.

As I opened them carefully, I realized they were printed articles. The first was an article on something called a Reikon. I scanned it quickly, then opened the next piece of paper. This one sparked my interest immediately. The title read: **'Tragic Suicide.'**

The article went on about a young girl—Serena Reilly, that was found dead in her home after slitting her wrist in the bathtub. My mind immediately jumped to my last attack in the bathtub. The story was very similar to what I thought I experienced. My hands were shaking as I looked back at the first article again. Reikons—they were souls—and something else about souls dying in a tragic way—they became these supernatural beings called an Yūrei. A spirit that could ultimately haunt the living. I suddenly froze as a horrifying thought surged my mind. That name...

I heard the bathroom door open, then Nathan stepped into the room drying his wet hair with a towel. He pulled the towel from this head and rested it around his neck—freezing the moment he saw the expression on my face. Then he saw the papers in my hands.

"Sophie,"

"What is this?" I asked, quietly.

"Don't be afraid. Just let me explain. This is why I wanted to talk to you, okay?"

"You know what I'm dealing with, don't you?" I asked, again. "Why wouldn't you tell me this earlier? Is this who I think it is?"

I could feel my heart begin to race. I wanted to know everything he knew.

"It says... these beings have some sort of unfinished business? Is that what I—"

"Soph, I'll tell you everything soon, I just—"

"No!" I butted in. "Just tell me, Nate. Is it her?!"

He didn't answer.

"Please don't make me say it," I cried.

When he still didn't respond, I snapped. "Is this your Serena?!" I shouted.

"Yes," He responded, quietly.

I went silent. It suddenly made sense—all of it. My fist clenched tightly to my side.

"You lied to me, Nate." I said. "You lied to me horribly—and not about something small—about something so huge—so important! Something that I could have—"

"Sophie, no. I was going to tell you." He interrupted. "That's why I wanted to talk to you tonight. Please, let me explain."

"I could've died, Nathan! Do you get that?" I shouted. I was furious the more I thought about it. "I could still die! And you knew all along what was following me, and you didn't tell me? How could you?"

He stepped towards me, but I immediately moved away.

"No, you're wrong. I just learned about it recently. I was going to tell you, I promise." He reached for me, but I pulled back again. "I didn't know before. Please, just sit down. Let's talk about this," he begged, but I shook my head.

"No... No, it's been her all along. That's why you've been sneaking off. That's why you never want to talk about your past. Have you seen her, Nate? Have you seen Serena? Because I definitely have."

My body trembled now as I continued to stare at him, waiting for a response.

"I only knew the moment she showed herself to me. I didn't believe it at first because I didn't know that she had died, Soph."

"She didn't just die, Nathan! She killed herself!" I tossed the papers at him.

"Now she's angry. She's angry with me and you. She'll never let us go. She wants me dead. Don't you get that? And you—you didn't tell me! Is it because you have no idea what to do with her? What's going to happen now, Nate? What if you have to choose between us?"

That sentence broke me. I couldn't bear the thought of Nathan choosing because I truly feared I would be the one to go. My hands stayed clenched as I went on with my questions and concerns.

"I can't even begin to process this. This is the worst thing you have ever done to me. I'm so mad at you! I could...."

I saw Nathan choke up at what I might say next. His lips quivered as he carefully chose his next few words. He eventually stepped forward and very quickly snagged hold of me, pulling me into his chest tight.

"Of course it would be you, Sophie. Don't be stupid. I love you. I'll always love you. You're my life now—not her." He breathed deeply.

I could hear his heart racing.

"It's just complicated. It just needs to be handled carefully and that's why we need Gabriel's help."

I wanted to believe him. I really did, but it just didn't add up in my mind. I pushed back from him, then turned to storm out of the room but Nathan cut me off at the doorway.

"Sophie, you promised. You promised we'd stick together no matter what." He said, desperately.

"I can't, I can't do this." I said, pushing past him.

He grabbed onto my shoulders, but I ripped from his hands and fell to the ground before him. I really couldn't handle this anymore. It was too much.

I felt myself falling into a panic attack. Nathan knelt in front of me.

"Sophie, please. You need to listen to me." He said, very kindly. "I'll get us through this. I won't let anything happen to you."

I shook my head, "You're going to leave me, Nate. I just know it," I said, dropping my head down.

"No, I'm not." He replied, lifting my chin up. "I swear it."

I began to cry.

"Sophie, just listen to me." He begged again. "I swear, I just found out about this recently. But I also learned something else," He paused as I looked up at him again worried. "You know that bracelet you found? The one with the cherry blossoms on it?"

I nodded. What was his obsession with my bracelet?

"It's the same one Serena wore long ago. There's no doubt about it. It's identical in every way."

I didn't blink. There was no way.

"I've never seen one like it since. And when I found out about her death and read those articles, it all kind of added up. It has to be hers, Soph. I'm so sorry I didn't see this sooner."

My eyes widened in fear thinking back to the day Nathan returned to me. The day I was in the shop ordering our slushies and that girl, the one who didn't pay. Her long blonde hair—her thin fingers…

Nathan interrupted my thoughts again.

"When you had myself and Gabriel around to watch over you, she could only haunt you in your dreams. But after I started to lose connection to your dream world and became more of a reality to you, she was able to break through with the attack in the bathroom. And when I finally became human once again, she made her move by dropping the bracelet for you to find. You found it right? You didn't buy it?"

I nodded, swallowing hard.

"Now she has a permanent connection to the real world. That's how she was able to finally show herself to me and now that I acknowledge her, she has linked herself to us both. We need the Archangels, Soph. This is way past anything we could ever deal with on our own." He spoke. "I have to find a way to stop her."

"But how?" I finally said. "How are we going to stop her, Nate?"

"I haven't figured that out quite yet. I'm hoping Gabriel will know. But Sophie, she's lonely. I really don't think she means to harm us. I mean, she's definitely upset and I want… I just want to help her."

"Help her?" I said, getting up from the ground. "Nate, of course she means to do us harm! At least to me she does. How are you going to help her? Seriously? She's out of control. Can't Gabriel just end her or something?"

Nathan stood up as I made my way over to the bed again.

"Sophie, she isn't just a spirit. It's Serena, someone very important to me."

I continued to glare at him. I didn't care. She was going to kill me.

"You just don't understand," he said.

"No Nathan, you don't understand. You're blinded by her!" I shot back at him. "She's gone! She isn't your girlfriend

141

anymore. She's just an angry spirit who wants me dead."

"I know that." He snapped back, "Please Soph, just let me try and help her, or at least reason with her. I can do it. I know I can."

I could feel it deep down. I was already losing him. The more we spoke about all of this, the more I felt Nathan and I tearing apart. I understood what he meant about his past with her, and I did feel bad about it, but the bigger picture here was that my life was in jeopardy. And to be honest, I felt a little insulted. Our past and our history was just as important—if not more! Did Nathan forget about everything we'd been through? Did he forget what Gabriel said? That we were fated to be together? My anger immediately changed its route with that last thought.

I took a deep breath, trying my best to understand Nathan's feelings. I also took into thought Gabriel's kind words from before. Although I didn't agree with Nathan one hundred percent, I had to help him. I had to be here for him. To show him how good we were as a team.

"The article mentioned jealousy," I began, reaching down to the floor and picking up the two pieces of paper. "Do you think she's jealous that she can't be with you now? Maybe she thought when she killed herself that you might get to be together? But she had no idea that you had become a guardian angel."

"Possibly." He said. A slight smile on his face.

I could tell he was grateful for my help—for trying to understand this all.

"But then you found me, and she saw our connection and didn't like it. Especially after you got your second chance. Now you're here with me in real life—as a couple. I'm sure it's really making her jealous. It has to be. She doesn't want us together, Nathan."

His eyes met mine again.

"She's still in love with you and she wants me out of the picture." I said, honestly.

"I won't let that happen, I swear." He assured me again.

But his eyes said something different. He seemed nervous.
I sat down on the edge of the bed.
"Let's talk with Gabriel as you suggested. Let's hear what he has to say."
It was true, we were going to need him. I was going to need him—to keep Nathan on my side so I didn't lose him. Nathan sat down beside me and leaned in for a kiss.
"We're going to be fine." He whispered. I nodded, unsure of what else to say.
"Do you trust me?" He asked. "You need to trust me, or we won't make it through this."
I stared quietly, then nodded again. "I trust you," I lied.
His face softened as he leaned in to kiss me again. I felt horrible. In a matter of minutes our relationship had completely changed again. He took my hand in his and called out to the angel of mercy.

We waited in silence for a few minutes. Gabriel didn't appear. Nathan called again. I was nervous, afraid that the Archangel would not come. He had warned us many times about our actions. Maybe he was fed up with us now. Then I heard his voice.
"For someone I believe is very intelligent, you do stupid things Nathan." He said from behind.
Nathan rose from the bed as Gabriel came around to meet us.
"I know. I'm sorry. I was just scared. Scared for Sophie and…" Nathan paused, looking down at me. "I worried that you—"
"Nathan, you cannot ask for trust from others and not give trust yourself," the Archangel interrupted. "If you did, you would see that I am always on your side. You have not given me the benefit of the doubt and worst of all, you have not given your full trust to Sophie either. It kills her. Don't you see that?"
My eyes fell to the ground. I couldn't look at either of them.
"I don't mean to," I heard him say.
Gabriel went on.

"Sophie is honest and true, the best kind of person there is. You are lucky to have her Nathan and you are even luckier to have this second chance. I know what you're going to ask me and yes, I will help you. But you will do things my way. I know everything about the information you have found and everything the two of you are thinking is true. You should be scared."

I felt that lump in my throat again.

"I know you wish to reason with Serena, but this path will not be an easy one."

Nathan nodded, surely prepared for the task at hand—but I wasn't.

"Are the two of you truly ready for whatever comes your way?" Gabriel asked, as if to read my mind.

"Of course, we can handle it." Nathan said, quickly. "Just tell me what I need to do."

I felt Gabriel's eyes burning into my skull. I knew he was still waiting for an answer from me. I couldn't look at him, because I couldn't give him the answer he needed me say. I heard him step closer to me. Then I felt his hand place down gently on my shoulder.

"It is you that I need the real answer from," he said, quietly.

I finally looked up at him. What was he expecting? Me to just jump on board and go after the girl who's trying to kill me? The girl that my boyfriend used to—or could possibly—still love? Of course I didn't want to do this. My entire life was slipping away into this supernatural dream world again. Was this really what my life was going to be about?

I then felt Nathan sit back down next to me on the bed. His soft hand turning my chin to look at him.

"Sophie," he spoke calmly. "Don't be scared. We can do this. I'm right here beside you and I'll never let you out of my sight."

I didn't answer.

"I don't have to read your mind to know what you're thinking sweetie." He smiled, then kissed me on the forehead. "I won't choose her. It's always going to be you."

I looked back up at Gabriel again, I needed his confident words to help me out—to make me believe.

"This will be a very hard road young one, and it will take a lot out of you. Are you truly ready for this?"

It wasn't exactly what I was hoping to hear. I wanted him to tell me that Nathan and I would make it through this. That we would be fine. That we would end up together. But that was all he gave me.

I sighed, "I can do it," I finally answered.

Gabriel stood silently, staring at me. Surely, he knew I was lying.

"You are stronger than you think, Sophie."

I was a little taken by his use of my name. He usually called me "young one". In fact, I couldn't remember a time he had ever used my name when talking to me. I had only heard it when he spoke to Nathan about me, but never used directly towards me. It sounded nice coming from him.

"I'll tell you what we are going to do, or should I say, what we are going to attempt to do." He then said. "We may need to try a few things. As I told you before, Serena is not going to be amenable as you might think."

I took a deep breath, sitting up a little straighter on the bed. Nathan and I needed to pay attention to this. Our life was in Gabriel's hands now.

"You are correct with your theory, Nathan. Serena has become one of those angry spirits you read of in the Japanese folklore. What most people don't understand is that most Japanese folklore is very accurate. People now-a-days have a hard time believing in what they cannot see. But from our point of view as angels, we see things that people would never begin to understand. You can blame that on your media," he smiled. "And it's true, Serena is still deeply in love with you, Nathan. When she chose to end her life, her thoughts were that she could be with you after she died. But after her spirit entered Purgatory, she somehow found you as a guardian. That's one part I'm confused about, how she was able to find you at all. This is why I say there must be another piece to this because we hid you very well after your death. When you began to watch over Sophie, her jealously manifested after seeing how close you two became. She heard every single word you said to Sophie from the darkness. But it isn't you Nathan that she's mad at. It's Sophie. She's mad because he chose you."

I relaxed a little from his words.

"Nathan wanted to be with you all the time and began appearing in your real life. That day you spent together walking under the cherry blossoms pushed her over the edge."

I remembered that day in great detail. It was right after Jake and I broke up—the day Nathan tried to cheer me up. It was the first day we really got to talk and hangout—to act more like good friends. I loved that day.

"That was something she had spoken so dearly to you about, Nathan."

My eyes turned to his.

"How she wanted to walk through them with you by her side. But instead, she watched you walk through the blossoms with Sophie."

Nathan's eyes began to tear up. He quickly wiped them away.

"Gabriel, if I had known she was watching... I thought—"

"It doesn't matter what you thought. What happened, happened. The final straw was when you almost kissed Sophie the day you left. She could see what was happening between you two. You broke her heart, Nathan. But sadly, she still wants you. She's certain that she can change your mind and make you want to be with her again. She does not understand that you two can never have a life together. But the spirits in Purgatory continue to feed her, just as she feeds them with her obsessive energy. She will not stop."

"So what can we do? Maybe if I could talk to her, I could explain—"

"She won't want to hear it, Nathan. She doesn't want to hear about your life now. She's living in the past. She wants Sophie out of the picture and will stop at nothing to make that happen."

"So, how can we reason with her then?" I spoke. "I mean, if

she's so set in stone?"

"I'm not sure we can, but for Nathan…" He paused. "I will try."

"Thank you," Nathan whispered.

"But know that if we attempt this and it fails, and she doesn't want to pass on willingly, we will have no choice but to force her. This could get ugly, and the Archangels will surely be ready with a trap to take her out brutally if we do not involve them in our plans."

Nathan's eyes widened at the thought.

"Do we really need to involve the Archangels? There has to be another way,"

"The only way to stop this kind of spirit is to resolve the conflict or emotional stress the spirit is in and let it pass. If the spirit denies the passing, then we do what we must to get rid of her. Those are the only two options, Nathan. I'm sorry."

Nathan sighed, dropping his head into his hands.

"But I fear the Archangels are already on her trail. If they get to her first, they will end her by any means," Gabriel warned. "So we must hurry."

"Then we have to try whatever we can—before they get to her." Nathan replied, worried. "I can't have her be treated like that. It was me that brought all this into her life. I won't let her end up like this—hunted down. She can't help what she's become, it's not her fault."

I looked at Nathan again, my heart aching for him. I could tell this was really tearing him apart. And as scared as I was of Serena, I wanted to help him. But the thought of Nathan and Serena in a room together talking, made me sick to my stomach. I didn't trust her. I felt like no matter what attempt we were about to make, this was surely going to end tragically. Gabriel then stepped in front of me again, his eyes glaring down at me as they did before.

"You need to let go of those thoughts. They will drive you crazy and eventually break you."

Nathan turned quickly to me, his hand grabbing my arm. I tried my best to block my thoughts from him.

147

"Sophie…" He said, a little taken back.

"It's nothing. I was just thinking, that's all," I lied again.

"Those are not just any thoughts. You have fears and you need to be very careful of the laws of attraction, young one."

Suddenly, the Archangel felt the need to speak to me as he did before.

"You need to be honest with him." He said, "You are a strong person, and you need to have faith in Nathan—and me." He then touched my hand. "I will not let you down, Sophie. I swear to you."

He used my name again, and instantly I believed him. It was a very bold statement coming from an Archangel. There was no way he could fail me, right?

"I will not let you down." He repeated, staring into my eyes. "You have my word."

It felt concrete—a solid promise. I had to believe him. I felt the tears begin to build up again the longer his hand lingered on mine.

"I trust you. I do." I whispered as a flash of emotion took over me.

Gabriel's hand slowly lifted to wipe a tear sliding down my cheek. Then another.

"Do not cry." He said, very quietly to me. "You've done that too much in your short time here on earth. It's your turn to be happy, so fight for it."

I nodded and then took a breath to calm myself.

"Give me a day or two. I want to talk with the Archangels. I'll tell them I plan to take Serena out. I will not fill them in on our details of how exactly, but just enough to assure them that I am on it. Perhaps it will buy us some time."

He glanced at Nathan once more.

"Please, please do not do anything until I come back." He begged. "Let's be smart about this. I will keep a close eye on you both. If Serena shows up again, I'll be here right away—or I will make sure someone else will—to protect the two of you. Can you give me your word?"

"I promise." Nathan replied. "But what do I do if she comes?

I mean, should I keep Sophie awake? How will I protect her?"
"Serena has already found every route into Sophie's world.
It will not matter if she sleeps or not, but if she does appear, distract her and try to stay calm. Especially you, Sophie. She can feel you. If she is able to overwhelm you, she can feed off of your energy and ultimately overpower you."
I swallowed hard. I didn't want Gabriel to leave. I felt safer with him here.
"Just stall her until I get here, and Sophie?" He paused.
My eyes met the Archangel's again.
"Do not try to speak with her. She will not want to hear anything you have to say, understand?" He warned.
I nodded. Then he was gone.

12
Confinement

Nathan got up from the bed and headed over to the closet to finish getting dressed.
"Where is it, Nate?" I asked.
He turned to me, sliding on a T-shirt.
"Where's what?"
"The bracelet. I want it gone."
When he didn't answer, I got up from the bed and began to search through his things. Then I opened my jewelry box and searched through the items a second time.
"It's not there," he said.
"Well, where the hell is it? This is so stupid. I mean, to think I thought that thing was... Everything is so messed up. It was supposed to be our—god, I'm so stupid," I rambled, upset that my keepsake had now turned into a bad omen.
"Sophie, stop for a second and talk to me. What are you talking about? What did you think?"
I turned quickly and snapped at him.
"The bracelet, Nate! I kept it because it was special to me. I thought it could be my little keepsake from the day you came back to me. It was the best day of my life. I never want to forget that feeling I had when I saw your face and—"
Nathan smiled at the thought. "It was a good day, I know."
"Where's the bracelet?" I asked again. "Please, I don't want it around us."
He reached into his pocket and pulled it out.
"Get rid of it," I said, closing my eyes in frustration.

"We might need it, Soph. I can't destroy it, but I'll keep it
far from us for now. Stay here for a moment," he said, then
quickly left the room.
While he was gone, I began to pace, thinking of all the
horrible things this girl had done to me. Then I thought of
what she might do if Nathan wasn't able to reason with her.
My anxiety was soaring. I quickly crawled into bed. With my
head resting back against the pillow, I took a few deep breaths
while staring at the ceiling. There was no way I was sleeping
tonight—or ever again. Not until this girl was gone for good.
I heard Nathan enter the room again. I turned over as he slid
into the bed next to me. His body rested behind me while his
arms held me tight.
"I love you," he said.
"This is going to get worse before it gets better, isn't it?" I
said, turning to him. He didn't respond.
He leaned in and began to kiss me. My arms wrapped around
his body, my fingertips digging into his back as his kisses
became more passionate.
"This might be the last night we get together, Nate," I said,
pulling back from him. "The last one before all hell breaks
loose." My body shivered as his lips ran down my neck to
my collarbone and then stopped. His eyes quickly returned to
mine.
"I just mean, I don't want any regrets. If something
happens…" I trailed off, hoping he understood what I was
getting at.
His face softened. "Sophie, nothing is going to happen. We
have all the time in the world." He smiled, then kissed my
nose. "We'll deal with this, and then our lives will continue as
before. I promise. Then we'll have our time—"
"No, Nate. If something goes wrong, we could—"
"Sophie, please stop thinking like that. I want you to see a
future with me, always. We don't have to rush anything. I
don't want it to be this way."
"But I want to. Please." I meant it this time. I was truly scared
that this would be it for us, and I couldn't live with myself if

Nathan and I hadn't taken that last step—the one I feared the most. I wanted to be with him. I wanted us to have this last moment. I slowly began to remove my clothes. I was dead serious about this. Nathan's eyes never moved from mine as I undressed.

"Please," I asked again.

His eyes closed for a moment. Then he began to remove his clothes. Pulling the covers up around us, he moved in close to me. His fingers laced through my hair as he stared into my eyes.

"I love you more than anything," he said, leaning in to kiss me. His lips stayed connected with mine as he moved over top of me. My heart began to race as his fingers traced my skin. My hands slid up his chest to his shoulders, so I could push him back down to the bed. I climbed over him, my long hair brushing across his face as I continued to kiss him. He slid his hand down to my hips. We had wanted this for so long—all of this. Every touch, every breath was perfect as we continued to consume each other for the rest of the night.

● ● ●

I felt a warm breeze blow across my skin. It lifted my long hair up into the wind—swirling it around and tangling it up. I slid my fingers through it, twisting it around and pulling it to one side where I could hold into it. I felt the touch of his hand on my shoulder, then he was beside me.

We walked quietly hand in hand. He was speaking about something, but I could barely hear him. His voice was so faint, I strained to hear him so I pulled at his hand to make him stop. He stepped in front of me and smiled. Then said very clearly, "I have to go Soph."

My heart stopped.

"No." I begged. "Not again. Nathan please,"

But he slowly began to step away. My hands scrambled to grab his once again, but he was out of reach and I was unable to move forward towards him.

"Nate!" I cried. "Please…" It was worse than the last time, if

that was even possible. "I need you, desperately." I shouted.
I felt a sickness building up inside of me as the tears poured
down my face. I clenched my chest, there was no way this was
happening again. Then *she* appeared.
Gracefully stepping in front of me her long, very blonde hair
blew beautifully in the wind, unlike mine. Serena batted her
eyelashes then smiled. Suddenly, Nathan was in sight again
and by her side. I watched as his hand slid into hers, pulling
her away.
"Nathan!" I called again. "Please, you were meant to be with
me. Not her. Me!" I cried, but they continued to walk away.
He didn't look back, not once, but she did. Her smile taunted
me. She had won. Above me, the clouds began to roll in and
suddenly everything was dark, windy and cold. Soon there was
no sign of light anywhere. It was pitch black and the wind had
stopped. Silence.
"Hello?" I said very quietly, my voice echoing as if I was in a
tunnel. "Is anybody there?" I couldn't see a thing.
"Hello?" A voice repeated, startling me.
Suddenly, a candle lit up between Serena's face and mine.
"So, I guess you know who I am now?" She asked, calmly.
I nodded and immediately remembered Gabriel's warnings
about not speaking to her. I had to be dreaming, but it felt very
real this time.
"Nathan—he's wonderful, isn't he?" Serena asked.
I nodded again.
"When he came into my life, I was so alone. He needed
someone and so did I. We have a very strong history. I'm sure
he's told you." Serena's eyes were glowing in the candlelight.
She was very beautiful. Even I had to admit that.
"What Nathan and I had—it was pure and true. Our lives
ended unfairly. We are the same person, understand? You do
not fit into his world, you only distract him."
My eyes started to water.
"He thought I was gone. He thought he had to move on, but
now he doesn't. Don't you see? We've found each other again
and now we can be together. He only thought he loved you,

but the real reason is… you somehow remind him of me and that excites him." She smiled again. "Why do you think he lies to you so much? He can't let go of me. The cherry blossom walk, and now the bracelet? Why do you think he won't get rid of it? He won't be able to let me go and as soon as I find a way to be with him, we will leave here. He will leave you, Sophie. He will always choose me."

I didn't want her to win. "No." I heard myself say.

"No?" Serena repeated with haste in her voice. "Of course he will. Why would he ever choose you? You're immature and have so much drama and uncertainty in life. You don't trust him and he's constantly trying to fit into your world. With me, he fits perfectly."

"You can't have him," I said, as clearly as I could. "You're wrong about him. He's not the Nathan you once knew. He's better now. He's happy—with me."

I swallowed hard as Serena stared into my eyes. I wanted her to know that I was going to fight for him.

"You're nothing but a stupid little girl," she said.

I know I wasn't supposed to be talking with her, but not talking felt like I was giving up. I needed to fight.

"You can't have him." I repeated.

Serena's eyes squinted as her hands clenched into a fist down low. I continued to stand my ground.

"How dare you," she said. "I will make your life hell!"

With one quick breath in, she blew out the candle between us and the room was black again. My hands searched the darkness around me, preparing myself for an attack. The fear came back just as quickly as it left a moment ago. I listened carefully as the sound of footsteps moved around the room. In the distance, I could hear a faint noise, a high-pitched sound. It grew louder and louder until it surrounded me in the dark room. I covered my ears as it screeched through me. Shrieks and screams circulated the room. Bouncing off the walls, taunting me as they did long ago in my dreams.

My nightmares had returned. I had to be dreaming. Except this time, Nathan could not save me. I hated these sounds. I needed him to wake me—now!

Suddenly, a quick sharp pain ripped across my arms. I screamed as they tore at my skin over and over again. My shaking hands tried desperately to cover my arms from the attacks, but I couldn't see anything. It felt like paper cuts, only a hundred times worse. Each cut felt deeper and deeper. I continued to scream and whip my hands throughout the darkness, trying desperately to fight off what I couldn't see. After one last horrific scream, everything went silent again.

My tormented body trembled as my eyes searched the darkness. Suddenly, the room around me became a little clearer. The darkness began to lift, and it seemed like I was in a very old hospital room. More specifically, a surgery room. It was disgusting, cold and smelt of mold and mildew. Still confused as to how I got here, I slowly got up and made my way across the room to a doorway.

Peeking out, everything was silent. Carefully, I stepped out of the room and began my way down the dark hallway, glancing over my shoulder every few steps. My arms burned and I felt the blood running down my skin. There was a lot, I was certain of it by how faint I felt. I had to stop for a moment, my body was weakening. Just then, those horrible daunting shrieks blasted again waking me from my tired state. I took off down another hallway. I needed to get out of here— wherever I was.

The screams became louder and louder the faster I ran. I wasn't sure how much longer I could hold on. I was so tired. As I turned the corner I noticed another door. I went for it. With luck it opened and the shrieks stopped just as it slammed shut behind me. I took a moment to catch my breath. Then turned and leaned my ear against the rusted door. It was silent again. I slid down to the floor exhausted. My head fell into my hands and I cried for a moment. How can I stop this? How was I ever going to get my normal life back? Looking down at my hands, there was blood everywhere, it all over my clothes. I paused—these weren't my clothes. Lifting my arms, I noticed I was dressed in some sort of cream-colored smock with matching pants. They looked like hospital garments now drenched in my blood.

"What's happening?" I said aloud. "If this is a dream, wake up Sophie. Come on, wake up," I continued to say.

Bang!

A huge thump against the door shook my body, then another, and another. I covered my ears and closed my eyes, hoping my weight against it could keep the door closed. This was the worst dream ever and I couldn't wake up. Serena was going to taunt me until I gave in, until I gave up Nathan, until I was... dead. I felt a sudden warm glow against my face. Afraid of what was in front of me, I slowly opened my eyes to a bedroom. I lowered my hands from my ears and got up to walk towards the bed. The covers moved slightly, stopping me in my tracks. I couldn't see very well, so I took another few steps closer. Walking around to the other side of the bed, I could see someone there. It was Nathan.

I felt a rush of happiness race through me. Was I half asleep now? Was he really safe, back in our own bed? I had heard stories about people having out of body experiences at night, it was called Lucid Dreaming.

He was sleeping so soundly. His hair, hanging slightly over his right eye. I was about to reach out and touch him, when a hand slid up from behind him. The long thin arm stretched around his shoulders and forced him to turn back to her. His eyelashes fluttered as I took a step back, awkwardly watching on. She met him with a kiss.

"No," I said, covering my mouth.

He pulled at her until she was on top of him. She leaned down with her legs straddled on either side of him and kissed him again. I couldn't move. Then she tilted her head my way.

"Too bad you wasted yourself on him," she half smiled, tracing her fingers down his neck to his chest. "He was picturing me the entire time,"

I found myself stumbling back towards the doorway. The pain inside my chest was making it hard to breathe. I desperately fumbled with the door handle when I heard him say,

"I love you, Serena."
In that moment, my heart stopped. I couldn't breathe, there
was no air. My hands clung to the handle as I thought for a
moment about giving up. I couldn't win this. She was too
strong.
   Suddenly, I felt the door unlocked and opened slightly. I
turned to look back, they were still there—all over each other.
I forced myself to leave the room and took off down the
hallway. I wasn't sure where the burst of energy came from,
but I needed to get as far as I could from the both of them. I
ran as fast as I could until I felt the floor below me become
slippery and wet. I crashed down hard, cracking my head back
against the ground. Everything became fuzzy and my eyelids
slowly began to close. I was done.
"Get up Sophie!"
Whose voice was that?
"Get up and run!" The voice yelled again—louder this time.
My eyes fluttered open for only a second, then closed again. I
couldn't concentrate. I couldn't get my vision straight. I was
too tired.
"Sophie, come on. Get up, please!" He pleaded.
"Nate?" I whispered. I thought I saw an image before me, but
my eyes couldn't focus.
"Get up, now!" He shouted.
Then suddenly, I felt a tight grip on my wrist.
He then yanked me from the ground. His touch burned the cuts
on my skin as he pulled at me. The hallway flashed in and out
of sight as I attempted to run with him. Yanking me around a
corner, he suddenly came to a halt, making me crash into his
body.
"Where are you going with her?" It was Serena, she was back.
My hand reached for the back of my head, I felt faint.
"Damn it, stay awake Sophie! I need you to pull it together. I
can only do so much!" He said, squeezing my wrist tighter.
"You can't save her. You have no power over me here. So hand
her over—now!" Serena demanded.
My hands loosened from his arm.

"I can't. I can't fight her anymore," I said weakly, then fell to the ground.

"No!" He shouted, "Get up, right now!" He continued to pull at me, but I couldn't move. I had nothing left.

"She's tired. Aren't you, Sophie?" I heard her say.

I nodded, my eyes closing on me again.

Serena stepped closer. "You want this all to be over, don't you? It's too much for you. All you ever wanted was a normal life. I can show you one, if you like."

Although my eyes were closed now, I could still hear her. She was right. I did want this to be over.

"Don't listen to her, Soph."

I felt the strange man kneel next to me, strategically placing himself between me and the ghostly girl.

"You could start a new life, a life with no supernatural beings. No angels. Just a normal, perfect, life. But you must start over completely."

"Leave her alone!" He shouted, then turned back to me. "Look at me, Soph. Please." He begged.

I could feel his warm hands holding my face. As scared as I was, and as tired as I was, and as much as I didn't care what happened to me next, I felt very safe in his grasp. He felt like Nathan long ago. "I need you to fight Soph... please." He repeated.

His voice, it reminded me of... my thoughts stopped as I felt my body being ripped away. I smashed hard against a wall. My eyes shot open in pain. Blurring in and out of focus, I tried my best to gain consciousness. When I finally did, I glanced down and saw a small surgical knife in my hand.

"Do it." Serena's voice persisted. "Do it, and you'll have your life back. A fresh, new life. I can make you forget everything. All the heartache and pain, I can make it go away. But you must first end this life. Then you can have your bliss,"

For a moment I understood everything she was saying to me. I wanted a fresh start, to try again and possibly do better. This was more than a normal human being should ever have to go through. I was mentally and physically exhausted. I wanted to rest. I wanted to sleep without fear of something coming after me. So maybe... that meant starting something new—on my own—without Nathan.

Moments earlier, I wanted to fight for him, but now... What I was feeling and fearing inside was more than I was prepared for. My weak hand lifted the knife towards my chest. The edge of the blade floated directly in front of my heart. It would be fast, wouldn't it? I took a deep breath.

"Sophie, no!" He shouted then lunged towards me, knocking the knife from my hands just as it was about to pierce my skin. His body tumbled over mine as we fell across the floor. Serena dashed for the knife. I then felt a quick slice of the blade across my collarbone. My body felt weightless as she dropped me back to the ground. Everything seemed much quieter for a moment as I lay there on the cold floor. Then I felt the blade against my skin again.

"Why can't you just leave already?" She said, ready to cut again. Suddenly, a blinding white light flashed before our eyes.

"Serena!" The Archangel's voice bellowed down the hallway. It echoed off the walls, sending chills down my spine. My eyes opened slightly to the sound of Gabriel's voice. Serena rose to her feet, pulling me along with her.

"Let her go now," He warned, appearing before us.

"This is none of your business, Gabriel," she said, frustrated.

"This is very much my business," he assured her. "Sophie is mine. You will not take her from me."

I tried hard to listen to the conversation. Did Gabriel just say, "I was his?" The Archangel stepped towards us, his eyes were set on mine. I felt a sudden urge to reach for him, but Serena spoke again.

"I'm sorry, her life is over now," she said tightening her grip on me. Just as she moved her hand to slice my neck with the blade, Gabriel lit up the room with a blinding light. The energy and heat coming from him warmed my skin.

The electrifying burst pounded us hard, blowing Serena far from me. I fell hard to the ground again. My heavy eyes finally closed just as I felt a pair of hands lift me from the floor. Resting against the strange man's chest, I knew I was safe.

"What should I do with her?" I heard him ask.

"Take her to Nathan." Gabriel responded. "He will not like what comes next, but it must happen. It's what's best for Sophie."

What was best for me?

The Archangel spoke again. "I will need you to be there for her. Nathan cannot protect her anymore. When this happens, he will...."

Their voices suddenly faded, and everything around us became very bright.

13

Me Without You

I began to slowly regain consciousness. I could hear Gabriel, and then Nathan speaking softly. My eyes adjusted to the light, blinking until they finally gained focus.
"Soph?"
I felt Nathan's soft hand against my cheek. It was definitely him.
"Nate?" My voice cracked.
I was instantly flooded with emotion. Everything I had thought about, everything I had seen...
"Hey, crazy girl, I'm here. I'm right here," he said, sitting down on the bed next to me.
"Where am I?" My throat felt sore and raw.
"You're in the hospital," he replied. "You had a dream..."
Then he paused. "I'm so sorry, Soph." His fingers brushed the hair from my face and tucked a few strands behind my ear.
I looked over to Gabriel who stood before us.
"You will be safe here. I'll be watching over you from now on. It's too easy now for Serena to get to you. She's become too strong."
The sound of her name sparked my fear again and I shot up from the bed. "Serena!" I said, frantically. "I saw her, she almost..." I felt the blood rush from my head, making me feel a little dizzy for a moment. Nathan's hands held me tight.
"She killed me. She had a knife, and my..."
Then I remembered the horrible feeling of the slices across my arms. I looked down at the bandages that were wrapped

around wrists all the way up to my elbows. My hand then rose to my collarbone, a small patch covered the cut. I could see the blood slightly leaking through the bandages on my arms. It was real. All of it really happened. The pain was real too. I clenched my teeth as I touched my collarbone once more.

"Don't." I felt Nathan's hand take mine. "I'm so sorry. She—"

"Who was it, Gabriel?" I blurted out, ignoring Nathan's words. "Who was in there with me? There was another man. I thought at first it was Nathan, but it wasn't. He was trying to help me."

"He works for me. I've assigned him to you. He's now your spirit guide. You need to trust him."

"Spirit guide?" Nathan repeated, confused.

"Yes, once and a while a person is assigned a spirit guide. He is not as powerful as an angel but can do some of the same things as us. He will be able to see into your dreams and protect you—to a point."

"What do you mean to a point?" Nathan spoke again.

"He guides her in whatever dream or situation she is in as best he can until an angel takes over. Think of him as the first line of defense." He smiled. "He's very good. I trust him with your life. I have assigned him to you so that I can help you Nathan and still keep Sophie safe."

"Spirit guide," I repeated, quietly. It sounded nice, comforting almost. "Sure, why not. I mean, I've had every other supernatural being in my life. Why not add that to the list," I said sarcastically, lying back down.

Just then a nurse knocked on the door, making Gabriel vanish from sight.

"You're awake," she said, kindly. "Do you need anything?" She asked, checking the bag of fluid hanging by my bed.

"I'm okay," I lied. "But maybe some water?" I asked, rubbing my throat.

"Sure, just let me attach another blood bag and I'll go get you some."

I watched as the nurse attached the bag. My eyes followed the tubing down. It led to a needle under a bandage attached to

162

my hand. Then I noticed a second bag hanging against the first one. That tube led down to a needle secured on my left hand.
"What's this for?" I asked, nervously.
"You lost a lot of blood last night. You're going to be light-headed for a while and very weak until we get you back to your old self. This second bag will help with your nutrition and help you sleep better."
Sleep? That was the last thing I wanted to do. She then reached over and felt my forehead.
"Visiting hours are almost over, Nathan. You have fifteen minutes left." The nurse said, as she turned to leave the room. "I'll bring some water in soon."
My eyes shot back to Nathan's.
"Visiting hours? You don't get to stay with me?"
"Not here, not in this wing." He responded.
"What do you mean not here? Where am I?"
"I told you, you're in the hospital," he repeated.
"Tell her the truth, Nathan. She deserves to know," Gabriel spoke from the corner of the room. He quickly appeared by the edge of my bed. "Nathan brought you in after your spirit guide left you to him. You had so many cuts and wounds. They immediately assumed you tried to kill yourself. They admitted you to the seventh floor to be monitored."
"What are you talking about? They think I tried to kill myself, and you let them believe that?" I complained. "So, I'm basically on suicide watch?"
"Sophie, there was no other way we could explain what happened to you. You have knife cuts all over and no witnesses. I'm sorry," Nathan said, taking my hand again.
"It's best for you to be here anyway. If you are on a suicide watch, they'll check in on you constantly and you'll have more eyes on you. That means less chances for Serena to attack." Gabriel added. "Then Nathan and I are free to go after her."
"What? You're going to ditch me here?" My eyes widened. "Nathan, you can't be serious. I would never leave you if you were here. You promised me,"

163

"Sophie, I don't like it any more than you do, but Gabriel has a point. Look, I promise, I'll be here every chance I can. I don't want to leave your side either but Soph, that attack last night... It was the worst ever. We need to act now. So, if that means I need to leave you for a bit to protect you, then I will."
"Nathan, we said we would do this together, remember? Now take me with you." I demanded.
I sat up in bed, studying how to get the needles out of me. Surely, they could break me out, couldn't they?
"Sophie, stop, you're going to hurt yourself. You need to rest." Nathan's hands removed mine from the bandages. "Please, lie back down. I'm sorry, but you're not going anywhere." He said, sternly.
I sighed, lying back in the bed again. I was already tired again. "Last night started so perfect," I said, quietly to him. "It's as if God—if there is one—doesn't want us to be happy, Nate."
"God does not wish that, Sophie." Gabriel interrupted, softly. "It is Fate. She is wielding her design, testing you both."
Nathan glanced at the Archangel, then brought his attention back to me. His face softened as he moved in closer to speak more intimately with me.
"It was perfect, the best moment of my life last night." He smiled, then whispered, "But we will have many more of those nights, I promise you."
I continued to stare at him, pleading for him to change his mind.
"I need you to stay strong, even if you don't see me every day. No matter what Serena says to you or says that I say. You have to believe my words only. Promise?" He begged quietly.
I nodded.
"I'll let you two say good night," Gabriel spoke again, stepping away from the bed. "I'll be here the whole night, Sophie. Do not be afraid." Then he was gone.
I sat there, quietly taking everything in.
"Kiss me," Nathan whispered, stopping my thoughts. His lips connected with mine only for a second, until the nurse entered again. "It's time to go Nathan," she said, placing a glass of

164

water on my nightstand. I watched as she grabbed a tiny bottle and needle from her front pouch.

"What's that?" I asked, nervously. "To help you sleep," My eyes shot back to Nathan's. He knew what I was thinking—what I was dreading.

"You'll be fine. Gabriel's here," he whispered.

"It's time to go, Nathan. Say good night," the nurse repeated as she left the room. Suddenly, my eyelids became very heavy and it was hard to speak. I fought against the medication, trying to keep my eyes on Nathan for however long I could. My breathing slowed as I felt his lips against my forehead.

"I love you," I whispered. Then it was black.

I slept without a single dream for hours, and when I finally woke, Gabriel was there just as he promised.

"This is weird," I yawned, stretching out in the bed. I then reached for my glass of water. Gabriel appeared by the nightstand and handed it to me.

"Thank you," I said, slowly taking it from him. My throat was still sore.

"What is weird?" He asked.

I swallowed another gulp before responding.

"Having Gabriel, the Archangel hanging around my room."

Gabriel smiled. "I want to share something with you."

I sat myself up a little more, intrigued by his words.

"You are a very rare soul, Sophie Reid. There are very few of you left in this world and we angels need you desperately."

I looked at him surprised and confused. "Need me? Why?"

"Because your heart is pure and true."

This again. That whole pure heart subject was annoying and confused me still.

"There is something inside of you that sees the good in everybody, even the ones that don't deserve it. You are a pure heart. You don't know it yet, but everything you need is right inside of you."

"Gabriel, I've heard Nathan speak about this before, but I don't understand."

"All humans are born this way, but most are tainted at a very early age, unable to return to their original state ever again. Life happens and unfortunately, changes you all—or should I say Fate happens." He paused. "But you, yours is still strong. Only someone like you could have guided an angel in the right direction, ultimately giving him that second chance."

"I still don't understand, what happened to them all?" I asked.

"Most people get taken over by the negativity in life and most times they become their own worst enemy. Their thoughts end up destroying their faith and core values, so they are of no use to us."

"No use to you?" I repeated.

"I will admit, I was a little worried when I saw your life take such a drastic turn a while back. The depression you had was strong, even with Nathan by your side. Those are usually the signs that a pure heart will die young. I didn't see that one coming. That was Fate's doing, but Nathan was very certain that you were special so I trusted him. I let Nathan continue guiding you, only after giving him fair warning to keep his head on straight."

I thought for a moment, "What do you mean guide an angel in the right direction? Is that all I am to him?"

"No, Sophie, Let me explain." He then sat down on the bed next to me. Having him so close and casual made me slightly nervous again.

"You see, Nathan is meant for something bigger in life. I've been waiting a long time for him."

"You mean, I'm going to lose him again?"

"No, I plan to make sure that the two grow old together and share a happy life. But Serena and Fate will surely test me. We all need to keep a clear mind to ensure we make it through this, so that you and Nathan can get your happy ending."

I rubbed my tired eyes, still confused with everything.

"Remember when I told you of the contract between God and Fate?"

I nodded.

"Well, He and the Archangels secretly believe that a prophecy will also happen. One that is meant to save us all from the hands of Fate." He paused. "I believe that Nathan is that prophecy."

I stared at Gabriel in disbelief.

"But until his time comes, we must deal with Fate as best we can and we must protect the ones who are pure in heart because they will ultimately save humanity when the prophecy comes true."

"Hold up," I said placing my glass back down on the nightstand. "You're saying that I'm going to restore humanity when Fate is gone?"

"Not exactly you, but your kind. Yes." He smiled. "Those who are pure in heart will be the ones to guide the others—ultimately improving the human race as a whole."

"Why can't you just end her?" I asked. "Fate, I mean."

"We've tried, but Fate is constantly spinning her web and each time a human falls down in life or fails her test, she creates a new path for them. She feels she is teaching you all a lesson."

"Pretty harsh lesson," I replied.

"This is also why Fate enjoys us, or should I say she's entertained by us. Our persistence to help humans when they are down only makes her game more exciting. But it's when we fail, that she truly lights up." He sighed. "It causes great pain to us when we lose one of you, when we fail to protect you from her path. We can never forget that she is always one step ahead of us, and she cares not for anyone or anything."

"Well, this sounds a little impossible," I sighed, looking away from him.

"Sophie, if I am right about Nathan and this prophecy is true, then soon enough Fate will be wiped from this earth, and He will lead us all to a better life. A world with love and order."

"That doesn't seem very fair Gabriel. Sometimes in life we are thrown off course due to no fault of our own. Why should we have to pay for that when we are only trying our best with the hands we've been dealt? How could we possibly ever know if we are doing the right things?" I asked.

"That is the game. Everyone is just a chess piece to her. She sets it up and then watches in delight as you all make your choices—right or wrong. It makes her happy that a gift from God could ultimately ruin you."

"Gift?" I repeated.

"The gift of free will," he replied.

"So this Fate, she basically plays with our lives and you guys try to keep everyone from making the wrong decisions in hopes of creating a better life for us all, against her design?" I questioned.

"Yes, along those lines." Gabriel smiled.

"Seems like an endless battle." I said, exhausted at the thought.

"It sometimes is, but when we find someone like you, a pure heart, we'll go above and beyond to keep you safe from her. You give us hope."

I smiled at him, it was nice to be such a positive influence to the angels.

"You know, when I came across Nathan, I immediately believed that he was the one we've been waiting for. There was a light inside of him I'd never seen before—in all my years. So I quickly figured out Fate's design for him. He had an extremely hard path ahead of him and I had a hard time trying to convince the rest of the Archangels that he was the one. I still do. That's when I presented you into the picture, and I'm thankful he chose you the moment he saw you. I knew you needed someone better than just any guardian and he needed someone better than just any human. Nathan immediately connected with you, better than I had hoped. And yes, Serena too was a very important part of his life. She helped him begin his journey to a better man, but her time is done. It is you that will truly make him great. Although, I didn't expect you two to fall in love and frankly, when I saw it happening, I was immediately worried for both of you because of my own past. But Sophie, that powerful connection you two have, the one you both didn't give up on, has done more for the both of you and us, then anyone could have ever imagined. You have set things in motion and ignited something so deeply inside of us all. Even if the other Archangels won't admit to it yet, you truly are meant to be together."

"Gabriel, this prophecy you talk about—"

"I'm sorry, I cannot say anymore in fear that Fate will hear us. It could endanger yours and Nathan's life even more if we talk too much on the subject. Please, just trust me."

I sat in silence for a moment again. I did trust him. I completely trusted Gabriel, but there was one more thing I still wanted to ask.

"Does Nathan know what he is to become?"

Gabriel shook his head no. "And he can never know. It must remain a secret between us. All of his actions must come from his own choices in life. That is the only way the prophecy can manifest itself."

"Do you think he can do it? Do you think that he can overcome Serena and actually defeat Fate?" I paused. "I ask this because—"

"I know why you ask this. I hear your fearful thoughts. He will succeed in everything, but we cannot lose faith in him. Nathan still hasn't faced his hardest days, and Fate will surely test him in more ways than one. She is getting suspicious already about my attendance to him. She knows he is special." He stopped, noticing the overwhelmed expression on my face. "I think that's enough for tonight,"

I quickly grabbed his hand, "What if he doesn't want what the future holds for him?"

He looked down at me as his other hand covered mine.

"As I said, if Nathan is the one, he will rise to the occasion without a second thought because he is just as pure and true as you. His heart will not let him fail." Gabriel then stood up from the bed.

"Where are you going?" I asked, worried. "You have a visitor,"

Then he was gone.

I looked towards the door then heard a very loud and upset voice from the hallway.

"Where is she? I demand that you let her out right now!"

Just then Charlotte barged through the door.

"Sophie? Oh my god, what is happening? Jesus! What happened to your arms!" She said, running up to me—the nurse chasing close behind.

"Excuse me! You need to leave. Visiting hours are over," she said, annoyed by my friend.

"I'm not going anywhere," Charlotte replied, pulling a chair up next to my bed.

I giggled, it was kind of a relief to see her. I looked up to the nurse. "Please, she's my best friend. Can't she stay for just a little bit?"

The woman stared at us—exhausted. "You have fifteen minutes,"

Charlotte smirked as she turned and left the room.

"Alright, will you tell me what's going on here? I got a call from Nathan that you were in the hospital? He said you had some sort of anxiety attack in your sleep and tried to kill yourself? That doesn't sound like you, Soph. He said you were practically asleep when you did it? That sounds like a load of crap to me," She said, furious.

I sighed, another story I had to go along with.

"It's true. I had some sort of nightmare. I was feeling really stressed. There's lots going on Charlotte, I can't explain it all."

"But Sophie, that's no reason to end your life," she said, sadly. "Look at your arms, they're all cut up." Charlotte touched them gently, the fear in her eyes was new to me. I suddenly felt guilty about everything, especially the lies.

"It's not that bad, I swear."

"Sophie, not that bad? They're completely wrapped up—and your neck—I can't believe you would do something like this." Her eyes began to water, "I'm so sorry," she said.

"For what? Charlotte, oh my gosh, don't cry. Why are you crying?" I asked, moving a little closer to her.

"Because I'm not a good best friend," She replied.

"What? What are you talking about?"

"If I was a good friend, I would know what's been going on

with you and you would talk to me. I'm so sorry. I've been wrapped up with Matt and I'm sorry I tried to push Alex on you. I'm sorry for everything," she continued to cry.

I couldn't help but smile at her affections. If she only knew the truth, and it was so like Charlotte to think that she hadn't done enough. She had been the friend I needed since the day I met her, even with giving Nathan a hard time.

"No, Char. This isn't your fault at all. You're the greatest friend anyone could ever have. I'm so lucky I have you," I finally said, then opened my arms for a hug. "Come here. Hug me! I demand it!"

Charlotte wiped her face and got up to hug me.

"When I got the call from Nate, I almost lost it. I was so scared that you were... You're my best friend. I don't want to lose you, and I want you to have someone to rely on, whether it's me or Nathan. I just don't want you to feel alone—not ever."

"I'm not. I know I have you both. I swear it has nothing to do with you. I'm just dealing with something from my past and only Nathan knows about it. It's hard and a little embarrassing for me to talk about, but don't ever think that you're not a good friend to me, okay?" I assured her again.

Charlotte nodded, then pulled herself together and leaned back in the chair. "Is there anything I can do for you? Do you want to talk about anything?" She asked, politely.

"No, I've done enough talking for now, thanks. But maybe later." I smiled.

She sighed in the chair.

"But... I could use some cheering up though, maybe some girl talk? What's new with you and Matt? Is everything going well?" I asked, changing the subject to a lighter one.

Charlotte blushed. "Are you sure? We can talk about something else if you want?"

"No, silly, I want to hear the good stuff. Come on, spill!" I laughed.

"Okay," Charlotte smiled, sitting up in the chair. "So, the other day when I was at work...."

171

I listened attentively as Charlotte went on with her stories. I wanted things to be as normal as they could—for now, because I knew this was just the calm before the storm.

14
Scrying Mirror

Six days went by, but it felt more like weeks with me
being stuck in this god-awful hospital room. Nathan had kept
up my story of suicide to keep me safe in here and I did as
he requested and played along—as embarrassing as it was.
Nathan only came just before visiting hours were over to see
me each day, so our time together was always short. Gabriel
had him on a mission, studying ways to interact with the dead
and working on his story to convince Serena to move on.
I missed him. I wasn't seeing him as much as I needed to. I
wanted to be home with him—helping if I could. This was
taking too long and it was making me anxious. Could they
really keep Serena out and for how long? Eventually, the
hospital would let me out and I would be open game once
again.

Gabriel had many late-night talks with me when I wasn't
drugged with all those sleeping meds. He kindly filled me in
on their plans and what Nathan was up to, so communication
and trust were always there. When Gabriel wasn't there,
Charlotte was, sometimes with Matt too. She kept me
entertained, but seeing Matt made me think of Alex. I hadn't
seen or heard from him since that day in our apartment. I still
wondered about him. He seemed to know about Serena, and
I still wanted to know why he attacked me? I wanted to ask
Charlotte about him, but I couldn't without giving anything

away. I had a horrible feeling about him.

When the ninth day came around, I started to really get restless. I needed to get out of here. I was tired of lying around in bed all the time and my wounds were healing nicely now.

Later that evening, Nathan came earlier than he usually did. It was only five o'clock and I was just waking up when he walked in.

"Crazy girl," he whispered, kissing me on the head.

My eyes slowly opened to see him smiling back at me.

"Nate," I said, lifting my arms to hug him.

Holding me tight, he sat down next to me.

"I miss you," I said.

"I miss you, too." He replied. "It's lonely at home without you," Brushing the hair from my face, he kissed me very gently on the lips, then another time, and once more.

"We've come up with a plan, Gabriel and I."

I suddenly became more alert, adjusting myself up in the bed to listen better.

"We're going to attempt something tonight. I'm hoping it will work and this will all be over."

"What? What's the plan?" I said, clearing my throat.

He reached over and handed me a glass of water.

"Slow down sweetie, I'll tell you," he said, motioning me to move over in the bed so he could sit next to me. I cuddled in close against him, handing him back the water to place on the nightstand.

"I was in the library and came across an old witchcraft book," I looked up at him oddly.

"I know, witchcraft, very silly sounding but go with me for a minute. You see, we can't just make contact by calling out to Serena. One, because we need to keep her hidden from the Archangels, and two, she's afraid of Gabriel. So, she most likely will never come. But your spirit guide suggested to Gabriel that we try a more superstitious approach. Something that would be so far-fetched to angels they might not think of it. Something they wouldn't see coming. He suggested a scrying mirror."

"A what?" I asked.

"A scrying mirror. It's an old spiritual way of getting in contact with the dead. Back in the olden days, it was even used to predict the future."

I looked at him oddly, did he really think that was going to work?

"Anything to do with witchcraft is usually off the radar for angels because they forbid it among their type. They would never suspect us to use it. Plus, most of those spells create a barrier that blocks anything from getting through while it's active. Which includes angels, depending on the strength. It's the perfect plan for us to connect with her."

I could tell Nathan was happy with their idea, but it seemed impossible that this witchcraft could actually work.

"Are you sure? I mean, what if the angels do see what you're trying to do? Who knows what they'll do to you, or what they'll do to Gabriel." I was nervous for them both. "You could all—"

"Sweetie, it's fine. They won't catch us. They know Gabriel would never work with witchcraft or anything like that, and remember, the barrier will be up so even if they are searching, they won't find us. We'll be fine. I have a good feeling."

I looked at him, his face was lit up. I had to trust him like Gabriel said.

"Okay then, what time are we doing this? After visiting hours?"

"Soph," Nathan said, calmly. "Not you. Just us, and definitely not here."

"What? But I can help. Nathan, please. I feel fine. Gabriel can sneak back in after visiting hours and—"

"No, Soph. We have it all planned out, and Gabriel will be right by my side the entire time."

I didn't like this anymore. I thought I was going to be able to help. I thought I would be there to protect him, to protect his thoughts from being manipulated by Serena. But by the look on Nathan's face no matter what I said, I wasn't going to win this argument.

I sighed, then leaned back from him a bit. "Fine."

Nathan leaned over and kissed my head.

"Thank you, and don't worry about anything happening to you either. Gabriel said your spirit guide will be here to watch over you tonight."

"Great," I replied, sarcastically. "Who is this spirit guide anyways? I mean, he was pretty rough with me in my last dream and Gabriel did say he only has half the powers of angels. What if he's not strong enough?"

"I'm sure Gabriel wouldn't trust you to him if he wasn't capable of protecting you, sweetie."

He then adjusted himself down to lie next to me. Cuddling close, he took a deep breath in.

"Let's just relax before I have to go, alright?"

"Nathan?" I said, as his face nestled into my neck. I could feel his warm breath on my skin.

"I can't wait until we're back in our own bed together, with Bruce too."

He kissed me on the neck then looked up at me.

"The second this is all over, we're going to spend an entire day together. We'll go home, have a nice hot shower, I'll make you the best meal of your life and then we are going to cuddle in bed with movies and never leave. I want you all to myself. I'm having some serious separation anxiety," he joked, rubbing my arms.

"I'd like that." I smiled. "Before we were together all the time and now it feels like each day we're getting further and further apart. I miss us, and more..." I hinted, locking lips with him again.

"I know. It's unfair." He breathed deeply. "But soon, sweetie." He then sat up from me.

"But before I go, I made you something."

I sat up again as he slid off the bed.

"I know you aren't allowed outside food, but since we're faking your craziness, I thought I would sneak some in. It's unfair to strip you of everything."

I watched as he reached into a bag he had beside the bed and

176

pulled out a large container. A smile grew on my face.

"Ah! Is that real food?" I laughed, clapping my hands like a child.

"Yes ma'am. I made it especially for you." He then opened it up for me to see. There was lasagna, a Caesar salad, and even a little cup of chocolate pudding with a tiny heart drawn on top with icing powder.

"Wait, there's one last part to this amazing meal,"

He carefully reached back into the bag and pulled out a container. He then reached down once more and pulled out two cups.

"Nate! You snuck in slushies!" I threw my arms around him. I was never so happy to see real food and a slushie in my entire life. He handed me a cup, pouring a little into it.

"Your straw," he smiled.

"Thank you," I said, giving him a kiss on the cheek. "This is really great Nate, seriously."

He passed me a fork and knife and watched as I dug in immediately. Even though it was a little cool, it was still amazing! The flavor activated every taste bud on my tongue.

"Aren't you going to have some?" I asked, stopping for a moment when I realized Nathan was watching me so attentively. I then held the fork up full of lasagna to his lips. He laughed at my persistence and took another fork out from the bag. "I've got my own. Let's eat."

The two of us sat on the bed, ate our meal, drank our slushies and talked like we used to talk back when things were normal. It was perfect.

When finished, Nathan packed his stuff up and got ready to leave. As he lifted the bag from the floor, I reached over and grabbed him by the wrist.

"Nathan," I said, very seriously, "Be careful. I need you."

He smiled at me.

"I will." He then leaned in for one last kiss.

"I'll see you soon, crazy girl."

Then he was gone.

The silence was defining as I sat alone in my bed. It was making me nervous. How was I ever going to rest tonight knowing what the two of them were up to? Would everything be settled after this? Was it as simple as that? Just then, I heard the nurse's voice.

"It's time for your meds, Sophie."

I rolled my eyes as she entered the room and pulled the regular bottles from her pouch. She injected them into the hanging bags attached to my hands. They still didn't trust me enough to give me the medication in pill form. Nathan must have made quite a convincing story. When the nurse was done, she set down another cup of water beside my bed. I felt pathetic, lying here helplessly. But soon enough the meds kicked in and without fail, I was back into a deep sleep.

Nightfall came quickly as Nathan headed down the street, a backpack filled with specific objects required to execute their plan slung over his shoulder. He reached an abandoned building, the exact location Gabriel gave him to meet. The heavy door slammed behind him as he stepped inside.

He began to make his way up a dark staircase in front of him. The dust in the building was almost unbearable and the smell of mold lingered in every corner. The steps creaked and echoed in the silence around him. When he reached the top of the stairs, he stepped forward into a massive round room surrounded by large glass windows. They rattled a bit from the windstorm growing outside. It looked like an old ballroom or something.

"Nathan, over here." Gabriel called. His voice quieter than usual. "Did you bring everything I asked?"

"I have it all," Nathan replied.

"Good. Let's set up. I don't want to waste any time."

As Gabriel began to explain the process, Nathan opened his bag and started to pull out each item.

"Remember, we must always move quickly, we never know what could happen when working like this."

Nathan nodded and pulled out the final few items: a black mirror, three white candles and Serena's bracelet.

He placed the three candles a row behind him, lighting each one as he set them down. He then placed the black circular mirror down in front of him, adjusting it slightly in a stand so he could look directly into it. Taking a deep breath in, he sat down in the middle of the protective barrier he was about to create and took Serena's bracelet in his hands.

"Now, calm your mind. Hold the bracelet tightly in your hand and think of Serena. Think of the times you shared together. Try to remember the conversations you had," Gabriel said, standing a safe distance back.

Nathan stared into the mirror without a single blink until his eyes became very heavy and finally closed. He thought back to one of the first few interactions he had with Serena. The windows suddenly stopped rattling around them and the room became very quiet. Gabriel kept his eyes peeled, then very faintly, the smell of fall filled the air.

Nathan opened his eyes to a classroom. He was back in university. Slowly, he stood up as the wind blew in from the windows to the left of him. He was the only one in the room. On his chair hung the sweater he wore that day and his backpack sat on the ground just below him. A rush of emotions flooded through him as he picked it up and headed for the door. Stepping into the hallway, things were livelier. Students were moving onto their next class. He began to make his way, trying to remember what his next class was.

Then he heard her voice.

"Hey, wait up!"

He turned to see Serena running behind him, carelessly bumping into students along the way. He had been here before in this very moment. He remembered how amusing she was, watching her barrel down the hallway towards him. He smiled as she approached.

"What are you doing?" He asked, it was the exact words he said before.

"I just... wanted to give you your pen back," she said,

stuttering over her words.

"You chased me down the hall like a lunatic just to give me back my pen?"

"I thought, well—you might need it," she answered, still out of breath.

He couldn't stop smiling. She was so innocent, so different, and exactly the way he wanted to remember her. Their interactions were always short and cute back then.

After Serena had gotten up the guts to speak to him in class and borrow a pen for the first time, her confidence only grew from there. She was always finding silly reasons to speak with Nathan or bump into him, but he didn't mind, because he too had a secret crush on her ever since he saw her that first day of school. He just didn't understand why someone like her would be interested in him.

She was so beautiful, smart and had a lot going for her and he was just some quiet loner that sat in the back of the room. She stuck the pen out in front of his face with a big grin.

"Keep it." He laughed. "I have tons,"

"Are you sure?"

"Ya, seriously. It's just a pen. I'm sure I'll survive."

He couldn't help but stare. All of his old feelings were coming back. He loved every second with her, no matter how silly it was. She was awkward at times and completely obsessed with Japan. She loved talking about her dreams and hopes for the future—this was the girl he once knew—the girl he loved.

Suddenly, it became dark as if he had closed his eyes. For a second, he couldn't see anything. Then, with a single blink, his eyes regained focus and he was back in the room with Gabriel.

"Keep trying, Nathan." He said, "I could hear you speaking to her."

Nathan's eyes softened at the thought.

He then took another deep breath in and glanced back into the mirror. Moments passed, and nothing happened.

"Concentrate, Nathan."

"I am," he replied, closing his eyes in frustration.

In a way, he was a little upset that Gabriel was listening in on his private moments, but he knew there was no other way to do this.

"Serena, where are you?" He whispered.

Beside him, Gabriel slowly lit a white light between his hands and pushed the energy towards Nathan, giving him a little boost to connect with the supernatural realm.

Nathan's eyes closed again and immediately began to race back and forth. Searching the darkness, he finally heard her voice.

"It's about time, Nathan. I thought you weren't coming," he heard her say. His eyes opened to Serena standing in a doorway.

"You're not Nate." She then said.

He watched as Serena stood quietly in front of the stranger, then with one blink, his vision changed. He was now seeing through her eyes, looking right at the man who had attacked her. He busted through the door, knocking her over. He watched as the man's fist came down hard against her face, over and over again. He could feel her pain, her fear and more.

"Where is he?!!" The man yelled but never gave her a chance to answer. The way he handled her started to make Nathan sick to his stomach.

"Stop! Please, I can't watch this!" He yelled, and instantly, he was back with Gabriel. It was quiet again. His heart raced as his head hung low to the ground tormented by the sights he saw and the memories flooding back.

It was all his fault. If he hadn't been doing what he was doing Serena would still be… He tried desperately to catch his breath. The pain in his chest ached badly. She had entered his life at the wrong time.

"You saved me Nathan," He then heard her say. His eyes shot open. In the mirror before him was her reflection. It looked like she was behind him now. He watched as her hand reached for his shoulder.

"Don't cry." She said, softly.

"I'm so sorry, Serena. It's all my fault. Everything. It's my fault you're like this. It's my fault you're dead and stuck where you are." His hand reached up to touch hers. To his surprise, she was actually there.

"Please," he said, turning to her. "Please tell me how I can help you."

"Nathan, I'm so alone," she cried.

Another tear slid down his cheek.

"I know. I'm sorry. I wish it were me in there instead of you. Please, let me help you get out."

"Then we can be together," she smiled.

He paused, the pain and guilt he felt from the reality of what he had to say next to her was torturing.

"I can't." He replied, staring back at her.

"Why not? I'm here, aren't I? I'm touching you. Don't you feel me?" She asked, leaning in close. Her breath was cold against his face. Then her lips touched his, ever so slightly.

"Serena, let us help you," Gabriel interrupted from behind. Startled, she immediately clung to Nathan.

"It's okay, I'm right here." He said, wrapping his arms around her. Her eyes shot back to the Archangel.

"Gabriel, why are you bothering us?" She asked. "Nathan and I have found each other again, so your business here is done. I will not bother you—or her, anymore."

"That's not how it works," he said sharply. "You are in two different worlds. You can never be together. You need to pass on and we can help you with that. Nathan will help you. You can say your proper goodbyes now."

"Gabriel's right. You need to move on." Nathan repeated sadly. "I want to help you because I love you, but we can't be together. I'm sorry. I'm sorry for everything,"

Her hands clenched tighter to his shirt.

"No, Nathan. Please," she whispered, then pulled him back in for another kiss. He couldn't help himself, it felt so natural between them. "I need you. I can't live without you."

"Enough!" Gabriel urged. "Nathan, step away from her! She is pulling you in."

Serena held on for dear life, ignoring the Archangel's words.

"Nathan! It is Sophie you are fighting for here. Sophie!"
The sound of her name shot Nathan's eyes back open. Staring
back at Serena. He suddenly felt a change between them. Her
eyes had grown cold in a matter of seconds.
"Don't tell me you love her more than me, Nathan? It can't be.
We are the ones meant to be. Tell me it's not true." She asked,
sadly.
"You are so special to me, but…" He paused.
"You said you loved me," Serena's eyes started to tear up as
they stood in silence for a moment.
"Yes, you did say you loved her. I heard you quite clearly."
Another voice stated from behind. "Hmm, now this is
awkward. Which girl do you love?" She spoke again in a
sarcastic tone.
Nathan and Serena turned to see a young woman standing
with her arms crossed casually. Gabriel quickly appeared
in between her and the two of them. Her eyes moved to the
Archangel on guard.
"Did you forget that I'm different from your brothers,
Gabriel?" She smirked. "Witchcraft. I like your approach.
Very nicely done, and you've even managed to keep the
Archangels in the dark, haven't you?" She applauded, "But
what will be your next move? Looks like she has quite a hold
on him," The young woman sighed, stepping towards Nathan
and Serena.
Gabriel again, placed himself between them.
"He isn't as strong as you hoped, is he?" She asked.
Gabriel still didn't respond. Nathan looked frantically at him
for answers as the woman leaned in closer to the Archangel.
"You're messing with my design," she whispered. "Bad idea."
"Gabriel…" Nathan called out, but Gabriel still didn't answer.
"You don't like my game?" She spoke again, staring into the
Archangel's eyes.
"I'm only trying to help you," He finally responded.
She smiled, then shot her glance to Nathan and Serena again.
"You, boy, come here." She demanded.
Serena held onto Nathan as he tried to step forward.

"Alright, well bring her with you if you must," the woman said, annoyed.

Nathan attempted to step forward again over the candles, but something blocked him. Gabriel turned quickly to see that Serena had already locked the circle. The simple protective barrier Gabriel had sent to Nathan with his white light suddenly lingered low on the ground before them. The darkness attached to her had pushed his light down.

"Serena, let him go or you will both pay the price." Gabriel pleaded.

"Well, this is just annoying." The woman spoke again. "Stupid young people and their feelings." She then pushed past the Archangel towards them.

"Nathan," She began, stopping at the edge of the circle. Gabriel was right behind her, but didn't make a move.

"Both of these girls are in your life now, but you can only have one. Choose right and you could live a long and happy life. But choose wrong and all three of you will die. The choice is yours and your time is running out," she warned.

"You know, this is quite a knot that's been tied here. Perhaps I should inform the Archangels. They may want to get in on this."

Gabriel's eyes widened.

"Now that would be fun, huh?" She continued to joke.

"Who are you?" Nathan asked, annoyed.

"Me? You honestly don't know who I am?"

He stood silent.

"I'm—"

"Fate," Gabriel interrupted sharply.

Nathan froze. He knew what this meant and immediately released Serena from his grip. The candles around them blew out quickly and the four of them waited silently to see who would make a move first.

"What? You're not happy to see me?" Fate smiled.

"I'm ecstatic to meet you. I mean, you have been playing quite a game here, Nathan. But now it's getting a little sloppy and I don't know how I feel about it. You see, I went to see your

184

other little girlfriend tonight. Sophie, is it?"
Nathan swallowed in fear.
"She's a cute little thing but her mind is all over the place.
She's a hard one to read, especially with all the meds they're
pumping into her. I'd be careful you don't do any long-term
damage."
"What did you do?" Gabriel interrupted.
Fate turned to him.
"Excuse me," she replied. "I was speaking to Nathan,"
Gabriel stared with fear in his eyes now.
"Well, since you asked so nicely," she said sarcastically, "I
think your spirit guide needs a little more training..."
"Where is she?" Gabriel snarled.
Nathan's heart stopped for a moment, his full attention was
on their conversation now. "What do you mean, Gabriel?" He
asked, worried. "What's happened to Sophie?"
Fate smiled again at the Archangel, then turned back to
Nathan.
"Well, I wanted to see for myself what kind of state she was
in. I mean seriously Nathan, this is just craziness. You got
girl number one who's dead and stuck in purgatory, and girl
number two being haunted by the first girl, and now girl
number two is all drugged up on meds in a suicide wing of
the hospital. This is stuff right out of a movie, I tell ya. Bravo
Nathan, you've made quite a mess here with this so-called life
you're trying to live. And as much as I find this entertaining,
it's starting to cause me some issues."
Gabriel stood restlessly behind her as she went on.
"I do like to be entertained, but only as long as it doesn't mess
up too much of my work. Since Nathan was brought into this
world, he's lived, died and came back as an guardian angel. I
believe you also revealed yourself to a few of Sophie's friends
back then too, didn't you?"
"They didn't know who I truly was." Nathan quickly replied.
"They thought I was an old friend of hers. I swear."
"Doesn't matter." Fate replied. "That's a big no-no. Even if
you're undercover. Your Archangel should have told you that."

She glanced back at Gabriel.

"But then, Nathan managed to get a second chance at life. Which is pretty much impossible. So, congrats to you on that too!" She clapped, then quickly sighed.

Her body twisted towards the Archangel again.

"You worked so hard on that one, didn't you? Must make you a little ticked that he's back here alive and involving himself with his past again. Kind of seems like a waste, huh?" She taunted.

"You know, Sophie's friends are starting to notice these odd little situations she gets herself into with Serena…. Too much of our world is being shared through Nathan's life. I'm a little worried that you don't have a good enough hold on him, Gabriel. I think I need to step in again." She said, looking back at Nathan. "Or should I leave it to the Archangels to take care of?"

Her index finger tapped her chin in a dainty manor.

"Where is Sophie?" Gabriel asked again, raising his voice to her. Her hands dropped, a little insulted by his tone.

"Well, I couldn't have you guys hiding her in the hospital forever. Eventually that would bring all your drama to that huge area with too many people that could get involved. So, I removed her while she slept. She didn't feel a thing, that poor soul."

Nathan's face dropped.

"Don't worry. She's safe."

"Where is she?!" Nathan shouted.

Fate suddenly appeared in front of him.

"Do not raise your voice at me!" She snapped. "You do not get to tell me what to do. This is my world. I own you!"

Nathan froze, his body trembling with fear and rage. Fate paused, then took a deep breath to calm herself. She cleared her throat, then spoke again in a much more pleasant manner.

"Now, since you are all in the searching mood, I added another person for you to find."

Gabriel and Nathan looked at each other, sadly knowing where she was going with this.

"This is where it gets exciting so listen up, because I'm going to lay everything out for you Nathan. You can choose to either look for Sophie or stay here and help Serena. And Serena, you can play too." Fate teased, adjusting her glance towards the ghostly girl. "You could stay here with Nathan…. Or, go after what you've wanted to get rid of all along. For now, she is in your realm."

Serena's eyes lit up.

"Oh, and one more thing." Fate smiled. "I lied, I already told the Archangels of what you're up to and now you are all on their target list. Better hurry and decide Nathan, before they get to one of your girls first."

Shocked at this massive twist, everyone remained silent for a moment. Fate spoke again.

"Which then leaves me with Gabriel." She said, turning to him one more time.

The Archangel stood furiously in front of her.

"Who will you choose to protect? Your spirit guide isn't strong enough for this, which leaves only you."

Gabriel watched as she paced around the room in delight of the game she created.

"Do you want to save Sophie, so she can be with Nathan? The one you fought so dearly for, or are you going to continue to help Serena who's stuck in purgatory? Ya know, she's getting help from someone very special… I'm surprised you haven't figured it out yet. Perhaps, it's because you've been so blinded by your precious Nathan,"

"What are you going on about? Just say it," Gabriel replied, annoyed by the conversation now.

"I have created a path for you too Gabriel, and I can't wait until you figure it out. You've already faltered once, will you do it again?" Fate smiled. "This is getting so exciting, isn't it? Don't worry, you're doing a fabulous job so far, not like before. But please, be sure to keep it within our world. I don't need everyone out there seeing all this supernatural stuff. It's kind of like seeing behind the curtain, ya know? We just can't have that. I mean, there's only so much mind erasing you can do." She said with a sigh.

Fate's eyes shifted and a large grin grew on her face.

"Looks like someone got a head start on you, good luck,"
Then she was gone.

Gabriel turned quickly back to Nathan. His eyes raced around
the room. "Where's Serena?" He shouted.

Nathan paused in fear. "You don't think she would've…"

Gabriel didn't respond.

"We have to find her—now! I have to find Sophie!"

"You can't, Nathan." He snapped. "You can't get to that world
anymore—neither can I. It's forbidden. There's only one
person who can get to her now. I'll be back. Go home and wait
for me there."

"No Gabriel, wait!" But he was already gone.

Nathan stood alone lost in horrible thoughts. How did Gabriel
not think of Fate in this equation. How were they so careless?
They had to find Sophie before it was too late. He quickly
gathered everything back into his bag and hurried down the
dark stair case.

Slamming through the doors of the building Nathan reached
into his pocket and pulled out his cell as he continued to
run. He opened the contact list and found the person he was
looking for. He knew it was against Fate's wishes, but he
needed help. His finger pressed on the name.

15
Helping Hands

When Nathan got inside, he threw his bag to the floor. "I'm so stupid!" He shouted. "Why did I get so caught up with Serena. I didn't even think of Fate. How did Gabriel miss that?" He stormed into the kitchen just as a knock came from the front door. "Come in!" He yelled.

The door opened, then closed again. He heard the lock snap shut, then footsteps across the floor until Charlotte entered the kitchen.

"Nathan," She spoke nervously. "What's happening?"

He turned to face her, trying to hold every emotion inside. She had never seen him like this.

"Nate? What's going on? Is Sophie okay?" She asked, stepping toward him slowly.

He started pacing again, trying to get a hold of himself before speaking but just as she touched him, he broke down.

"I screwed up, Charlotte. I'm sorry. I think I lost her."

Charlotte looked at him in fear. "You're scaring me, what do you mean lost her Nate? Where's Sophie?"

He shook his head no as she stood confused with what he was trying to tell her.

"It's okay. Whatever it is, we'll figure it out."

After Nathan caught his breath, Charlotte sat him down at the table and pulled a chair up in front of him. She then spoke very calmly, "Look Nate, I know we've had our differences,

189

but the one thing we have in common is Sophie and both of us would do anything for her, right?"

He nodded.

"Good. Then you need to trust me. You need to tell me everything that's been going on. Everything that Sophie said she couldn't tell me. It's the only way I'm going to be able to help you."

"It's not that simple, Charlotte. If this were as easy as depression or something like that, I would. But what I want to tell you is going to be impossible for you to believe, or even begin to understand."

"Just try. I promise I'll keep an open mind okay? Please," she begged.

Nathan sat quiet for a moment. He knew to get her involved would be a bad choice given Fate's warning and he didn't want to get Gabriel in trouble either, but he needed someone to talk to. He also thought that Charlotte could be of good use for when he got Sophie back. Because they were definitely going to get her back.

Nathan took a deep breath, "Everything I want to tell you is impossible to believe. Please understand this, but it's true and when we get Sophie back she will confirm all of it. Okay? Can I trust that you will have some faith in me?"

"What? When we get Sophie back?" She repeated. "Where is she?"

"Charlotte, please. Can you just trust me?" He repeated.

"Okay, okay, yes. Just tell me." She snapped.

He sighed, deciding where to begin.

"You know how Sophie told you that we knew each other from long ago?" She nodded. "Well that part is true, but I wasn't just a friend. I watched over her... like a guardian." He paused.

"What do you mean watched over her? Like family or something?"

"No. As her guardian angel."

Charlotte smiled. "That's really cute, so you felt like her guardian angel? No wonder she's so caught up about you,"

190

Then her smile faded. "But I'm still confused,"
"No. What I'm saying is…" He took another deep breath.
"I was sent from heaven to watch over Sophie as her actual
guardian angel. I died long ago and was brought back by the
Archangel Gabriel to become a guardian. The reason I was
watching over Sophie was because she was very depressed—
suicidal, but then something dark began to follow her,
something that wanted to hurt her. With Gabriel's help, I was
able to keep her safe and help her grow strong again. That's
when she began to really live and change inside—of course,
with the help of good friends like you as well. Then, when she
was confident enough and settled, my job was over. I was out
of time, and I had to say goodbye."
Charlotte stared at him, completely taken back by his words.
She definitely wasn't expecting this much of a story, and he
could tell that she wasn't buying any of it by the expression on
her face. He continued anyway.
"It was the hardest thing I've ever had to do because I had
fallen in love her. Completely and madly in love with her—
which was not allowed. I thought we'd never get a chance
together but somehow, by the power of Sophie's love and
the pure heart that had grown strong inside of her she got
me a second chance at life. Something that's pretty much
impossible for any angel. Which is why I suddenly appeared
back in her world—your world—for good. We couldn't
believe it. It's truly a miracle that we can be together now. You
have no idea." Nathan paused again. "Charlotte?"
"Give me a sec," she uttered, "I'm thinking,"
"There's more," he hesitated.
She looked back at him and braced herself.
"That thing that was after Sophie, well it's back and it's
all my fault. It's an angry spirit stuck in the purgatory
world. The Archangels and I have been trying to stop her
but unfortunately, we've failed each time and now Fate has
stepped into the picture and taken Sophie from us and released
her into purgatory where this spirit can reach her."
Charlotte quickly stood up from the chair.

"Whoa okay, hold on a sec, Nate. Spirits? Archangels, and purgatory? I mean okay, I know that some crazy tragic things have happened to Soph, but this Nathan—you can't be serious? Am I really supposed to believe that you were an angel that came back to life?" Her eyes locked on his. He nodded.

Her hands dropped dramatically letting out a huge sigh. When Nathan didn't argue back, she sat down again.

"Okay," Charlotte said, sitting up straight. "Let's just say there is an evil spirit after Sophie. I mean, I'm not gonna lie, some freaky shit has happened while I was with her and it doesn't add up, but what does this spirit want? Why Sophie?"

"She's in love with me and she wants Sophie dead."

"Now that's just stupid," Charlotte blurted out. "What is this, some kind of horror movie? You want me to believe that a spirit that's in love with you is after Sophie? That doesn't make any sense—I mean, what's her motive?" Charlotte laughed a bit, thinking how ridiculous this was getting now.

"She's the same girl I loved when I was alive in my first life, before I was a guardian. Her name is Serena. Our relationship didn't last long before I was killed." He paused as Charlotte stared at him in disbelief. "Then, sadly, she killed herself thinking she could be with me again, but I had already become an angel and was watching over Sophie. Seeing us together upset her very much. She wants Sophie gone.

"Nate, wait. She said? You mean you've spoken to this spirit?" Charlotte asked, nervously.

"Yes, she finally showed herself to me. I had no idea she was the one doing all the harm and now that Sophie knows the truth, she's more scared than ever."

"When was she here last?"

"The night of Sophie's attack. That's why Sophie's in the hospital. That's why I made up the story about her attempting suicide. If we kept her in a public place there would be less of a chance that Serena would show herself."

"Who's we?" Charlotte asked, trying to wrap her head around all of this.

"Gabriel and I," Nathan answered. "He's an Archangel. He's trying to protect us."

"Okay, wait, you mentioned fate too. Do you mean... like someone's fate? Are you saying that Fate is a real being?"

"Yes, and she's very powerful—more powerful than God."

"God? Alright, I'm tapping out. This is just insane, Nathan! How do you expect me to believe all this? I mean really?"

"I know, Charlotte. I warned you that it would be hard to believe, but Serena attacked Sophie. That's why she had all of those cuts on her arms. She came very close to killing her and she would've succeeded if Gabriel hadn't stepped in."

Charlotte stood up and began to pace around the kitchen. "This is just crazy. I mean, what do I say to this?"

"Nothing. You say nothing," he begged. "I just need you to help me even if you don't believe me."

She stopped and turned to him. "Nathan, you must know how this sounds, right? I mean, I like you as a person, but I always felt you were a little off—like something wasn't quite right. I couldn't put my finger on it before but now..." she paused. "You made my friend insane and now she's totally cracked and gone missing!" Charlotte's voice rose in fear.

She paced again, anger pulsing through her. She slammed her fist down on the counter frustrated.

"Damn it!" She said, holding her hand that now ached. Nathan's face softened a little, amused by Sophie's fiery friend. Charlotte marched back over to him.

"Well, I guess I have no choice do I? I have to believe you. I need to help my friend and if that means I need to play along with your silly story then I will, but know this," she warned, pointing her finger in Nathan's face. "If anything happens to Sophie, I will make you pay so dearly for it."

Nathan smiled. "I believe you," he said, relieved.

"So then what's my part in all of this?" She asked, sitting back down in front of him.

"Gabriel and I will find Sophie, and when we do, I need you to stay with her twenty-four seven, take her to work with you if you have to. Just don't leave her alone. This gives Serena less

of a chance to get her. Then Gabriel and I can go after her."
Charlotte leaned back in the chair—annoyed with him still.
"I don't understand why those so-called Archangels don't just
mutilate her ass. Aren't they supposed to be super powerful or
something?" She pushed.
"I want to try and help Serena before they get to her. She can't
help what she's become and it's all my fault. She's just scared
and alone."
"Nathan, that seems a little selfish, don't you think?"
Charlotte huffed. "Just let the angels take care of her. I mean,
Sophie's already missing. How much more are you going to
watch her go through before you throw up the white flag and
do what's right?"
"I am doing what's right." He snapped back. "I'll handle this,
I promise. Trust me, Charlotte,"
She rolled her eyes, "Fine."
"Thank you. So here are some things you need to understand."
Nathan spoke, getting straight to the point. "One, Serena finds
Sophie more easily in her dreams, so sleeping is a tough one,"
"But she's been sleeping so much at the hospital?" Charlotte
stated.
"Yes, but she was drugged. Her mind is too thick to get
through and the nurses monitored her sleep. Plus, we had
Gabriel."
"And where was this Gabriel when Sophie went missing?"
Charlotte shot back.
"With me, unfortunately."
Charlotte rolled her eyes another time. "Okay, go on."
"Second, Serena has been very good at controlling Sophie's
thoughts, making her believe things are real when they're not.
The more Sophie believes her, the more physical harm Serena
can do, hence the cuts on her arms. She has now reached a
point that she can do physical harm to Sophie and make it
stay. So, if you get caught in a situation with her like that, you
need to try and keep Sophie's mind clear and in the present—
listening only to you."
"Alright, anything else?" Charlotte asked, feeling

overwhelmed now.

"Be aware of Fate. She is the most powerful being and controls all of us. Also, please know that stepping into this situation, knowing what you know, could alter your fate as well if you choose to help us. We're not allowed to share the information I have, so doing so has put you in harm's way. If you don't want to help, I completely understand. It's a big thing to ask anyone—to risk their own life for someone else. If you choose not to, I can ask Gabriel to come and erase everything I've told you, and you can go back to normal. It's your choice."

Charlotte sat still, pondering over her options.

"I'll do it," she finally answered. "Soph's my best friend. She would do it for me, no matter how far-fetched the story. Just tell me what to do and I'll do it."

"Thank you, Charlotte," he smiled. "Oh, one more thing."

"How can there possibly be any more?" She sighed.

"You must never ever tell anyone else about this. No one. Not even Matt. You have to swear, Charlotte."

"I understand, Nate. As if I would tell anyone about this anyway. Any normal person would think I'm a total nutcase."

"I'm just making sure—for your own safety and ours," Nathan said, kindly. "Okay, now we wait. Gabriel said he would meet me here, hopefully with news."

"Gabriel? The Archangel—is coming here?" Charlotte repeated, raising her eyebrow at him.

Nathan smiled, then got up and walked over to the counter. "Do you want some tea? Or a beer?" He joked.

"I'm definitely going to need a beer now thanks to you," Charlotte replied, dropping her head back in exhaustion.

Nathan grabbed two bottles from the fridge and joined her at the table again. He popped the cap and handed her the bottle. "It really means a lot to me that you're here, Charlotte. Seriously. I knew you would come. Even if you don't like me very much."

"Nate, it's not that I don't like you," she paused. "I just don't understand you. I know nothing about you, and if what you

195

say is really true then I have so much more to process about you before I begin to trust you. You have to understand where I'm coming from and knowing what I know about Sophie's past? I mean, of course I'm going to be protective of her. She needs someone to watch out for her. I want to trust you, but I will always do what's best for my friend first—no offense."

"None taken." He replied. "That's why I have total trust in you. You always think of Sophie first. But I promise, I am the best person for her. You'll see."

16
The Other Side

My senses were on high alert as I felt around for
something—anything but found nothing in the pitch black.
My eyes searched the darkness nervously. There was a
sickening feeling building up inside of me, a feeling of great
sorrow and it hurt very badly. I listened carefully, the silence
was deafening. Then I heard a faint whisper, then another, then
a second voice joined in, but they were still too quiet to make
out the words.
"Who's there?" I said, bravely.
I immediately regretted speaking aloud because the voices
silenced the second they heard me. I had made myself known,
instead of staying hidden.
Suddenly, a blinding light forced me to cover my eyes. It
burned bright for a moment, then faded quickly. I began to
see shapes—shapes of trees. It looked like I was in the woods
somewhere. My eyes squinted, trying to make out the large
objects lingering in the hazy distance. Behind the healthy
trees that surrounded me, stood a bunch of tall and very dead
ones. They looked torched and were dripping with some sort
of black ooze. Some of them drooped and smelled of rotten
bark. I covered my nose. Slowly, the gloomy world around me
became much clearer. I got up from the ground with my hands
out, balancing myself with each step. I felt a little dizzy.
I began to walk.

The faint whispers whistled around me again. Their quiet voices trying to feed my brain with meaningless words. Whatever was lingering around me was not happy. Soon a heaviness filled my body again. I stopped. It was so cold here—where ever I was. But how did I get here? I had to be dreaming again. Was I still at the hospital? Did they not give me enough meds to keep the dreams away this time? I had to try something to find out.

"Nathan?" I whispered first, hoping that if I was still in the hospital, Gabriel might wake me up. The whispers around me stopped for a moment, then began again, taunting me with his name.

"Stop it," I said. I didn't actually need Nathan, I needed someone stronger. "Gabriel?" I called a little louder. "Gabriel, where are you?" I shouted.

The voices didn't repeat the Archangel's name. Then I heard another voice, one that stopped the others.

"Sooophiee,"

I turned in fear, staying alert from all sides.

"Sooophiee," She taunted again.

This time it was louder and much closer.

"I know it's you," I said, figuring I might as well get this over with. "Serena?"

I waited again. The cold wind whipped through the loose strands of my hair. It felt awful to say her name aloud.

"Sophie," the voice said once more, but much lower.

"I can feel you around me. Please don't do this," I begged. Everything went silent, but only for a moment before the whispers started again. My name hurled around the dead woods that grew darker by the moment. Even the few trees that looked alive when I first arrived suddenly drooped with darkness now. I covered my ears, spinning around and searching for whatever might appear. It was getting too dark!

Suddenly, my legs were pulled out from under me, and I fell hard to the ground and screamed in fear as I attempted to get away from whatever was grabbing at me. I could feel hundreds of hands all over my legs pulling and scratching, dragging me backwards in the dirt. I kicked and screamed for dear life. "Gabriel! Gabriel, help me!" My voice broke in fear, the dust in the air choked me as the wind pounded against my face now. The hands crawled up my legs until their long bony fingers covered my mouth, blocking my voice and my airway. I felt like my heart was going to stop right then and there if not from lack of air, then definitely from fear alone. Worst of all, I knew he wasn't coming for me. I didn't have my guardian angel anymore. I continued to choke as the dust burned my eyes until finally, I passed out.

My body shivered in the cold as my eyes slowly flickered open again. Around me were four walls. I was lying on a bed with dirty sheets that smelled of mothballs. My wrists and ankles were bound to the bed, making it impossible to escape. I struggled pulling at the ropes, but they were too thick, and my skin burned from the rubbing sensation. My heart began to race as the tears built up in my eyes. I did my best to hold it in. I needed to concentrate. I couldn't lose it just yet.
I searched the room. It resembled the hospital room I was in before but this one was much worse. This room was full of spiders and rotted tile that leaked dampness in. The smell was nauseating.
"Looks like those cuts aren't going to heal as nicely as you hoped, huh?" A voice suddenly said.
Slowly, a figure approached.
A small light above me illuminated, creating a soft glow as Serena stepped to the edge of the bed. My body froze up.
"Had to make sure that you couldn't get away on me this time," She smiled. "You know, this is so much easier with you here in my world than me always trying to break into yours. It was so nice of Fate to drop you off,"
I looked at her, confused.
"Oh wait, that's right, you don't know where you are yet." She teased. "Poor thing, you must think you're dreaming again?"
My eyes grew wide.
"I bet you're hoping that your precious Gabriel will save you,

huh? Must be nice having an Archangel watch over you. You must feel very special." She then stopped, and a serious look came over her face. "Well not this time,"

"Where am I?" I heard myself say.

Serena smiled again, "You're stuck, like me."

"Stuck?"

"Yes. You've heard of purgatory, haven't you? I'm sure you'll find it an exciting place being a horror movie fan as you are. This is the place where souls linger. You should know that. So I'd watch your back, things are not always as they seem here."

Serena walked around the bed to the other side, dragging her long fingers along the edge, brushing my body as she went. Her touch sent shivers up my spine.

"Why are you working with him? Gabriel does not know what's best. Are you sure you can trust him?" She stopped at the head of the bed to look down into my eyes.

"You cry too much. It's annoying," she said, rudely. "Why can't you just leave him alone? That's all I ask. It's not too big of a request, is it? I mean, I was with him first."

"I can't," I replied, "It's not just me. He won't leave my side."

"You haven't even tried hard enough!" Serena shouted.

"You're still here!" She then snagged the rope tied around my left wrist and yanked it tighter. It dug into my skin. The scars on my wrist started to tear open and blood began to drip to the floor as I screamed in pain.

"Stop, please!"

Serena walked around again to the other side of the bed. "Nathan wants to be with me. He just doesn't know how to tell you. You're so damn needy. He feels sorry for you. You need to just leave!" She shouted again, tightening the other side as well.

I screamed again.

She then reached over and aggressively grabbed my chin. "I really do owe Fate for dropping you at my doorstep. I'm going to enjoy every moment with you, as will they..."

My eyes flickered around the room as the whispers I once heard now grew into terrifying growls.

"There's a lot of them you know, and guess what? They love fresh meat—humans I mean." She stopped for a moment to listen to their growls. My eyes shot back to hers.

"I apologize if it gets out of hand," she said, stepping back from me. I felt desperation rip through my body.

"Wait, Serena. Please! Don't leave me here. I can help you. Please don't do this. You're only hurting Nathan. Think of Nate!" I cried, trying a new approach as the voices grew louder around me.

Serena paused. "I am thinking of Nathan. I always think of Nathan." She said not looking back at me. Suddenly, her body darted towards me again with a small sharp object in her hands. My eyes closed immediately in fear.

When nothing happened, I slowly opened them again to Serena's face directly over me.

"I hate you," She whispered, then quickly sliced my lips with a piece of glass.

It burned horribly. I could taste the blood draining into my mouth.

"Try kissing him with those lips," she said, furiously. "I should cut each part of your body until you are useless to him—until you are no more." Her hands shook in rage, then quickly grabbed my neck. I gasped for air as her fingers dug into my skin, but then she let go.

I gasped again frantically. I didn't want to go through this anymore. All of this torture was worse than death itself.

"Just kill me already!" I screamed.

If I truly was in purgatory, there was a good chance no one was coming for me, and I didn't want to rot here like Serena.

"No," She replied. "I'm going to take my time with you, just as you slowly tortured me over the years."

I struggled again, trying desperately to free myself as she walked away. Then I heard her speak again,

"She's yours to play with for now. Just don't kill her—not yet." Then she was gone.

The taunting sounds ripped around the room as my heart raced in fear. The bed began to shake as the dark shadows climbed up it. Then like before, I felt their bony rotten hands grabbing at me. With their sharp nails cutting into my skin again, I screamed with the bitter taste of blood sliding down my throat. My lungs ached and my entire body hurt like it never had before. As they climbed on top of me, slowly tearing me apart, my teeth clenched in raging pain. They were everywhere. Then I tasted the rot as their nails reach into my mouth, tearing my gums down until they gripped onto my bottom lip. My eyes widened in terror, then it went black.

●●●

With no sign of Sophie, each week went by more painfully for Nathan. He became obsessed with reading witchcraft books and using the scrying mirror on his own. Charlotte was at his place every day, helping him search for anything that might lead them to their friend's whereabouts.

Charlotte still had not seen any proof of Gabriel yet and it was making her nervous. Nathan said the Archangel was busy, erasing the minds of those from the hospital making them forget that Sophie was ever there. But she was beginning to wonder how long she could play along with Nathan's story. She really wanted to call the cops. Her best friend had been missing for way too long now. She had covered for Sophie by calling her agent and her job, telling them she had gone home to Ontario for a family emergency but didn't know when she would return. But how long could she really do this? It was frustrating and making her sick to her stomach with worry.

It was late one night when Charlotte threw her purgatory book to the floor. "This is hopeless, Nate. Look, I don't mean to be rude, but I've been very patient with all this and—"

"Please, Charlotte. Keep reading," He begged, not looking up at her.

"No, I really think now is the time to call the cops. We need more help."

"We have help! Gabriel is looking for her. I told you that," he replied, glancing up at her.

"We haven't even seen or heard from this Gabriel yet, and I'm beginning to think there's something else going on here, Nathan." Slowly, she stood up from the table.
"You better tell me right now, or I'm walking."
When he didn't answer, she shoved her chair back and started to make her way past him. He quickly grabbed her by the arm. "You can't leave, Charlotte. You have to help me. We have to find her," he begged.
"I'm sorry, but I'm beginning to think we aren't going to. We don't know where to look anymore. I've done everything you've suggested, but nothing is working, Nathan. I'm not sure how much I believe you anymore, I'm sorry. I'm going to the cops."
"I said no cops!" He shouted, quickly standing up. "You need to trust me!"
"Let me go!" She yelled, shoving him back but his grip was too strong.
He tried desperately to hold onto her as she continued to pull. She yanked once more and this time he accidentally release her arm. Charlotte slipped from his grip and fell back against the chair making it slide out from under her. Before she hit the ground, she felt the grasp of someone's hands.
"Nathan!" Gabriel shouted, lifting Charlotte to her feet.
She turned quickly to face him. A little scared, but also stunned by his beauty and perfect posture, she studied the strange man before her.
"Where did you come from?" She asked, nervously.
"I'm Gabriel, but Nathan has already told you that. Hasn't he?"
"You're Gabriel? The Archangel?" She repeated.
He nodded.
"Well shit, where do I sign up for heaven?" She joked.
A small smirk grew on the Archangel's face. He then stepped past her, towards Nathan. "Sit down, Charlotte," he said, without looking back at her.
She surprisingly did as he requested.
"Nathan, you're changing and it's not helping you. You need

to keep your head on straight."

Nathan took a step back from him, "Keep my head on straight? Are you kidding me? I'm the reason the first girl I loved is dead and now the new love of my life is lost somewhere in purgatory, and I can't do shit without my powers. I'm useless—to everyone. I've read and read, and researched everything over and over again—and still I have nothing. I mean nothing! Nothing that has gotten me anywhere closer to Sophie's location."

His hands were shaking.

"Nathan, calm down. I told you this was going to be a long road." He reached for him, but Nathan moved across the room and began pacing the kitchen.

"Gabriel, she could be dead by now. If Sophie's dead, I won't be able to live with myself."

"We will find her, Nathan."

Gabriel then quickly appeared beside him before he could move again and placed his hand on Nathan's back.

"Calm yourself,"

Charlotte sat in awe as a small white light lit up behind Nathan's back where Gabriel's hand rested. She watched as Nathan's gasps for air slowly calmed. Running his hands through his hair, Nathan took a deep breath.

"I think you should try to get some sleep. You are of no use to us if you are exhausted."

"I think that's a good idea, Nate." Charlotte agreed. "You'll feel better in the morning, and we'll start bright and early. Hell, I'll even keep reading tonight if it makes you feel better,"

"We can't stop," he repeated, "Please."

"We won't." She assured him. "I'll find something, don't worry. Go get some sleep,"

After a moment, Nathan slowly made his way down the hall towards the bedroom. He sat down on the edge of the bed just as Gabriel appeared before him again.

"You can't be like this, Nathan. It will help no one, and you can never act like that with Charlotte. She is your only friend right now and Sophie's best friend. You need her. She is doing you a great favor. Be gracious to her."

"I just thought that we'd have her back by now. Gabriel, this is killing me. I don't want to be mad at Serena but Sophie, she's probably scared and she—"

"Nathan, we will find her. I spoke with her spirit guide today. He mentioned a possible way to reach her. Remember, he can get into many places I cannot. He said he was going to attempt something tonight."

Nathan looked up at him. "He's found a way into purgatory?"

"I'm not sure. But if he has, he will go alone. You need to trust us."

"I do trust you Gabriel, but I haven't even met this so-called spirit guide."

"You will, soon. Now get some sleep or I will call you off this completely."

Nathan sighed, then pulled the shirt from over his head and chucked it to the floor. "Fine, good night," he said, rudely. Gabriel smirked shaking his head, then disappeared from sight. It wasn't long before sleep took Nathan that night.

He had only gotten a few hours sleep when a cold feeling rushed through his body. He woke up to complete darkness. Even the hallway was dark. He wondered if Charlotte had gone to bed. He looked over at the clock. It was three fifteen in the morning. He rubbed his eyes and continued to lay there staring up at the ceiling. Suddenly, the wind picked up through the window and blew across the room violently. Nathan sat up in fear as picture frames and loose objects from their shelves fell to the floor. Just then, Gabriel appeared by his bedside. "Get up, now!" He shouted over the wind.

Nathan froze, confused with what was happening. Then out of nowhere, a flash of blue light blinded them both. It illuminated the room numerous times until a figure appeared in the middle of it. Gabriel disappeared then reappeared in front of the light just as Charlotte busted into the room. She hurried behind Gabriel and covered her eyes. As the wind continued to pick up, she quickly gripped onto the Archangel's arm for stability.

"Nathan! Get up!" He shouted once more before the blue light ignited fiercely before them. Then everything went black and the wind came to a dead stop. It was silent.

Charlotte's hands continued to clench onto the Archangel's arm in fear. The moonlight shone directly through the window now and slowly the room became more visible to everyone. In front of them, was the silhouette of a man crouched over. He was holding something in his arms. Covered in blood and dirt, his beaten body looked like he'd been through a vicious fight. He slowly raised his head to the Archangel,

"I got her," he said, out of breath. "She's barely alive," Brushing the bloody hair back from the lifeless body in his arms, he revealed Sophie's beaten face.

Nathan leaped from the bed and ran to his side in horror.

"Give her to me," he said, carefully taking the body into his arms. Charlotte covered her mouth in fear.

"Sophie. Sophie, open your eyes," Nathan pleaded. The body was frail in his arms. "What's wrong with her? Why isn't she waking up?" He shouted.

Charlotte began to cry silently as she stepped past Gabriel towards them.

"If you knew what she has been through—what they did to her..." The strange man began. Nathan started to cry as he held the lifeless body in his arms. He lifted her up against his chest, kissing her head softly.

"Don't you die, Sophie. Don't you leave me! Do you hear me?" He said, sternly.

Gabriel slowly approached and knelt next to the body. He touched her forehead gently. His face was worried.

"Get her cleaned up," he said, calmly. "Let's get something into her system."

Nathan nodded lifting her up and heading straight for the bathroom. Charlotte watched as her friend lay close to dead in Nathan's arms.

Gabriel turned to her.

"Charlotte, go make her something easy to eat. Something you can feed to her and get some water too." He waited for Charlotte's reply, but she didn't move.

"Charlotte, now!" His voice chimed, snapping her out of her shocked state.

She quickly looked down at the man still crouched over on the floor below them. His eyes met hers. She froze again.

"Alex?" Her voice shook.

He half smiled, "Go, Charlotte. Do as Gabriel says."

17
The Aftermath

In the bathroom, Nathan carefully placed the body down to the ground, resting her gently against the tub as he reached over to turn on the water.

When the tub was full, he turned back to the tortured body. His hands shook as he gently removed her bloody torn clothes—one piece at a time. The cuts were everywhere. His thumb traced what used to be tiny, beautiful pink lips. He remembered how they felt. So soft and... He cringed. They were now cracked with tiny scabs from cuts that had attempted to heal. Her entire body lacked of hydration. Reaching down to the fragile hands he once knew, her nails were barely there. They were either torn away or extremely worn down and some of her fingers were broken too.

"Jesus Sophie," Nathan said, looking away. It made him sick to his stomach—the thought of her being tortured like this. Carefully, he lifted her body into the tub. The water immediately turned dark from the blood and dirt. With a small cloth, he began to wash the lifeless body, every inch of it, being extra careful on the areas with open wounds.

Slowly, with one hand behind her head and his other on her torso, he slid her body downward into the water to rinse the grime from her once long and beautiful flowing hair. When he was done, he lifted her from the water and wrapped her tightly in a plush towel.

Entering the bedroom, Nathan carried Sophie's body over to the bed and placed her down.

"Get her something to wear," Gabriel said, resting his hand on her cheek.

Nathan left her with him and quickly searched the drawers for something she might be comfortable in. He returned with a T-shirt and a pair of sleeping shorts. Gabriel turned as Nathan dressed her. He then wrapped her in a few warm blankets. Movement in the room startled Nathan for a moment, he had forgotten about the strange man that appeared with Sophie. Their eyes finally connected, "Alex?"

"Hey," He replied, with shaky hands. "I'm sorry I didn't get her to you sooner. She was really hard to find,"

"Alex," Gabriel spoke, "Go get cleaned up."

Alex nodded, then did as he was requested.

When the bathroom door closed, Gabriel turned back to Nathan. "This situation needs to be taken care of immediately. Next time, she will surely be dead." He said, "Move aside," Nathan backed away as Gabriel sat down next to the lifeless body. With his hand placed gently against her cheek, a small light began to glow against her face. He slowly moved the light over her cracked and scabby lips, they instantly healed—leaving nothing but a tiny scar. He then lifted each of her hands very carefully into his own, a second light lit up between them. Nathan watched as her nails began to grow back and the odd few broken fingers snapped back into place. Gently, he placed them back down and slid them under the covers.

"I cannot heal her completely, but this will help," he said, standing up from the bed. "I am more worried for when she wakes. She will not know where she is and it may cause terror in her. She won't be able to comprehend what happened and I fear she won't forget any of it anytime soon. But we can't take her back to the hospital anymore so you and Charlotte must care for her here. We must end this, Nathan. The sooner the better, for all our sake."

He crossed the room, then looked back once more from the

doorway. "I'll be back in the morning. You are safe for the night. Alex will stay with you. Rest with her. Try to make her as comfortable as possible."

Then he was gone.

Moments later Charlotte returned with a cup of soup and a bottle of water. She placed the tray on the nightstand and then sat down on the bed next to Nathan. The two of them stared at Sophie quietly.

"I'm sorry I didn't believe you," She whispered.

Nathan glanced at her.

"But this... This is too much." She said, "She doesn't deserve this. It's just Sophie. Goofy, sweet and loyal Sophie. She just wants to be happy. She didn't want a life like this. She deserves better, Nathan." She wiped her eyes, trying to hold back the tears.

"I know," He agreed.

Just then, Alex entered the room with a towel wrapped around his waist.

"How is she?" He asked.

"The same," Nathan replied, turning to him. "So... You're her spirit guide?"

Alex nodded. Nathan stared at him for a moment.

"Then thank you. Thank you for bringing her back to me."

"You're welcome," He replied with a slight smile. "Um, Nate...do you think you can lend me some clothes? Mine are sort of—"

"Sure." He replied, getting up from the bed and heading over to his drawers. He then handed Alex all the essentials.

Charlotte couldn't help but stare at Alex's perfectly sculpted body as he tossed on a shirt.

"I just wish I could've gotten to her sooner," he sighed. "In the morning, I'd like to speak with you both. You should know what they put her though, so you understand how to deal with her when she wakes. But for now, we all need some rest. She won't be waking anytime soon and you'll need your strength if you're going to continue to fight this."

Nathan nodded.

"Come on, Charlotte. Let them be." Alex said, pulling a pair of jeans up under his towel. "You need to rest too."

She looked down at her friend once more, then got up from the bed and followed him out of the room.

Nathan pulled the covers up tight around Sophie once again. Lying back in the bed next to her, he felt fear for the first time. He was scared—of her. Scared for what she may do when she woke up. He had no idea of what really happened in purgatory, but he knew it was bad—really bad, and what came next was going to be the hardest thing their relationship would ever face. He carefully pulled her body close against his. She was still—too still. Nathan's eye lids eventually grew heavy, and it wasn't long before sleep took him as well.

● ● ●

It was dark for only a moment until Gabriel lit up the room with candles. He had gotten Alex to research more into witchcraft, considering Nathan's first attempt to make contact was a success. He was hoping to find a spell that would hide them and their actions from the Archangels.

As expected, Alex succeeded in creating a secret room, hidden away from everyone and everything. Here they were safe to talk and plan their next move. Alex paced around the room with a single book in his hands.

"Alex, tell me what you did to find Sophie," Gabriel asked, demanding his attention. Alex stopped and turned to the Archangel.

"Well, I came across this type of bridge spell."

"Bridge spell?" Gabriel repeated.

"Yes. As you know because I am a spirit guide, I can enter the real world as a human or the supernatural world as a spirit. I am myself practically a bridge, so I thought this spell would work best for us. It enhances my abilities."

"Go on." Gabriel said, intrigued.

"So, when I read about this bridge spell, it spoke about mediums who wanted to cross into other worlds like purgatory or even heaven to make contact with the dead. They were spells only advanced mediums could cast. At first, they were used to help people, but then they became a game for some. They were not just talking to the dead but physically going there to see them."

Gabriel's eyes widened.

"They say, sometimes you leave your body entirely to go to these places. That there's even a risk of separating your soul from your body and with that, a possibility of losing yourself forever. I don't know why anyone would take that chance, but I figured in our situation, this was our only shot. So, I went ahead and cast it. Almost immediately I entered their world." Alex paused again, taking a breath.

"I'm not going to lie Gabriel, purgatory scared me. It was the most horrifying place I have ever seen. At first it starts off calm and interesting, just long enough to trap you. It messes with your mind. The spirits stuck in there—they're angry and vicious with revenge and hatred."

"Where was Sophie when you found her?"

"I searched for what seemed like forever. I felt like I was in there for years," He paused, his hands began to shake again. "It does that to you. It makes you think you've been gone for a long time, when truly it's been only a few minutes or days in the real world. That's one thing we need to watch out for when Sophie comes to. She will be under the impression that she had been tortured for many years when in fact, she was only there for a few weeks."

"Either way, long enough." Gabriel interrupted.

"Agreed." Alex replied, trying to regain his thought. "They chased me for what seemed like forever. Their long arms grabbed at me with razor sharp nails. They cut through my skin like butter. I just kept heading to the darker areas, thinking if Serena had her anywhere, it would be in the worst part there could be. I eventually came across an old, abandoned building. Once inside, the spirits taunting me stopped and all was silent."

Alex rubbed his arms, remembering the cold, eerie feeling

from that realm.

"I looked everywhere Gabriel—in every corner. Until finally, in the last room, I found her. She was tied to a hospital bed that was disgustingly dirty. It looked as if they had tortured her many times. They hadn't fed her or given her water in what seemed like months. She was already unconscious when I found her. I actually thought that she might have been… Anyways, I tried to revive her, but Serena showed up."

"Serena?" Gabriel repeated.

"Yes, but I felt as if she wasn't alone. I felt someone else there too. She kept whispering to someone, but I could only see her. At times, I could hear two voices at once when she spoke. It was if someone else was speaking through her. It was the scariest thing. I tried to get my bearings, but most of my powers were weakened in there."

Gabriel continued to listen attentively as Alex went on with his story.

"When I finally managed to get a few spurts of power, I fought back with everything I had and ripped Sophie from the bed and ran. She was like a banshee after us. The anger inside of her was horrifying. Even worse, the other spirits in there were feeding off of her energy. The moment you step into purgatory you feel every single emotion that each spirit in there has. Or at least I did, and it was overwhelming."

Gabriel stepped towards him and touched him on the shoulder. "Be calm, you are safe now."

"There's something else, Gabriel." He paused. "Those spirits, they look for the one with the most anger—the most sorrow. The one with the most power to feed off. That energy is spread throughout them all. They are constantly firing each other up like a wolf pack or something. They work together and they grow stronger with each spirit that enters purgatory and for someone like me—like us, we almost feel defeated the moment we enter into their world. They sense us. They taste our light and—"

Gabriel touched him again to calm him.

"I was running low on what power I had left, and they were

right on my tail. Every part of me was bleeding from them ripping at me as I ran with Sophie in my arms. Eventually they took me down." He stopped.

"Gabriel, there were like dogs, biting at us as if they hadn't eaten in months. It was so painful. I tried desperately to hang onto Sophie as they dragged her away from me. They were everywhere! I eventually tore myself from them and reached for Sophie's poor wrist. I was able to drag her up and take off again. With my last burst of energy, I cast my spell and prayed to God at the same time. I felt a sudden energy fill me, a warmth—I actually thought it was one of you..."

Gabriel looked at him oddly.

"Then I was here, with Sophie in my arms." He looked up at the Archangel sadly, "Somehow, it worked. I have no idea how, but somehow it did."

Gabriel crossed his arms in deep thought for a moment, then reached for the spirit guide again.

"You did very well, Alex. But now we need to make our next move. We need to stop Serena," he said, very clearly. "On our own,"

"Our own?" Alex repeated.

"Nathan may not be strong enough for this, I think its best if he stays out of it from now on. He needs to worry about Sophie. She's been through too much already and we are very lucky to have her back. We won't be so lucky next time." Alex nodded.

"Now that's a shitty thing to do, Gabriel—Angel of Mercy," Fate teased from behind. "You promised him that you would work together and now you're planning on sneaking behind his back to kill the girl he loves? Harsh." She snickered.

The two of them stood guard, startled by Fate's sudden appearance. She casually made her way towards them.

"So many lies in this world. People just can't seem to keep their word anymore,"

The Archangel's eyes followed her closely.

"Nice job, Alex. Very well played. Busting into purgatory like a knight in shining armor and saving the girl."

"What do you want, Fate?" Gabriel asked, impatiently.
He wondered how she was able to find them so quickly. They
were sure Alex's secret room was hidden from all—even her.
"Well, I was just listening in on Alex's story, it's good, huh?"
She smiled. "But I think you're missing one little detail
that Gabriel might find interesting," she said, staring at the
nervous spirit guide.
"I've told him everything," Alex managed to get out.
"Come on. Everything? Don't you think Gabriel may want to
know who he's really killing before he takes Serena out?"
"What are you talking about?" Gabriel replied.
"Go on, Alex. Tell him who was really in there with Serena..."
She urged.
The spirit guide's eyes shot to the Archangel.
"You might remember a young girl, named Anna?" She paused
for Gabriel's reaction.
The look in his eyes softened. "Anna?" He repeated, quietly.
"I knew you'd love this..." She smiled.
"Gabriel no," Alex said, cutting in before Fate could speak
again. "The only reason I didn't mention it was because I
know our task at hand. I thought that if you knew this, you
might become distracted and Sophie, she needed us!"
The Archangel's eyes changed again, they were disappointed.
"I know of your past with Anna. The Archangels told me the
day I was given to you. Michael warned me that a young girl
almost cost you your wings. He was just teaching me how
important my job was—that I mustn't ever get side-tracked,
which is what I was trying to do, Gabriel. I'm so sorry. But
Nathan is our priority here. If I had told you, your head
wouldn't be clear to fight."
"Enough Alex!" Gabriel growled. "Tell me everything."
The room was quiet—awkwardly quiet as the Archangel
awaited the new information.
Alex sighed, "When I told you that Serena was talking with
someone, I actually heard her call out to Anna. The two of
them know each other. They tried to mess with my mind—
both of them. They told me not to trust you, that you were

215

fated for evil. Anna said you made the wrong choice before with her and she ended up dead."

Gabriel's face was expressionless. He closed his eyes, trying to regroup his thoughts.

"I'm actually surprised you didn't sense this sooner, Gabriel." Fate interrupted, pleasantly. "You have the same look on your face now that Nathan once had when he first saw Serena. I guess you were too wrapped up in your precious Nathan to see the bigger picture here, huh?" She stepped closer to him. "Gabriel," She whispered. "I know what you think of this Nathan, what you think he might become..." She then straightened herself up. "I'm not stupid. ya know?"

The Archangel's eyes rose to meet hers as she turned from him.

"When will you damn angels learn that I allowed you to be here. I know everything that goes on in any realm. I see and feel every thought and emotion your silly human creations conjure up including your own. He will not become what you think and here's why," she said, turning back to the Archangel again. "Your precious humans are weak. They cannot survive the life I wield, so they will never grow strong enough to overcome me. Not ever." She assured him, then turned to Alex.

"You see, when Gabriel found his so called 'the one', I of course had to make my move and change Nathan's fate. So, I introduced to him Serena—for a very good reason too. Serena is very special but you don't know why, do you Gabriel? You thought you had lucked out with another possible pure heart. Didn't you?"

"What are you going on about, Fate?" Gabriel finally spoke, annoyed with the conversation. "Spit it out already! Enough games!"

"Serena! Oh my god, do I need to spell it out for you?" She snapped. "She's an ancestor of Anna's. Which is why I chose her. Their connection runs blood deep, making them quite a powerful team. I still can't figure out why you couldn't feel Anna when you were around Serena. Perhaps she kept herself hidden from you for a good reason. Clearly, she still has an effect on you—clearly, she's waiting for something." She said, noticing the change in the Archangel's body language. He wasn't standing as tall and strong as he usually did. He began to sweat and his breathing had picked up profoundly in the last few minutes. Fate smiled, pleased with herself.

"Perhaps she seeks revenge on you for abandoning her?" Alex's fist clenched as he watched Fate continue to taunt his leader.

"You see, it's quite beautiful—this game." She said, tossing back her long black hair from her shoulders. "I fed Nathan a new path with Serena. Then he died, which I thought might have put a damper in your plan, but then you went and made him a guardian." She huffed, crossing her arms at him. "Well played by the way. So I played my next hand and told Anna of Serena's sad story which only broke her tortured heart even more. Especially after I convinced Serena to kill herself." She smiled.

Alex stepped closer to Gabriel as the Archangel stared Fate down.

"But what surprised me, was how angry of a soul Anna actually was. She immediately latched on to Serena and now wields her hateful ways through her. Of course, only after I told her how Serena was connected to Nathan, and how Nathan was ultimately connected to you. We're all just tied together by a big red ribbon, aren't we my friends?" She laughed. "You see, Anna may not have been able to get to you as an Archangel, but she can definitely get to you through Serena, Sophie and Nathan."

Gabriel stepped towards her, but Fate's hand rose as she spoke again.

"I'm not done," she said, stopping the Archangel in his tracks. "Of course, when you made Nathan a guardian, I changed my hand again...I had an ace sitting in the wings." She smiled. "Sophie."

Gabriel froze.

"You would have never found such a pure heart on your own,

217

Gabriel. I keep most of those hidden from you Archangels. Why do you think they are so hard to find?"

Gabriel's fist tightened.

"Then you showed Sophie to Nathan as I hoped you would, thinking she was the one who was going to change him into what he needed to be next. It was just too easy to control you all and poor Sophie, being nothing but a pawn in this wicked game. She sure has taken a beating in all this, hasn't she?"

Alex quickly grabbed the Archangel by the arm.

"Gabriel, even if what she says is true... If you believe Nathan is the one, then he is." He said, sternly. "And even if she wielded this impossible chain of events, you could still change it. I know it. Don't let her distract you,"

Fate's eyes shot to the spirit guide and with one flick of her hand, she threw him across the room. He smashed against the wall, then hit the ground hard.

"He cannot change anything. He is blinded like Nathan and always will be. Think about it, Gabriel. You want to protect your precious Nathan, but to do so, you need to end Serena. But now she's much more than just Serena. Keep in mind that most of what Serena does is controlled by Anna. Which means that resolving Serena's issues doesn't just fall upon Nathan, but now you as well. And while the two of you are being stupid, little Sophie over there—the pure heart you've been looking for—is being torn apart and most likely will not survive this journey to the end. Sophie is fated to Nathan, who is fated to Serena, who is fated to Anna, who is in turn, is fated to you. Now you must make it through all of these connections before reaching your Sophie—who could change your Nathan into what you need him to be. The one that you think could change the world." She snickered. "Those chances are very minimal, Gabriel. You must know that? I've truly made the ultimate game."

"Why tell us all this?" Alex asked, getting up from the ground painfully and moving cautiously towards them again.

"Because, if you lay all your cards on the table, it makes for a much more exciting game. When people start to react in panic mode, the things they do—especially for love, are outstanding."

Alex looked at the Archangel again.

"So Gabriel, are you going to kill Serena then? Or should I say Anna, without resolving your issue?"

He didn't respond.

"You know, she thinks you don't love her. That you chose God instead, because you were afraid."

"Gabriel, don't listen to her. She's just trying to make this more complicated than it really is. We can figure this all out, I promise."

"Shut up boy," Fate snapped again.

"Enough!" Gabriel said, raising his voice. "I don't like to be played with. You've done your work here, Fate. Now go. I will make my choices. If it means I need to kill Anna to keep Nathan alive, then I'll do it. I will not be played with like a doll."

Fate stared at him with a grin.

"Finally, something out of you. Aright then boys, have fun with your magic games." Then she was gone.

Gabriel quietly turned to Alex,

"We will find a way to end them both. Nathan is our top priority—always. We must all make sacrifices in life to do what's right."

Alex nodded sadly.

"Continue your research. See if there's any possible chance of getting us both into purgatory. Perhaps together we will be stronger against the spirits. If we can get there, we could possibly end this by ourselves keeping everyone here in the real world safe.

"But Gabriel... the rules. The Archangels will—"

"Alex, do as I say. I know the consequences, and keep a close eye on Nathan and Sophie until I return. We have no other choice."

18
Witchcraft & Angels

The wind blew in hard throughout the abandoned building as Gabriel lit three candles behind him without a single touch. He then placed the scrying mirror in front of him and pulled out a small handmade necklace from his pocket. The string was knotted tightly together in a unique design that had a single bead in the middle. He held it tightly in his hands and stared into the black mirror. Minutes went by with no response. He knew by doing this that the Archangels would never forgive him, but there was so much happening now and this time, he did not want things to end the same way. Suddenly, a cool breeze circulated around him twice, then seemed to settle before him. He stared into the mirror as a landscape began to manifest in the glass. He recognized it immediately. It was the last day he spent with Anna. The day he told her he had to go. She was crying—begging him to stay. The image faded, then another appeared. The angel realm and Michael. He was scolding him. It changed once more, back to Anna in the woods. There were men following her, taunting her. She was running towards town for help, but before she could reach the tree line one of the men grabbed her. He couldn't hear the dialogue, but it got rough fast. He saw Anna struggling to break free from them. They persistently chased her into an open field and when they finally caught up to her, they toppled her to the ground. She was kicking and screaming, doing everything she could to get away from them. Their disgusting hands were all over her. The rage began to build inside of the Archangel as he watched on. Eventually, they beat her until she didn't move. Her lifeless body was on the ground—helpless and alone now.

He would never forget that horrible feeling in his gut that day. That inkling that led him to find her body, moments too late. The mirror went black again and Gabriel closed his eyes in pain. All these horrible images made him furious. Suddenly, a new image appeared in the mirror. This time it was Serena. She was looking straight at him.

"Now you've deceived everyone, haven't you?" She spoke. "Everyone you care about..."

He didn't answer her.

"What, nothing? Gabriel, the great Angel of Mercy has no words of wisdom to say? Do you feel bad about what you just saw? Are you regretting your choices now?"

He suddenly felt a presence. Turning quickly, he found Serena behind him.

"You know, when Anna first came to me, she told me her story. She told me everything about you. It was very surprising to think of an Archangel falling in love. A little unfair as well—for the one he is in contact with. To put someone through that, knowing you can never be with them is just selfish."

He still didn't speak.

"She's an ancestor of mine, you know." Serena paused. "It's unfair that two innocent women were treated like this."

Gabriel's expression softened.

"She said you planned it all," Serena's words caught him off guard.

"That you were waiting for Nathan to die all along. So not only did you allow heartache to an innocent soul once with yourself, but twice with Nathan and I—and by choice." She said, disgustedly.

"Not a very noble angel move, is it?"

"It's not like that." He finally said. "You do not understand.

There is something much bigger happening here,"
Serena turned from him.

"You know, when Nathan died, I felt like my whole world crumbled before me. I had no one." She said, sadly. "The night I decided to end my life, I heard a voice in my head. She spoke very quietly and clearly to me. I remember not being afraid at that moment. I was too far gone. Sitting in the bathtub with a blade at my wrist... The water had already turned cold. I had been there for almost three hours, pondering over what to do. She spoke of Nathan—"

"Serena that voice—" Gabriel interrupted, but Serena ignored him. Turning back to the Archangel, something changed in her eyes.

"She said if I killed myself, I could have a chance at being with him again. Anything, anything would be better than not having him at all. I wanted to take that chance. So I did."

"You should have lived out your life, Serena." Gabriel replied, stepping out from his barrier towards her.

"She said it would take a while and it did, but I finally found him. She also warned me that I would have some obstacles, one being you." She continued, taking a step back from him. "That I had to be very careful not to get caught by the Archangels."

"Serena, stop. You must understand that sometimes people are not meant to be together,"

"No, you don't understand!" She shouted. "You don't know what it's like having the person you love, the person who instantly changed your world, be taken from you out of nowhere with no explanation. She's the only one who gets me. Don't you understand the torment you have put upon us? Don't you see how it destroys a person's soul when you rip out their heart?"

"It is Fate," The Archangel's voice began to rise.
Serena quickly grabbed her chest,
"It hurts so badly inside. I would do anything to fix it—to make the pain stop." Her eyes met his again. "I need Nathan. He can make this go away. You can't stop me, not with Anna

222

by my side. Not unless you kill her too."

"My situation was complicated, Serena. You cannot compare it to yours. I was already an Archangel. I didn't mean to find her. It just happened. Neither of us are to blame for what happened," He sighed.

"I wanted Anna more than anything, but it just wasn't meant to happen. I serve God and that is my path. That is my fate."

"You choose your own destiny. You could have chosen her, but you didn't!"

"No, I couldn't!" He yelled defensively, then turned to walk away. The conversation was upsetting him now.

"So you choose to walk away again?"

The dueled voices made him stop in his tracks. Slowly, he turned to see Anna where Serena once stood. Her long Auburn hair flowed beautifully over her shoulders. Her earthy scent filled the air as she stepped closer to him. He watched as her hazel eyes glowed under her long, beautiful lashes.

He felt every defense mechanism inside of him begin to break down, piece by piece. She was beautiful. He stood perfectly still as she slowly came towards him. She stopped within arm's reach and looked up at him sadly.

"You left me," her voice broke. "You left me to die, Gabriel,"

His eyes closed, "I'm sorry," he whispered. "I'm so sorry."

He then felt her small delicate hand touch his cheek gently. It was cold.

"Look at me," she spoke again.

He swallowed hard, then opened his eyes to her.

"You can fix this. You can still be with me if you choose right this time." Her words were gentle and kind as she stared at him with hope.

"Don't be an Archangel, just be you. Then we can be together. Don't you want that? You've been alone for so long. Let me be with you, Gabriel. Please." She begged. Her hands slid over his firm chest as he stood his ground. Many thoughts raced through his mind—mainly how forbidden this moment was.

"You've already come this far—dark magic, lies…. Gabriel, it's like you've already chosen." She smiled. "Come be with me. It's what you were meant to do, that's why we are here now. This is our fate."

Her hands moved over his muscular shoulders and down his arms. She then laced her small fingers between his. He suddenly felt a little sluggish, like he was being pulled down to her. Her cool touch against his warm hands sent a shiver up his spine. He closed his eyes, trying to regain his thoughts, but she continued to pull at him.

"Gabriel, the great angel of Mercy..." She whispered, then leaned up and connected her lips to his. He felt his arms naturally slide around her waist and pull her body against him. With her fingers clasped around his neck she secured him in that moment. The taste of her lips, the softness of her skin as his fingers traced her bare arms were like a drug, he couldn't stop. Even if every fiber within him screamed to repel back— to get out of there—to remember who he was! A servant of God!

Suddenly, he felt her ripped from his grasp as loud thunderous sounds filled the room around them. His eyes opened and desperately began to search for her. A blinding light ignited in the middle of the room as a figure appeared before him. The two stood face to face as the light eventually dimmed.

"This is a new route for you, brother," Michael sighed. "Witchcraft? Making your spirit guide study into subjects that are forbidden by us? Why go to this extent?" He asked, approaching slowly. The room was silent now.

"We seem to have a bigger problem than anticipated, don't we?" He hinted, "I am thankful that you let your guard down with that girl. Otherwise, I would never have found you. I'm very disappointed, brother."

"I'm trying to help these spirits." Gabriel responded quietly. "They are lonely and deserve a fair passing, not one that is brutal and harsh as their past life."

"Kissing Anna, that's what you call helping? I do remember telling you once before that you were forbidden to ever see her again. Do you remember?" Michael asked.

"Of course, and I apologize," Gabriel lowered his head.
Michael began to pace around the magical barrier Gabriel had deactivated in his weakness seconds before. He studied the area, a little intrigued.

"If this Nathan is who you think he is, the prophecy could come true and we will all be set free." He stopped to look at Gabriel. "You cannot afford to mess this up. You are meant for more, just as Nathan. This is an easy choice."

Gabriel still didn't respond. Michael then made his way back to the Archangel.

"If the spoken day comes, we will be prepared to fight and we can only do so if we have everyone ready. We must stay on track. You are losing yourself to this girl again. I will not let the rest of us suffer for one angel's mistakes. Don't you see that I am trying to help you? Do not let her blind you."

Michael looked deeply into his brother's eyes.

"I have not lost my way." Gabriel spoke again, "I just wish to do both, and I truly believe there is a way to help them pass more peacefully but I need you to have faith in me and trust that I know what I'm doing."

Michael sighed again, "I saw what happened to that girl, Sophie."

Gabriel's eyes softened.

"Letting her get taken into purgatory, then sending your spirit guide in after her? Do you know how many laws you have broken? And do you know what could become of that girl when she awakes? She will not be the same person. You are bringing too much of the other side into this world. It will mess everything up and more importantly you could fall, Gabriel." He paused, letting his words sink in. Then his tone changed. "I should punish you now, before you can do anymore harm to us...."

Gabriel stood silently, staring back at the Archangel.

"Your Nathan he is barely holding himself together."

Gabriel agreed silently.

"You will lose him if you continue on like this. His mind and determination will be lost. We can't afford for any of that to happen, especially if he is who you think he is."

"I know." Gabriel replied. "I won't let him—"

"No, you won't." Michael interrupted. "We won't."

Gabriel looked back at him nervously.

"We will handle things our way from now on. I've tried to help you, to teach you, but you insist on doing things your own way. I have no choice but to show you differently now. Please know that this is only to protect our future. It's what's best for us all."

Gabriel's eyes widened, "Michael wait," He then searched the room for Anna. "Where is she?"

"Well, this feels a little like déjà vu, doesn't it?" A sudden voice piped up from behind.

Gabriel shot around to see the Archangel Uriel with Anna in his arms. She struggled beneath his strong grasp. Gabriel stepped toward him,

"Let her go. She is mine to deal with,"

"We warned you, Gabriel. We don't have time to play. There is a prophecy we must try to fulfill, remember? You said it yourself. She needs to go, so I'll gladly take care of her for you," Uriel smirked, pulling her chin up and preparing to snap her neck.

Anna's eyes grew wide. Although a spirit like her could not be killed with such an easy attack, it would definitely bring her great pain. Especially from Uriel.

Gabriel bolted at the Archangel just as his fingers began to tighten around the girl but was quickly snagged from behind by Michael who tossed him to the ground. He shot back up and went directly towards Anna again.

"Do not make us fight you, brother," Michael said, appearing between them. Gabriel skidded to a stop.

"Please, I can't let her go through this again," Gabriel begged, then noticed the blank stare in both his brother's eyes. He knew what that meant. He had no choice, "I'm sorry..." was all he said. He then raised his hands, but before he could ignite his energy, Michael blasted him back.

Thrown hard to the ground, Gabriel suddenly found himself

underneath Michael as he raised his hand again—prepared to
fight until a tiny red ribbon wrapped quickly around Michael's
neck and yanked him back. Another beam of light shot across
the room. This time from Uriel as he tried to break Michael
free from the hands of Fate. Anna scrambled to get to her
feet. Gabriel reacted immediately and appeared by her side.
She clung to him desperately, trying to catch her breath. He
watched as the two Archangels and Fate went head-to-head.
Blasts of light were no match for Fate's disappearing act. She
was nearly impossible to catch. He worried for his brothers
as he watched them fail with each attack they attempted. He
needed to help them.

Appearing behind Fate, Gabriel grabbed onto her just as she
turned. Her long thin hands clenched onto him and threw him
like a rag doll over her shoulder. He tumbled across the floor
and skidded to a stop. Before he had a chance to get up, Fate
was on top of him—pinning him down. Staring deep into his
eyes, she warned him very clearly,

"Do not fight me you ignorant man. I'm helping you, can't
you see that?"

His eyes tightened in disbelief. "Why would you help me?" He
asked, gripping onto her wrist. Her fingers tightened around
his neck. She smiled, then her eyes shot to the left, then back
to the right as his brothers charged from both sides.

They gripped onto her for only a second before she launched
herself back, taking the two of them with her. Their bodies hit
hard against the back wall as Fate landed strategically on her
feet again. She was fast and agile like a cat.

"Come on boys, give me a little more of a challenge." She
snickered, dusting the dirt from her tall black boots. She then
slowly crouched over as if she was beginning a race and took
off towards them again. Gabriel quickly got to his feet and
appeared between Michael and Uriel as Fate charged them.
Just as she was about to reach them, she vanished into thin air.
Their eyes searched the room, but found no trace of her—or
Anna. Gabriel hurried over to the place she stood last. Fate
reappeared again, surprising the Archangel and slamming him

back against the wall. Her fingers laced around his neck with one hand. In her other, was a thin red ribbon. She released him for only a second to take hold of the other end of the ribbon. She then stretched it out long against his skin. He didn't dare swallow or move an inch. For this one item, this one small insignificant little ribbon had seen many deaths by her hands. The Archangels watched many lives end with a single slice.

"I could end you now if I wanted to," she said, a little winded. "Choose your side, time's running out."

Suddenly, Fate's head was ripped back with a quick jerk. She roared, twisting herself around to the boy behind her. Immediately, her hand reached out and grabbed Alex by the chest. Her fingernails dug in through his shirt and into his skin. He crippled over in pain.

"Watch how you touch me," She warned, then released her hand from his chest and gripped onto his neck. She raised him from the ground, his feet dangling in the air now.

The three Archangels charged, but just before they reached her, she disappeared from sight—dropping Alex's body hard to the ground. Behind them, the sound of shattered glass startled them. The scrying mirror was smashed into a million pieces. Alex's eyes grew wide as he tried to catch his breath.

"Don't you see what you have gotten yourself into, brother?" Michael pleaded. "This will surely end badly for us all."

Uriel carefully made his way around the magic circle. The candles were blown out and the shattered glass had somehow managed to remain within the protective barrier.

Michael appeared by his brother, "Don't touch it. The darkness still lingers," he said. They both took a step back. Michael then glanced back at Gabriel and Alex, silently pleading with them to listen to his words. Uriel stepped towards them again clearly upset.

"Come brother," Michael said, touching his arm gently and stopping him in his tracks. "We have business to attend to." Uriel snarled, then they were gone.

Gabriel quickly turned to Alex and held out his hand. "Are you alright?" He asked, pulling him up from the ground.

"I'm fine." He replied.

Gabriel reached out and touched Alex's chest gently. With a soft glow, the Archangel's energy healed the wounds.

"I wish you would've told me what you were going to do. I would have helped you, Gabriel."

"Thank you." He replied, "But it was a stupid mistake. Let's move on." He then rested his hand on the spirit guide's shoulder as they began to leave.

"I really could have helped you." Alex repeated.

"I know, next time." Gabriel smiled.

19
The Awakening

Nathan and Charlotte stayed close over the next few days watching Sophie sleep. They took turns, feeding and hydrating her as Gabriel suggested. The body seemed to be healing, but the mind—it was hard to tell.

Charlotte was more than overwhelmed. Everything had changed in her life, instantly. It seemed very unfair to both her and her best friend. She still couldn't wrap her head around it all, but it didn't matter what she thought, there were bigger things happening now. The more she watched over her friend, the more her job and personal life suffered. She told lie after lie, trying to hold onto everything she could—even her relationship. Matt soon became very suspicious about her absence. He didn't understand why he couldn't spend time with her, especially if she was going through so much personal stuff as she said she was. Eventually, he got fed up and it ended their relationship.

Nighttime was the hardest for her. For at night, Charlotte thought about her hopes and dreams. She thought about all that she had worked for to get to where she was today. But every time she thought about her future, she worried more about what supernatural being might appear in those moments now and who was physically around her each day that she couldn't see? It made her anxious—about everything. It felt impossible to wish for a normal life now, especially for her best friend. It was unfair for anyone to be put through this much in life. It was too much drama, too much stress and mostly—not enough love to make someone feel worth something. The world around her was so much different now. There was no going back to the way things used to be, ever again

●●●

His eyes opened to a familiar bathroom—Serena's. He was in the same spot he sat when he took care of her the night of the attack. In the tub, was the bloody water left over from her beaten body. He leaned over, the sour smell of the water made him cover his mouth in disgust. Slowly, he reached out towards the water to see if it was really there when suddenly, the touch of a hand on his shoulder startled him. He fell back in fear as a young woman stepped in front of him. She was beautiful, but not Serena.

"Hello Nathan," she said, politely.

He stared back at her, "Who are you?"

As she knelt down in front of him, he slid slightly back from her on the floor. She smiled, clearly entertained.

"My name is Anna."

"Anna?" He repeated. "Gabriel's Anna?"

She smiled, "Gabriel's Anna... Hmm, that's nice sounding. Does he call me that?"

He didn't respond. Anna continued to stare at him. Nathan sat still, unsure of what to say next. Tucking her long hair behind her ear, Nathan noticed how pale her skin was. It was much fairer than Serena's and she was dressed much differently too. Her garments seemed to be close to the 1900's era.

"Nathan, do not be afraid of me." She said, interrupting his thoughts. "I am here to help you."

"Help me, with what?"

"Serena." She replied. "She told me your story, it's very tragic. I'm so sorry for what you had to go through together. It's not very fair, is it?" She stated with an understanding voice.

"No, it wasn't," he agreed.

She tilted her head and blinked twice. Her hazel eyes were bright and ghostly looking staring back at him. For a moment, he felt as if he recognized her from somewhere, but where? "Do you know who I am? I mean, other than Gabriel's Anna?"

"I'm sorry, I don't."

Her arms wrapped around her knees like a child. Her long, cream-colored lace dress barely touched the floor, exposing her very white feet.

"I am an ancestor of Serena's, and I want to help you both any way that I can because I too have been through the same thing—with Gabriel." She sighed. "It was unfair how your story ended and it can really take a toll on someone when they have unfinished business. It can make the spirit angry and sad. I don't want that for Serena. Do you?" She asked, reaching out to touch his knee but he moved back again. She sighed, a little insulted. Nathan's eyes softened, he then slid a bit closer to her, making her head raise again.

"So, you want to help me make Serena understand and pass on?"

"In a way, yes." She smiled, "I've come to you because I want to offer you a choice,"

He looked at her oddly.

"Serena and I are stuck here in purgatory, and I know you've been searching with Gabriel, trying to make contact, correct?"

He nodded.

"Well, you're missing one important thing..."

He waited patiently.

"Me." She spoke, softly. "Well technically, any supernatural spirit can help you, but they must have access to both sides and not an angel. They don't count. That's why you haven't been able to get here yet. Gabriel is not allowed. So if you want to save Serena, you will have to come to purgatory on your own and I can help you with that."

"But Alex, he was able to—"

"No." She interrupted, harshly. Her face was tense. She took a breath and spoke again. "I mean, he cannot go back. He will not survive a second round. No one does."

"Then how?" He asked.

She held out her hand to him.

"All you must do is come with me, I'll take you there. Together we will find her."

"Right now? It's as simple as that?" He said, doubtfully.

"Yes, with me it is."

"Where's Serena now?" He asked.

"She's stuck there, waiting for you. She really needs you, Nathan." Her hand dropped to her side. "She loves you more than anything in the world. You owe it to her to get her out of there."

"There—as in purgatory?" He repeated.

"Yes," she answered again.

"But you're here now, and I've seen Serena in real life... so why can't she just come out?"

Anna rose from the ground. "Because we are only able to latch on for short periods of time, then we are sucked back. That's why we need your help to bring us out permanently." She insisted.

"Us?" Nathan repeated.

Anna paused to regroup, then smiled,

"Yes. Us. I too want to pass on, Nathan. I want to help her understand so she doesn't get stuck there and tormented like I have been for many years. Please say you'll help us. I've tried to contact Gabriel, but the Archangels are always there. I need a proper passing, a beautiful one, as does Serena. We deserve it, don't you agree?" She begged.

Nathan thought about it for a moment. He knew the Archangels would never agree.

"What should I do about Gabriel? I'm sure if he knew, he would want to help—"

"No. Only you." She quickly cut him off. "Like I said, angels cannot go there. It's forbidden. You don't need to inform him. There's no point. He will only try to stop you. If you truly want to save Serena, this is the only way. It has to be you and you alone." She begged again.

He thought long and hard for a moment. Could he really do it on his own? As confident as he was about helping Serena, he worried about everything else in there he had to face—as a human—not an angel.

"I need some time." He spoke again. "I can't leave Sophie on her own. Let me get her settled with someone, then I'll go."

"No! There isn't enough time for that. Forget about Sophie. Soon Serena will be nothing if you leave her there too long. You must act now. My offer is for now," Anna quickly held out her hand again. Nathan rose to his feet.

"Please, give me a few days. I'll go, I swear. I won't tell Gabriel or Alex. It will just be me, and I'll help you both. I promise."

He did want to help Serena. He wanted to help them both if he could and secretly, he feared that this might be the best shot he was going to get to sneak into purgatory. Anna was right, Gabriel would never let him go alone. He would only try and stop him. He had no choice but to keep this quiet.

"Fine," Anna replied. She then reached into the right pocket of her frail vintage dress and pulled something out.

"Here, take this." In her hand was a small brownish-red bead. "When you're ready, go somewhere alone so no one can see you. Hold this bead tightly in your hand and call for me." She grabbed his hand and pushed the bead into it. "It will open a portal for you and I will be waiting on the other side, but I suggest you hurry. You don't have much time left and neither do we."

He could barely hear her last few words as she faded away, then he woke.

●●●

Daylight shone through the bedroom windows making his eyes squint from the light. Sophie was still asleep against him. He opened his hand. There inside was the bead. He carefully leaned over, opened the nightstand drawer and placed it inside. It would be safe there for now. He then heard the front door. It had to be Charlotte. He had given her a key to come and

go as she pleased. He listened as she made her way down the hallway towards their bedroom. She knocked on the door.
"Come in,"
"Hey Nate, how's she doing this morning?" She asked, sitting down on the edge of the bed
"No change," Nathan sighed, stretching out.
"This doesn't seem right. Shouldn't she be awake by now?" Nathan didn't answer.
Charlotte hesitated for a moment, "What if she doesn't wake up?" She said, looking up at him.
"We can't think that way," He replied, slipping out from under the covers. "Look, I'm going to have a shower and freshen up. Can you stay with her?"
"Sure," She answered. Quietly, she climbed into the bed and rested her head down on the pillow facing her friend. She watched her breathe silently and slowly.
"Come on Soph, wake up. I need my best friend back,"
No response came from the lifeless body in front of her. Charlotte listened as Nathan turned on the shower. She continued to talk to her friend, but nothing changed. The others had said this was pointless, but it made Charlotte feel better if she talked to Sophie as if she was awake. Her eyes soon became heavy and just for a moment, they closed.

It seemed like only a second had passed when she opened her eyes again, this time to the not so lifeless body staring back at her. Startled, Charlotte flew back on the bed then fell to the ground. Slowly, she got up and peeked over the edge of the mattress.
I stared at her. The vision took a moment to become clear in my mind, then I recognized her.
"Sophie?" She said, quietly, "You're awake..."
Sophie... That's my name. My name is Sophie—I think.
I watched her eyes began to water.
"It's me," She spoke again. "It's Charlotte. You're back home with Nate and I. Every thing's going to be okay,"
Back at home? Charlotte... Nate?

235

His name made me flinch.

"How are you feeling? Do you need anything?"

I didn't respond.

"Sophie?"

The moment her hand reached for me I shot back in the bed— my body vibrating in fear.

"Okay, okay. Sorry." She froze. "I didn't mean to scare you. It's okay. I won't touch you. Let's just talk, alright?"

Talk? They had never talked this much before, not before everything changed. Not before the pain... My body tensed up as the sound of a door opening stole my attention—*Nathan.* His vision made me gasp. I knew what was coming next. *Not him...he's the last thing before... Before the pain came. He brought the pain. I can't. Not again!*

"Sophie?"

Before he could take another step towards the bed, I let out a horrifying scream. Charlotte covered her ears in fear as he darted around the bed. I scrambled back against the headboard, then fell hard to the floor with a thump. I scurried back into the corner of the room, curling my legs up tight into my chest.

"Don't touch me! Don't touch me! Please don't touch me!" I screamed.

"Nathan stop!" Charlotte yelled. "You're scaring her!"

I wanted him to disappear before what came next. There was always something next.

"Sophie," he said, calmly. "Sweetie it's me, Nate."

Nate... No. His vision only came with pain, the pain was coming. I can't listen to him. I began to scratch my skin. It burned. He reached for me again,

"Don't touch me," I repeated.

"Soph, it's me." He begged, "You're safe. You're home. This is your bedroom,"

That's what he said last time. It's never home and I am never safe. My chest began to heave. I was having a hard time breathing. Just do it already. Get it over with. This vision was too long—too painful already.

"You're safe, we promise." Charlotte spoke up, moving in closer. "Let us help you, please. No one will hurt you."
Lies.
Just then a blinding light lit up the room and two visions appeared within it.
"Don't push her or she'll crack," a voice said.
I know that voice.
Nathan slowly reached out again, I screamed bloody murder the moment he touched my arm. He struggled to hang onto me as I fought back against him kicking, screaming, scratching and pushing him away with all my might, but he kept at me.
"You make me sick," I said sharply, then spit at him.
He stopped, staring back into my horrified eyes.
"Stop it! Stop looking at me! Kill me already!" I growled.
I gripped onto my hair and began to pull, grunting in pain before him. *Hurry up, end this!* My hands then dropped to my bare legs, where my nails began to dig into the skin.
"Sophie, stop!" He shouted.
Why wasn't this ending? Why wasn't he dead by now? Where was she?
"I can't... I can't do this anymore." I cried.
Everyone was too quiet, they kept staring at me. Why were they staring at me? I wanted them out of here—now!
"Don't touch me. Don't touch... me," I repeated, numbly.
Nathan turned. "Help her, Gabriel!" He pleaded.
The Archangel stepped forward, but another man quickly intervened. Slowly, the strange man approached.
My eyes grew wide the closer he got.
You...I know you.
He crouched in front of me, forcing fake Nathan to release me and take a few steps back. I continued to scratch and dig at myself as my eyes locked on his. *Those eyes, I've seen them...*
His hand touched mine.
Dirt, the dirt, the bed, it was him. He hurt me, he ripped me from the bed. He was there, with them....
Just as the man brought his other hand forth, I belted out again. My scream pierced the room and even frightened

myself. He suddenly shouted over it, grabbing onto my arms. "Sophie!"

I continued to scream.

"Sophie, look at me." He shouted, again.

No, no, no, they're coming. He was there before. They were fighting over me—pulling at my body—the pain. So much pain!

"Sophie, look at me now!"

This time, the sound of his voice sent a jolt through my body and silenced me.

His voice. My teary eyes opened again to him.

His face, he wasn't...

"That's it... You know me, Soph." He said, very calmly. "I helped you. Remember?"

Helped me?

"Think hard. I was there with you, fighting for you." He continued.

Fighting for me—with me?

"You're okay." He said, "You're home now, for real this time. It isn't a vision. It isn't a trick."

A trick...

"You know me..." He repeated.

"I know you..." I repeated.

Alex.

His hand touched mine again.

"Alex," I cried aloud. He smiled back at me.

I immediately fell into his arms and held on for dear life. He was there, fighting for me—fighting with me. He pulled me away from them. The warmth of his familiar body comforted me. I had been in his arms before. I remembered now. My nails dug into his shoulders. I needed to feel him deeply. I needed to know he wasn't going to diminish beneath me. He didn't.

I could smell him. I could feel him breathing too.

"I'm real...and I'm not going anywhere." He said, stroking the back of my head. I wanted him to hold on tighter. I needed to feel more. I wanted him to crush me in his arms. This feeling was unlike anything I'd felt before. His hand held the back of my head so gently it made me cry with happiness, even harder than I thought possible. I couldn't possibly be safe, but this moment was too real, he was too real. I couldn't let it go.

I eventually looked up from his embrace as Charlotte glanced over at Nathan. They didn't seem real to me yet. I couldn't let my guard down.

"Don't take offense to this, Nathan." Alex then spoke, "Sadly, each of you were used in a game to torment her every second in there. First appearing as someone she loves, a casual setting like this, then ultimately turning into a spirit that would tear her apart. She watched all of you torn apart, dismembered and killed right before her eyes many times. Any contact in there only brought profound pain, no matter how wonderful it looked at first. She can't trust what she sees right now, even you Gabriel." He spoke.

His voice was soothing.

"I wasn't a big part of her life. So, I was never a vision in her torture. They couldn't use me in their game, understand?" He asked, looking back at them

I couldn't make sense of what Alex was saying.

"You must work with her slowly for she will think that everything is not what it seems for a while still."

"Are you saying... she sees me as a threat?" Nathan finally said.

"Possibly," Alex replied. "Who knows what she's seeing. Her mind could conjure up anything at this point. We can't even begin to imagine or understand what she's seen or been through."

I watched as fake Nathan's eyes changed before me. They became tense and upset.

"I would never hurt her. I just..."

Charlotte made her way over to Nathan and rested her hand on his arm.

"Nathan, why don't you let me speak with her for a moment, alone." Alex then suggested. "Let's not overwhelm her right away,"

I gripped onto Alex tighter, still worried for when things would change.

"What's the big secret? Why don't you just talk to her right here in front of us?" Nathan said, suspiciously.

I don't like his tone.

Suddenly, the Archangel appeared before him. His quick movement startled me.

"Slowly, Gabriel." Alex reminded.

The Archangel looked at us, then back to Nathan.

"We understand how badly you want to see Sophie, but right now she doesn't recognize you and you're scaring her." He paused, looking over at Charlotte who was in tears now. He then touched each of their shoulders.

"We need to get some information out of her that she might not say if she's around the two of you. It's nothing personal. Please, wait for us in the kitchen."

Nathan didn't move. He continued to stare at me. I didn't like him staring at me. I wanted him to leave.

"Scaring her?" He huffed.

I tucked myself into Alex again.

Gabriel's hand tightened on his shoulder, "Nathan, every thing's going to be fine. Let us help her." The Archangel repeated, "Please, trust us."

Trust, there's no trust. All lies!

"It will only take a moment," Alex assured him. "Then I'll bring her out to you."

Why was he still staring at me?

Slowly, Nathan stepped back and headed towards the door with Charlotte close behind.

"Wait," Gabriel said, calmly. "Charlotte, can you please make her some tea for when we come out?"

She nodded, then gave Nathan a little push to exit the room.

I felt his body adjust beneath mine until he was sitting on the floor. I was still in his lap, arms laced around his neck.

"You did it..." He whispered. "You made it back to us."

I couldn't open my eyes. His warmth, his voice was too intoxicating. It felt good, it felt right, but mostly—safe.

As long as I heard his voice, I knew they couldn't get me.
"You came back for me…" I said, my voice was shaking.
"Of course," He replied, stroking my hair.
I didn't want to let go or open my eyes. I just wanted to feel what I felt in his arms from here on out, until it was over. But suddenly, I felt him loosening his grip on me. I tightened mine, making him gasp a little.
"Sophie," he whispered. "I need for you to listen to me like you did before. Do you remember?"
No, I can't remember. I need quiet.
"You need to listen very carefully, even if you don't believe me right now. I need you to open your heart and listen to my voice. You can do it? You've done it before, in there. Do you remember?" He asked again.
Listen, with my heart…
I nodded in his arms, opening my eyes to him. I remembered his voice, even when I couldn't see him. I could hear him, I could feel him close by.
"I didn't let you down before and I won't let you down now. I'm going to help you get through this. You can trust me. I'm your spirit guide. I will always protect you."
His words. *I trusted these words.*
"No one will take you from us ever again. Do you understand?"
Don't let them take me…
"As long as you hear my voice, you're safe. Know that I am always real to you, Sophie."
I nodded. His words lit up my heart. I hadn't felt my heart react like this in a very long time.
"Gabriel is here too," He then said, "The real one."
My eyes shifted to the large man standing off to the right of us. I felt Alex's hand touch my chin, bringing me back to him.
"He's here to help, so you need to tell us what happened in there. I know it's hard and scary, but you can help us end this. It's what you want, isn't it? For none of this to ever happen again—to have your normal life back?" He smiled, brushing his thumb across my cheek.

I felt my eyes begin to tear up. It hurt so badly inside.
The pain. Stop the pain. Make it stop. Don't let them take me.
"And when we are done, if it is still too much to bear I will erase it all. Everything. Any memory of being in that horrible place will be pulled from your mind.
"Why not now?" I said, aloud. "Take it away now...please." I begged. His eyes softened.
"I can't, not yet."
"Why?" I said, tightening my grip on him.
"Because we need your help to finish this and unfortunately," he paused looking deep into my eyes, "You aren't in the right frame of mind to decide this yet. I don't want you to give up so easily, Sophie. Please, trust me."
I looked back to the Archangel, a new feeling filling my chest. A painful one. *Lies.*
"You..." I snarled at the Archangel. "You said that you would protect me, that I should trust you." I clenched my chest, the words were hard to say aloud. "You let them take me. You let her take me!"
"I know." Gabriel replied quietly. "I'm truly sorry, Sophie." He stepped towards me. "There were some things I did not see. Things I should have been ready for. I have no excuse."
Lies.
"I just thank God that we have you back. I will not let you down again. I swear on my life."
"God? What God?" I said, disgustingly. "I saw no God where I was."
The Archangel's eyes frowned at me.
"There is no God," I repeated.
He didn't respond, but I didn't care. He was wrong. He let me down. I couldn't trust him anymore. *There is no God.*
"I'm sorry for all that you've been through," He spoke again.
Lies...
"I will do my best to regain your trust back if it's the last thing I do."
I shook my head no then glanced back to Alex. My hands were still tightly gripped to his shirt.

"Sophie, you must tell us everything you can. Do you remember how you got in there?" He asked, touching my hand that began to scratch at my arm. I fought back, pushing his away, then eventually stopped for a moment in thought.

The hospital, the bed—her...

"I just woke up there. One minute I was in the hospital and the nurse, she gave me my sleeping medication. The next minute I woke up..."

Her! Spirits, blood...their nails!

My fingers began to scratch at my neck, I remembered her grip. She strangled me. Alex's hand rose again to pull mine down.

"One thing at a time," Gabriel said, "Be calm."

My eyes shot at him just as a glass of water appeared in his hand. He extended it towards me.

Pondering for a moment, I cautiously reached for it. My hands were shaking. I snagged it and attempted to chug it down. I was so thirsty, but the water burned my throat, making me cough some of it back up. Alex removed the glass from my hand and handed it back to Gabriel.

I gripped desperately back onto him.

"I don't want to talk about this," I begged. "Please,"

"I know, but you must." He replied.

No, she will hear. She will hear us.

"Do you trust me, Sophie?" Alex asked again.

My fingers laced again into my hair, tugging at the strands.

"Stop," he repeated, pulling my hands down. "Calm down,"

My eyes began to search the room. Alex touched my face again. "Look at me."

My eyes moved again as the Archangel stepped back from us.

"I'll leave her with you. Perhaps she will do better without me here." He suggested. "I'm going to check on the others. Bring her into the kitchen when she's ready. Let's feed her and get her some more water."

Alex nodded as Gabriel left us alone. An immediate weight lifted from my shoulders and I fell back into Alex's chest.

In the kitchen, Nathan paced quietly around the room as Charlotte made tea. When Gabriel finally entered, he ran to him.

"How is she? What did she say?" He asked, anxiously.

"Calm down, Nathan. She's speaking a bit, but she gets easily overwhelmed and having you like this won't help her. You need to be as normal as possible, so pull yourself together." Charlotte brought the tea over to the table and sat down.

"How long will it take for her to feel safe around us? It feels horrible that she sees us as a threat."

"There's no telling, that depends on her and how we work with her. There are no guarantees with any of this but Nathan, you need to make her trust you again if you are to end up together. You must be patient. You too Charlotte, she needs you both."

"This is bullshit. Why can't you just leave her with me? She knows me and I know if we had time alone, she would feel that connection again. Please!" He begged. "I know her, I know she'll come back to me. You can't keep her from me!"

"Nathan, sit down. Now!" Gabriel demanded, startling the two humans.

Charlotte reached over and touched Nathan's arm as he sat down in the chair next to her.

"She'll be fine Nate, she'll remember soon. She loves you." She assured him, but his eyes were fixed on the Archangel.

"Please Gabriel, let me see her." He begged, again.

"Be patient," He repeated. "Alex must help her come to terms first. She needs to understand that it is you and not a dream."

"Yes, and I'm sure she'll want to be with you right away as soon—"

"Charlotte, she won't even touch me!" Nathan snapped. "This is killing me to sit here and watch this. I just need to talk to her by myself. I can get through to her, I know it." He repeated, getting up from the table.

"Nathan, sit down please." Alex demanded calmly entering the kitchen.

Nathan did as he requested, watching our every move. I held tight to his arm as he guided me in. The sight of Nathan made me nervous again. He directed me towards the kitchen table. Charlotte quickly stood up and pulled out her chair.

"Here Soph, sit," she said, politely. "Drink some tea. It's your favorite."

Tea... I like tea? I can't remember.

Slowly, I sat down. They continued to stare at me. It was making me anxious. I felt Alex's hand pull from mine and I was forced to sit on my own.

"Sophie was able to give me a bunch of information that we could use to our advantage." He said, calmly. "She's still a little on edge, so please have patience with her and Sophie, you need to remember that Charlotte is your very best friend. You can trust her,"

Charlotte, my best friend.

"And Nathan, he is your boyfriend." He then said, making my eyes shift to his across the table from me. His eyes were beautiful—too beautiful—too real. *He's too close.*

"You love them both, very much,"

I felt myself growing tense in the chair. It was too open here. Too many people were around me. There was too much pressure in my head, it was beginning to hurt. I pressed my forehead down into the palms of my hands.

"You guys may need to remind her of this a few times. She's probably going to have a few more episodes that throw her back into that world."

My fingernails began to dig into my forehead. Alex reached down and touched the back of my head. "Don't do that," He whispered.

My head raised once again to Charlotte who sat down directly across from me—beside Nathan. Her smile was faint and just as scared as I was feeling. I could see it. I was scared just looking at her. Then I heard Alex's voice again.

"You can't let her out of your sight. Not for a minute and you must bear through her bad moments. It's very important that you all become her rock."

Nathan.

I felt my eyes adjust to his again, the one I feared the most right now. He always made it turn on me. He made me feel the most pain. I wanted desperately to look at him, but at the same time, I didn't want to see him at all. I felt a sickening feeling creeping up inside of me. I wanted to rip it out. My fingers gripped onto the table and my nails began to dig into the wood.

"It's your fault," I said under my breath, then looked up at Nathan. Everyone was silent.

"You did this to me,"

"Sophie..." He began.

The look in his eyes confirmed that this was not my Nathan in front of me. He was different. He was much colder. My Nathan would've had sweet words to calm me. He always knew what to say. He always knew what to do. This was not my Nathan. The twisted feelings inside of me made me cripple over in pain like a horrible stomachache.

"Soph," Nathan spoke again, reaching out for my hand.

"Don't touch me!" I screamed in fear. "I hate you,"

Then I felt a huge lump choke up my throat, stopping me from saying anything more. I began to sweat profoundly. It pushed its way up and out of my mouth. I threw up everywhere on the floor. My hands shook as I gripped one onto the table and the other to the back of the chair trying to stabilize my trembling body. My stomach was rejecting the little bit of water I had earlier. In the corner of my eye, I saw Charlotte jump up from her chair in fear.

"I can't do this," My head hung low, "It hurts so bad."

Then I felt Alex's presence by my side again. His hands laced through my hair, pulling it back from my shoulders. I wiped my mouth, disgusted with myself—embarrassed.

"Alex," I pleaded. "Please, make it go away. Erase my memories. Erase everything. I don't want to remember anything or anyone. I just want this gone." I begged again but choked on the vomit rising up in my throat a second time. I threw up again, continuing to cry as he rubbed my back.

Please stop this...

My eyes rose again to Nathan slowly backing away from the

table. He then exited the room. I sat quietly, trying to catch my breath. Alex sat down in front of me, being cautious of where he stepped.

"He didn't... He didn't—die." I managed to get out.

Alex stared back at me, a slight smile on his face.

"No, and he won't because he's real Sophie. He's really there. You don't need to be afraid of him, or anyone else in this room. It's over now."

Lies...

I knew that part wasn't true.

20
The Uprising

"Nathan, you mustn't get upset." Gabriel said, entering the bedroom after him. "That's not Sophie talking back there,"
"Of course it is!" Nathan shot back. "If Sophie hadn't met me in the first place, none of this would be happening to her,"
"She would also be dead by now, Nathan." Gabriel reminded. "Remember that. If she didn't have her guardian angel her depression would have taken her eventually. She would've killed herself. She was doomed either way—until you. Always remember that. You two keep each other alive. You need each other."
"She's almost gone, Gabriel. That's not my Sophie in there." Sitting down on the edge of his bed, his head fell into his hands. "I did this to her. I did this, and I don't know how to fix it."
"It will take time, but you will get her back." Gabriel assured him. His hand rested on Nathan's shoulder.
"She will most likely have more bad days than good still to come and she will surely have many more mean words to say to you, but you must not forget the real person she is inside. She loves you more than anything. You are her world as she says," Gabriel smiled trying to cheer him up.
Nathan wiped his eyes then brushed the Archangel's hand from his shoulder.
"I'm sorry, Gabriel. I can't just sit around here and do nothing," he said, getting up from the bed.

"Nathan, it's better if you just wait. Be calm. We will find an answer."

"But Sophie won't even look at me, do you get how that feels? I feel like we are losing everything that is special about us. Everything that holds us close. I feel her slipping away from me and you want me to do nothing?"

Before the Archangel could respond, a loud crash came from the kitchen. Nathan turned and raced down the hallway.

Gabriel appeared just as he reached the kitchen. The Archangel disappeared, then reappeared in front of Charlotte. I pulled a knife on her.

She's moving too quick. Something isn't right. She's one of them, she's going to change…

I felt cold inside. I wanted to jab this knife into her and make that horrible spirit disappear. I had to save myself, before she kills me.

"Move," I said in a deep tone, but the Archangel stood still.

Beware of Gabriel…he is against you…

I turned quickly, noticing movement from behind. I sliced my knife through the air.

Alex.

"Back off, I don't want to hurt you!" I said, glancing back to the Archangel I no longer trusted.

"Sophie, it's Charlotte." Alex said, very calmly. "You don't want to hurt her."

Wrong.

"That's not Charlotte!" I said, scratching at my throat.

"She's your best friend," He went on.

No!

Then I saw Nathan.

They're all too close. All of them, I can't trust any of them.

"Stop messing with me. Everyone just shut up! Just stop talking. Stop talking to me!" I yelled, then quickly shoved Charlotte to the ground and turned the knife on myself.

"No!" Alex shouted.

My hand swung back out towards him. "Stay away." I warned, bringing the knife back to my chest.

There here, I can feel them... ripping at my skin!
"Stop it!" I screamed, my body seizing up. "They're all over me. I can't stop them—it hurts!" The knife shook in my hand. I had to stop it. Quickly, I sliced the blade across my arm then screamed at the sight of blood.
She's here... she did this...
I quickly turned the knife to my stomach, but before I could add pressure, someone toppled me to the ground. The sight of him on top of me made me lose it completely.
Nathan!
He was fighting against me. I screamed in pain as he wrestled my arms back against the ground until I dropped the knife. Gabriel kicked it across the floor. His grip on me was hard and forceful, a way my Nathan would never have handled me. I continued to scream and fight against him. I felt my hands reach up and grab onto his biceps, attempting to force him off me, but he was too heavy. He groaned as my nails dug into his skin, making blood appear instantly.
"Sweetie, stop," he said. His legs straddling my body, using all his strength to hold me down.
"Let me go. I hate you! I hate you so much!"
The words were pouring out. So many thoughts, immediate reactions and emotions coming out all at once. Then I felt him pull me up against his chest. My arms continued to wail on him. I hit him as hard as I could. It was exhausting,
Eventually, I slowed feeling unable to fight anymore. My hands slid down his sides to his waist. He continued to hold me as I tried desperately to catch my breath. His embrace tightened. My breathing was deep now as I tried to stay conscious. His scent was familiar for just a moment. Then suddenly, an image flashed across my mind.
Hand in hand, we were walking with a little dog. I continued to shake as I blinked myself back into his arms. Trembling, I soon found myself gripping onto his shirt. I had done this before. I had been in his grasp like this before. Another vision flashed.
The bathroom floor. We were holding each other, trying to

understand each other. Sadness filled my heart, I began to cry. There was something so heart breaking about being in his arms and it wasn't just my sadness, I felt his.

My head rested against his chest. The sound of his heart beating crushed me even more. I felt his arms tighten again. Closing my eyes, I breathed him in. My eyelids were too heavy to keep open, but I could hear his voice speaking to me. "I'm here," He whispered, "I'm right here."

I felt weightless for a moment until my body sank into a soft mattress. Then I felt warmth all around me. I was too weak, too exhausted to open my eyes. Sleep was taking me again. Then I heard the Archangel speak,

"I can hear your thoughts, Nathan. You can't leave her. Not now, not when she needs you the most."

"I don't know what you're talking about." Nathan replied, getting up from the bed.

"We will make a new plan soon enough. Do not try and fix this on your own."

Nathan stood silently.

"Why are you trying to block me from your mind..." Gabriel said, trying his best to read the details of Nathan's plan but for some reason, he couldn't.

"She needs you," He urged.

"The more time we waste, the more torture Sophie endures. Don't you see that?" Nathan replied.

"I do, but I also see her needs and fragile state. Alex and Charlotte can only do so much. You need to concentrate on your relationship. That is the key here before anything else or you will lose her."

Nathan didn't respond.

"She loves you. You know that. Even if she says hateful things, deep down her soul knows it's you that makes things safe for her. Trust me. I can still feel her emotions. Her pure heart still exists. Couldn't you feel it holding her in your arms just now? It's just her mind that is lost and it is to be expected. It's trapped and confused, a result from purgatory alone. We must make her believe in us again. We must bring the old

Sophie back."

Nathan finally spoke, "What's happening to Sophie is killing me, Gabriel. I need to fix it. I need to help Serena too. I hate what's happened to her. I feel guilty for both of them. This is my mess and I have to be the one to correct it. I owe it to both of them. I mean, at some point you must have felt the same about Anna?"

"I did, I do. I understand completely."

Their words were starting to fade. I could barely make them out anymore. What where they planning? I can't hear...

Then I felt someone sit down next to me on the bed, but my eyes were too heavy to open.

"Look at her, she is so fragile. I fear one wrong move will break her. This is why I beg you to wait—just a little longer. She cannot be without you. Not right now. I need you to trust me on this. I'll talk with Alex and..."

Then it went silent. Dead silent.

●●●

Back in the kitchen, Charlotte was cleaning up the mess. Alex hovered close. She moved quickly and was clumsy with everything, knocking things over—she was a complete mess. He watched silently.

"Charlotte?" He finally spoke, watching her wipe down the counter that was already clean. She didn't answer.

"It's going to get worse before it gets better," he said. "It's not Sophie in there. It's Sophie's body, but her mind is gone. She's just confused. We just need to bring her back. Her heart is still the same. She just can't get past her mind yet and she's probably begging for you not to give up."

Charlotte stopped and threw the dishrag in the sink.

"I know," she said softly, turning towards him. "It's just hard when you're sad because you miss your friend, but you're also terrified of her at the same time. It's messing with my head. I hate that I don't know how to fix her." Her head dropped and she began to cry. Alex moved in close, reaching out to touch her back.

"I'm sorry. This is so embarrassing. Can you just go," She asked, wiping her eyes. "I don't want you to see me like this." He turned her to face him.

"You're allowed to cry Charlotte. Sophie isn't the only one suffering right now." His kind words made her break. He wrapped his arms around her tightly.

"I don't know if I can stay here tonight, Alex."

"Don't worry. I'll be right here with you,"

He could feel her tears begin to dampen his shirt.

"If it makes you feel safer, I'll crash on the floor of your room to make sure nothing happens to you. Okay?" He then paused, realizing how odd that might have sounded.

"I mean, no pressure. If that's weird or whatever." He stuttered.

She smiled.

"After everything that's happened in my life recently, nothing is weird. I would really appreciate it. I just don't want to be alone. I feel silly saying I'm afraid of my best friend killing me in the middle of the night. Sounds like a plot of a horror movie, huh?" She smiled again, wiping some tears away. "I miss her, Alex."

"She's not gone forever," he replied, wiping one last tear from her cheek. He then took her hand in his and led her towards the spare bedroom.

Stopping at the doorway he spoke again,

"Get ready for bed. I know it's a little early, but I feel like sleep is not going to come easy to us over the next little bit. We should always sleep when she sleeps—just to stay safe."

Charlotte nodded.

●●●

My mind raced. I felt cold and distant from everything I knew, but I also felt a strange familiarity as I slept. I could feel a presence around me as I subconsciously fought back the nightmares trying to get into my head. I felt myself reach out in bed for something—anything to remind me I was safe, that I was supposedly home in my own bed. Then I felt his hand take mine as it used to in dreams long ago. I felt the gentle brush of his fingertips as he pushed the loose strands of hair from my face and tucked them behind my ear.

"Nathan," I breathed, "don't leave me,"

I felt his body closer now. My hand reached for his waist. I pulled myself in closer and rested my head on his chest.

The sound of his heart made my eyes flutter open. I breathed quietly, listening to the familiar sound. It was special to me once—I think. No, I'm sure of it. His heartbeat was so rare, so perfect. Something we had created together. My hands reached up further to his arms, pulling at him. I heard him moan in pain very faintly. My head rose from his chest, startling him a bit.

"What's wrong?" I asked quietly, then slid the shoulder of his t-shirt up. The tiny cuts were fresh. "What happen to you? Are you okay?" I asked, worried.

He looked at me confused, then smiled.

"Oh, I just hit my shoulder off something. It's just a little sore." He replied.

Staring at him, I remembered that it bothered me to see him in pain, no matter how little it was. My fingers traced his shoulder around the cuts as I moved up against him. He remained still. I could feel his heart beginning to race beneath me. This moment caused me some mixed emotions—being so close to him and having his body react to my every touch.

I stared at his lips. If I kissed him, would he vanish? Would this wonderful moment just beginning between us suddenly change for the worse? I couldn't decide. Everything inside of me wanted to connect to him, I think.

"It hurts so bad, Nate," I whispered.

His eyes softened. "I know," He replied, carefully reaching out to touch my face. When I didn't flinch, he pulled me up closer. Our foreheads touched gently, resting against one another.

Then the pain grew inside of me again, creating that same sick feeling from before.

"You're going to forget about me... Because I can't stop this." I spoke.

254

"What? Sophie, no." He whispered back.

"I'm so sorry, it just hurts so bad." I repeated.

I felt him move back from me, adjusting himself up in bed more so he could look me in the eyes. The expression on his face made me feel horrible. Like I was causing him pain, the same if not more than what I was feeling inside.

"Sophie, I will never forget about you." He said very clearly to me, his hands holding my face so I couldn't look away from him. I felt my eyes beginning to tear up as he held onto me.

"I'm going to make the pain go away very soon, I promise. Don't you give up on me though, okay? I need you to hang in there."

He's going to make the pain go away.

I nodded, then placed my head back down against his chest. I wasn't sure if I believed him.

"I know you're still in there," he spoke again, kissing the top of my head. The sensation from that simple act shot me back to times he had done that before in this very bed. Lying here, just like this. It made me feel safe. I was remembering now, remembering our almost perfect life.

"I love you, crazy girl." I then felt his arms tighten around me. Mine did the same. I only hoped I could continue to feel safe like this. I feared sleep, I feared closing my eyes, in case they came for me again.

Keep me safe...

I was losing my battle to sleep again fast. I heard myself whisper one last thing, "I love you..." Then I was out.

The next morning, I felt the gentle touch of lips against my forehead. I froze for a moment. *Where am I?* My head shot up from his chest.

"Sophie, relax. Everything is fine."

I stared at Nathan. *It looks like Nathan.*

"You moved into me last night. You were scared. We do this all the time. You're completely safe," he said very calmly. "I love you."

You love me....
I repeated out loud, then twice more.
Nathan stared at me worried.
"No, this is all going to flip on me any second now. I know it."
I quickly pulled back from him in the bed, covering my eyes.
"I can't watch. Please, I can't watch you die again,"
"Soph? What are you talking about, sweetie?" He said, taking
my hands carefully from my face.
I flinched from his touch.
"They aren't going to kill me." He assured me.
I didn't believe him. I could barely breathe from the pain
building up inside. My eyes met his again.
"Every time you were lying here with me, I would think it was
perfect and that I was safe back at home. Then you would start
to bleed—everywhere, and they would rip you apart right in
front of my eyes.... Every, single, time." I began to cry at the
thought.
"I watched you die a hundred times, Nathan. Brutally. I can't
do it anymore. Please, I need Alex... I need him to—"
"Jesus Sophie," he said, pulling me into him. "I'm not going
to die. Not this time, I'm right here. I'm real, and you are
never going back to that place—ever. No one will touch you
again." I felt his lips kiss my head over and over again. "We're
going to get through this, I promise."
"Promise you won't leave me?" I asked. I needed to hear it
again.
"I promise." He said, holding me in his arms.
I was drowsy again. I felt overwhelmed and tired. I soon
passed out in his arms.

Hours later I awoke again, this time in a full panic. I flew
up in bed, trying to catch my breath. It felt as if I was being
strangled. My fingers frantically scratched my neck, trying to
release the tension that wasn't physically there.
Nathan woke up immediately. I felt his hands on my arms,
pulling at me.
"Sophie! Sophie, breathe!" He yelled.

My body fell back down to the bed. There was no air, I couldn't breathe. I felt darkness fall over my eyes and slowly the life slipping out of me.

The muffled sound of his voice got further and further away and soon I couldn't hear him at all. Everything became very hollow as my body lay there in the darkness. At first, I could feel his hands on my skin even though I couldn't see them. But soon I became numb and eventually, I couldn't hear or feel Nathan at all.

It was quiet for quite some time. I thought I had died. Then I heard muffled voices in the distance. They slowly grew louder and louder. There were too many of them.

They were here.

The ones I feared. I tried to scream, to call for help, but my voice was silent. I was back there—with them. They had come for me.

Suddenly, I felt the softest touch against my lips, then warm air filled my body. It pushed the voices back and the darkness began to lift around me. I heard his voice much clearer now. Another burst of air pushed its way through my lungs and shot my eyes open. The brightness of the sun blinded me as I sat up and gasped for air.

"Sophie, breathe. Listen to me… breathe." He said, over and over again.

When my eyes regained focus. I was back in my bedroom. Nathan was by my side, his hands held my face. Alex was on the other side of me. I quickly pulled back from both of them and slammed myself into the headboard. Both of them raised their hands, releasing me—giving me my space.

Charlotte busted into the room, "What's happening?!"

"She's fine," Alex said, taking a breath himself. "We're all good." He then held out his hand for me.

I stared at it for a moment, looking back and forth between them. They were both still here, I was still here, in my room. Cautiously, I placed my hand in his and he helped me out from the bed.

"You need to eat something." He said, as I clung to his arm.

257

"Come to the kitchen."

Nathan jumped from the bed and quickly grabbed Alex by the arm. Charlotte carefully reached for my hand, then led me down the hallway slowly. I watched as the two of them stayed behind.

"Thank you," I heard Nathan say.

"You're welcome." Alex replied. "Are you alright?"

Nathan's pause worried me as we got further down the hallway.

"I have to do something today," he spoke quietly. "It won't take long. Will you be okay with Sophie for a few hours?"

Charlotte guided me into the kitchen and soon I couldn't hear them at all. What were they talking about? Where was Nathan going?

21
Come What May

It was about two in the afternoon by the time Nathan reached his destination. He would have been there sooner, but he had one little stop to make on the way there at a local jewelry shop. He walked through the doors of the small cafe he had visited before and he ordered the same drink, an Angel's Dream Tea Latte, but two of them this time. Then he waited.

Fifteen minutes past, he began to worry that she wouldn't show. It had been quite some time since he saw her last. She would be much different now—he hoped. He had learned of this angel and her story from Gabriel after assisting him one evening with her. Secretly, Gabriel and the Archangel Chamuel were helping a Fallen angel grow again, and as a guardian. Nathan was asked to assist once and a while, even if it was only to lend an ear. They were helping her heal, like she used to do for others long ago.

Since becoming a human again, Nathan had lost all touch with her. But he still remembered how to summon her. A simple prayer and a single emerald stone were used to call upon the former Archangel Raphael when one wanted to heal. But Raphael was much different now. She was healing herself from a tragic event long ago. Raphael's story was just as tragic as Gabriel's. After the Archangel had obeyed his brothers and returned to the throne leaving Anna behind, Raphael soon experienced the same emotional test of her own. The only difference being, she had failed it in the eyes of her brothers.

Raphael had fallen in love with a man in the mid 1900's. A writer named William, who had continuously called upon her with prayer, night after night. On his desk, sat a small green stone on a white piece of material. This simple man intrigued the Archangel hidden in the darkness. Not only with his good looks, but also with his words. For quite some time, she sat silently watching over him—giving him strength.

He was sick. An illness that had given him only a few months left to live. He only prayed for enough strength to finish his novel, to be able to share his story of love and strength with the world. It was unfortunate, the path given to him. Raphael always stayed close listening in on his thoughts, secretly making him comfortable while he continued to write. This wonderful man wrote of loyalty, faith and following your dreams until the bitter end. But what caught her heart, was how he wrote of love—true love and finding the one you were meant for.

He believed that some souls were connected for eternity. He called them twin souls. These souls would pass through time secretly searching for the other—each and every lifetime they lived. He believed that one soul would always find the other, no matter the obstacle or distance between them. She thought that was beautiful, truly a creation and reflection of God.

Then one night, when he was very weak, she appeared in front of him. He didn't fear her, he expected her. His head fell into his hands at the sight of her. Quietly, he sat in his chair at the writing desk as she approached. Her long, wavy, beautiful brown hair flowed over her shoulders. Her green eyes sparkled in the candlelight. Around her neck was a simple silver chain with a single emerald stone to compliment the green silk dress she wore that hung long to the ground. An impeccable vision that calmed his heart immediately.

"I knew you'd come for me," he said. "If I had the strength, I would bow down to you on my knees."

She smiled, then stepped before him slowly lowering herself to the ground. On her knees, she took his hands in hers.

"I wish to bow before you," Her voice hummed. "For your strength, your love and all that you are."

William held her hands tightly, "Thank you..." He whispered.

"Worry not, I am not here to take you." She smiled.

He looked at her surprised.

"I wish to help you. You must finish what you've started."

He sighed, "I fear I do not have the strength,"

Her hand slid from his and gently touched his face. Skin that was once youthful and full of life, now felt worn even at his young age. His hair was course as well. It just couldn't shine they way it used to. The sickness had left him weathered, dull, and weak.

"I see you..." She spoke again. "I see in you in there. You still have much life left,"

His eyes closed from the warmth of her touch.

Although William was only in his early 30's he moved and felt twice the age. He longed for his old self. Deep inside, he wasn't ready to leave this world yet. He hadn't done or experienced all that a normal life had the beauty of experiencing. He hadn't even fallen in love.

She was mesmerized by him yet saddened at the same time. How could a soul like his have such torture put upon it? It was surely the doing of only one person—Fate. She was unfair and too harsh in the eyes of the angels. Especially to Raphael, it pained her as the angel of healing to see such beauty, such perfection created by *Him*—tormented and ruined like this. This man's heart and soul had captured her completely. She wanted desperately to help him, to heal him, no matter the cost. Slowly, she stood up from him and pulled him to his feet. His hand braced the writing desk for balance. She took both his hands in hers and stepped back, making him rely on her for strength.

"Please," He said, "I can't."

Her hand slid down to his waist as the other slid up to his heart. He gripped her arms tight a little startled as her eyes lit up before him.

"You are much stronger than you think," She whispered,

stepping towards him again.

He silently doubted her. His once blue and full of life eyes now sunk in a light gray colour and eventually closed before her.

"If I must go, then let me go with you." He spoke.

Raphael's expression softened as she waited for him to open his eyes.

"I am grateful for all that you have given me up until now. I am grateful for your strength. For I know, you have been watching over me. I have felt your presence here before." She continued to stare at him.

"Please, it would be an honor to be taken by you." He begged kindly.

She felt his heart beneath her hand weakening by the second. She smiled again as his body trembled.

"You are truly beautiful." He whispered, still mesmerized by her presence. "Like the angel in my story,"

Her body gently pressed against his, the warm breath of the angel feathered against his neck. Even her wonderful scent made him weak in the knees. Then he felt her lips brush up against his earlobe as she whispered to him once again.

"I am the angel in your story,"

Her words brought a silence to the room around them as her eyes met his again. She then leaned up and gently rested her lips against his. A sudden energy ignited between them. Electrifying his body from head to toe.

The room became very warm, and the scent of lavender mixed with a summer breeze filled the air. He felt his veins begin to pulse with adrenaline as his stomach turned once, then surprisingly settled inside.

The blood raced through his body straight into his hands and suddenly, his grip on the angel was much stronger. With his lips still attached to hers, he carefully slid his hands up to the angel's beautifully sculpted face. Her skin was soft, almost too delicate to touch. An unexpected breeze in the room sent the smell of spring flowers through her hair directly into his lungs. His lips pressed a little harder against hers. A slight

262

smile grew on the angel's face. She tasted as sweet as honey. Her hands pulled him closer, forcing life to fill his body once again.

"You are magnificent," He whispered between their kisses. He then stopped for a moment to catch his new breath.

She looked up into his now crystal blue eyes and smiled again.

"You are the magnificent one, as you always were." She said, touching the side of his face.

He then looked down at his youthful and very healthy body. His fingers nervously ran through his full, thick head of hair that was now perfectly shaped. He couldn't believe it. He felt no more pain, no agony. He was alive and his heart was beating stronger than ever.

"It's a wonderful feeling, isn't it?" She asked.

"More than I could ever describe." He replied, reaching out for her again. "How can I ever thank you? How could I ever repay you?"

She rested her hands against his strong chest.

"William, you must simply continue to be you. Finish your novel. Share your words of love and life with the world. Make a difference."

He nodded with tears in his eyes.

"And you?" He said, "Please tell me this isn't the last time I will see you." His hands traced her arms gently.

She could feel it, just beneath his chest, the glowing light. His soul was igniting within. His pure heart had fully returned to him. He felt amazing, his presence, his touch... She leaned up and gently kissed him again, this time much differently than before. Something inside of her had lit up as well.

A feeling she had never felt, something she wasn't familiar with. She had heard of feelings like this in a story from Archangel Gabriel once before. She was sure it was the same thing he spoke about. It was overwhelming this connection she was having with this man. She now understood what Gabriel meant, what he had felt with Anna. This simple man had stolen her heart so quickly. She had healed many before him, but none had connected to her like this. None had captured

263

her mind, heart and soul all at once. She didn't leave him that night, she stayed. Ultimately changing her fate, along with his.

This simple act of love and free will had casted Raphael into purgatory after that night for many years. With Michael leading the throne now, he gave the Archangel a choice, just as he once did for Gabriel. Only Raphael chose differently. She refused to give William up. She begged, trying to make the Archangels understand that she could give both her love to this man and to God. But Michael couldn't see it. He saw her choice of wanting more than just God as an act of greed, like Lucifer long ago. It was the last anyone saw of Raphael, until many years later. Just before Nathan was turned into a guardian—someone had secretly released Raphael from purgatory. The angels felt her presence the moment she was back. She was ruined, changed, and terrified. Terrified of everyone and everything. Chamuel found her first and only told Gabriel.

The two of them secretly worked with her, helping her stay hidden from the rest of the Archangels until the time was right. Until she was ready to face them and plea for her place back alongside them. The two of them believed she truly belong with them and would do anything in their power to help her redeem herself, but when that day would come no one knew. The idea had crossed Nathan's mind late last night. Right now, Raphael was the only person who could ever understand what Sophie was going through. Whether she was ready or not, he needed her help. He also hoped in some way, maybe this could be the redeeming moment she had been waiting for.

Suddenly, a tap from behind, startled him. Then a young girl with beautiful freshly colored brunette hair, sat down beside him at the table. A smile grew on her face as she breathed in the wonderful scent of the angel's dream tea latte.

Nathan smiled at her. "I'm sorry, it got cold." He said.

Her hand floated over the mug. Instantly, the foam lifted back to life. She then blew gently over the drink and steam began to rise. "It's perfect." She replied.

"How are you?" He asked, relieved that she came.

"A lot better, thanks." She then took a small sip of the tea. "Mm, it's delicious."

He smiled again.

"I like the new look, it suits you." He complimented.

Her hair was much shorter now, it barely touched her shoulders, but still had a slight wave to it. Her green eyes were lighter, but still glittered when the light caught them just right. She seemed very healthy and confident, but not as delicate as she used to be. Her attire now consisted of black leggings, a dark green lace camisole and a black leather jacket. On her feet were a pair of tall black riding boots.

As a guardian, Nathan remembered feeling the warmth of being around her. He only wished he had met her when she was at her best—at her purest. But she was amazing now for all that she had been through—for all that she had survived. Which is why he needed her.

"It was nice of you to keep in contact with me over the years. I want to thank you for your words of encouragement, always." She said, humbly. "The three of you have never given up on me. I needed that. I still need it." She admitted.

"It's no problem," He said, taking her hand. "I'm glad you're doing well. I'm sorry I haven't seen you lately, a lot has changed." He began.

"I can tell. You are much different now. Human." She smiled back. "You are lucky to have found her, to have things turn out the way they did for you. She is very special. Chamuel has told me much about her. He speaks of how genuine and wonderful your love for each other is." She said, with a slight sadness to her voice.

"You're right." He agreed. "I am lucky to have her, she's very special to me. Which is why I humbly ask for your help," Raphael took another sip of her tea, then smiled at him again. "Go on... do not be nervous."

Nathan thought about where to begin and how to explain all that had happened. He didn't know how much the Fallen had learned of his life since he had become human again.

"The angels are talking about you a lot up there and Gabriel is in a lot of trouble." She spoke again.

Nathan looked at her oddly.

"My healing has allowed me to listen in once and a while to the angel realm," She smiled. "I miss it..."

"That's wonderful." Nathan replied.

"Michael and Uriel are watching you all very closely, which is never good. Watch out for him—Uriel—he's quick and has very little patience."

"Yes, I've seen it." Nathan replied. "Have they seen you yet? I mean, now that you are this?" He then asked.

She nodded.

"They are aware I'm here, we've spoken one or twice." She began, "Chamuel has asked them for a second chance, a chance to redeem myself, but no answer has come from the thrown yet."

"In time," He said, touching her hand again. "They will see the greatness that has returned to you and surely give you your moment to redeem yourself. Have faith."

She smiled again, then moved the cup of tea to the side. She looked him directly in his eyes.

"Tell me what you need." She said. "I need to hear everything and please know that I'm on your side, even if the Archangels come after us. I will not let you or your Sophie down."

He smiled, her words comforted him, especially with his recent choice of action. He then spent the next few hours filling Raphael in on everything that had happened over the past year. All of the good things, and the bad. There were many conversations in regards to how they should proceed with Sophie and of course about purgatory. Since Raphael was the only one ever to have survived purgatory, other than Alex recently, she was the best to get answers from. For Alex wasn't a choice for him right now. He would never abandon or go against Gabriel's words.

Nathan continued to listen as Raphael told him all that she could to help and as she spoke, Nathan slowly began to worry about Gabriel understanding his motives and of course, his actions to come. It was all for Sophie's sake alone. He had to understand, wouldn't he? Guilt began to grow inside his chest as he continued to talk to Raphael. The feeling of betrayal filled his body. It suddenly felt wrong to be going behind Gabriel's back and with someone he had worked so hard to help. Someone that was just getting back on her feet again. The reason Raphael fell in the first place was a matter close to Gabriel's heart. He was very protective of her, Chamuel too—being the angel of love. He wondered for a moment, if bringing Raphael into this situation might harm her healing.

"Nathan," She interrupted, touching his arm.

He snapped back to their conversation.

"You're letting your mind run away with thoughts. Calm yourself. Do not worry about me, I want to do this." She assured him.

"You've got your powers back," He said, quietly.

"Some," She smiled, then her face grew more serious. "Your pain, it hurts very badly inside. It aches my heart." She said, placing her hand against her chest. She then looked up at him, "I'm sure she feels it too."

"I'm not so sure about that." He replied, sadly.

Raphael reached out and wrapped her arms around him tightly. When she finally released him his eyes began to tear up. He quickly wiped them.

"I have a gift for you." He said, reaching into his pocket and pulling out a small white tissue. He placed it on the table and pushed it towards her. Her delicate hands slowly opened the tissue to reveal a silver chain. She carefully picked it up, letting it dangle in the sunlight shining through the windows. Hanging in the middle of it was a single emerald stone. An electric shade of green that glistened in the light. Her eyes shot back to him.

"I thought you could use a new one for your new journey. Perhaps it will help you feel a little more like your old self." He said, remembering back to when Gabriel had told him of her necklace and how it represented her light within. He knew it wasn't the same as a gift from God, but the meaning behind it was just as strong.

She quickly attached it around her neck without saying a word. Her face lit up as she touched the stone against her skin. She reached again for Nathan's hand, this time pulling him up from the chair. Her smile grew as she stared into his eyes. "Let's go see her," She insisted.

On their walk home, Nathan still had some questions on his mind. "Raphael," He hesitated. "Who was it that pulled you from purgatory?"

She took his hand in hers, guiding their walk as if she knew where he lived.

"I don't know." She said, very lightly. "My mind was lost at the time I was pulled out. I had no awareness of where I was or who anyone was—not even Gabriel. Actually, I'm pretty sure that I tried to kill him a few times." She smirked.

Nathan pondered for a moment.

"I only ask because, who would have the strength to get into purgatory and pull you out? I mean, if Archangels cannot go there unless banished," he paused, thinking of the last person that went into purgatory. "Of course, could it have been another spirit guide like Alex? A more experienced one?"

"Possibly," she replied.

"Sophie seemed to remember flashes of Alex appearing in purgatory. She remembered him fighting for her. Are you sure you can't remember anything? It could be very helpful." He tried again.

"I'm sorry, I was in there so long…" She said, with a frown.

Nathan rubbed her hands, he didn't mean to press her so hard. "Raphael?" He asked, again. "How did you deal with the memories and flashbacks from purgatory?"

"It took me a very long time, but I had a lot of help from my two brothers—and you." She smiled. "To be honest, I'm still working on it. An image, a sound, anything can rattle me. Most of the time I have the strength to shake it off and tell myself it's not real, but I constantly have to work at it." She sighed. "Tell me Nathan," She then said. "How is Gabriel? I

miss him so. I haven't seen him in quite some time. He's been very busy. It will be nice to work alongside him once again."
"He's well. He knew I kept in touch with you as a guardian, but I don't think he will be expecting you. I hope it will please him," Nathan laughed a little.
Raphael linked her arm through Nathan's as they continued their talk the entire way home. Nathan only hoped bringing the Fallen angel into the equation was a good choice, a choice that wouldn't make matters worse.

When they arrived back at home, Charlotte was making dinner in the kitchen with Alex. Their day had been peaceful so far. The smell of pasta filled the air as Nathan walked into the kitchen with Raphael close behind. Alex stopped everything the moment he felt her presence.
"Raphael," a smile grew on his face. He then turned to her. Charlotte pulled her head out of the fridge and stared.
"Who are you?"
"Charlotte, this is Raphael. She was once an Archangel…"
He began. He wasn't sure how much to tell her or how much Raphael felt comfortable with.
"Once?" She repeated, slowly making her way over to the table.
I heard their voices from the living room where I sat in silence staring out the window.
"We can trust her," Alex added. "Actually, she might be just what we need for Sophie."
I felt their gaze on me, even before I turned to them. Her eyes met mine immediately. She began to make her way across the room towards me. I turned on the bench in front of the window as she approached, Nathan was close behind.
"You must be Sophie," She said, very kindly.
As she knelt before me, for a split second, I saw a glimmer of the same fear in her eyes that I felt in my mind. Then it was gone.
Who are you?
My eyes locked on hers.

She then touched my hand. Her eyes lit up the moment we connected. She glanced back at Nathan and the others, a smile on her face. Her eyes then returned to mine once again.

"You are most beautiful, my darling. I can see why he loves you so."

Charlotte took a step forward but Alex grabbed her wrist at the edge of the living room. Keeping her still.

She continued to stare into my eyes.

"I have seen all that you have young one. I know the fear you hold inside. I know the pain you are bearing,"

Pain...

"What is she talking about?" Charlotte asked, feeling a little protective of her friend. She pulled her arm from Alex and stepped closer, trying to listen better.

"I'm sorry for what you have gone through, but it will get better. I will help you—your friends will help you. Most importantly, Nathan will help you. He loves you and I know love when I see it."

Her grip on my hands was tight.

"You must fight for it," She then whispered.

Fight...

Her words confused me.

"Yes, her friends will help her." Charlotte repeated, joining my side. She then sat down on the bench staring back at Raphael.

"I am only here to help. I will not hurt your friend."

"Well, I don't know you enough to believe that." Charlotte quickly responded. "She's been through too much. She doesn't need another person coming into her life and telling her what to do. She needs to heal and remember who she was."

A smile grew on the Fallen's face. Slowly, she stood up.

"I like this one." She said, turning to Nathan.

He chuckled beneath his breath. Just then, Gabriel appeared. She stared at him pleasantly.

"You're here," he spoke.

"Thanks to Nathan," she replied.

Gabriel glanced to him, a little surprised.

"It's good to see you again." He said. "You are very much

welcome here." Gabriel then changed the subject immediately.
"Charlotte, can you take Sophie out of the room?" He asked.
"This will be too much information for her to listen to,"
I looked at him nervously, my fingers gripped onto the bench
below me.

Lies...

I felt my friend begin to peel my fingers from the wood. She
helped me up and guided me past them all without a single
word.

He's going to trick you...

I gripped onto the wall as we passed through the kitchen,
towards the hallway.

"Wait! What's happening here?" I said, feeling a little anxious
about them all in my home. What secrets were they keeping
from me? Why was I being removed?

Alex was immediately at my side. "Soph, it's fine. We're just
going over some stuff that could help you. You should take
a rest. You've been up all day," He said, gently touching my
face. But their looks were upsetting me. They were staring at
me—plotting something.

"Come on, Soph," Charlotte said, taking my arm again.

RUN!

I pulled free of her grip and took off down the hallway.
When I reached the bedroom, I quickly slammed the door shut
behind me and locked it. I heard their footsteps coming down
the hallway, then a bang at the door. It startled me.

"Sophie, open the door." Nathan said, trying his best to remain
calm.

"No. Make those people go away. There's too many of them.
They're going to turn on us!" I screamed, then searched
the room for something. I grabbed the small chair from our
writing desk and nudged it under the door handle. I couldn't
let them get to me. My body was vibrating, energy pulsing
through me. My arms whipped around and slid everything
from the top of the dresser to the floor. I then grabbed the
sheets from my bed and began to tear at them, pulling them
from the bed. I grabbed onto the writing desk and tipped it

over. I wanted to rip everything apart. I began to crack my fingers, undecided on what to go for next when I heard the Archangel's voice.

"Sophie, open this door, or we'll open it for you," Gabriel warned.

There was no way I was letting any of them in. Then I heard that woman's voice through the door.

"This is exactly the stage I went through after coming out of purgatory. I thought everyone was after me. Too many sounds, voices or quick actions really brought out the anxiety in me. It made me crazy,"

"Enough of this," Gabriel then blasted the door open with a white orb.

I could hear their footsteps entering the room as I hid from them. Suddenly, I felt a grip on me. My mouth was covered and I couldn't move. Then Nathan appeared before me. The look on his face scared me.

"Wow, you've got a lively one here, don't you?" Fate teased, holding me tightly in her arms. "They really messed with her head, huh?"

Nathan froze. The others quickly appeared behind him.

Slowly, she pulled me up to my feet, her hand secured around my mouth. Her grip was strong, stronger than any I had felt before. My body was pulsing beneath her.

"Don't worry. She can still breathe. I just had to shut her up. She kept rambling on and on..."

"What do you want, Fate?" Gabriel asked.

"You have quite a crew going here, don't you? I mean spirit guides, angels, humans and now a Fallen? This is getting complicated, isn't it?" She said, moving towards them.

I felt myself tripping over my feet as she shoved me along. Nathan backed away as she stepped closer.

"I think I specifically said to not bring anyone else into this ridiculous situation that you seem to make more difficult by the day." She reminded them, then turned to Nathan again.

"But well played Nathan, bringing Raphael back into the picture. We're all getting very good at this game, aren't we?"

Fate paused as if she heard something.

A smile then grew on her face.

She quickly tossed me across the room, but just before I hit the ground, somebody caught me.

"I heard you coming," She said, as the Archangel held me in his arms. "Now this is going to be fun."

Alex immediately appeared beside Uriel and ripped me from his grasp. I gripped onto him in fear of the strange angel in my room. The Archangel turned to us, an annoyed look on his face as he raised his hand in our direction. My eyes squinted as the bright light blasted towards us. Our bodies slammed hard against the wall and slid to the ground. I glanced up to see Charlotte running towards us.

"No no, don't touch," Fate said, appearing behind and grabbing her quickly.

Gabriel charged Fate. She dropped Charlotte the moment she spotted him. He slammed her back into the wall, his hand gripped tightly around her neck.

"Why must you make things so complicated all the time?" He yelled.

She struggled under his grip, trying to get her words out. Her eyes glanced at Uriel heading her way. She quickly raised her hand and the deadly red ribbon slid out from the tip of her index finger. It shot directly at him, wrapping itself around his neck and holding him in his place. Her eyes then returned to Gabriel's.

"Because you're all so stupid... when it... comes... to... love. It's the best game... in life," She said, trying to breathe through his grip. Then out of nowhere, she tossed him back like a rag doll.

"Totally joking, your grip wasn't that hard to get out of. I just wanted to give you a glimpse of hope. But then I realized, I don't like losing," She said, sarcastically.

She started to walk towards him again but Nathan quickly jumped in, toppling her to the ground with all this strength. She tossed him over until she was on top of him.

"You stupid boy, as if you could take me down. Nathan,

273

Nathan, Nathan, what am I going to do with you?" She complained, looking down at him. "Your girlfriend's kind of a nut case. Not sure if she's worth it anymore. What do you think?" She asked. From her fingertip, another red ribbon appeared. Nathan's eyes grew wide.

Suddenly, a hand ripped Fate from Nathan's body. He scrambled away to see Serena in front of him.

"Don't touch him," she said, ready to attack again.

The sound of her voice was like an arrow that struck my heart. The pain shot through me as quickly as the fear returned. Then I lost it.

The sight of her—this was the turn in the dream I had been waiting for. She had come for me. I scrambled to get up from the floor but Alex grabbed onto me, then Charlotte too from the other side. They tried their best to contain me. I wanted out! I needed out now!

From the doorway, Raphael glanced at me. Her eyes were cold for only a moment until Uriel exploded from the ribbon's grip. His eyes raced around the room, he didn't know who to go for first— Serena or Fate. Then his eyes met Raphael's.

Suddenly, Serena lunged again in Nathan's defense, but Fate raised her hand and forcefully threw her back against Nathan, who was just getting up from the ground. He caught her just in time as her body flew into his. I watched as Nathan held onto her. I watched as she wrapped her arms around his neck as I used to. Memories flooded my mind, words I had said to him, words he had said to me. The promises we made.

"Nathan!" I yelled, unsure of what I was doing.

He turned immediately.

The look in my eyes seemed to softened his expression. I knew he knew what I was trying to say. I was letting him in for the first time in a long time. Letting him read my mind like he used to. I wanted him to hear my thoughts—my fears, everything. I just wanted him.

"It's okay, sweetie. I'm fine," he said. "Don't worry."

A tear fell from my eye just before Serena's glance caught mine, then the coldness returned. I gripped onto my hair and pulled at it. Nathan glanced to Serena, her eyes were locked on mine—controlling my thoughts.

"That's enough of that," Raphael said, stepping in and pulling Serena from his grip. As she wrapped her arms around her, Serena's body changed into a completely different person—Anna. She fought back hard against Raphael, but couldn't break free.

Uriel suddenly appeared by Anna's side ready to end her in the hands of the Fallen Archangel until Gabriel broke through them and ripped her from them both. He then disappeared into thin air. Alex's eyes searched the room for Gabriel, but he didn't reappear. He knew he definitely didn't have enough power to beat Fate on his own and now grew nervous of the situation at hand.

Fate waited patiently for the next move from Uriel as I continued to scream in fear. He was about to lunge again in rage when he heard his brother.

"Uriel!" Michael said sternly, making the Archangel stop in his tracks. "Leave them be,"

Uriel looked to Nathan and then Raphael, still a little surprised by her appearance alongside them. He then glanced back at Fate.

"Trust me..." he heard Michael speak again.

Annoyed by the indecisive feeling inside, the Archangel did as his leader requested. Fate, a little surprised by the departure of the Archangel, slowly walked towards me. The others rose to their feet, ready to fight again—even Charlotte. But Fate quickly released multiple ribbons that laced around each of them, pulling them back down to the ground and holding them in place. She continued to approach and I continued to scream. I scrambled back as Fate got closer until I couldn't go any further. With my back against the wall, I curled my knees up into my chest in fear. I could hear Alex shouting, telling me to be strong, but I wasn't. She crouched down before me.

"You excite me, Sophie." She said first, "You make this game very fun, but I'm wondering if it's too much fun. As much as I love what's happening here, I see this getting out of hand very soon. You see, even I have to follow some rules."

I heard the sound of someone running towards us. I glanced to the right of Fate, Raphael had broken free and was charging her. Fate raised her hand and with a flick of her fingers tossed the Fallen angel back against the wall.

"Nice try, I'll keep my eyes on you. I feel you're going to cause me a lot of grief," she said, giving a nasty glance back at the Fallen angel. She then turned back to me.

"I should end you now. Maybe I'm ready for a new game. I do still have Serena and Anna to play with but you, you're becoming a little annoying and I can see that you've mentally checked out, so I don't see the point in keeping you around." Nathan fought desperately against the ribbons holding him down.

"Let's put you out of your misery why don't we? Then we can move on to more exciting things, huh?" Fate said, raising her hand to my forehead.

From the corner of my eye, I noticed Nathan struggling beneath the ribbons that held him down. His was sweating profoundly and his breathing was deep. The restraints were too strong for him—for everyone. I was done for.

"Well, you had a good run Sophie my dear. Don't worry, this will all be over in just a minute,"

My eyes met Nathan's again, sadly this time. He was about to watch me be killed. Just as I watched him be killed many times in purgatory, and none of them could do anything about it. I closed my eyes in fear, remembering his face one last time. Suddenly, a flood of emotions filled my body, but they were not my own. They were Nathan's. I could feel his pain, his fear, and the heat. Something was happening to him. Something was pushing through his body. I felt a sudden jolt of energy. My eyes shot open and connected with his immediately.

Save me....

Just then, Fate stood up and took three steps back as a massive light grew from her hand. I screamed once more in fear. Everything inside of Nathan lit up at the sound of my voice

and like Uriel, he exploded from the ribbon and ran towards
me—throwing himself in front of the ball of light that
smashed up against us—blinding everyone in the room.
As the light burned against his body, I heard him groan in
pain, trying desperately to keep me hidden from its power.
He tucked me in as close as he could to his body. My hands
gripped onto his shirt in fear as a bright red light began
to glow all around us. Then I could hear him. I could hear
Nathan's thoughts, his fear, his love for me. This light,
was awakening everything between us. I heard previous
conversations we had, I saw our past, and our once almost
perfect future. The rush of emotions overwhelmed me and the
heat was almost too much as the red light slowly it pushed
Fate's back.
Her eyes grew wide in fear as she watched her own energy
coming towards at her. The orb burn brightly. Alex and
Raphael stared in amazement as the ribbons that held them
down suddenly disintegrated from sight. They immediately
rose to their feet. Alex quickly pulled Charlotte up and close
against him as they watched the fire-like, red energy continued
to push Fate back. But just before it singed the tip of her boot,
she vanished from sight.
   The power from Nathan faded as quickly as it appeared,
leaving everyone speechless. Nathan slowly raised his head.
"Nate," Alex called to him, unsure if he should approach.
"Nathan, are you alright?"
The sound of Alex's voice made me look up from Nathan's
chest. He was breathing deeply, looking directly into my eyes.
His eye lashes fluttered a few times and his pupils sparked
with a hint of red between the blinks. He then swallowed hard,
clearing his throat. "We're fine," he finally replied.
I felt his hands tracing my skin, looking for wounds as I
continued to stare at him. I felt something different in his
arms. Something jolted through him and electrified me at the
same time. He felt it too, I could tell.
"Are you...okay?" I whispered.
For some reason in that moment, my mind was very clear.

I knew everyone around me. I knew where I was and what was happening. I knew him. He was my Nathan—yet not at the same time. This power he ignited was creating a ripple effect inside him. I reached up and touched his face. He blinked a few times.

"Your eyes..." I said, seeing a few more sparks ignite within them. He quickly closed them. I pulled him down to me and held him close. His heart was racing, faster than ever before.

"What just happened? What was that light?" I heard Charlotte ask.

Raphael stepped towards us and knelt down. Surely, she could see a new fear in my eyes as her hand touched the back of Nathan's neck.

"He's burning up," She said, quickly removing her hand. "Nathan, what are you feeling right now?"

His head rose slowly, "I don't know..." He replied, "I thought I was going to lose her,"

Raphael looked to me, then smiled softly. "Are you alright, Sophie?"

My body began to shiver in his arms, it was wearing off—the awareness. I closed my eyes, trying my best to hold on to it. I began to scratch at my wrist a little bit. Raphael's hand stopped me. "Hold tight, concentrate on where you are,"

I stared at her. Nathan quickly removed the hoodie he was wearing and wrapped it around me. I felt as if my body temperature had dropped dramatically in the last few seconds, but the heat of his body warmed me as he lifted me from the ground. I laced my arms around his neck.

"Be careful," Alex worried.

"Please, leave us for a moment." Nathan replied.

"Come," Raphael spoke quickly, "Let's talk in the kitchen,"

She then guided everyone out of the room. Before closing the door behind her, she turned to Nathan.

"Please, join us when you are settled."

Nathan nodded, placing me down in the bed.

She then closed the door.

I watched as he pulled the covers up tight around me. I tried to catch his eyes in his movements, but he kept them hidden from me. Raphael and the others hadn't seen it. They hadn't seen his eyes change, but I did. I grabbed onto his wrist, forcing him stop, forcing him to look at me. When he finally did, his eyes were back to their normal shade of dark brown.

"What?" He whispered. "Are you alright?"

I pulled at him until he joined me in the bed.

"Don't leave me," I whispered.

My mind was flickering in and out of this moment. I thought if he was close, I might be able to hold on to it a bit longer. He seemed to have a little control over me. It wasn't even a matter of figuring out where I was at each point. It was a matter of who I felt safe around and right now, it was him— completely. I hadn't felt this aware in a long time. That energy, it had shocked me back into this world—our world—I think. I curled up close to him.

"You scared me," I said.

"Soph?" He tilted my head up to look at him. "Is it really you? Do you know where you are?"

"I'm not sure, but I know you scared me." I said, lacing my fingers through his. His hand pulled from mine to touch my face.

"It sounds like you," He smiled a bit.

"I'm sorry. I'm so sorry." I began. "I know I've been hard to deal with," He immediately reacted and shook his head no. He was about to interrupt me but I needed to get this out while I could. "I have," I repeated. "I see the fear in all of your faces. You're always on edge and you should be." I said, nervously.

"But, I'm starting to see images, images from our past. I remember some of our plans, Nathan."

I tried to smile as he continued to listen carefully.

"But the moment I see her, it gets—"

"I know," He said, leaning his forehead against mine.

"I remember this." I said.

He sighed, closing his eyes. His fingers laced through my hair.

"There's so much more,"

"I know, I'm sorry... I can't remember it all," I felt a small pain lingering in the pit of my stomach. I pushed it back down, trying to stay in our conversation.

"Listen to me," He then said. "You don't have to figure everything out right now, okay? You have time and you have me, Charlotte, Alex, Gabriel, and now Raphael to help you stay on track. We're going to bring you back. I swear."

My hands trembled against his chest.

"I want to remember. I don't want to be scared anymore, Nate." He held my face close to his.

"I want so badly..." He paused.

I knew what he wanted, because I wanted it too.

"I want to kiss you Sophie with every fiber in my body, but I don't want to scare you,"

"I want that as well," I replied.

His lips hovered close to mine for a moment, a second later he pulled back from me.

"I'm sorry, I can't." He sighed. "This moment is too precious for me to take a chance on ruining it."

With his hand still on my cheek, I felt his thumb brush my bottom lip.

"Your mind may be scrambled from purgatory, but know that your emotions and heart are true. You need to trust that. That is who you are, Soph. Your heart hasn't changed and I know it's going to be hard to choose which one to listen to but promise me you'll listen to your heart over your head, alright?" He begged.

"When I saw you holding Ser—" I paused. I can't say her name. "Her," I continued. "My heart felt like it was going to burst out of my chest." I admitted, sadly. "It hurt so badly. All I wanted to do was take you from her. I wanted your arms around me, Nate. That overwhelming feeling that I needed you silenced my thoughts and that's why I called out for you. I remembered our promises to stick together through this and to not give up on each other. I could hear our voices and conversations running through my head. They were much louder than the horrible ones."

"I am always yours, Sophie." He whispered. "Never think

differently and I'll keep reminding you so you don't forget," he smiled.

I took a breath, relaxing in his arms for a moment.

"I think you should get some rest," He then said.

As tired as I was, I was afraid if I slept I would forget all of this. He stared at me, reading my thoughts.

"You won't forget, I'm not going anywhere."

I fought hard again my heavy eyes trying to close.

"Promise me," I whispered. "Promise me you'll be here when I wake up."

"I'll be here," he said softly.

Then I was out.

22
Forever & Always

"How did he do that?" Alex spoke beginning to pace around the kitchen.

"I believe it came out of fear of losing Sophie," Raphael replied. "Love is the most powerful force in the universe,"

"What about Gabriel?" Charlotte added, clearly pissed off. "Does anyone else find it insane that Gabriel peaced in the middle of our attack? Isn't he supposed to be protecting us and who was that other chick? The one he disappeared with?"

"Anna, a secret love from long ago." Alex responded, silencing everyone.

Nathan entered the room.

"How is she?" Raphael asked stepping towards him.

"She's sleeping now." He replied, heading towards the fridge. He opened it, there wasn't much food inside. He couldn't remember the last time he went shopping. He took out a bottle of water, twisted the cap off and began to chug it down.

"And how are you feeling?" Raphael spoke again, reaching out to touch the back of his neck gently as he continued to down the water. She then reach for his forehead with her right hand. "Your temperature seems to have returned to a normal level. That's good."

"Nathan, what happened back there?" Alex interrupted. "How did you do it? How did you beat Fate?"

Nathan placed the empty water bottle down on the counter, then reached into the fridge for another.

"I don't know," he said. "It just happened."

"Please Nathan, sit with us for a moment." Raphael insisted, guiding him over to a chair. The four of them sat around the table in silence, waiting for someone to speak. Just then Gabriel appeared in a blinding light. Charlotte jumped up, startled. Alex touched her arm, assuring her she was safe. When the Archangel's light faded, Charlotte's eyes tore into Gabriel.

"What happened to you? You ditched us!" She shouted, stepping towards him.

"I had to get Anna—I mean Serena, out of there." He replied. "I knew you would be okay with Alex and Raphael by your side,"

"Are you kidding me?" Charlotte replied pulling her arm from Alex's grip and coming at him again. "Two of us are human, and I have no idea about this one.." She said pointing to Raphael. "And Alex," she paused looking over at him. "No offense, is a just a spirit guide! How the hell were any of us to stand up against Fate?! And did you forget about that other friggin' guy? What was his name, Uriel? Who the hell was he? Clearly he didn't like us either!" She hollered. "How am I supposed to trust you? How is Sophie—"

Alex got up and took Charlotte's hand again, trying to calm her. He motioned to Nathan, the expression on his face was bothersome. She quickly got the hint and followed him back to the table, her eyes still locked on the Archangel.

"It was a little chancy, Gabriel," Alex finally added.

"I'm sorry. But you are all fine, aren't you?" He replied, looking around at them.

"Barely," Charlotte huffed again, rolling her eyes.

Raphael smiled, amused.

Gabriel then glanced to Nathan who was quiet across the table. He immediately felt the weight of everyone's eyes. The chair scuffed across the floor as he stood up.

"Excuse me," He said, exiting the room.

Alex jumped up quickly, but Gabriel motioned him to sit back down.

"Let him be, something is stirring inside of him." The Archangel said in a worried tone.

"You missed it, Gabriel." Raphael finally spoke catching his attention. "You're definitely right about Nathan. He broke through. We all saw it."

Gabriel's eyes widened.

"Fate was about to end Sophie and Nathan threw himself in front of her. A force I'd never seen before ignited from his body. It was like fire, burning back against Fate's power. It was remarkable, she retreated the moment before it touched her."

He looked to Alex, who nodded confirming her words.

"His power was clearly much stronger than hers. She was afraid, Gabriel."

The Archangel stood quiet for a moment. "So he's broken through? He's not supposed to—not yet," he said, under his breath.

"What do you mean he's not supposed to?" Raphael asked, confused.

"He must have been completely overwhelmed by emotion and fear for that to happen. I should have been here so he didn't feel that. He can't break through, not yet," Gabriel repeated. "Raphael, he's supposed to have much more time before any of this shows itself. That's why we are here. If he's like this now, then we risk him changing for the worse. He's too vulnerable right now. They will use him against us. If he is truly at a changing point, then we need to begin the training now."

Everyone was silent, especially Charlotte.

"He needs to prepare. He needs to learn how to control himself so he doesn't..." He then stopped looking over at Charlotte. Raphael got up from the table and joined the Archangel's side. Alex could feel what Gabriel was thinking, he then remembered the prophecy and the other part that went along with it. The part they didn't speak about. The part about what "the one" would be come if he didn't stay pure—if he changed when he wasn't supposed to. He then turned to Raphael, exchanging quiet thoughts.

"It won't happen," She said, aloud. "We won't let it."

"Agreed." Gabriel responded.

"What are you guys talking about? What's happening to Nathan?!" Charlotte asked, getting worked up again.

The three of them ignored her.

"I'm going to enter purgatory and end this once and for all." Gabriel then said.

"What? You can't go! It's suicide!" Alex pleaded. "There must be another way. Give me some time, please, I can—"

"No. I need to get into their world and stop them there." He said, sternly.

Charlotte couldn't believe what she was hearing.

"I can't let you go, Gabriel." Alex spoke sternly.

"Spirit guides do not give orders to Archangels." He replied sharply.

Alex frowned. "I understand that, but..." he then turned to Raphael. "You must know what I'm trying to say," he pleaded again, hoping she would back him up.

"I do. I understand completely." She replied. "But Gabriel is not as weak as you think. He's very smart, and I believe that if he chooses to do this, then he will succeed."

"No, Gabriel please..." Alex spoke again. "I've seen it. It will do nothing but ruin you and all that you are and if it doesn't by some miracle, the Archangels will banish you for sure upon return!"

"Alex," the Archangel spoke, raising his hand to him. "I am willing to face whatever consequences that come from my actions. This is our only way and I need for you to keep this quiet. Do not tell Nathan, or anyone else. He will want to come and he isn't strong enough."

"I'm so confused with what is happening here," Charlotte said, dropping her head down to the table.

"Gabriel, please!" Alex pleaded a third time. "You are the angel of Mercy, this world needs you! It's forbidden for a reason. You may not return as yourself, don't you understand? It's not just you that will suffer from this."

Gabriel sighed, staring back at him, then glanced over to Charlotte. "You as well, must keep this conversation quiet. All of it." He repeated.

Charlotte's head popped up from the table and stared back at him, a little insulted. "Who would I tell? Honestly..." She sighed again.

"I will return soon with a plan. Take care of Sophie and Alex, work with Raphael and do your best to prepare me for what I'm walking into. That is an order!"

Alex didn't speak. He turned from Gabriel and got up from the table making the Archangel reappear in front of him.

"I will be fine," He said, resting his hand on the spirit guide's shoulder. "Have faith in me, as I do in you..."

He then disappeared from sight.

Alex ran his hands through his long hair, then turned back to Raphael.

"Can someone please tell me what the hell is going on here?" Charlotte snapped. Alex sighed, then sat down next to her again. "Don't worry. I'll fill you in,"

"Finally!" She replied, slamming her hands down on the table, annoyed. She then looked to Raphael.

"Let's start with you, Missy. Spill it!" She demanded, kicking the chair out from the other side of the table. Raphael smiled, then made her way over to sit down.

"Where should I begin?" She said to herself.

"How about you start from the beginning? Like the very beginning. Why were you "once" an Archangel? What happened to you, and don't leave anything out!" She glanced over to Alex. "Then you're going to explain this whole Nathan thing to me,"

He nodded in silence. They had no choice, Charlotte was already involved. It was better now if she knew everything and was prepared for what could happen next.

●●●

I stretched out in bed as the sunlight through my bedroom
windows warmed my face. Slowly, my eyes opened. I was in
my room. I was sure of it. It felt nice to not wake in panic,
and I was aware of it. Then I noticed I was alone in the bed.
The immediate thought made me shoot up nervously. I glanced
around the room. My hand traced the spot on the bed where
Nathan was last. My eyes shifted to his pillow. On top, was a
very small, beautiful, purple velvet bag with a note attached to
it. I pulled up the long sleeves of Nathan's hoodie and reached
for it. Carefully, I unfolded the note. It read:

*"I may not be your guardian angel anymore, but I'm still watching over you. I
will always protect you. I hope this gift reminds you daily that I am always with
you." - Love, Nathan*

I smiled, admiring how nicely the gift was put together
for a moment. Placing the note down next to me, I pulled
at the silver ribbons to open it. Reaching my fingers down
into the small bag, I felt them brush across a chain. I pulled
it out of the bag, letting the object hang from my fingers
in the sunlight. It was a silver chain with a diamond angel
wing hanging in the middle of it. It was gorgeous. Holding
it between my fingers, a memory sparked. I froze deep in
thought and closed my eyes. A conversation on a plane...
The first time Nathan appeared to me in real life.
"Trust you?" I heard myself say, *"I don't even know you."*
"Well, what do you want to know?" I heard him reply.
His voice made me smile. Then the memory changed.
Cherry blossoms. I could smell them all around me.
"A second chance...." My voice whispered.
Then I was back in my bedroom once again. My eyes opened
to the sparking necklace before me. Our life together seemed
so long ago. The bedroom door opened. Nathan.
His hair was wet from the shower. I smiled at the sight of him.
"It's beautiful," I said. "Thank you."
He made his way over and climbed across the bed to me.
"I'm glad. I want you to wear it always, so you don't forget

that you have me with you every step of the way," he then
moved himself behind me. Gently, he lifted my hair back and
off to the side. I felt the brush of his fingers as he took the
necklace from my hand and laced it around my neck. My arms
rested on his legs around me. When he was done, he laid my
hair back in place then wrapped his arms around me.
I held tight to him for a moment, until he slid out from behind
me.
Sitting in front of me now, his fingers touched the glittering
wing that hung against my chest.
"I love this," I whispered, touching his hand.
"I love you." He replied. Then his smile faded.
"What?" I asked, nervously. "What is it?"
"Sophie," He spoke quietly. "Can I... kiss you?"
I felt my cheeks blush at his simple request.
His hand moved from my chest and gently touched my
face. He was careful and slow with every movement. My
heart began to race. This is Nathan, my Nathan, my world I
repeated to myself just in case. He stopped just before my lips,
hesitating for only a moment—his warm breath felt nice on
my skin. Then I felt the connection.
His lips pressed gently at first, then a little more pressure
came. A warmth filled my body from head to toe. My mind
shot back to our first connection. A day I hadn't thought about
in a very long time. The day he returned to me. It was the
same feeling then as it was right now in this very moment.
My hand reached up to his neck, holding him tight. The
sensation was indescribable. He tasted perfect. Then, I felt
him pull back from me.
My hands lingered in the air in front of us as I opened my eyes
to him. He waited for my reaction. I was breathing deeply, but
not in fear this time, in relief. It felt good. My eyes adjust up
to his as a worried look grew on his face.
"Did you feel it?" I asked.
He looked at me confused a little.
"It felt like the day you returned to me," I said.
A smile grew on his face.

"I felt it." He replied, "I feel it every time, Soph."
I smiled back at him, then leaned up and kissed him again.
He embraced me immediately. Happy to reconnect. I moved
myself onto his lap, straddling him. His arms tightened
around me as a new vision shot through my mind. Our bodies
intertwined with nothing between us. He suddenly gasped and
pulled back from me. Startled from his quick reaction, I stared
into his eyes—nervously.
"I think that's a little too fast, Soph…" He said, then noticed
the look in my eyes. His hands pulled my arms from around
his neck. He then laced his own around my body, so I couldn't
escape from him.
"I'm not saying it's bad," He spoke, cautiously, "I'm just
saying it might be a little too much right now. I want to take
this slow. I don't want to overwhelm you," He smiled, and
then kissed my nose. He then leaned in and hugged me tight.
"Thank you," He whispered.
I didn't answer.
"I needed this. I've needed you—for so long." He spoke again.
My arms tightened around him.
"I need you." I whispered back. "I love you, Nate."
He immediately pulled back again to look at me.
"Are you reading my mind?" I asked.
He smiled, then nodded.
"Did I mean it?"
He nodded again.
"Come on, let's get you some breakfast." He said, lifting me
off of him and getting up from the bed. He then held out his
hand to me.
I was still for a moment. I didn't want to leave the room.
Everything seemed quiet in here—quiet and safe. I felt myself
slowly changing back when I was alone with him. I didn't
want to be around anyone else.
"Please," He said, waiting for me.
Sliding out from the bed, I zipped the hoodie up higher and
took his hand. He then guided me down the hall to the kitchen.

Entering the room, I suddenly felt a little nervous, but Nathan held tight to my hand. He walked me over to the counter, then turned my body towards him. I felt his hands on my hips as he lifted me up to sit on the counter.

"Wait here." He said, stepping away from me. He quickly grabbed the pancake mix from the cupboards and then some milk from the fridge.

Quietly, I watched as he mixed up the batter, lit up the stove and pulled some dishes down from the cupboard beside me. This familiar moment was peaceful.

"Nathan," I spoke quietly.

He stopped and looked at me.

I wasn't sure what I wanted to say, my mind was fuzzy again.

He stepped towards me, "What, crazy girl?" He smiled.

Crazy girl... I loved it when he called me that.

Reaching out to his face, I gently brushed a few strands of his hair off to the side. His hair was long, longer than before. He moved in closer, placing himself between my legs that hung off the counter. My fingers traced his face, he was beautiful and still waiting for a response from me. I didn't really need anything, I just wanted to look at him—to touch him.

His hands slid up to my thighs as I leaned in and kissed him on the forehead. I heard him chuckle a bit from the touch.

"Hmm, not as fun," I said, staring back down at him.

He shook his head and smiled, agreeing with me. I then leaned in, this time for his lips. I wanted to taste him again. I breathed him in as our lips caressed one another. When I finally stopped, I lingered close to his face. My fingers traced the shape of his lips until his hand reached up and took mine. He kissed it, then slowly stepped back from me to finish making breakfast.

"I hope you didn't forget about the most important job?" He then said.

I looked at him confused, until he placed a bottle of syrup down next to me. I smiled, I hadn't forgotten.

My thoughts were suddenly interrupted as Charlotte entered the room, followed by Alex. I had forgotten for a moment that they were here.

"Are you making pancakes?" She asked, sitting down at the table. Then I noticed movement from the living room. Raphael.

I began to rub my hands together nervously until everyone sat down at the table. I watched as Nathan finished breakfast, then set the table for everyone. He placed down some juice and a large plate of pancakes in the middle of everyone.

They all seemed to be enjoying the meal, but my nerves were kicking in as I watched on from the counter. Raphael glanced over with a smile on her face.

"Come on," Nathan said appearing in front of me again. "Let's eat with them."

I looked to the table, then back at Nathan. His hands embraced me as I slid off of the counter. My hand laced into his as we made our way over. He then pulled out a chair next to Charlotte and sat me down.

"Here Soph, have some juice." She said, pouring a little bit into the glass in front of me.

"Thank you." I heard myself say.

"You're welcome."

"I'll be right back," Nathan then whispered into my ear. My eyes watched as he walked over to Raphael and leaned down.

"Walk with me for a moment?" I heard him say.

Raphael nodded, then got up from her chair to follow him out of the room. Alex touched my hand from across the table.

"Did Nathan give you that necklace?" He asked, kindly.

Charlotte turned to me, leaning down to see it better.

I pulled my hand from his and touched the diamond wing that hung low.

"Sophie, it's beautiful." She said.

"I love it," I spoke quietly.

Charlotte glanced back at Alex and smiled again. My interaction with them was the most normal it had ever been in quite some time. Alex then dropped two pancakes on my plate and pushed the container of butter over to me.

Stepping out into the sunlight, Nathan began to make his way down the street towards the local park.

"She's looking well today," Raphael said, happily.

"She is." Nathan replied, sitting down on a bench. "I could feel the old Sophie in there for just a few moments." He then paused. "She let me kiss her." He smiled.

Raphael sat down next to him and took his hand in hers. "That's wonderful."

"I know, which is why I need to tell you something."

Raphael waited patiently for what he wanted to say.

"I think she's strong enough now and she has Alex, Gabriel, you, and Charlotte to help her keep moving in the right direction..."

Raphael looked at him oddly.

"I found a way to end this," He then said. "I'm going into purgatory—alone."

She didn't respond right away. Her hand slowly slid from his and she eventually stood up from the bench.

"Nathan, I'm sorry, but you can't. I won't let you go. Not there and definitely not alone." She said, sadly. "I understand why you want to do this, but it's much too dangerous, especially now—for you I mean."

"What are you talking about?" He said, getting defensive. "Of course I can go... I'm the one who found the way in! It's happening, no matter what you say,"

"How did you find this way in, Nathan?" She then asked. "Who brought you this answer?"

He hesitated for a moment, unsure of what to say. Raphael reached for his hand quickly. His eyes shot to hers as she read his mind.

"Anna," She said, aloud.

He quickly stood up. "I know how crazy it sounds, but I need to end this. I need to do it for Sophie. Whether I survive or not, she deserves a normal life. She deserves for me to try for her."

She didn't respond.

"This will work, Raphael. I know it."

"I'm worried it will be too much for you," She sighed, "and with your—"

"My what?" He interrupted. "My self-control? Is that what you're all worried about? I'm fine. I know what needs to be done. I'm just going to help Serena pass on. I've done my research. I can do this Raphael. Trust me."

"Yes." She admitted. "I'm worried that your feelings will get in the way and you'll make a wrong decision, Nathan."

He turned away from her in disbelief. He thought for sure that she of all people would understand him, possibly even help him. Why didn't anyone believe he could handle this?

"Raphael, I'm very aware of everything I feel for Serena." He said, turning back to her. "I truly am and yes, I would do almost anything for her, but Sophie—it's hard for me to explain what she does to me. She makes me feel whole inside. I can't imagine a world without her. So yes, I want to help Serena. But the bigger picture here is that I will say goodbye to Serena so I can be with Sophie. I know when I see Serena it's hard because all of my feelings come rushing back, and they are very strong. But they are not as strong as my feelings for Sophie. Please. I beg you, trust me."

She continued to stare at him.

"Read my mind, you'll know it's true." He then waited for her to do so, but she didn't. She just smiled back at him.

"Then you must do what you think is right." She finally replied. "But Sophie, she does not see the big picture yet. She's worried about losing you. You know that, right?"

"I know. I see it in her eyes every time I look at her," He replied.

"And you'll risk breaking her trust by going this route," Raphael waited again, letting the thought settle for a moment.

Nathan nodded. "I'm hoping our relationship is strong enough to work it out when I get back." He said, quietly.

"I hope so too, but you still can't go alone." She replied.

He looked at her again, worried for what else she was thinking.

"I will go with you."

It was the last thing he expected to hear from her.

"No, Raphael." He couldn't bare it. There was no way he could force her back into that world. She had worked too hard to get where she was now to be thrown back into it.

"You can't. You just started this new life and you're doing so well. Why would you ever want to go back? It could break you this time." He said, sadly.

"It won't." She replied. "I know better than anyone what's in there—what could happen. I'm fully prepared. More then you could ever be."

"But we just got you back. Please, let me go alone. I can do this."

She shook her head no. "If you wish for me to not speak of this to Alex or Gabriel, then you will allow me to assist you on your journey."

Nathan sighed. He needed to go alone, it's what he promised Anna. "Please, just give me a few days to see if I can do it on my own. Then if you don't hear from me, tell them. And if you come after me then, so be it. And if you don't, then that's okay too."

Raphael stared at him.

"Do you remember the day you were taken from William?" Nathan then said, trying a new tactic on her. He hated to go there, but he had no choice.

Her face softened.

"I'm sure it was the most horrible feeling in the world, wasn't it? To lose him—the one you love. To know that you would never see him again."

She didn't speak.

"I've already left Sophie once and believe me, this time will be much worse. But I know I have a chance to save her and this can finally be over—for everybody. I need to try Raphael. Sophie and I didn't make it this far to lose everything."

He continued stared at her.

"Our love can survive this, I know it. Please don't let me lose her. That alone, will surely kill me."

Her eyes began to tear up as she silently stared back at him.

"Please," He pleaded again.

"Alright," She finally agreed. "When do you need to go?"

Nathan sighed in relief, then stepped towards her to wrap his arms around her.

"Gabriel will not like this at all," She said, holding him tight. "And you're going to get me into a lot of trouble. So you better come out alive," She warned.

"I will," He assured her.

Slowly, she pulled back from him.

"I want to leave tomorrow."

"Well, you might want to think about getting Sophie out of the house before you go. I don't see that being an easy exit. As for Gabriel, I can distract him. He's already making his own plans anyways."

Nathan hugged her again. "Thank you."

"Thank me later when you come home to us. Please don't make me regret this, Nathan."

"I won't." He replied. "Now let's get back before they begin to worry."

On their way home, Nathan made a quick stop at the corner store to purchase five slushies. As they continued their walk, Nathan handed one of the drinks to Raphael.

"Trust me, you'll like it." He smiled, then popped a straw into the lid. "Drink."

He watched as her face lit up the moment the slush entered her mouth. She then pressed her palm to her forehead.

"Is this fun for you?" She asked, fighting her first battle against brain freeze.

"You have to drink it slower, so that doesn't happen." He laughed.

He hoped this simple, normal pleasure might relax everyone—even if just for a moment. He wanted one last memory with them all before he secretly departed this world. He only hoped he was making the right choice, and could truly return to them once this was over and done with.

Returning home, I heard Nathan enter the living-room. I was gazing out the window while Charlotte and Alex sat on the couch watching television.

"She's been like that since you left." Alex said, quietly.

Then I felt his hand on my shoulder.

"Sophie,"

I turned to him.

"Look what I brought you." He sat down beside me on the small bench under our windowsill. I smiled at him, happy that he was back. He then placed the cup into my hands.

"It's your favorite, berry-cola mix."

"Thank you," I replied quietly, taking the slushie from him. I placed my lips down on the straw and carefully sucked up the slush. The moment the flavor hit my tongue my eyes widened with pleasure. Nathan leaned in and kissed my forehead. I then handed the drink back to him and turned to look out the window again.

"Sophie," He spoke, touching my arm.

I didn't look at him. I was thinking, of what, I wasn't too sure—but something. He gave my arm a little shake, trying to get my attention. When I finally looked at him, he smiled.

"Listen, I was thinking, since there has been so much craziness around this place, I thought it might be a good change of scenery if you go stay with Charlotte for a few days. You guys could rent some movies like you used to and have a girl's night or whatever. Just not scary ones though, okay?" He said, turning to Charlotte.

I glanced over at them, their eyes were wide with shock. I didn't know how I felt about their expressions. Alex quickly touched Charlotte's arm. My eyes adjust back to Nathan's, confused.

"Nathan?" Alex spoke, suspiciously.

"It was me," Raphael interrupted. "I suggested for Nathan to get Sophie out of the house for a bit, hoping maybe some fresh air and a change of scenery might do her well," She said in a positive tone.

"Okay Well, we can't just leave them alone." He replied,

turning to Charlotte. She was silently pleading for him not to leave her. Although she saw recent changes in my behavior, I knew Charlotte still feared being alone with me. I could see it on her face, always.

"Of course not," Raphael replied. "You must go with them. They can't be left unprotected,"

I continued to study Nathan as he watched their conversation. When his eyes met mine again, he spoke before I could.

"Well, Soph? What do you think? Wanna pack up some stuff and hang at Charlotte's for a bit?"

"But you won't be there," I said, sadly.

"No, but I'm really close. I think it will be good for you. Please do it for me, Soph." He said, touching my face gently.

I placed my hand against his, holding it still. I then slid his hand to my lips and kissed it once.

"If you think it's best." My lips lingered on his hand. "Will I be safe?" I then asked, without looking up at him.

"I promise you will," he answered, tilting my head up to him.

"Okay," I replied, getting up from the bench. I then numbly headed off towards my bedroom.

Alex glanced at Nathan still confused and completely surprised by how quickly I agreed to his idea.

"Nathan, what's going on?" Charlotte asked, not buying his story for one second.

"Nothing. I just think we're on a roll with making her feel better. Maybe if she gets out and does something that's normal for her it will completely snap her out of it. I'm just trying everything I can think of Charlotte."

She stared at him for a moment, unsure of this idea.

"Don't worry. I'll be right there with you." Alex said, taking her hand.

"As will I," Raphael added. "And we'll talk more about our plan for purgatory, alright?"

"But what will you be doing Nathan? Why aren't you coming with us?" Charlotte spoke again.

"Gabriel wants to work with me on his own. He says he has stuff we need to discuss, I can't come." He lied.

Charlotte sat for a moment in thought, then vaguely remembered the conversation at the kitchen table a while ago. It made sense. She sighed, then got up from the couch to gather her things.

I stood awkwardly in my bedroom. I wasn't sure what to pack. I didn't even know where to start, I was just frozen in the middle of the room. I had forgotten where my clothes were hidden and what I essentially needed for each day. For the last few days I had Nathan around to dress me, to tell me what to wear, when to eat, and so on. I was suddenly lost and frightened at the thought of not having him there. I climbed onto the bed a little stressed now. Pulling the covers up around me, I heard Nathan enter the room.

"What are you doing my love?" He laughed softly, then sat down beside me.

"I think I'm going to miss you too much." I said, sitting up and curling my knees into my chest. "I know it's only for a few days, but I feel like it's going to be forever."

"It won't be forever, Soph. I promise." He said, rubbing my back. "Please try and relax. It will be fun and good for you. You want to get better, right?"

I sighed, tilting my head towards him. He smiled, leaning his head down against mine.

"Just keep my necklace on and I'll always be with you."

I then watched as he slid from the bed to help me pack. He pulled a small duffel bag from the closet then headed for the dresser to get my clothes. Last, he entered the bathroom for some daily essentials. He knew where everything was. He knew everything I would need. He knew me, he knew us— better than I right now. I had to trust him.

When he was done, he zipped up the bag and turned to me.

"You ready?" He asked, holding out his hand for me.

His eyes were glistening as I pulled myself out from under the covers. I still felt like there was something wrong. But before I could ask, he pulled me in tight against his chest.

His breathing was different. It bothered me a little.

"Is everything alright, Nathan?"
I heard him swallow hard before answering me.
"Yes..." He said, clearing his throat.
I pulled back from him and looked up into his eyes.
"Then why are you crying?" I asked, nervously.
His eyes were watering.
"I'm not," He replied, wiping them. "I'm just a little sad. I'm really going to miss you, but I know it's what's best for you. We have to do this."
"No we don't," I replied. "I can stay here with you. I'll try harder, I promise." I begged. He pulled me in close again.
"No Soph, it's not that. You're doing amazing. We just need to take this next step. It won't be long and we'll be back together soon enough. So I need you to do this. I need you to try."
"Okay," I responded holding him tight.
He then pulled back from my arms and reached down for the duffel bag. I slowly took it from him as he handed it to me. We then walked towards the doorway. I stopped again, glancing up at him. I didn't want to go.
"I love you, crazy girl." He managed to get out, "You, are my world."
I smiled. "I love you... more."
As I left the room and made my way down the hallway, I watched as he slid his hands into his pockets. His head then dropped. I immediately wanted to rush back into his arms, but I did my best to do as Nathan requested. Even if it felt wrong. Soon he was out of sight, and I was at the front door with Charlotte and Alex. I only hoped this was the right choice for us.

23
May Angels Lead You In

The next day Nathan slept in a very long time. He needed every bit of energy he could build up. It was a lonely sleep on his own. He missed Sophie with every second that passed. Raphael had kept her side of the bargain and distracted Gabriel well. So far, everything was going as planned. He only needed a little more time to get out.

Eventually, he got up from bed, showered, then cleaned up the apartment so it was ready for when he returned, because he was certain he was coming back. He then started to pack a small bag.

Before zipping it up, he looked around the room once more. The bead from Anna was the only thing left he needed. He headed over and opened the nightstand to retrieved it from inside. Holding it in his hand, he hoped that all of this was going to be worth it in the end. Heading back over to his bag, he quickly snatched it up and tossed it over his shoulder. He then stopped for a moment in the doorway and did something he had never done before as a human. He closed his eyes and prayed.

"If you are with me right now, then please, help me through this. I don't want to lose her, but I fear she will never forgive me. Please help me God, if you truly mean well for us. Protect us both until we are back together again. I know I've been lost for a while now and my faith has suffered, but I really need

300

you—now more than ever." He then opened his eyes. It was silent. Nathan sighed, then grabbed his jacket off the back of the door. Sliding it on, he placed the bead into his right pocket, then zipped it up before leaving the room.

He made his way into the living room and stopped at the coffee table. He knelt down and reached under it for something. Taped up underneath it, was Serena's bracelet. He tore it from the wood, removed the loose pieces of tape and placed it in his other pocket. Making his way back into the kitchen, he placed his bag down on the table and removed his wallet for one last errand before he left.

Heading down the street, Nathan quickly cut through the park as he usually did. He couldn't help but think if this would be the last time he would ever walk this route. He loved Vancouver and all that it had brought to his life so far. He desperately wanted a future here. He swallowed hard as he entered the flower shop.

Inside, he was surrounded by the scent of perfection. Flowers that had grown to their full potential in life. He headed over to the glass cabinet and picked out two purple roses and one white one. The purple meant a love that longed for each other, and the white one meant a love for eternity. He then thoughtfully wrote a message to Sophie on a small piece of paper to go along with them:

"Please wait for me, Soph. I'll be back for you crazy girl and remember what I said. I love you more than anything. You are my world". - Love, Nate.

The lady at the cash then wrapped the roses with baby's breath and greens before tying them together with a white ribbon. Nathan paid for the flowers and hurried on his way.

The walk home was nerve-racking. He needed to get out before Gabriel caught onto his plan, or Alex for that matter. He crossed back through the park, picking up speed when suddenly a figure stepped out from behind a tree and blocked him. "Where are you going?" Gabriel asked, calmly.

Nathan froze.

"And do not lie to me." The Archangel warned.

Nathan had no choice but to speak the truth, for if the Archangel truly wanted to know, he would read his mind but he was giving him a chance to explain.

"I'm going into purgatory, alone. My plan is set. If I stay, Sophie will surely die. I have to try." He said, a little winded.

Gabriel looked at him, clearly upset and annoyed by Nathan's thick-headed actions. He then carefully chose his next few words, fearing he may lose him for good if he spoke too bluntly.

"That is true. She will die if nothing is done, but that is why Alex and I are making a plan. We can handle this. You can't. You aren't stable enough."

"I can, Gabriel." Nathan replied.

"When the Archangels find out about this," Gabriel paused, "if you are even able to return—they will come for you and I would not be able to protect you. There are so many things that can go wrong—"

"I'm going, Gabriel." Nathan repeated. "You can't stop me."

The Archangel paused once again, collecting his thoughts.

"You are certain this plan of yours will work?"

Nathan nodded.

"And you will not listen to any more of my ideas?"

Nathan shook his head no.

"You know that you could lose her over this?"

"I know, and I'm willing to take that chance. Anything is worth the chance if I can save her, if I can give her back her life. You must understand by now, Gabriel. I won't live without her. I have to try, even if she doesn't want me afterwards. You must feel the same about Anna? Don't you? Don't you want to fix what you've done so she can finally be happy and move on? No matter the consequences?"

Gabriel walked towards him and stopped directly in front. He opened his eyes and stared into Nathan's.

"No matter the consequences," he said, confidently. "I'm

coming with you. We will end this together," He then said.
Completely overwhelmed by the Archangel's reaction, Nathan
sighed in relief.

"I told you I would be with you the entire way and I intend to
keep my word. You are like family to me, Nathan. I will not
let you down. I must protect you until the very end. No matter
what you choose."

Emotions rushed through Nathan. He suddenly felt more
confident with his choice simply from their positive
conversation. Knowing he now had the Archangel Gabriel by
his side.

"So how are you getting in exactly?"

Nathan slowly reached into his pocket and pulled out the
small bead. By the reaction on Gabriel's face, he recognized it
immediately.

"Where did you get that?" He asked.

"Anna, she came to me in my dreams."

Gabriel continued to stare at the bead, knowing what had
become of his precious Anna and how she controlled Serena's
every move. Clearly she had fooled Nathan. He reached out
and closed Nathan's hand around the bead.

"She will not like what you're about to do." He warned again.
"Sophie, I mean."

"I know," Nathan replied.

"It is a big sacrifice you are about to make, one that could end
very badly. There are no guarantees. So you must make sure
your heart and mind are prepared for what will come from
this."

"I'm well aware of everything. I only pray that God will help
me. That I'm making the right choice. I mean, it feels right,"
Nathan admitted, quietly. "I just have to drop these off. Then
we will go."

Gabriel nodded and let Nathan lead the way.

On their walk home, Gabriel paused for a moment. He had
something else to tell Nathan and he had to do it now.

"She will be there when you get home," he began.

"What?" Nathan stopped, turning back to him. "I sent her to Charlotte's. She won't be back for a few days. How—"

"Fate paid a visit to her this morning, but Raphael and I intervened." Nathan's face became worried.

"Don't worry. She didn't hurt anyone. She came to play her game. She told us of your plan and that Raphael had known about it all along. She did this to light a fire underneath us, to make things more complicated, perhaps to start a fight."

"Gabriel, I'm sorry we lied to you, but—"

"I understand why you chose this. I do. I cannot stop you if you are that determined. But lying to us, will never turn out good. I'm not mad at you or Raphael, but I had to stop you and try to change your mind one last time."

Nathan swallowed in fear, "So she knows what I'm doing?" He asked. "Is she mad?"

"It was hard to tell. She was quiet and immediately began to pack up her stuff. Charlotte tried to stop her, but she threatened them all. She's probably home by now. I just want you to be prepared for what she might do, or say..."

Nathan thought long and hard about what he was about to face. Gabriel then placed his hand on his shoulder.

"She will be angry, but try to understand where she is coming from. She will say things she doesn't mean and some she will. But you need to stay confident with your choices. If you are to make it through this, you must have faith in yourself, not meaningless words said out of fear."

Nathan nodded, then stepped away from Gabriel—dreadfully continuing his walk home.

●●●

I heard him enter the apartment. A sudden fear filled my gut. I listened as he made his way down the hallway towards us and into the kitchen. I was sick to my stomach waiting for him—Charlotte was by my side. His travel bag was sitting in the middle of the kitchen table.

"Sophie," He spoke, nervously.

"What's this, Nate?" I asked, pointing to his bag.

304

"Where are you going?"

He stared at me as I waited patiently for an answer. No matter what he came up with, there was nothing he could say that would make me feel better about what I knew he was going to do. I watched as his eyes moved to Charlotte's.

"What is this, Nate?" I asked again, a little louder.

He still didn't speak.

"Answer me!" I shouted.

Out of the corner of my eye, I saw Charlotte's hand covered her mouth as she continued to stand silently beside me. The silence from both of them annoyed me. I needed someone to speak.

"No!" I screamed, slamming my fist down on the table. "You promised me! You promised me, Nathan!"

I then stormed up to him. My mind wasn't lost in this moment. It was very awake and very aware of what was happening. Everything inside of me hurt. A feeling I was oh so familiar with now.

"How could you?" I shoved him once. "You're going after her, aren't you? You're not going to listen to anybody... You're just going do what you want, aren't you?" I could feel my eyes tearing up.

"Sophie, sweetie...." He stumbled over his words. "Please," He begged. "Please try to understand."

Tears slid down my face as the anger rose inside of me. I tried desperately to push it back down so I could speak again.

"No. I'm done, Nathan. I'm done trying to understand."

Nathan's eyes looked to Charlotte again, but she remained silent.

"How could you? How could you do this to me after everything we've been through? After everything I've been through." I paused. "It wasn't enough that I almost died?"

"Of course, Sophie! That's why I'm doing this!" He shouted back. "I don't want to lose you!" He yelled in defense.

"If you don't want to lose me, then don't leave me! Don't tell me goodbye. Stay with me Nate, if you want us—if you want us to truly be—then you won't walk out that door. I told you, I can't survive without you, Nathan. You'll kill me if you leave now." I begged. I didn't care if I hurt his feelings, I wanted to. He needed to understand.

"Sophie, please don't say things like that. You know I want us to be. I'm doing this to save you."

"No. That's bullshit!" I snapped. "I can't live like this anymore." Even I was surprised by how present I was in this very moment, but I needed to be, I needed to do everything I could to make him stay. I continued to stare him down. I knew he hated every single word I was saying right now. I could feel it.

"You'll have to choose, Nate. Her or me!"

I had taken it to the next level by jabbing him right in the heart with something I knew he never wanted to do. But I had no choice.

"I'm telling you to choose. Right now." I repeated, as tears streaked my face and dripped from my chin.

Nathan wiped a tear that was about to fall from his eye, then carefully reached past me to grab his bag off of the table.

I shoved him back, knocking the flowers from his other hand. They fell to the floor.

Slowly, he knelt down and picked them up.

"Please, don't do this." I begged, again.

Placing the flowers down on the table, he reached again for the bag. His hands were shaking as he pulled it past me. He then turned and began to walk away. I quickly ran after him, grabbing him just before he reached the door. I ripped the bag from his hand and tossed it down.

"Nathan, look at me!" I demanded.

He stopped and turned to me, he was crying. I was crying. The way he looked at me pulled at my heart. I quickly wiped my eyes, then cleared my throat. He waited painfully for what I might say next. Something even I didn't expect, but it's what I felt in that horrible moment.

"I hate you." I said, very coldly. "I hate you, Nathan."

He didn't respond. He couldn't even look at me.

"I hate you!" I shouted, shoving him again—and then another

time. At first he let me go at it. He let me release all the pain inside upon him. Then his arms wrapped around me tightly. I fought back, crying harder than ever before.

"Sophie stop, please." He said, holding tight. "I love you, and I'm coming back. I promise."

"No you won't..." I cried, "I know it..."

"I will, Gabriel's coming with me. He's going to help me. We can make it, Soph."

Nathan glanced up to see Charlotte's confused look on her face. He only hoped she would pass the information onto Alex, just in case they didn't make it back.

"Promise me you'll wait for me." He then said. "I know I don't deserve it, but I swear to you that it will be worth it. I won't fail you again. Please Sophie, it will kill me if I know I've lost you but someone has to end this."

I pushed myself back from him violently.

"We were supposed to stick together, Nate. You broke our promise." I then reached up to the necklace hanging around my neck and yanked it off. I tossed to the ground before him. "I hope it kills you, because I definitely won't be here if you leave now. I hope you feel the pain that I've felt from you— for as long as I've known you."

They were the meanest words I had ever said and I said them to him. I felt a sharp pain in my heart as I tried desperately to hurt him—to make him understand what I was feeling.

He could barely speak after hearing that. I had hit him hard. Nathan swallowed in pain, watching the angry tears continue to fall down my face.

"I wish I never met you, Nathan," I then said.

"Sophie, you don't mean that." He replied, softly.

"Get out," I said, wiping another tear from my cheek.

"Soph," he begged, stepping back towards me. "Please..."

"I said get out! Just get out, Nathan! I never want to see you again!"

It was his worst fear. Even Charlotte couldn't believe what I was saying to him, but I couldn't stop myself. I hated him right now. I couldn't stand the sight of him. The darkness lingering inside me from long ago suddenly broke through again, and alongside the heaviness of purgatory racing through my veins I was filled with unbearable rage and hatred like I'd never felt before.

Nathan slowly knelt down and picked up his bag, then the necklace from the ground. He slid it carefully into his pocket. Turning from us, I felt my heart sink even lower than possible. My teeth clenched and my breathing picked up at the sight of him turning the door knob. Then he stopped, making my heart skip a beat. He glanced back at me and spoke once more.

"I love you, Sophie. With all my heart."

Then he was gone.

I gasped for air and dropped to the ground. Hanging my head low, I surely thought I would die from pain alone. He was gone. Gone for good. I had lost him. I began to panic. I couldn't catch my breath. I was crying so hard that every part of me ached. Then, I felt her arms around me as she slid herself down by my side. My hands reached for her as I fell hard into her chest.

"Sophie... I'm so sorry." She said, holding me tight.

I could hear her quiet sobs.

"Charlotte...." I cried, "I lost him,"

My world had crumbled in front of me once again and this time, he wouldn't be there to pick up the pieces.

The room was silent. There was no one around but the two of us. No spirits, no angels, and no Nathan.

Find out what happens next in:
Don't Tell Me Goodbye
The second novel in
The Guardians Of Your Heart Series

The Guardians Of Your Heart Series
by Becca Blue

Stay With Me
Don't Tell Me Goodbye
You're Not Alone

About the Author

Becca Blue is a writer, director, photographer and graphic designer whose work blends emotional depth with a touch of the supernatural. She is the author of The Guardians of Your Heart series and the children's series My Dog Bruce. Her first award-winning film, All I Need, became the prelude to The Guardians of Your Heart, establishing her signature style of love, loss, and redemption. When she isn't writing or making her next film, she's taking photos, traveling with her pets, and helping other indie authors publish their own stories as Becca holds a diploma in Graphic Design and Interactive Media.

Find Becca on Social Media:
Facebook.com/beccablueauthor
Facebook.com/sakurabluestudio
TikTok: @beccablueauthor

www.ingramcontent.com/pod-product-compliance
Lightning Source LLC
Chambersburg PA
CBHW070535120726
47909CB00007B/2144